W9-BWL-568

If you have a home computer with Internet access you may:
- request an item to be placed on hold.
- renew an item that is not overdue or on hold.
- view titles and due dates checked out on your card.
- view and/or pay your outstanding fines online (over $5).

To view your patron record from your home computer click on Patchogue-Medford Library's homepage: www.pmlib.org

THE LANGUAGE OF FLOWERS

THE LANGUAGE OF FLOWERS

A NOVEL

VANESSA DIFFENBAUGH

THORNDIKE
WINDSOR
PARAGON

This Large Print edition is published by Thorndike Press, Waterville, Maine USA and by AudioGo Ltd, Bath, England.

Copyright © 2011 by Vanessa Diffenbaugh.

The moral right of the author has been asserted.

Thorndike Press, a part of Gale, Cengage Learning.

Thorndike Press® Large Print Basic.

The text of this Large Print edition is unabridged.

Other aspects of the book may vary from the original edition.

Set in 16 pt. Plantin.

LIBRARY OF CONGRESS CATALOGING-IN-PUBLICATION DATA

Diffenbaugh, Vanessa.
  The language of flowers / by Vanessa Diffenbaugh.
    p. cm. — (Thorndike Press large print basic)
  ISBN-13: 978-1-4104-4171-3 (hardcover)
  ISBN-10: 1-4104-4171-7 (hardcover)
  1. Young women — Fiction. 2. Florists — Fiction. 3. Flower
language — Fiction. 4. San Francisco (Calif.) — Fiction. 5. Large
type books. I. Title.
PS3604.I2255L36 2011b
813'.6—dc22

                                                              2011027757

BRITISH LIBRARY CATALOGUING-IN-PUBLICATION DATA AVAILABLE

Published in the U.S. in 2011 by arrangement with The Ballantine Publishing Group, a division of Random House, Inc.

Published in the U.K. in 2012 by arrangement with Pan Macmillan Ltd.

U.K. Hardcover: 978 1 445 87028 1 (Windsor Large Print)

U.K. Softcover: 978 1 445 87029 8 (Paragon Large Print)

Printed in the United States of America
1 2 3 4 5 6 7 15 14 13 12 11

For PK

Moss is selected to be the emblem of maternal love, because, like that love, it glads the heart when the winter of adversity overtakes us, and when summer friends have deserted us.

— HENRIETTA DUMONT,
The Floral Offering

CONTENTS

Part One / Common Thistle 11

Part Two / A Heart Unacquainted . . 149

Part Three / Moss 311

Part Four / New Beginnings 431

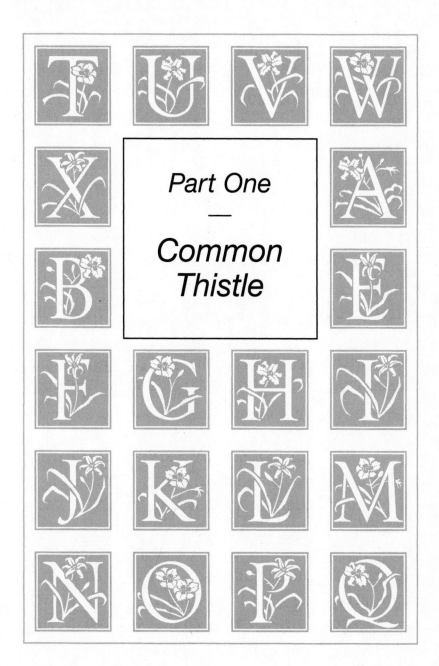

Part One

—

*Common
Thistle*

1.

For eight years I dreamed of fire. Trees ignited as I passed them; oceans burned. The sugary smoke settled in my hair as I slept, the scent like a cloud left on my pillow as I rose. Even so, the moment my mattress started to burn, I bolted awake. The sharp, chemical smell was nothing like the hazy syrup of my dreams; the two were as different as Carolina and Indian jasmine, *separation* and *attachment.* They could not be confused.

Standing in the middle of the room, I located the source of the fire. A neat row of wooden matches lined the foot of the bed. They ignited, one after the next, a glowing picket fence across the piped edging. Watching them light, I felt a terror unequal to the size of the flickering flames, and for a paralyzing moment I was ten years old again, desperate and hopeful in a way I had never been before and would never be again.

But the bare synthetic mattress did not

13

ignite like the thistle had in late October. It smoldered, and then the fire went out.

It was my eighteenth birthday.

In the living room, a row of fidgeting girls sat on the sagging couch. Their eyes scanned my body and settled on my bare, unburned feet. One girl looked relieved; another disappointed. If I'd been staying another week, I would have remembered each expression. I would have retaliated with rusty nails in the soles of shoes or small pebbles in bowls of chili. Once, I'd held the end of a glowing metal clothes hanger to a sleeping roommate's shoulder, for an offense less severe than arson.

But in an hour, I'd be gone. The girls knew this, every one.

From the center of the couch, a girl stood up. She looked young — fifteen, sixteen at most — and was pretty in a way I didn't see much of: good posture, clear skin, new clothes. I didn't immediately recognize her, but when she crossed the room there was something familiar about the way she walked, arms bent and aggressive. Though she'd just moved in, she was not a stranger; it struck me that I'd lived with her before, in the years after Elizabeth, when I was at my most angry and violent.

Inches from my body, she stopped, her chin jutting into the space between us.

"The fire," she said evenly, "was from all of us. Happy birthday."

Behind her, the row of girls on the couch squirmed. A hood was pulled up, a blanket wrapped tighter. Morning light flickered across a line of lowered eyes, and the girls looked suddenly young, trapped. The only ways out of a group home like this one were to run away, age out, or be institutionalized. Level 14 kids weren't adopted; they rarely, if ever, went home. These girls knew their prospects. In their eyes was nothing but fear: of me, of their housemates, of the life they had earned or been given. I felt an unexpected rush of pity. I was leaving; they had no choice but to stay.

I tried to push my way toward the door, but the girl stepped to the side, blocking my path.

"Move," I said.

A young woman working the night shift poked her head out of the kitchen. She was probably not yet twenty, and more terrified of me than any of the girls in the room.

"Please," she said, her voice begging. "This is her last morning. Just let her go."

I waited, ready, as the girl before me pulled her stomach in, fists clenched tight. But after

15

a moment, she shook her head and turned away. I walked around her.

I had an hour before Meredith would come for me. Opening the front door, I stepped outside. It was a foggy San Francisco morning, the concrete porch cool on my bare feet. I paused, thinking. I'd planned to gather a response for the girls, something biting and hateful, but I felt strangely forgiving. Maybe it was because I was eighteen, because, all at once, it was over for me, that I was able to feel tenderness toward their crime. Before I left, I wanted to say something to combat the fear in their eyes.

Walking down Fell, I turned onto Market. My steps slowed as I reached a busy intersection, unsure of where to go. Any other day I would have plucked annuals from Duboce Park, scoured the overgrown lot at Page and Buchanan, or stolen herbs from the neighborhood market. For most of a decade I'd spent every spare moment memorizing the meanings and scientific descriptions of individual flowers, but the knowledge went mostly unutilized. I used the same flowers again and again: a bouquet of marigold, *grief;* a bucket of thistle, *misanthropy;* a pinch of dried basil, *hate.* Only occasionally did my communication vary: a pocketful of red carnations for the judge when I realized I

16

would never go back to the vineyard, and peony for Meredith, as often as I could find it. Now, searching Market Street for a florist, I scoured my mental dictionary.

After three blocks I came to a liquor store, where paper-wrapped bouquets wilted in buckets under the barred windows. I paused in front of the store. They were mostly mixed arrangements, their messages conflicting. The selection of solid bouquets was small: standard roses in red and pink, a wilting bunch of striped carnations, and, bursting from its paper cone, a cluster of purple dahlias. *Dignity.* Immediately, I knew it was the message I wanted to give. Turning my back to the angled mirror above the door, I tucked the flowers inside my coat and ran.

I was out of breath by the time I returned to the house. The living room was empty, and I stepped inside to unwrap the dahlias. The flowers were perfect starbursts, layers of white-tipped purple petals unfurling from tight buds of a center. Biting off an elastic band, I detangled the stems. The girls would never understand the meaning of the dahlias (the meaning itself an ambiguous statement of encouragement); even so, I felt an unfamiliar lightness as I paced the long hall, slipping a stem under each closed bedroom door.

The remaining flowers I gave to the young woman who'd worked the night shift. She was standing by the kitchen window, waiting for her replacement.

"Thank you," she said when I handed her the bouquet, confusion in her voice. She twirled the stiff stems between her palms.

Meredith arrived at ten o'clock, as she'd told me she would. I waited on the front porch, a cardboard box balanced on my thighs. In eighteen years I'd collected mostly books: the *Dictionary of Flowers* and *Peterson Field Guide to Pacific States Wildflowers,* both sent to me by Elizabeth a month after I left her home; botany textbooks from libraries all over the East Bay; thin paperback volumes of Victorian poetry stolen from quiet bookstores. Stacks of folded clothes covered the books, a collection of found and stolen items, some that fit, many that did not. Meredith was taking me to The Gathering House, a transitional home in the Outer Sunset. I'd been on the waiting list since I was ten.

"Happy birthday," Meredith said as I put my box on the backseat of her county car. I didn't say anything. We both knew that it might or might not have been my birthday. My first court report listed my age as approximately three weeks; my birth date and location were unknown, as were my biological parents. August 1 had been chosen for purposes of emancipation, not celebration.

I slunk into the front seat next to Meredith and closed the door, waiting for her to pull away from the curb. Her acrylic fingernails tapped against the steering wheel. I buckled my seat belt. Still, the car did not move. I turned to face Meredith. I had not changed out of my pajamas, and I pulled my flannel-covered knees up to my chest and wrapped my jacket around my legs. My eyes scanned the roof of Meredith's car as I waited for her to speak.

"Well, are you ready?" she asked.

I shrugged.

"This is it, you know," she said. "Your life starts here. No one to blame but yourself from here on out."

Meredith Combs, the social worker responsible for selecting the stream of adoptive families that gave me back, wanted to talk to me about blame.

2.

I pressed my forehead against the window and watched the dusty summer hills roll past. Meredith's car smelled like cigarette smoke, and there was mold on the strap of the seat belt from something some other child had been allowed to eat. I was nine years old. I sat in the backseat of the car in my night-gown, my cropped hair a tangled mess. It was not the way Meredith had wanted it. She'd purchased a dress for the occasion, a flowing, pale blue shift with embroidery and lace. But I had refused to wear it.

Meredith stared at the road ahead. She didn't see me unbuckle my seat belt, roll down the window, and stick my head out until my collarbone pressed against the top of the door. Tilting my chin up into the wind, I waited for her to tell me to sit down. She glanced back at me but didn't say anything. Her mouth remained a tight line, and I couldn't see her expression underneath her sunglasses.

I stayed this way until Meredith touched a button on her door that made the window rise an inch without warning. The thick glass pressed into my outstretched neck. I flew back, bouncing off the seat and sinking down onto the floor. Meredith continued to raise the window until the wind rushing through the car was replaced by silence. She did not look back. Curling up on the dirty carpet, I pulled a rancid baby bottle from deep beneath the passenger seat and threw it at Meredith. It hit her shoulder and flew back at me, leaking a sour puddle onto my knees. Meredith didn't flinch.

"Do you want peaches?" she asked.

Food was something I could never refuse, and Meredith knew it.

"Yes."

"Then get in your seat, buckle your seat belt, and I'll buy you whatever you want at the next fruit stand we pass."

I climbed onto the seat and pulled the seat belt across my waist.

Fifteen minutes passed before Meredith pulled off the freeway. She bought me two peaches and a half-pound of cherries, which I counted as I ate.

"I'm not supposed to tell you this," Meredith began as we turned back onto the road.

Her words were slow, the sentence drawn out for effect. She paused and glanced back at me. I held my gaze out the window and rested my cheek against the glass, unresponsive. "But I think you deserve to know. This is your last chance. Your very last chance, Victoria — did you hear me?" I didn't acknowledge her question. "When you turn ten, the county will label you unadoptable, and even *I* won't keep trying to convince families to take you. It'll be group home after group home until you emancipate if this doesn't work out — just promise me you'll think about that."

I rolled down the window and spit cherry seeds into the wind. Meredith had picked me up from my first stay at a group home just an hour before. It struck me that my placement in the home might have been purposeful — in preparation for this exact moment. I hadn't done anything to get kicked out of my last foster home, and I was in the group home only a week before Meredith came to take me to Elizabeth.

It would be just like Meredith, I thought, *to make me suffer to prove her point.* The staff at the group home had been cruel. Every morning the cook made a fat, dark-skinned girl eat with her shirt pulled up around her neck, her bulging belly exposed, so she would remember not to eat too much. Afterward, the housemother, Miss Gayle, chose one of us to stand at the head of the long table and explain why our family didn't want us. Miss Gayle picked me only once, and since I was abandoned at birth, I got away with saying "My mother didn't want a baby." Other girls told stories of the awful things they'd done to siblings, or why they were responsible for their parents' drug addictions, and almost always they cried.

But if Meredith had placed me in the group home to scare me into behaving, it hadn't worked. Despite the staff, I liked it there. Meals were served at regular hours, I slept under two blankets, and no one pretended to love me.

I ate the last cherry and spit the seed at the back of Meredith's head.

"Just think about it," she said again. As if to bribe me into contemplation, she pulled over and purchased a steaming basket of fish and chips and a chocolate milkshake from a drive-through. I ate quickly, sloppily, watching the dry landscape of the East Bay turn into the crowded chaos of San Francisco and then open up into a great expanse of water. By the time we crossed the Golden Gate Bridge, my nightgown was covered in peaches, cherries, ketchup, and ice cream.

We passed dry fields, a flower farm, and an empty parking lot, and finally came to a vineyard, the vines neat stripes on the rolling hillside. Meredith braked hard and turned left onto a long dirt driveway, increasing her speed on the bumpy road as if she couldn't wait another moment to get me out of her car. We went flying past picnic tables and rows of carefully tended, thick-trunked grapevines growing on low wires. Meredith slowed slightly at a turn before picking up speed again and driving toward a gathering of tall trees in the center of the property, dust billowing around her county car.

When she stopped and the dust cleared, I saw a white farmhouse. It stood two stories tall with a peaked roof, a glass-enclosed porch, and lace curtains covering the windows. To the right was a low metal trailer and more than one slumping shed, toys, tools, and bikes scattered between them. Having lived in a trailer before, I immediately wondered if Elizabeth would have a foldout couch or if I would have to share her bedroom. I didn't like listening to people breathe.

Meredith didn't wait to see if I would get out of the car voluntarily. She unbuckled my seat belt, grabbed me under my arms, and pulled me kicking to the front of the large house. I expected Elizabeth to come out of the trailer, so I had my back to the front porch and didn't see her before feeling her bony fingers on my shoulder. Shrieking, I bolted forward, sprinting on bare feet to the far side of the car and then crouching down behind it.

"She doesn't like to be touched," I heard Meredith say to Elizabeth with obvious annoyance. "I told you that. You have to wait until she comes to you." It angered me that she knew this. I rubbed the skin where Elizabeth had grabbed me, erasing her fingerprints, and stayed out of sight behind the car.

"I'll wait," Elizabeth said. "I told you I would wait, and I don't intend to go back on my word."

Meredith began to recite the usual list of reasons she couldn't stay to help us get to know each other: an ailing grandparent, an anxious husband, and her fear of driving at night. Elizabeth's foot tapped impatiently near the rear tire as she listened. In a moment Meredith would be gone, leaving me exposed in the gravel. I crawled backward, low to the ground. Darting behind a walnut tree, I stood up and ran.

At the end of the trees I ducked into the

first row of grapes, hiding within a dense plant. I pulled down the loose vines and wrapped them around my thin body. From my hiding spot I could hear Elizabeth coming toward me, and by adjusting the vines I could see her walking along one of the aisles. I let my hand drop from my mouth with relief as she passed my row.

Reaching up, I picked a grape from the nearest bunch and bit through the thick skin. It was sour. I spit it out and smashed the rest of the bunch one at a time under my foot, the juice squishing between my toes.

I didn't see or hear Elizabeth come back in my direction. But just as I began to smash a second bunch of grapes, she reached down into the vines, grabbed me by the arms, and pulled me out of my hiding spot. She held me out in front of her. My feet dangled an inch above the ground while she looked me over.

"I grew up here," she said. "I know all the good hiding spots."

I tried to break loose, but Elizabeth held firmly to both my arms. She set my feet down on the dirt but did not loosen her grasp. I kicked dust onto her shins, and when she didn't release my arms, I kicked her ankles. She did not step back.

I let out a growl and snapped my teeth toward her outstretched arm, but she saw me coming and grabbed my face. She squeezed my cheeks until my jaw loosened and my lips puckered. I sucked in my breath in pain.

"No biting," she said, and then leaned forward as if she would kiss my pink puckered lips but stopped inches from my face, her dark eyes drilling into mine. "I like to be touched," she said. "You'll have to get used to it."

She flashed me an amused grin and let go of my face.

"I won't," I promised. "I won't ever get used to it."

But I stopped fighting and let her pull me up the front porch and inside the cool, dark house.

3.

Meredith turned off Sunset Boulevard and drove too slowly down Noriega, reading each street sign. An impatient car honked behind us.

She'd been talking continuously since Fell Street, and the list of reasons my survival seemed unlikely stretched halfway across San Francisco: no high school diploma, no motivation, no support network, a complete lack of social skills. She was asking for my plan, demanding I think about my own self-sufficiency.

I ignored her.

It hadn't always been this way between us. As a young child I'd soaked up her chatty optimism, sitting on the edge of a bed while she brushed and braided my thin brown hair, tying it up with a ribbon before presenting me like a gift to a new mother, a new father. But as the years passed, and family after family gave me back, Meredith's hopefulness chilled. The once-gentle hairbrush pulled, stopping and starting with the rhythm of her lecturing. The description of how I should act lengthened with each placement change, and became more and more different from the child I knew myself to be. Meredith kept a running list of my deficiencies in her appointment book and read them to the judge like criminal convictions. Detached. Quick-tempered. Tight-lipped. Unrepentant. I remembered every word she said.

But despite her frustrations, Meredith had kept my case. She refused to transfer it out of the adoptions unit even when a tired judge suggested, the summer I turned eight, that perhaps she'd done all she could. Meredith negated this claim without pause. For a buoyant, bewildered moment I thought her reaction had come from a place of hidden fondness for me, but when I turned my gaze I saw her pale skin pink in embarrassment. She had been my social worker since birth; if I was to be declared a failure, I was, by extension, her failure.

We pulled up in front of The Gathering House, a peach, flat-roofed stucco house in a row of peach, flat-roofed stucco houses.

"Three months," Meredith said. "I want to hear you say it. I want to know you understand. Three months' free rent, and after that you pay up or move out."

I said nothing. Meredith stepped out and slammed the car door behind her.

My box in the backseat had shifted during the drive, my clothes spilling out onto the seat. I piled them back on top of the books and followed Meredith up the front steps. She rang the bell.

It was more than a minute before the door opened, and when it did a cluster of girls stood in the entryway. I clutched my box tighter to my chest.

A short, heavy-legged girl with long blond hair pushed open the metal screen and stuck out her hand. "I'm Eve," she said.

Meredith stepped on my foot, but I didn't reach for her outstretched hand. "This is Victoria Jones," she said, pushing me forward. "She's eighteen today."

There was a mumbling of happy birthdays, and two girls exchanged eyebrow-arched glances.

"Alexis was evicted last week," Eve said. "You get her room." She turned as if to take me there, and I followed her down a dark, carpeted hall to an open doorway. Slipping inside, I closed the door and turned the lock behind me.

The room was bright white. It smelled like fresh paint, and the walls, when I touched

them, were tacky. The painter had been sloppy. The carpet, once white like the walls but now mottled from use, was streaked with paint near the baseboard. I wished the painter had kept going, painted the entire carpet, the single mattress, and the dark wood nightstand. The white was clean and new, and I liked that it had belonged to no one before me.

From the hall, Meredith called me. She knocked, and knocked again. I set my heavy box down in the middle of the room. Pulling out my clothes, I piled them onto the closet floor and stacked my books on the nightstand. When the box was empty, I ripped it into strips to cover the bare mattress and lay down on top. Light streamed through a small window and reflected off the walls, warming the exposed skin on my face, neck, and hands. The window was south-facing, I noticed, good for orchids and bulbs.

"Victoria?" Meredith called again. "I need to know your plan. Just tell me your plan and I'll leave you alone."

I closed my eyes, ignoring the sound of her knuckles against the wood. Finally, she stopped knocking.

When I opened my eyes, an envelope lay on the carpet near the door. Inside, there was a twenty-dollar bill and a note that read:

Buy food and find a job.

Meredith's twenty-dollar bill bought five gallons of whole milk. Every morning for a week I made my purchase at the corner store, drinking the creamy liquid slowly throughout the day as I wandered from city parks to schoolyards, identifying the local plants. Having never lived so near the ocean, I expected the landscape to be unfamiliar. I expected the dense morning fog, hovering only inches from the soil, would cultivate an array of vegetation I had never before seen. But except for wide mounds of aloe near the water's edge, tall red flowers reaching for the sky, I found a surprising lack of new-ness. The same foreign plants I'd seen in gardens and nurseries all over the Bay Area — lantana, bougainvillea, potato vine, and nasturtium — dominated the neighborhood. Only the scale was different. Wrapped in the opaque moisture of the coast, plants grew bigger, brighter, and wilder, eclipsing low fences and garden sheds.

When I finished a gallon of milk I would return home, cut the jug in half with a kitchen knife, and wait for night. The soil in the next-door neighbor's flower bed was dark and rich, and I transferred it into my improvised flowerpots with a soupspoon.

Poking holes in the bottoms of the jugs, I set them in the center of my bedroom floor, where they would get direct sun for only a few hours in the late mornings.

I would look for a job; I knew I needed to. But for the first time in my life I had my own bedroom with a locking door, and no one telling me where to be or what to do. Before I started searching for work, I'd decided, I would grow a garden.

By the end of my first week I had created fourteen flowerpots and surveyed a sixteen-block radius for my options. Focusing on fall-blooming flowers, I uprooted whole plants from front yards, community gardens, and playgrounds. Usually I walked home, my hands cradling muddy root balls, but on more than one occasion I ended up lost, or too far from The Gathering House. On these days I would sneak onto a crowded bus through the back door, push my way onto a seat, and ride until the neighborhood became familiar. Back in my room, I spread out the shocked roots gently, covered them with the nutrient-rich soil, and watered deeply. The milk jugs drained right onto the carpet, and as the days passed, weeds began to sprout from the worn fiber. I hovered, watchful, plucking the invasive species almost before they could push their way out of the darkness.

Meredith checked in on me weekly. The judge had declared her my *permanent connection,* because emancipation legislation required a connection and they couldn't dig anyone else out of my file. I did my best to avoid her. When I returned from my walks, I surveyed The Gathering House from the corner, walking up the front steps only when her white car wasn't parked in the driveway. Eventually she divined my tactic, and in early September I unlocked the front door to find her sitting at the dining room table.

"Where's your car?" I demanded.

"Parked around the block," she said. "I haven't seen you in over a month, so I figured you must be avoiding me. Is there a reason?"

"No reason." I walked to the table and pushed someone's dirty dishes out of the way. Sitting down, I placed fistfuls of lavender — which I had uprooted from a front yard in Pacific Heights — on the scratched wood between us. "Lavender," I said, handing her a sprig. *Mistrust.*

Meredith spun the sprig between her thumb and forefinger and set it down, uninterested. "Job?" she asked.

"What job?"

"Do you have one?"

"Why would I have one?"

Meredith sighed. She picked up the lavender I'd given her and launched it, tip first, in my direction. It nose-dived like a poorly constructed paper airplane. Snatching it off the table, I smoothed its ruffled petals with a careful thumb.

"You would have one," Meredith said, "because you've looked for one, and applied, and been hired. Because if you don't, you'll be out on the street in six weeks, and there won't be anyone opening their door for you on a cold night."

I looked to the front door, wondering how much longer until she'd leave.

"You have to want it," Meredith said. "I can only do so much. At the end of the day, you have to want it."

Want what? I always wondered when she said this. I wanted Meredith to leave. I wanted to drink the milk on the top shelf of the refrigerator labeled LORRAINE and add the empty jug to the collection in my room. I wanted to plant the lavender near my pillow and go to sleep inhaling the cool, dry scent.

Meredith stood. "I'll be back next week when you least expect me, and I want to see a thick stack of job applications in your backpack." She paused at the door. "It'll be hard for me to put you out on the street, but you should know that I'll do it."

I did not believe it would be hard.

I walked into the kitchen and opened the freezer, poking through egg rolls and frost-bitten corn dogs until I heard the front door close.

I spent my final weeks at The Gathering House transplanting my bedroom garden into McKinley Square, a small city park at the top of Potrero Hill. I'd found it while pacing the streets for help-wanted signs, and been distracted by the park's perfect combination of sun, shade, solitude, and safety. Potrero Hill was one of the warmest neighborhoods in the city, and the park was located at a peak, with a clear view in every direction. A small, sandy play structure sat in the middle of a manicured square of lawn, but behind the lawn the park became forested and steep, tumbling downhill in a tangle of shrubs overlooking San Francisco General Hospital and a brewery. Instead of continuing my job search, I'd transported my jugs one at a time to the secluded spot. I chose the location for each planting thought-fully — shade-loving plants under tall trees, those desiring sun a dozen yards down the hill, out of the shadows.

The morning of my eviction I awoke before dawn. My room was empty, the floor still damp and dirty in patches where the milk jugs had been. My imminent homelessness had not been a conscious decision; yet, rising to dress on the morning I was to be turned out onto the street, I was surprised to find that I was not afraid. Where I had expected fear, or anger, I was filled with nervous anticipation, the feeling similar to what I'd experienced as a young girl, on the eve of each new adoptive placement. Now, as an adult, my hopes for the future were simple: I wanted to be alone, and to be surrounded by flowers. It seemed, finally, that I might get exactly what I wanted.

My room was empty except for three sets of clothes, my backpack, a toothbrush, hair gel, and the books Elizabeth had given me. Lying in bed the night before, I'd listened to my housemates picking through the rest of my belongings like hungry animals devouring the fallen. It was standard procedure in foster and group homes, the scouring of things left behind by rushed, weepy children. My housemates, emancipated, carried on the tradition.

It'd been years — nearly ten — since I'd participated in the scavenging, but I could still remember the thrill of finding something edible, something I could sell at school for a nickel, something mysterious or personal. In elementary school I began to collect these small, forgotten things like treasures — a silver charm with an engraved *M,* a watch-band of fake turquoise snakeskin, a quarter-sized pillbox containing a blood-encrusted molar — stuffing them into a mesh zippered bag I'd stolen from someone's laundry room. The objects pressed through the tiny holes of the fabric as the bag grew full and heavy.

For a short time I told myself I was saving these objects for their rightful owners — not to give them back but to use as bribes for food or favors if we landed again in the same home. But as it grew I began to covet my collection, telling myself the stories of each object over and over again: the time I lived with Molly, the girl who loved cats; the bunkmate whose watch had been ripped off and arm broken; the basement apartment where Sarah learned the truth about the Tooth Fairy. My attachment to the objects was not based on any connection with the individuals. More often than not I had avoided them, ignoring their names, their circumstances, the hopes they had for their futures. But over time the objects came to read like a string of clues to my past, a path of bread crumbs, and I had a vague sense of wanting to follow them back to the place before my memories began. Then, in a rushed, chaotic placement change, I'd been forced to leave the bag behind. For years afterward I'd refused to pack up my belongings, arriving at each new foster home stubbornly empty-handed.

Quickly, I began to dress: two tank tops followed by three T-shirts and a hooded sweatshirt, brown stretch pants, socks, and shoes. My brown wool blanket would not fit in my backpack, so I folded it in half, wrapped it around my waist, and secured a pleat with a safety pin at each inch. The bottom I gathered and pinned in bunches like a formal petticoat, covering the whole thing with two skirts of varying lengths, the first long and lacy orange, the second A-line and burgundy. I studied myself in the bathroom mirror as I brushed my teeth and washed my face, satisfied to see that I was neither attractive nor repulsive. My curves were well hidden beneath my clothing, and the extra-short haircut I'd given myself the night before made my bright blue eyes — the only remarkable feature on an otherwise or-dinary face — look uncannily large, almost frightening in their dominance of my face. I smiled into the mirror. I didn't look home-less. Not yet, at least.

I paused in the doorway of my empty

room. Sunlight shone off the white walls. I wondered who would come next, and what they'd think of the weeds sprouting from the carpet near the foot of the bed. If I had thought of it, I would have left the new girl a milk jug full of fennel. The feathery plant and licorice-sweet smell would have been a comfort. But it was too late. I nodded goodbye to the room that would no longer be mine, feeling a sudden gratitude for the angle of the sun, the locking door, the brief offering of time and space.

I hurried into the living room. Through the window I saw Meredith's car already in the driveway, the engine off. She studied her reflection in the rearview mirror, her hands clutching the steering wheel. Spinning around, I snuck out the back door and onto the first bus that passed.

I never saw Meredith again.

4.

From the brewery at the bottom of the hill, steam rose smokelike into the sky day and night. I watched the spread of white while I weeded, the image infusing my contentment with an edge of despair.

November in San Francisco was mild, McKinley Square quiet. My garden, except for a sensitive matilija poppy, survived the transplant, and for the first twenty-four hours I imagined I could be satisfied with an anonymous life, hidden in the safety of the trees. I listened as I worked, prepared to run at the sound of footsteps, but no one wandered off the manicured lawn, no one poked a curious face into the forest where I crouched. Even the playground was empty except for a fifteen-minute window before school, when closely monitored children swung (one, two, three times) before continuing down the hill. By the third day, I could match the children's voices with their names. I knew who listened to their mother (Genna), who was loved by their teacher (Chloe), and who would rather be buried alive in the sandbox than sit through another day of class (Greta, little Greta; if my asters had been in bloom, I would have left her a bucketful in the sandbox, so desolate was the voice that begged her mother to let her stay). The families couldn't see me, and I couldn't see them, but as the days passed I began to look forward to their visits. I spent the early mornings thinking about which child I would have been most like, had I had a mother to walk me to school every morning. I imagined myself obedient instead of defiant, quick to smile instead of sullen. I wondered if I would still love flowers, if I would still crave solitude. Questions, unanswerable, swirled like water at the roots of my wild geraniums, which I soaked deeply and often.

When my hunger grew to the point of distraction, I climbed onto buses and rode to the Marina, Fillmore Street, or Pacific Heights. I toured high-end delis, lingering at polished marble countertops and sampling an olive, a slice of Canadian bacon, or a sliver of Havarti. I asked the questions Elizabeth would have asked: which olive oils were unfiltered; exactly how "fresh" was the albacore, the salmon, the sole; how sweet were the season's first blood oranges? I accepted additional samples, feigned indecision. Then, when the attendant turned to another customer, I walked out the door.

Afterward, my hunger barely appeased, I wandered the hills, looking for plants to add to my growing garden. I searched private yards as often as public parks, slipping beneath canopies of morning glory and passionflower. On the rare occasion I settled near a plant I could not identify, I pinched a stem and carried it quickly to a crowded restaurant, where I waited for a customer to leave before taking my place at her table. Sitting before abandoned plates of half-eaten lasagna or risotto, I placed the distressed bud in a sweating water glass, its weakened green neck drooping against the lip of the glass. As I ate small, saucy bites, I thumbed through my field guide, studying the parts of the plant and answering questions methodically: *Petals numerous or not apparent? Leaves swordlike, emerging from one another, or heart-shaped? Plant with copious milky juice, ovary hanging to one side of flower, or without milky juice, ovary erect?* When I had deduced the plant family and memorized its common and scientific name, I pressed the flower between the pages and looked around, hoping to find another half-empty plate.

The third night, sleep evaded me. My empty stomach churned, and for the first time, my flowers offered no reassurance. Instead, the dark floral silhouettes were reminders of the time I'd had to look for a job, the time I'd been given to start a new life. I pulled my blanket tighter around my head and closed my eyes, drifting in and out of consciousness, refusing to think about what I would do when the next day arrived, or the day after that.

In the middle of the night, I was startled awake by the sharp smell of tequila. My eyes snapped open. The heath bush I'd transplanted from an alley off Divisadero stretched its needled arms over my head. Between the new growth and glowing bell-shaped blossoms, I saw the outline of a man bend over and snap a stem of my helenium. His tequila bottle leaned over as he did, alcohol splashing out of the top and landing on the shrub concealing my body. A girl behind him reached for the bottle. She sat down on the ground with her back to me and tilted her face to the sky.

The man held out the flower, and in the moonlight I could tell he was young: too young to be drinking, too young even to be

44

out after dark. He ran the petals along the top of the girl's head and down the side of her face. "A daisy for my darling," he said with an attempted southern drawl. He was drunk.

"That's a sunflower, dumb ass," the girl said, laughing. Her ponytail, tied with a ribbon that matched her shirt and pleated skirt, swung back and forth. She plucked the flower from between his fingers and smelled it. The small orange blossom was missing half its petals; she scattered the remaining few until the center bobbed, abandoned in the night air, and then flicked it into the forest.

The boy sat down close to her. He smelled of sweat masked by drugstore cologne. She threw the empty bottle into the bushes and turned to him.

Without pause, the boy began to devour the girl's face with sloppy smacking sounds, his hands underneath her shirt. His tongue pushed open her mouth, and I thought she would gag, but instead she feigned a moan and grasped at his greasy hair. My own stomach lurched, a slice of salami high in my throat. I held one hand over my mouth and the other over my eyes, but still I heard them. Their kissing sounds were wet and aggressive, traveling to where I lay with such

precision that they felt like ravenous fingertips, gouging my lips, my neck, my breasts.

I curled up into a tight ball, the bed of
leaves crackling beneath my body. The couple kept kissing.

From the bus stop the next morning, I
watched a tall woman with a bucketful of
white tulips slip a key into the lock of the
neighborhood flower shop. She flipped on
the light and the word BLOOM, created with
bundled sticks, emerged backlit from the
large picture window. Crossing the street, I
approached her.

"Out of season," I said, nodding to the
tulips.

The woman raised her eyebrows. "Brides."
She set the bucket down and looked at me as
if waiting for me to speak.

I thought of the lovers tangled under my
heath. They had collapsed even closer to
me than I'd thought, and I'd stepped on the
boy's shoulder blade before I could locate
them in the shrubs. Neither one had moved.
The girl's lips rested on the boy's neck as if
she'd passed out in the middle of a kiss; the
boy's chin pointed up, his head pressed back
into tangles of helenium as if he'd been enjoying it. In an instant, my illusion of safety
and solitude had vanished.

"Can I help you?" the woman asked. She ran impatient fingers through spiky gray hair.

It occurred to me that I had forgotten to apply my hair gel, and I hoped I didn't have leaves stuck in my hair. I shook my head self-consciously before I spoke. "Are you hiring?"

She looked me up and down. "Do you have experience?"

Running my toe along a deep line in the concrete, I considered my experience. Jam jars full of thistle and duct-taped spikes of aloe didn't count for much in the world of flower arranging. I could spew scientific names and recite histories of plant families, but I doubted either of these would impress her. I shook my head. "No."

"Then no." She looked at me again, and her gaze was as unwavering as Elizabeth's had once been. My throat tightened, and I clutched at my brown blanket petticoat, afraid it would come loose and pool at my feet.

"I'll give you five dollars to unload my truck," she said. I bit my lip and nodded.

It must be the leaves in my hair, I thought.

5.

The bath was already drawn. It made me feel uneasy to think that Elizabeth knew I would arrive dirty.

"Do you need my help?" she asked.

"No." The bathtub was sparkling white, the soap nestled among seashells in a reflective metal dish.

"Come down when you're dressed, then, and be quick." A clean outfit was arranged for me on a white wood vanity.

I waited until she left, tried to lock the door behind her, and saw that the lock had been removed. I pulled the small chair from the vanity and propped it under the doorknob, so at the very least I would hear her coming. Taking my clothes off as fast as I could, I submerged myself in the hot water.

When I came back downstairs, Elizabeth was sitting at the kitchen table, her food untouched and her napkin on her lap. I was dressed in the clothes she had purchased,

a white blouse and yellow pants. Elizabeth looked me over, undoubtedly taking in their enormity. I had rolled the pants down at the waist and up at the legs, and still they hung low enough to show my underwear, if my shirt hadn't been so long. I was a head shorter than most of the girls in my third-grade class, and I had lost five pounds earlier in the summer.

When I told Meredith the reason for my weight loss she'd called me a liar, but she pulled me from the home anyway, launching a formal investigation. The judge listened to my story and then to Ms. Tapley's. *I will not be made a criminal for refusing to cater to the demands of a picky eater,* she had written in her testimony. The judge proclaimed the truth to lie somewhere in the middle, his eyes on me stern and accusing. But he was wrong. Ms. Tapley was lying. I had more faults than Meredith could list on a court report, but I was not a picky eater.

For the entire month of June, Ms. Tapley had made me prove my hunger. It started on my first day in her home, the day after school let out. She helped me unpack my things in my new room and asked, in a voice kind enough to arouse my suspicion, to know my favorite and least favorite foods. But I answered anyway, hungry: pizza, I said, and frozen peas. For dinner that night, she served me a bowl of peas, still frozen. If I was truly hungry, she said, I would eat it. I walked away. Ms. Tapley locked the refrigerator and all the kitchen cabinets.

For two days I left my room only to use the bathroom. Cooking smells pushed under my door at regular intervals, the phone rang, and the TV grew louder and softer. Ms. Tapley did not come to me. After twenty-four hours I called Meredith, but my reports of starvation were so common that she did not return my call. I was sweating, shaking, when I returned to the kitchen table on the third night. Ms. Tapley watched my weak arms attempt to pull the heavy chair away from the table. Giving up, I slid my paper-thin body into the crack between the table and the back of the chair. The peas in the bowl were shriveled and hard. Ms. Tapley glared at me over the top of a dish towel as grease popped on the stove, lecturing me about foster kids eating because they were traumatized. *Food is not for comfort,* she said as I placed the first pea in my mouth. It rolled down my tongue and stuck in my throat like a pebble. Swallowing hard, I ate another, counting each pea as it went down. The smell of grease and something frying kept me going. Thirty-six. Thirty-seven. After the thirty-eighth pea, I vomited them back into the bowl. *Try again,* she said, gesturing to the half-digested peas. She sat down on a bar stool in the kitchen and pulled steaming meat out of the pan, taking hot bites and watching me. I tried again. The weeks continued this way until Meredith came for her monthly visit; by then the weight was already lost.

Elizabeth smiled as I entered the kitchen.

"You *are* beautiful," she said, not attempting to conceal the surprise in her voice. "It was hard to tell underneath all that ketchup. Do you feel better?"

"No," I said, though it was not the truth. I couldn't remember the last home that allowed me to use the bathtub; Jackie may have had one upstairs, but kids were not permitted on the second floor. Before that was a long series of small apartments, the narrow shower stalls crowded with beauty products and layers of mold. The hot bath had felt good, but now, looking at Elizabeth, I wondered what it would cost me.

Climbing up onto a chair, I sat at the kitchen table. Set out was enough food for a family of six. Big bowls of pasta, thick slices of ham, cherry tomatoes, green apples, American cheese stacked in clear plastic sleeves, even a spoon full of peanut butter on a white cloth napkin. It was too much to count. My heart beat audibly; my lips curled into my mouth, and I bit my upper and lower lip together. Elizabeth would force me to eat everything on the table. And for the first time in months, I wasn't hungry. I looked up at her, waiting for the command.

"Kid food," she said, gesturing to the table shyly. "How did I do?"

I didn't say anything.

"I can't imagine you're hungry," she said, when she could see that I wasn't going to respond. "Not if your nightgown was evidence of your afternoon."

I shook my head.

"Eat only what you want, then," she said. "But sit at the table with me until I've finished."

I exhaled, momentarily relieved. Dropping my eyes to the table, I noticed a small bouquet of white flowers. It was tied with a lavender ribbon and placed on top of my bowl of pasta. I studied the delicate petals before flicking it off my food. My mind filled with stories I'd heard from other children, tales of poisoning and hospitalizations. I glanced around the room to see if the windows were open, in case I needed to run. There was only one window in the room of white wood cabinets and antique appliances: a small square above the kitchen sink, with miniature blue glass bottles lining the windowsill. It was shut tight.

I pointed to the flowers. "You can't poison me, or give me medicine I don't want, or hit me — even if I deserve it. Those are the rules." I glared across the table when I said it and hoped she felt my threat. I had reported more than one person for spanking.

"If I were trying to poison you, I would give you foxglove or hydrangea, maybe anemone, depending on how much pain I wanted you to feel, and what message I was trying to communicate."

Curiosity overcame my dislike of conversation. "What're you talking about?"

"These flowers are starwort," she said. "Starwort means *welcome*. By giving you a bouquet of starwort, I'm welcoming you to my home, to my life." She twirled buttery pasta on her fork and looked into my eyes without a glimmer of humor.

"They look like daisies to me," I said. "And I still think they're poisonous."

"They aren't poisonous, and they aren't daisies. See how they only have five petals but it looks like they have ten? Each pair of petals is connected in the center." Picking up the small bouquet of flowers, I examined the little white bundle. The petals grew together before attaching to the stem, so that each petal was the shape of a heart.

"That's a characteristic of the genus *Stellaria*," Elizabeth went on, when she could see that I understood. "Daisy is a common name, and spans many different families, but the flowers we call daisies typically have more petals, and each petal grows separate from the others. It's important to know the difference or you may confuse the meaning. Daisy means *innocence*, which is a very different sentiment than *welcome*."

"I still don't know what you're talking about," I said.

"Are you done eating?" Elizabeth asked, setting down her fork. I had only picked at the slabs of ham, but I nodded. "Then come with me and I'll explain."

Elizabeth stood and turned to cross the kitchen. I stuffed a fistful of pasta into one pocket and dumped the bowl of small tomatoes into the other. Elizabeth paused at the back door but did not turn around. I pulled up my kneesocks and lined the American cheese between my socks and calves. Before jumping down from the chair, I grabbed the spoon of peanut butter, licking it slowly as I followed Elizabeth. Four wooden steps brought us down into a large flower garden.

"I'm talking about the language of flowers," Elizabeth said. "It's from the Victorian era, like your name. If a man gave a young lady a bouquet of flowers, she would race home and try to decode it like a secret message. Red roses mean *love;* yellow roses *infidelity.* So a man would have to choose his flowers carefully."

"What's infidelity?" I asked as we turned down a path and yellow roses surrounded us on all sides.

Elizabeth paused. When I looked up, I saw that her expression had turned sad. For a moment I thought something I said had disturbed her, but then I realized her eyes were directed at the roses, not at me. I wondered who had planted them. "It means to have friends . . . secret friends," she said finally. "Friends you aren't supposed to have."

I didn't understand her definition, but Elizabeth had already moved along the path, reaching out for my peanut-butter spoon to drag me with her. I snatched my spoon back and followed her around another bend.

"There's rosemary; that's for remembrance. I'm quoting Shakespeare; you'll read him in high school. And there's columbine, *desertion;* holly, *foresight;* lavender, *mistrust.*" We took a fork in the path, and Elizabeth ducked under a low-hanging branch. I finished the last of the peanut butter with one slow lick, threw the spoon into the bushes, and jumped up to swing on the branch. The tree did not sway.

"That's an almond tree. Its spring blossoms are the symbol of indiscretion — nothing you need to know about. A beautiful tree, though," she added, "and I've long thought it would be a great place for a tree house. I'll ask Carlos about building one."

"Who's Carlos?" I asked, jumping down. Elizabeth was ahead of me on the path, and I skipped to catch up.

"The foreman. He lives in the trailer between the tool sheds, but you won't meet him this week — he took his daughter camping. Perla's nine, like you are. She'll look out for you when you start school."

"I'm not going to school," I said, struggling to keep up. Elizabeth had reached the center of the garden and was making her way back to the house. She was still pointing out plants and reciting meanings, but she walked too fast for me to keep up. I started to jog and caught up with her just as she reached the back porch steps. She crouched down so that we were eye to eye.

"You'll start school a week from Monday," she said. "Fourth grade. And you aren't coming inside until you bring me my spoon."

She turned then and went inside, locking the door behind her.

6.

Tucking the florist's five-dollar bill into the empty space beneath the cup of my bra, I paced the neighborhood. It was still early, and there were more bars than coffee shops open as I walked through the Mission District. On the corner of 24th and Alabama, I slid into a pink plastic booth and spent two hours eating donuts and waiting for the small shops on Valencia Street to open. At ten o'clock I counted my remaining money — one dollar and eighty-seven cents — and walked until I found a fabric shop. I purchased half a yard of white satin ribbon and a single pearl-topped pin.

When I returned to McKinley Square it was late morning, and I crept toward my garden on silent grass. I was afraid the couple would still be sprawled across my flowers, but they were gone. The imprint of the boy's back in my helenium and the tequila bottle protruding from a dense shrub were

57

all that remained.

I had only one chance. It was clear to me that the florist needed help; her face had been as pale and lined as Elizabeth's in the weeks before the harvest. If I could convince her I was capable, she would hire me. With the money I earned I would rent a room with a locking door and tend my garden only in daylight, when I could see strangers as they approached.

Sitting under a tree, I studied my options. The fall flowers were in full bloom: verbena, goldenrod, chrysanthemum, and a late-blooming rose. The carefully tended city beds around the park held layers of textured evergreen but little color.

I set to work, considering height, density, texture, and layers of scent, removing touch-damaged petals with careful pinches. When I had finished, spiraling white mums emerged from a cushion of snow-colored verbena, and clusters of pale climbing roses circled and dripped over the edge of a tightly wrapped nosegay. I removed every thorn. The bouquet was white as a wedding and spoke of prayers, truth, and an unacquainted heart. No one would know.

The woman was locking up when I arrived. It was not yet noon.

"If you're looking for another five dollars, you're too late," she said, gesturing to the truck with her head. It was full of heavy arrangements. "I could have used your help."

I held out my bouquet.

"What's this?" she asked.

"Experience," I said, handing her the flowers.

She smelled the mums and roses, and then poked the verbena, examining the tip of her finger. It was clean. Starting up the hill to her truck, she motioned for me to follow.

From within the truck she withdrew a nosegay of stiff white roses, packed close and tied with pink satin. She held the two bouquets side by side. There was no comparison. She tossed me the white roses, and I caught them with one hand.

"Take those to Spitari's, up the hill. Ask for Andrew, and tell him I sent you. He'll let you trade the flowers for your lunch."

I nodded, and she climbed inside the truck. "I'm Renata." She started the engine. "If you want to work next Saturday, be here by five a.m. If you're even a minute late, I'll leave you behind."

I felt like sprinting down the hill, overcome with relief. It didn't matter that I'd been promised only a single day's work, or that the money would probably only be enough to rent a room for a handful of nights. It was something. And if I proved myself, she would invite me back. I smiled at the sidewalk, my toes jittering in my shoes.

Renata pulled away from the curb, then slowed to a stop and rolled down her window. "Name?" she asked.

"Victoria," I said, looking up and suppressing a smile. "Victoria Jones."

She nodded once and drove away.

The following Saturday, I arrived at Bloom just after midnight. I had fallen asleep in my garden with my back against a redwood, keeping watch, and I bolted awake at the sound of approaching laughter. It was a band of drunken young men this time. The nearest, an overgrown boy with hair past his chin, smiled at me as if we were lovers meeting at a prearranged location. I avoided his eyes and walked quickly to the nearest streetlamp, then down the hill to the flower shop.

While I waited I applied deodorant and gel, then paced the block, forcing myself to stay awake. By the time Renata's truck turned up the street, I had checked my reflection in parked car mirrors twice and reordered my clothing three times. Even with all of this, I knew I was beginning to look and smell like a street person.

Renata pulled up, unlocked the passenger door, and motioned for me to get inside. I sat as far away from her as possible, and when I slammed the door it rattled against my fleshless hip.

"Good morning," said Renata. "You're on time." She U-turned and drove down the empty street the way she had come.

"Too early to wish me a good morning?" she asked. I nodded, rubbing my eyes, pretending I'd just awakened. We drove in silence around a roundabout. Renata missed her turn and went around twice. "It's a little early for me, too, I guess."

She drove up and down the one-way streets south of Market until she pulled in to a crowded parking lot.

"Follow close," she said, getting out of the truck and handing me a stack of empty buckets. "It's crowded in there, and I don't have time to waste looking for you. I have a two o'clock wedding today; the flowers have to be delivered by ten. Luckily, they're just sunflowers — won't take long to arrange."

"Sunflowers?" I asked, surprised. *False riches. It wouldn't be my wedding flower of choice,* I thought, and then rolled my eyes at the absurdity of the words *my wedding.*

"Out of season, I know," she said. "You

61

can get anything — anytime — at the flower market, and when couples throw money at me, I don't complain." She shoved her way through the crowded entry. I followed close behind, cringing as buckets and elbows and shoulders brushed my body.

The inside of the flower market was like a cave, hollow and windowless, with a metal ceiling and cement floor. The unnaturalness of the sea of flowers within, far from soil and light, set me on edge. Booths overflowed with seasonal flowers, everything blooming in my own garden but cut and displayed in bunches. Other vendors sold tropical flowers, orchids and hibiscus and exotic plants I couldn't name, from hothouses hundreds of miles away. I plucked a passionflower and tucked it in my waistband as we rushed past.

Renata flipped through sunflowers as if they were pages of a book. She argued over prices, walked away, and returned. I wondered if she had always been an American, or if she had been raised in a place in which bargaining was a way of life. She had a trace of an accent I couldn't place. Other people walked up, handed wads of cash and credit cards, and left with their buckets of flowers. But Renata kept arguing. The vendors appeared to be used to her, and argued only

halfheartedly. They seemed to know that in the end she would win, and in the end she did. She stuffed bundles of orange sunflowers with two-foot stems in my buckets and raced to the next booth.

When I caught up with her, she held dozens of dripping calla lilies, tightly rolled petals of pink and orange. The water from the stems soaked though the thin sleeves of her cotton blouse, and she threw the flowers in my direction as I approached. Only half landed in the empty bucket; I folded over slowly to gather the fallen flowers.

"This is her first day," Renata said to the vendor. "She doesn't yet understand the urgency. Your lilies will be gone in another fifteen minutes."

I slid the last flower into the bucket and stood up. The vendor was selling dozens of varieties of lilies: tiger, stargazer, imperial, and pure white Casablancas. I brushed a bead of pollen from where it had fallen on the petal of an open stargazer, listening as Renata negotiated the price of her purchases. She was spewing numbers far below what the surrounding customers had paid, barely pausing for a response, and stopped suddenly when the vendor agreed. I looked up.

Renata pulled out her purse and waved

a thin stack of bills in front of the vendor's face, but he didn't reach for them. He was looking at me. His eyes traveled from the top of my stiff hair down my face, flitting around my collarbone and heating my covered arms before resting on the sticky brown pollen on my fingertips. His gaze felt like an invasion. I squeezed the lip of the bucket I held, my knuckles white.

Renata's hand jutted into the still quiet, her cash flapping impatiently. "Excuse me?"

He reached out to grab the money but did not pause in his bold exploration of my body. Continuing down my layers of skirt, he studied the stripe of leg visible between my socks and stretch pants.

"This is Victoria," Renata said, flicking her fingertips in my direction. She paused, as if waiting for the flower farmer to introduce himself, but he didn't.

His eyes snapped back to my face. Our eyes met. There was something unsettling in them — a flicker of recognition — that captured my attention. Looking him over, my first impression was of a man that had struggled as much as, if differently than, I had. He was older than me, I decided — five years, at least. His face had the dusty, lined look of a manual laborer. I imagined he had planted, tended, and harvested his flowers himself. His body was lean and muscular as a result, and he neither flinched nor smiled as I examined him. His olive skin would be salty. The thought caused my heart to race from something besides anger, an emotion I didn't recognize but which made the core of my body warm. I bit the inside of my lip and pulled my eyes back to his face.

He withdrew a single orange tiger lily from a bucket.

"Take one," he said, handing it to me.

"No," I said. "I don't like lilies." *And I'm no queen,* I thought.

"You should," he said. "They suit you."

"How do you know what suits me?" Without thinking, I snapped the head of the lily he held. Six pointed petals fell, the flower's face examining the hard floor. Renata sucked in her breath.

"I don't," he said.

"I didn't think so." I rocked the full bucket of flowers I carried, dispersing the heat radiating from my body. The motion drew attention to my shaking arms.

I turned to Renata. "Outside," she said, motioning toward the front of the building. I waited for her to say more, sinking with dread at the thought of being fired on the spot less than an hour after starting my first job. But Renata's eyes were fixed on the growing line at the next booth. When she glanced back and saw me unmoving, her eyebrows pinched together in confusion.

"What?" she asked. "Go wait by the truck."

Pushing through a thick crowd, I made my way toward the exit. My arms strained under the weight of the full bucket, but I carried it through the parking lot without stopping to rest. At Renata's truck I set the bucket down, sinking, exhausted, onto the hard concrete.

7.

From behind the dark windows, Elizabeth watched. I was sure of it, even though I couldn't see the outline of her body behind the glass. The back door remained locked. Shivering, I watched the sun drop out of sight. I would have ten minutes, no more, before I was left to root for the spoon in darkness.

I'd been locked out before. The first time I was five years old, my protruding stomach empty in a house with too many children and too many bottles of beer. Sitting on the kitchen floor, I had watched a tiny white Chihuahua eat her dinner from a ceramic bowl. I inched closer, overcome by jealousy. It was not my intention to eat the dog's food, but when my foster father saw me, my face only centimeters from the bowl, he picked me up by the back of my turtleneck and threw me out. *Act like an animal, be treated like an animal,* he'd said. Pressing my body against the sliding glass door, I'd absorbed the heat of the house and watched the family prepare for bed, never imagining they'd leave me there all night. But they did. My body quivered, cold and afraid, and I kept thinking about the way the little dog shook when she was scared, her triangular ears vibrating. My foster mother sneaked downstairs in the middle of the night and tossed a blanket through a high kitchen window, but she did not open the door until morning.

Sitting on Elizabeth's steps, I ate the pasta and tomatoes from my pockets and thought about whether I would look for the spoon. If I found it and gave it to Elizabeth, she might still make me sleep outside. Doing as I was told had never been a guarantee that I would get what I was promised. But I had glimpsed my room on the way downstairs, and it looked more comfortable than the splintering wood steps. I decided to try.

Slowly, I meandered through the garden until I came to the place I'd tossed the spoon. Kneeling under the almond tree, I felt around with my hands, thorns cutting my fingers as I reached through the thick brush. I parted tall stalks and pulled petals off thick shrubs. I tore leaves, broke branches. Still, I didn't see it.

"Elizabeth!" I screamed, growing frustrated. The house was quiet.

The darkness was becoming thick, heavy. The vineyard seemed to stretch in all directions, an inescapable sea, and all at once I was terrified. With both hands I reached for the trunk of a dense bush, thorns piercing my soft palms as I pulled as hard as I could. The plant uprooted. I continued, pulling up everything I could grab, until the earth was bare. In the overturned soil the spoon lay alone, reflecting moonlight.

Wiping my bloody hands on my pants, I grabbed the spoon and ran toward the house, tripping and falling and picking myself up without ever letting go of my prize. I bounded up the steps, pounding the heavy metal spoon against the wooden door relentlessly. The lock turned, and Elizabeth stood before me.

For just a moment we looked at each other in silence — two pairs of wide, unblinking eyes — then I launched the spoon into the house with as much strength as I could gather in my thin arm. I aimed for the window over the kitchen sink. The spoon flew just inches past Elizabeth's ear, arched high toward the ceiling, and bounced off the window before clattering into the porcelain sink. One of the small blue bottles teetered on the edge of the windowsill before it fell and shattered.

"There's your spoon," I said.

Elizabeth took a barely controlled breath before lunging at me. Her fingers dug into my lower rib cage, and she transported me to the kitchen sink, all but throwing me inside. My hip bones pressed against the tile countertop, and my face hovered so close to the shattered glass that for a moment the whole world was blue.

"That," Elizabeth said, lowering my face even closer to the glass, "belonged to my mother." She held me completely still, but I could feel the anger filling her fingertips, threatening my descent into the glass.

With a jerk she pulled me out of the sink and set me down, letting go before my feet touched the ground. I fell backward. She stood above me, and I waited for her hand to fall on my face. All it would take was one slap. Meredith would return before the mark could fade, and this final experiment would be over. I would be declared unadoptable, and Meredith would stop trying to find me a family; I was ready — past ready.

But Elizabeth dropped her hand and stood up straight. She took a step away from me.

"My mother," she said, "would not have liked you." She nudged me with her toe until I stood up. "Now get yourself upstairs and into bed."

So, I thought, disappointed, *this is not the end.* My body filled with a palpable dread, heavy and overwhelming. It *would* end. I did not believe there to be even the slightest possibility that my placement at Elizabeth's would be anything but short, and I wanted to have it over right then, before spending a single night in her home. I took a step toward her with my chin pushed forward in defiance, hoping my proximity would push her over the edge.

But the moment had passed. Elizabeth looked over my head, her breathing even.

With heavy steps I turned away. Pulling a slice of ham off the table, I climbed the stairs. The door to my room was open. I leaned for a moment in the empty frame, taking in all that would be temporarily mine: the dark wood furniture, the circular pink rag rug, and the desk lamp with a pearly stained-glass shade. Everything looked new: the puffy white eyelet comforter and matching curtains, the clothes hung in neat rows in the closet and folded into stacks in each dresser drawer. Crawling into bed, I nibbled the ham, salty and metallic-tasting from where my bleeding hands gripped. Between bites I paused to listen.

I had lived in thirty-two homes that I could remember, and the one thing they all had in common was noise: buses, brakes, the rumbling of a freight train passing. Inside: the warring of multiple televisions, the beeping of microwaves and bottle warmers, the doorbell ringing, a curse uttered, the snap of deadbolts turning. Then there were the sounds of the other children: babies crying, siblings screaming upon separation, the yelp of a too-cold shower, and the whimper of a roommate's nightmare. But Elizabeth's house was different. Like the vineyard settling in the dusk, inside the house was silent. Only a faint, high-pitched buzz traveled through the open window. It reminded me of the squeal of electricity on wires, but in the country I imagined it to come from something natural, a waterfall, maybe, or a band of bees.

Finally, I heard Elizabeth on the stairs. I pulled the covers over my head and around my ears so that I couldn't hear her footsteps. Startling, I felt her sit lightly on the edge of my bed. I peeled the blanket an inch away from my ears but did not uncover my face.

"My mother didn't like *me*, either," Elizabeth whispered. Her tone was gentle, apologetic. I had an urge to peek out from underneath the covers; the voice that burrowed through the down was so different from the one that had held me over the sink that for a moment I didn't think it belonged to Elizabeth.

"We have that much in common, at least." Her hand rested on the small of my back when she said this, and I arched away from her, pushing my body into the wall that lined the side of the bed. My face pressed into the slab of ham. Elizabeth kept talking, telling me about the birth of her older sister, Catherine, and the seven years of stillbirths that followed: four babies total, all boys.

"When I was born, my mother asked the doctors to take me away. I don't remember this, but my father told me it was my sister, only seven years old, who fed, bathed, and changed me, until I was old enough to do it myself." Elizabeth continued to talk, describing her mother's depression and her father's devotion to her care. Even before she had learned to speak, Elizabeth told me, she had learned exactly where to place her feet as she tiptoed the hallways, to avoid the squeak of the old wood floors. Her mother didn't like noise, any noise.

I listened as Elizabeth spoke. The emotion in her voice interested me — I had rarely been spoken to as if I was capable of understanding another's experience. I swallowed a bite of meat. "It was my fault," Elizabeth continued. "My mother's illness. No one kept that a secret from me. My parents didn't want a second daughter — girls weren't believed to have the taste buds required to discern a ripe wine grape. But I proved them wrong."

Elizabeth patted my back, and I could tell she had finished speaking. I took my last bite of ham. "How was that for a bedtime story?" she asked. Her voice was too loud in the quiet house, pretending an optimism I knew she did not feel.

Poking my nose out from underneath the covers, I took a breath. "Not great," I said.

Elizabeth laughed once, a sharp exhale. "I believe you can prove everyone wrong, too, Victoria. Your behavior is a choice; it isn't who you are."

If Elizabeth really believed this, I thought, there was nothing but disappointment in her future.

8.

Renata and I worked most of the morning in silence. Bloom had a tiny storefront with a bigger work space in back, a long wooden table, and a walk-in refrigerator. There were six chairs around the table. I chose the one closest to the door.

Renata placed a book in front of me, titled *Sunflower Weddings.* I thought of an appropriate subtitle: *How to Begin a Marriage Steeped in the Values of Deceit and Materialism.* Ignoring the book, I created sixteen matching table arrangements with the sunflowers, lilies, and a tangle of wispy asparagus fern. Renata worked on the bridal-party bouquets, and when she finished those, she began a floral sculpture in a corrugated metal bucket longer than her legs. Every time the front door squeaked open, Renata ducked into the showroom. She knew her customers by name and chose flowers for each without direction.

When I was done, I stood in front of Renata and waited for her to look up. She
glanced at the table where the full vases sat
in a straight line.

"Good," she said, nodding her approval.
"Better than good, actually. Surprising. It's
hard to believe you haven't been taught."

"I haven't," I said.

"I know." She looked me up and down in
a way I disliked. "Load up the truck. I'll be
done here in a minute."

I carried the vases up the hill two at a
time. When Renata had finished, we carried
the tall vase together, laying it down gently
on the already-full truck bed. Walking back
into the shop, she removed all the cash from
the register, closing and locking the drawer.
I expected her to pay me, but instead she
handed me paper and a pencil.

"I'll pay you when I get back," she said.
"The wedding is just over the hill. Keep the
shop open, and tell my customers they can
pay next time." Renata waited until I nodded, and then walked out the door.

Alone in the flower shop, I was unsure of
what to do. I stood behind the manual cash
register for a few moments, studying the
peeling green paint. The street outside was
quiet. A family walked by without pausing,
without looking in the window. I thought

about opening the door and dragging out a few buckets of orchids but remembered the years I'd spent stealing from outdoor displays. Renata would not approve.

Instead I walked into the workroom, picked stray stems off the table, and tossed them in the waste bin. I wiped down the table with a damp cloth, swept the floor. When I could think of nothing else, I opened the heavy metal door of the walk-in, peering inside. It was dark and cool, with flowers lining the walls. The space drew me in, and I wanted nothing more than to unpin my brown blanket petticoat and fall asleep between the buckets. I was tired. For an entire week I'd slept in half-hour stretches, pulled out of sleep by voices, nightmares, or both. Always, the sky was white, steam from the brewery billowing above me. Each morning, minutes passed before I pulled myself from panic, smoke-filled dreams dispersing into the night sky like the steam. Lying still, I reminded myself I was eighteen and alone: no longer a child, with nothing more to lose.

Now, in the safety of the empty flower shop, I wanted to sleep. The door clicked shut behind me, and I slunk onto the floor, leaning my temple against the lip of a bucket.

I had just found a comfortable position when a voice came muted through the walk-in. "Renata?"

I jumped to my feet. Running my fingers quickly through my hair, I stepped out of the walk-in, squinting into the bright light.

A white-haired man leaned against the counter, tapping his fingers impatiently.

"Renata?" he asked again when he saw me.

I shook my head. "She's delivering flowers to a wedding. Can I help you with something?"

"I need flowers. Why else would I be here?" He waved his arm around the room as if to remind me of my occupation. "Renata never asks me what I want. I wouldn't know a rose from a radish."

"What's the occasion?" I asked.

"My granddaughter's sixteenth birthday. She doesn't want to spend it with us, I'm sure, but her mother is insisting." He pulled a white rose from a blue bucket and inhaled. "I'm not looking forward to it. She's turned into a sulky one, that girl."

Mentally, I scanned the flower choices in the walk-in, surveyed the showroom. A birthday present for a sulky teenager: The old man's words were a puzzle, a challenge.

"White roses are a good choice," I said, "for a teenage girl. And maybe some lily of the valley?" I withdrew a long stem, ivory

78

bells dangling.

"Whatever you think," he said.

Arranging the flowers and wrapping them in brown paper as I had seen Renata do, I felt a buoyancy similar to what I'd felt slipping the dahlias under the bedroom doors of my housemates the morning I turned eighteen. It was a strange feeling — the excitement of a secret combined with the satisfaction of being useful. It was so foreign — and decidedly pleasant — that I had a sudden urge to tell him about the flowers, to explain the hidden meanings.

"You know," I said, attempting a casual, friendly tone, but feeling the words catch in my throat with emotion, "some believe lily of the valley brings a return of happiness."

The old man wrinkled his nose, the expression a combination of impatience and disbelief. "That would be a miracle," he said, shaking his head. I handed him the flowers. "I don't think I've heard that girl laugh since she was twelve years old, and let me tell you, I miss it."

He reached for his wallet, but I held up my hand. "Renata said to pay later."

"Okay," he said, turning to go. "Tell her Earl came in. She knows where to find me." The flowers jolted in their buckets as he slammed the door.

When Renata returned an hour later, I had assisted a half-dozen people. On the piece of paper she'd given me was a complete record of transactions: customer names, flowers, and quantities. Renata scanned the list quickly and nodded, as if she'd known exactly who would come into the shop and what they would request. She slipped the piece of paper into the cash register and extracted a wad of twenty-dollar bills, counting out three.

"Sixty dollars," she said. "Six hours. Good?"

I nodded but didn't move. Renata looked into my eyes as if waiting for me to speak. "Are you going to ask if I need you next Saturday?"

"Do you?"

"Yes, five a.m.," she said. "And Sunday, too. I don't know why anyone would want to get married on a Sunday in November, but I don't ask. It's usually a slow time of year, and I've been busier than ever."

"Next week, then," I said, closing the door gently as I walked outside.

With money in my backpack, the city felt new. I headed down the hill, looking into shop windows with interest, reading menus and scanning room prices at cheap motels south of Market. As I walked, I thought about my first day of work: a quiet walk-in full of flowers, a mostly empty storefront, and a boss with a direct, unemotional style. It was the perfect job for me. Only one exchange had made me uncomfortable: my brief conversation with the flower vendor. The thought of seeing him again the following Saturday made me nervous. I decided I would have to arrive prepared.

In North Beach I stepped off a bus. It was early evening, the fog just beginning to spill over Russian Hill, transforming headlights and taillights into soft orbs of yellow and red. I walked until I found a youth hostel, dirty and cheap. Presenting my money to a woman behind a desk, I waited.

"How many nights?" she asked.

I nodded to the bills on the counter. "How many can I have?"

"I'll give you four," she said, "but only because it's off-season." She wrote up a receipt and pointed down the hall. "The girls' dorm is to the right."

For the next four days I slept, showered, and ate the remains of tourists' lunches on Columbus Avenue. When my nights ended at the hostel, I moved back to the park, worried about the overgrown boy and the dozens of others like him but aware that I had few other options. I tended my garden and waited for the weekend.

On Friday I stayed awake, worried I might sleep late and miss Renata. I wandered the streets all night, pacing outside the club at the bottom of the hill when I got tired, the music vibrating against my falling eyelids. When Renata's car pulled up, I was leaning against the locked glass door of Bloom, waiting.

She barely slowed enough for me to jump into the truck, and started her U-turn before I closed the door.

"I should have told you four," she said. "I didn't check my book. We need flowers for forty tables today, and the wedding party is over twenty-five people. Who has a wedding with twelve bridesmaids?" I couldn't tell if she was asking me or if it was a rhetorical question. I stayed silent. "If I married, I wouldn't even have twelve guests," she added, "at least not in this country."

I wouldn't have one guest, I thought, *in this country or any other.* She slowed at the roundabout and remembered her turn.

"Earl came in," she said. "He wanted me to tell you his granddaughter was happy — he said it was important that I said 'happy' and not some other word. He said you did something with the flowers to bring it out of her."

I smiled and looked out the window, away from Renata. So he had remembered. Surprisingly, I did not regret the decision to divulge my secret. But I didn't want to tell Renata. "I don't know what he's talking about," I said.

She glanced from the road to my face and back again, one eyebrow raised in question. After a stretch of silence, she continued. "Well, Earl is a funny old man. Angry, mostly, but occasionally soft in ways you wouldn't expect. He told me yesterday he's old enough to have given up on God and come back around."

"What did he mean by that?"

"I'm guessing he thinks you consulted with Him before choosing the flowers last weekend."

I snorted. "Ha."

"Yeah, I know. But he told me he's coming back today, and he wants you to pick out something for his wife."

I felt a quick thrill at having been given a new assignment.

"What's she like?" I asked.

"Quiet," Renata said, shaking her head. "I don't know much more than that. Earl told me once that she was a poet, but she rarely speaks and never writes anymore. He brings her flowers nearly every week — I think he misses the way she used to be."

Periwinkle, I thought, *tender recollections.* It would be hard to make into a bouquet but not impossible. I would wrap it with something tall and sturdy-stemmed.

The flower market was not as crowded as it had been the week before, but Renata still burst through as if the last bouquet of roses was on the auction block. We needed fifteen dozen orange roses and more stargazer lilies than would fit in the buckets I carried. I walked the flowers outside and came back for a second load. When everything was locked in the truck, I returned to the bustling building, looking for Renata.

She was at the booth I had been avoiding, arguing the price of a bunch of pink ranunculus. The wholesale price, scrawled on a small black chalkboard in nearly unreadable print, was four dollars. She flapped a single dollar bill above the tubs of flowers. The vendor neither responded nor glanced in her direction. He watched me walk down the aisle until I stood before him.

Our interaction the week before had plagued me, and I'd scoured McKinley Square until

I found the right flower to defuse his unwarranted interest. I took off my backpack and withdrew a leafy stem.

"Rhododendron," I said, placing the clipping on the plywood counter before him. The cluster of purple blossoms was not yet open, and the buds pointed in his direction, tightly coiled and toxic. *Beware.*

He studied the plant, then the warning in my eyes. When he looked away, I knew he understood the flower was not a gift. He picked it up with his thumb and index finger, and tossed it into a trash bucket.

Renata was still bargaining, and with a quick motion of his hand the vendor stopped her. She could have the flowers, he said with an impatient gesture, waving her away.

Renata turned to go, and I followed.

"What was that, Victoria?" Renata asked when we were out of earshot. I shrugged and kept walking. Renata glanced back at the booth, then at me, then again at the booth, her eyes puzzled.

"I need periwinkle," I said, changing the subject. "They won't sell it cut. It's a groundcover."

"I know periwinkle," she said, nodding to a back wall, where plants sat in buckets, their roots intact. She handed me a wad of cash and didn't ask any more questions.

Renata and I worked frantically throughout the morning. The wedding was in Palo Alto, a wealthy suburb thirty-five miles south of the city, and Renata had to take two trips to deliver all the flowers. She took the first half of the arrangements while I worked on the second. While she was gone I kept the door closed and locked, the light off in the showroom. Customers lined up outside, awaiting her return. I was content in the dark solitude.

When she returned I was busy examining my work — pinching pollen and trimming an occasional awkward leaf with sharp scissors. Renata glanced at my bouquets and nodded to the stream of people behind her.

"I'll start the bridal party; you take over the shop." She handed me a laminated price list and a small gold key to the cash register. "And don't think for a second I don't know how much is in there."

Earl was already at the counter, waving to me. I walked over to where he stood.

"For my wife," he said. "Didn't Renata tell you? I only have a few minutes, and I want you to pick out something that will make her happy."

"Happy?" I asked, looking around the

room at the available flowers. I felt disappointed. "Is that as specific as you can be?"

Earl tilted his head and was thoughtful for a moment. "You know, now that I think about it, she's never really been a *happy* woman." He laughed to himself. "But she was passionate. And smart. And interested. She always had an opinion, even about things she knew nothing about. I miss that."

It was the request for which I had prepared. "I understand," I said, setting to work. I pinched tendrils of periwinkle at the roots until they hung in long, limp strands, and grabbed a dozen bright white spider mums. I wrapped the periwinkle tightly around the base of the mums like a ribbon and used florist's wire to create loose curlicues of the leafy groundcover around a multilayered explosion of mums. The effect was like fireworks, dizzying and grand.

"Well, that will deserve a response of some kind," Earl said as I handed over the flowers. He passed me a flat twenty. "Keep the change, sweetheart." I consulted the price list Renata had given me and put the twenty in the drawer, withdrawing a five-dollar bill for myself.

"Thanks," I said.

"See you next week," called Earl.

"Maybe," I said, but he had already gone

out the door, slamming it closed behind him.

The store was abuzz, and I turned my attention to the next person in line. I wrapped roses, orchids, mums of every color, and handed bouquets to couples, elderly women, and teens sent on errands. While I worked I thought about Earl's wife, tried to bring forth an image of the once-passionate woman: her tired, withdrawn, unsuspecting face. Would she react to the wild bouquet of mums and periwinkle, *truth* and *tender recollections*? I felt sure she would, and imagined the relief and gratitude on Earl's face as he boiled water for tea, provoking the opinionated woman he had missed into a discussion of politics or poetry. The image quickened my fingers and lightened my steps as I worked.

Just as the shop emptied, Renata finished the bridal party.

"Load up the truck," she ordered. I transported armfuls as quickly as I could. It was almost two. Renata climbed behind the wheel, directing me to keep the shop open until she returned in an hour.

The delivery took much longer than Renata had expected. At half past five she stormed into Bloom, spewing anger over boutonnieres and bow ties. I kept quiet, waiting for her to pay me so that I could leave. I'd worked twelve and a half hours without a break, and I was looking forward to a locked room and possibly even a bath. But Renata didn't reach into her purse.

When her frustrated monologue ended, she opened the cash register, thumbing through wrinkled bills, checks, and receipts. "I don't have enough cash," she said. "I'll stop at the bank on the way to dinner. Come with me. We'll talk business."

I would rather have taken her money and fled into the night, but I followed her outside anyway, aware of the precariousness of my position.

"Mexican food?" she asked.

"Yes."

She turned toward the Mission. "You aren't much of a talker, are you?" Renata asked.

I shook my head.

"At first I thought you just weren't a morning person," she said. "My nieces and nephews, don't try before noon, but after that just pray for a moment of silence."

She glanced at me as if she was waiting for a response.

"Oh," I said.

She laughed. "I have twelve nieces and nephews, but I rarely see them. I know I'm supposed to make an effort, but I don't."

"No?"

"No," she said. "I love them, but I can only handle them in small doses. My mother always jokes that I didn't inherit her maternal gene."

"What's that?" I asked.

"You know, that bit of biology that makes women coo when they see a baby on the street. I've never had that."

Renata parked in front of a taqueria, and two women fussed over a stroller by the door as if to prove her point. "Go order anything you want," she said. "I'll pay when I get back from the bank."

Renata and I ate until eight p.m. It was enough time for her to eat a taco and drink three large Diet Cokes, and for me to eat a chicken burrito, two cheese enchiladas, a side of guacamole, and three baskets of chips. Renata watched me eat, a satisfied smile flicking across her face. She filled the silence between us with stories of her childhood in Russia, describing a flock of siblings traveling across the ocean to America.

When I finished eating, I leaned back, feeling the heaviness of the food in my body. I had forgotten how much I could consume, and also the complete paralysis that accompanied my overeating.

"So, what's your secret?" Renata asked.

I squinted my eyes in question, tightened my shoulders.

"To staying thin?" she asked. "When you eat like that?"

It's simple, I thought. *Be broke, friendless, and homeless. Spend weeks eating other people's leftovers, or nothing at all.*

"Diet Coke," she said, filling the silence as if she didn't want to hear my answer, or already knew it. "That's my secret. Caffeine and empty calories. Another reason I never wanted children. What kind of baby would develop on that?"

"A hungry one," I said.

Renata smiled. "I saw you out there today, working with Earl. He left pleased. And he'll come back, I imagine, week after week, looking for you." *Would I be there?* I wondered. *Is this Renata's way of offering me a permanent job?*

"That's how I built my business," she said. "Knowing what my customers wanted even before they did. Anticipating it. Wrapping up flowers before they came in, guessing the days they'd be in a hurry, the days they'd want to browse, talk. I think you have it in you, that kind of intuition, if you want it."

"I do," I said quickly. "Want it."

I remembered Meredith's words then —

"You have to want it" — at The Gathering House and hundreds of times before. You have to want to be a daughter, a sister, a friend, a student, she had told me, again and again. I hadn't wanted any of those things, and none of Meredith's promises, threats, or bribes had altered my conviction. But suddenly I knew I wanted to be a florist. I wanted to spend my life choosing flowers for perfect strangers, my days steadily alternating between the chill of the walk-in and the snap of the register.

"I'll pay you under the table, then," Renata said. "Every Sunday. Two hundred dollars for twenty hours of work, and you work whenever I tell you. Deal?"

I nodded. Renata stretched out her hand, and I shook it.

The next morning, Renata leaned against the glass doors of the flower market, waiting for me. I checked my watch. We were both early. The wedding that day was small, no bridal party and less than fifty guests at two long tables. We wandered around, looking for shades of yellow. That had been the bride's only request, Renata told me. She wanted sunlight in flowers, just in case it rained. The sky was dry but gray; she should have married in June.

"His booth's closed Sundays," Renata said as we walked, gesturing in the direction of the mysterious vendor.

But as we approached his empty stall, a hooded silhouette appeared, perched on a stool and leaning against the wall. He stood when he saw me, bending over the flowerless buckets, his image reflected in the still circles of water. From the pocket of his sweatshirt he withdrew something green and spindly. He held it up.

Renata greeted him as we passed. I acknowledged his presence only by reaching out to grasp what he had brought me, keeping my eyes on the ground. When I was safely around a corner, out of view, I looked into my hand.

Oval, gray-green leaves grew from a tangle of lime-colored twigs, translucent balls clinging to the branches like drops of rain. The clipping fit exactly in the palm of my hand, and the soft leaves stung where they touched.

Mistletoe.

I surmount all obstacles.

My puncture wounds scabbed in the night and attached themselves to the thin cotton sheets. Emerging from sleep, it took me a moment to locate the burning in my body and even longer to remember the source of the injury. I squeezed my eyes shut, waiting, and it hit me all at once: the thorns, the spoon, the long drive, and Elizabeth. I yanked my hands out from underneath the covers with one fast tug and studied my palms. The cuts had reopened; fresh blood seeped out.

It was early, and still dark. I felt my way down the hall to the bathroom, my hands leaving bloody streaks on the walls where I touched. In the bathroom, Elizabeth was already up and dressed. She sat at the vanity and looked in the mirror as if she would apply makeup, but there was no makeup on the counter, only a half-empty jar of cream. She dipped her ring finger, the nail flat and short, into the cream and smoothed it under her brown eyes, along her defined cheekbones, and down the bridge of her straight nose. Elizabeth's skin was unwrinkled and glowed with the dark warmth of summer, and I guessed she was much younger than her high-collared shirt and middle-parted, tightly wrapped hair made her look.

She turned when she saw me, her profile sharp in the mirror.

"How did you sleep?" she asked.

I stepped forward, holding my hands so close to her face she had to lean back to focus.

She inhaled sharply. "Why didn't you tell me last night?"

I shrugged.

Elizabeth sighed. "Well, give me your hands. I don't want them getting infected."

She patted her lap for me to sit down, but I took a step backward. Retrieving a small bowl from underneath the sink, Elizabeth filled it with peroxide and reached for my hands, dipping them one at a time. She watched my expression for pain, but I clenched my teeth and held my face perfectly still. My wounds turned white and frothy. Elizabeth emptied the basin, refilled it, and submerged my hands again.

"I'm not going to let you get away with

anything here," Elizabeth said. "But if you couldn't find the spoon after a true attempt, I would have accepted a genuine apology." Her voice was stern and direct. In the sleepy haze of early morning, I wondered if I had imagined her gentle tone of the night before.

She dipped my hands in again, watching the tiny white bubbles form for the third time. Running my hands under cold water, she patted them dry with a clean white towel. The small punctures looked deep and empty, as if the peroxide had eaten away perfect circles of flesh. With white gauze, she began wrapping my wrist, working her way slowly toward my fingers.

"You know," Elizabeth said, "when I was six, I learned the only way to get my mother out of bed was to act out. I behaved atrociously, just so that she would get up and punish me. When I was ten, she tired of it and sent me to boarding school. The same won't happen with you. Nothing you could do would make me send you away. Nothing. So you can go on testing me — hurling my mother's silver around the kitchen, if that's what you have to do — but know that my response will always be the same: I will love you, and I will keep you. Okay?"

I looked at Elizabeth, my body tight with

suspicion, my breath lost in the steamy bathroom. I didn't understand her. Shoulders tense, her sentences sharp and clipped, she spoke with a formality I'd never encountered. Yet behind her words was an inexplicable softness. Her touch, too, was different; the thorough way she cleaned my hands, without the heavy, silent burden in the actions of all my other foster mothers. I didn't trust it.

Silence stretched between us. Elizabeth tucked a strand of hair behind my ear and looked deeply into my eyes for an answer.

"Okay," I said finally, because I knew it was the fastest way to end the conversation and leave the heat of the small bathroom.

The corners of Elizabeth's mouth turned up. "Come on, then," she said. "It's Sunday. On Sunday we go to the farmers' market."

She turned my body and led me back to my bedroom, where she slipped my gauze-wrapped hands out of my nightgown and into a white smocked sundress. Downstairs, she made scrambled eggs and fed me small bites on a spoon that looked identical to the one I'd launched across the room the night before. I chewed and swallowed, following directions, still trying to reconcile Elizabeth's contrasting tones and unpredictable actions. She did not try to start a conversation over breakfast, just watched the eggs travel from the spoon into my mouth and down my throat. When she finished feeding me, she ate a small plate of eggs herself, washed and dried the dishes, and put them away.

"Ready?" she asked.

I shrugged.

Outside, we crossed the gravel, and she helped me into her ancient gray pickup. The aqua plastic upholstery peeled away from the piped edging, and there were no seat belts. The truck lurched down the driveway, dust and wind and exhaust whipping through the cab. Elizabeth drove less than a minute before turning in to what had been an empty parking lot when I had passed in Meredith's car. It was now full of trucks and fruit stands, families wandering up and down the aisles.

Elizabeth went from stand to stand as if I wasn't there, exchanging cash for heavy bags of produce: pink-and-white-striped beans, tan-colored pumpkins with long necks, purple potatoes mixed with yellow and red. When she was busy paying for a bag of nectarines, I stole a green grape off an overflowing table with my teeth.

"Please!" exclaimed a short, bearded man I hadn't noticed. "Sample! They're delicious, perfectly ripe." He tore off a bunch of grapes and placed them in my wrapped hands.

"Say thank you," Elizabeth said, but my mouth was full of grapes.

Elizabeth bought three pounds of grapes, six nectarines, and a bag of dried apricots. On a bench facing a long, grassy field we sat together, and she held out a yellow plum a few inches from my lips. I leaned forward and ate it out of her hand, the juice dripping down my chin and onto my dress.

When only the pit was left, Elizabeth threw it into the field and gazed to the far side of the market.

"See the flower stand over there, the last one in line?" she asked me. I nodded. A teenager sat on the open bed of a pickup truck, his feet in heavy boots hanging above the blacktop. At a table in front of him, roses lay wrapped in tight clusters.

Elizabeth continued. "That's my sister's stand. See the boy? Almost a young man now, it seems. That's my nephew, Grant. We've never met."

"What?" I said, surprised. From Elizabeth's bedtime story, I'd assumed the sisters were close. "Why not?"

"It's a long story. We haven't spoken in fifteen years, except to divide up the properties after my parents died. Catherine took the flower farm; I kept the vineyard." The teenager jumped off the back of the truck and made change for a customer. Long brown hair fell in front of his face, and he pushed it away from his eyes before shaking hands with an old man. His pants were slightly too short, his long, thin limbs the only feature I could find to resemble Elizabeth from the distance at which we sat. He seemed to be alone running the flower stand, and I wondered why Catherine wasn't there.

"The strange thing," Elizabeth said, following the boy's movements with her eyes, "is that today, for the first time in fifteen years, I miss her."

The boy threw the last bunch of roses to a couple passing by, and Elizabeth turned to me, snaking her arm around my back and pulling me closer to her on the bench. I leaned away, but she dug her fingers into my side, holding me still.

10.

On my chest bone, the mistletoe rested. I studied its irregular rise and fall. Neither my heartbeat nor my breath had returned to normal since reading the stranger's response in my palm.

I didn't remember what I'd done with the buckets of yellow flowers. I must have done something, though, because by noon they were settled in the back of Renata's truck, bouquets of sunshine rolling down the freeway to brighten someone's near-winter wedding, and I had stretched out alone on top of the worktable. Renata had asked me to keep the shop open, but no one came in. It was usually closed on Sundays, and I kept the door unlocked but the light off. I wasn't technically disobeying Renata, but I wasn't exactly inviting business, either.

My forehead was wet with sweat even though the morning had been cold, and I was frozen in a state of fascination resembling terror. For years my message-laden flowers had been faithfully ignored, an aspect of my communication style that gave me comfort. Passion, connection, disagreement, or rejection: None of these was possible in a language that did not elicit a response. But the single sprig of mistletoe, if the giver did indeed understand its meaning, changed everything.

I tried to sedate myself with rationalizations of coincidence. Mistletoe was thought to be a romantic plant. He had visions of me tying it with a red ribbon to the wooden frame of his stall and positioning myself underneath it for a kiss. He didn't know me well enough to know I would never permit such closeness. But even though we had exchanged only a handful of words, I couldn't shake the feeling that he somehow did know me well enough to understand that a kiss was out of the question.

I would have to respond. If he presented me with a second flower, the meaning again perfectly matched, I would no longer be able to explain away his understanding.

My legs trembled as I climbed off the table and wobbled into the walk-in. Settling among the cool flowers, I debated my reply.

Renata returned and began ordering me

around the walk-in. There was another job, a small one, to be delivered down the hill. She retrieved a blue ceramic vase while I gathered the leftover yellow flowers.

"How much?" I asked, because price guided our arrangements.

"It doesn't matter. But tell her she can't keep the vase. I'll stop by for it next week." Renata slid a scrap of paper toward me as I finished the arrangement, an address scrawled in the center. "You take it," she said.

On my way out the door, my arms around the heavy vase, I felt Renata slip something into my backpack. I turned. She had locked the door behind me and was heading toward her truck.

"I don't need you again until next Saturday, four a.m.," she said, waving goodbye. "Be prepared for a long day, no breaks."

I nodded, watching her get in her truck and drive away. When she turned the corner, I set down the vase and opened my backpack. Inside was an envelope with four pressed hundred-dollar bills. A note read: *Payment for your first two weeks. Don't disappoint me.* I folded the cash and put it in my bra.

The address led me to what looked like an office building, only two blocks down the hill from Bloom. The glass windows of the storefront were dark. I couldn't tell whether there was a business inside, closed on Sundays, or whether there was no business at all. When I knocked, the doors rattled on metal hinges.

A window opened on the second floor, and a disembodied voice floated down. "I'll be a minute. Don't go anywhere." I sat down on the curb, the flowers at my feet.

Ten minutes later, the door opened slowly, and the woman who opened it was not out of breath. She reached for the flowers.

"Victoria," she said. "I'm Natalya." She resembled Renata with her light milky skin and water-colored eyes, but her hair was acetaminophen-pink and dripping wet.

I handed her the flowers and turned to go.

"Change your mind?" she asked.

"Excuse me?"

Natalya stepped back as if to let me through the door. "About the room. I told Renata to tell you it's literally a closet, but she seemed to think you wouldn't mind."

A room. The cash in my backpack. Renata had staged an intervention, and all without letting on that she understood. My instinct was to walk away from the open door, but the reality of having nowhere to walk to was insurmountable.

"How much?" I asked, stepping back-ward.

"Two hundred a month. You'll see why."

I looked up and down the street, unsure what to say. When I turned back, Natalya had already walked through the empty storefront and was climbing steep stairs.

"Come or don't," she called, "but either way, close the door."

I took a deep breath, exhaling through floppy lips, and stepped inside.

The one-bedroom apartment above the empty storefront looked as if it was designed to be office space, with thin commercial carpet over cement floors and a kitchen with a long bar and short refrigerator. The window over the kitchen was open and framed a view of a flat roof.

"I can't legally rent this room," Natalya said, pointing to a half-door positioned on the wall near the living room couch. It looked as if it would open to a crawl space or a small water heater. Natalya handed me a key chain with six keys, all numbered. "Number one," she said.

Kneeling, I opened the low door and crawled inside. The room was too dark to examine. "Stand up," Natalya said. "There's a string hanging down from the light." I grasped around in the darkness until I felt the string on my face. I pulled.

A bare lightbulb illuminated an empty blue room, blue as a painter's palette on a boat in the middle of the sea, bright as illuminated water. The carpet was white fur and almost looked alive. There were no windows. The room was big enough to lie down in but not big enough for a bed or a dresser, even if I could have found one that fit through the small door. One of the walls held a row of brass locks, and when I looked closer, I saw that the locks bridged the space between the wall and a full-size door. Light seeped through the seam. Natalya was right; the room was literally a closet.

"My last roommate was a paranoid schizophrenic," Natalya said, gesturing to the deadbolts. "The door opens into my room. Those are the keys to all the locks." She pointed to the key ring in my hand.

"I'll take it," I said. I reached out into the living room and set two hundred-dollar bills on the arm of the couch. Then I closed the half-door, turned the lock, and lay down in the center of the blue.

11.

The sky felt bigger at Elizabeth's. It curved from one low horizon line to the other, the blue seeping into the dry hills and dulling the yellow of summer. In the corrugated roof of the garden shed it reflected, and in the round metal trailer, and in the pupils of Elizabeth's eyes. The color felt inescapable and as heavy as her sudden silence.

I sat in a lawn chair on a garden path, waiting for Elizabeth to return from the kitchen. Earlier that morning, she'd made peach-banana pancakes, and I'd eaten until I'd folded onto the kitchen table, unable to move. But rather than her usual stream of questions, some of which I answered, some of which I ignored, she'd been eerily quiet. She'd only picked at her food, pulling out the grilled peaches and leaving the rest of her pancake in a pool of syrup.

My eyes closed, I'd listened to the squeak of Elizabeth's chair pushing back, her socked feet crossing the wood floor, and our stacked plates settling into the kitchen sink. But instead of the sound of running water that usually followed, I'd heard an unexpected clicking noise, and when I looked up, Elizabeth was leaning against the kitchen cabinets, her attention on an old-fashioned telephone. She twirled the spiraling cord that attached the receiver to the base and then stared at the dial as if she'd forgotten the number. After a time, she began to spin the dial again, but when she reached the sixth number she paused, curled in her lips, and hung up forcefully. The sound aggravated my full stomach, and I'd sighed.

Elizabeth startled, and when she turned, she looked surprised to see me sitting there, as if in her focus on the phone call she couldn't make, she'd forgotten my very existence. Exhaling, she pulled me off the kitchen chair and into the garden, where I waited.

Now she emerged from the back door, clutching a muddy shovel in one hand, a steaming mug in the other.

"Drink it," she said, handing me the cup. "It'll help your digestion."

I grasped the mug between my gauze-wrapped hands. It had been a week since Elizabeth cleaned and wrapped my puncture wounds, and I'd grown accustomed to the helplessness of the gauze. Elizabeth cooked and cleaned while I lay around day after day, doing nothing; when she asked me how my hands were healing, I told her they felt worse.

Blowing on the tea, I took a careful sip and then spit it out.

"I don't like it," I said, tipping the cup forward and letting the liquid spill onto the path in front of my chair.

"Try again," Elizabeth said. "You'll get used to it. Peppermint blossoms mean *warmth of feeling*."

I took another sip. This time I held it in my mouth a little longer before spitting it over my armrest. "You mean warmth of bad taste."

"No, warmth of feeling," Elizabeth corrected me. "You know, the tingling feeling you get when you see a person you like."

I didn't know that feeling. "Warmth of vomit," I said.

"The language of flowers is nonnegotiable, Victoria," Elizabeth said, turning away and putting on her gardening gloves. She picked up the shovel and worked the soil where I had uprooted a dozen plants in my search for the spoon.

"What do you mean, 'nonnegotiable'?" I

asked. I took a sip of peppermint tea, swallowed it, and grimaced, waiting for my stomach to settle.

"It means there's only one definition, one meaning, for every flower. Like rosemary, which means —"

"Remembrance," I said. "From Shakespeare, whoever that is."

"Yes," said Elizabeth, looking surprised. "And columbine —"

"Desertion."

"Holly?"

"Foresight."

"Lavender?"

"Mistrust."

Elizabeth put down her gardening tools, took off her gloves, and knelt down next to me. Her eyes were so penetrating, I leaned back until my lawn chair started to tip backward, and Elizabeth's hand flew out to clutch my ankle.

"Why did Meredith tell me you couldn't learn?" she asked.

"Because I can't," I said. She took hold of my chin and turned my face until she could look directly into my eyes.

"Not true," she said simply. "Four years of elementary school and you haven't learned simple phonics, Meredith warned me. She said you'd be put in special education, if you could make it at a public school at all."

In four years I'd done kindergarten twice and second grade twice. I wasn't faking inability; I'd just never been asked. After the first year, my reputation of silent volatility was such that I was isolated from every class I entered. Stacks of photocopied worksheets taught me letters, numbers, simple math. I learned to read from whatever picture books slipped out of my classmates' backpacks or I stole from classroom shelves.

There had been a time when I believed school might be different. My first day, sitting at a miniature desk in a neat row, I realized the chasm between me and the other children was not visible. My kindergarten teacher, Ms. Ellis, spoke my name softly, with emphasis on the middle syllable, and treated me like everyone else. She partnered me with a girl who was tinier than I was, her thin wrists brushing mine as we walked in line from the classroom to the playground and back again. Ms. Ellis believed in feeding the brain, and every day after recess she placed a paper cup with a sardine on top of each desk. After we ate our sardine, we were to flip the cup upside down to see the letter written on the bottom. If we could say the letter's name and sound, and think of a word that started with the letter, we could have a second sardine. I memorized all the letters and sounds the first week and always got a second sardine.

But five weeks into school Meredith placed me with a new family, in a different suburb, and every time I thought of the slippery fish, I angered. My anger flipped desks, cut curtains, and stole lunch boxes. I was suspended, moved, and suspended again. By the end of that first year, my violence was expected, my education forgotten.

Elizabeth squeezed my face, her eyes demanding a response.

"I can read," I said.

Elizabeth continued to search my face, as if she was determined to dig out every lie I had ever told. I shut my eyes until she released me.

"Well, that's good to know," she said. She shook her head and went back to gardening, slipping on her gloves before dropping into shallow holes the plants I'd uprooted. I watched her work, replacing the topsoil and patting gently around each trunk. She looked up when she finished. "I've asked Perla to come over to play. I need a rest, and it would be good for you to make a friend before school starts tomorrow."

"Perla won't be my friend," I said.

"You haven't even met her!" Elizabeth said,

exasperated. "How do you know if she'll be your friend or not?"

I knew Perla would not be my friend because I had never, in nine years, had a friend. Meredith must have told Elizabeth this. She'd told all my other foster mothers, and they warned the children in their homes to eat quickly and sleep with their Halloween candy tucked deep inside their pillowcases.

"Now come with me. She's probably already waiting by the gate."

Elizabeth led me through the garden, to the low white picket fence at the far edge. Perla leaned against it, waiting. She was close enough to have heard every word we said, but she didn't look upset, just hopeful. She was only an inch or two taller than I was, and her body was soft and round. Her T-shirt was too tight and too short. Lime-colored fabric stretched across her stomach and ended before the waistline of her pants began. Deep red lines circled her arms where the elastic bands of her cap sleeves had been, before they inched up and got lost in her armpits. She dug out the elastic bands and pulled down her sleeves one at a time.

"Good morning," Elizabeth said. "This is my daughter, Victoria. Victoria, this is Perla." The sound of the word *daughter* made my stomach hurt again. I kicked dust at Elizabeth until she stepped on both my feet with her right shoe, her fingers clamping down on the back of my neck. My skin burned under her touch.

"Hi, Victoria," said Perla shyly. She picked up a heavy black braid from where it rested on her shoulder and chewed on the already-wet ends.

"Good," said Elizabeth, as if Perla's quiet words and my stubborn silence had established something. "I'm going inside to rest. Victoria, stay out here and play with Perla until I call you."

Without waiting for a response, she walked into the house. Perla and I, alone, stared at the ground. After a time, she reached out hesitantly and touched the tip of my wrapped hands with a thick finger. "What happened?"

I pulled at the gauze with my teeth, all at once desperate to use my hands again. "Thorns," I said. "Unwrap them."

Perla pulled at the edges of the tape, and I shook loose of the material. The skin, uncovered, was pale and wrinkled, the scabs small, dry circles. I picked at the edge of a scab with a fingernail, and it flaked off easily, fluttering to the ground.

"We'll be in the same class at school tomorrow," Perla said. "There's only one fourth grade."

I didn't respond. Elizabeth thought I would start school. But she also thought I would be her daughter, and thought she could force me to have a friend. About all of this, she was wrong. I walked toward the garden shed. Perla's heavy footsteps followed. I didn't know what I would do, but suddenly I wanted Elizabeth to understand exactly how wrong she'd been about me. Snatching a knife and a pair of clippers from a shelf by the shed, I crept around the side of the garden.

On the other side of the almond tree, I followed a pattern of gray-and-green succulents until they faded into gravel. There, at the place the dusty dirt road collided with the lush garden, was an enormous, tangled cactus. It was bigger than Meredith's county car, and the trunk was brown and scabby-looking, as if it had been cut over and over again by its own spines. Each branch was built like a collection of flat hands growing one out of the other, right, then left, then right again, so that each branch was balanced enough to stand straight and tall.

I knew what I would do.

"Nopales," Perla said, when I pointed to the cactus. "Prickly pear."

"What?"

"It's a prickly pear; see the fruit on top? In Mexico, they sell them at the market. They're good, as long as you peel them well."

"Cut it down," I ordered.

Perla stood still. "What? The whole thing?"

I shook my head no. "Just that branch, the one with all the fruit. I want it, to give to Elizabeth. But you have to do it, or I'll hurt my hands." Perla still didn't move but looked up at the cactus, twice as tall as she was. Flaming red fruit grew like swollen fingers on top of each flat palm. I shoved the knife in her direction, its dull blade pointed low toward her abdomen.

Perla reached out, tested the point of the blade with her soft finger, then stepped closer to me and took the knife by its handle.

"Where?" she asked quietly. I pointed to a place just above the brown trunk where a long green arm began. Perla rested the blade against the cactus and closed her eyes before leaning forward with the weight of her whole body. The skin was tough, but once she broke through the outer layer, the knife slipped through easily and the branch fell to the ground. I pointed to the fruit, and Perla cut off each one. They lay on the ground, bleeding red juice.

"Wait here," I commanded, running

through the garden to where I had discarded the dirty gauze.

When I returned, Perla was right where I'd left her. I held the fruit with the gauze, picking up the knife and carefully removing the spines from each prickly pear as if I was skinning a dead animal. I held the ripe, edible fruit out for Perla.

"Here," I said. She looked at me with confusion.

"I thought you wanted these?" she asked. "For Elizabeth?"

"So take them to her, if you want," I said. "This is the part I need." I wrapped the strips of spiny skin in the gauze.

"Now go home," I said.

Perla cupped the fruit in her hands and walked away slowly, sighing, as if she expected something more from me for her act of loyalty.

I had nothing to give her.

12.

Natalya was Renata's youngest sister. There were six siblings, all girls. Renata was second in the birth order, Natalya last. It took me all week to gather this information, and for this I was grateful. Most days Natalya slept until late afternoon, and when she was awake she was quiet. She told me once she didn't like to waste her voice, and the fact that she considered conversation with me a waste did not offend me at all.

Natalya was the vocalist for a punk band that, as she put it, had "made it" only within a twenty-block radius of the apartment. The band had a spirited following in the Mission and a few scattered fans around Dolores Park, and were unknown in every other neighborhood and every other city. They practiced downstairs. The rest of the block comprised offices, some leased and some empty, but all closed after five. Natalya provided me with a box of earplugs and a pile of pillows. Between the two I could reduce the music to only the vibration of the sound on the fur carpet, making it feel even more alive. Most nights her band didn't start practicing until after midnight, so I had only a few hours of attempted oblivion before I rose.

I didn't work until the following Saturday, but every morning that week I found myself wandering the streets around the flower market, watching wholesalers back overflowing trucks into the crowded parking lot. I wasn't looking for the mysterious flower vendor; at least, I told myself I wasn't. When I did see him, I slipped down an alley and ran until I was out of breath.

By Saturday I had settled on a response. Snapdragon. *Presumption.* I got to the flower market at four a.m., an hour before Renata, with a five-dollar bill and a new mustard-colored knit hat pulled low over my brow.

The flower vendor was bent over, unloading bushels of lilies, roses, and ranunculus into white plastic tubs. He didn't see me approach. I took advantage of the time to return the unabashed stare he had released on my body the first day we met, scanning from the back of his neck down to his muddy work boots. He wore the same black hooded sweatshirt he had the first day we met, dirtier this time, with white-speckled work pants.

They were the kind with the loop to hold a hammer, but the loop was empty. When he stood up I was standing directly in front of him, my arms overflowing with snapdragons. I had spent five dollars on the flowers, and at wholesale prices that bought me six bunches, mixed bouquets of purple and pink and yellow. I held the flowers high so that the tip of my hat ended where the snapdragons began, hiding my face completely.

I felt his hands close around the bottoms of the stems; his fingers, where they touched my own, were the temperature of the early-morning November sky. Fleetingly, I had the desire to warm them: not with my own hands, which weren't any warmer, but with my hat or socks, something I could leave behind. He withdrew the flowers, and I stood exposed in front of him, heat rising in pink patches to my face. Turning quickly, I walked away.

Renata was waiting for me at the door, flustered and frantic. She had another big wedding, and the bride was straight out of a Hollywood blockbuster, demanding and irrational. She'd provided Renata with a pages-long list of flowers she liked and disliked, specifying color with paint swatches and size in centimeters. Renata tore the list in two and handed half to me with an envelope of cash.

"Don't pay full price!" she called after me as I hurried away. "Tell them it's for me!"

The next morning, Renata sent me to the flower market alone. We had arranged flowers and tied nosegays until five for a six-o'clock wedding, and the stress had launched her into bed rest. Her shop was to be open every Sunday from now on; she'd created a new sign and told all her regulars I would be there. She gave me cash, her wholesale card, and a key. Taping her home phone number to the cash register, she told me not to bother her for any reason.

When I arrived at the flower market, the sky was still dark, and I almost didn't see him standing to the right of the entrance. He was still, and flowerless, his head bent to the ground but his eyes up, waiting. I walked to the door with a purposeful step, eyes on the metal handle. The market would be busy and loud, but outside it was nearly silent. As I passed he raised a hand, holding up a rolled paper tied with a yellow ribbon. I took the scroll like a runner taking a baton, never breaking stride, and opened the door. The noise greeted me like the roar of a crowd. When I peeked back over my shoulder, he was gone.

Inside, his booth was empty. I crouched inside the white wood, untied the ribbon, and unwrapped the scroll. The paper was visibly old, yellowed and flaking at the corners. It resisted straightening. I held the two bottom corners down with my big toes, the top corners with my thumbs.

The paper held a drawing in faded graphite, not of a flower but of the trunk of a tree, its bark textured and peeling. I ran my fingertip along the bark; although the paper was flat, the drawing was so realistic I could almost feel the rough knobs. In the bottom right-hand corner were the words *White Poplar* in a curving script.

White poplar. It was not a plant I knew by heart. Taking off my backpack, I withdrew my flower dictionary. I scanned the *W*'s first, then the *P*'s, but neither *white poplar* nor *poplar, white* was listed. If there was a meaning, I wouldn't be able to glean it from my dictionary. I rerolled and tied the scroll with the ribbon, but stopped midway through the bow.

On the underside of the ribbon, in a scratchy hand I recognized from flower prices on a chalkboard, were the words *Monday, 5 p.m., 16th and Mission. Donuts for dinner.* The black ink had spread into the silk so that the words were almost unreadable, but the time and place were clear.

I bought flowers that morning without thinking, without bargaining, and when I opened the shop an hour later, I was surprised by the things I carried.

The morning was slow, and I was grateful. I sat on a tall stool behind the register and flipped through a heavy phone book. The number listed for the San Francisco Public Library had a long recorded message. I listened to it twice, jotting down hours and locations on the back of my hand. Main Library closed at five p.m. on Sundays, as did Bloom. I would have to wait until Monday. Then, based on the meaning I uncovered, I would decide whether or not to meet for donuts.

At the end of the day, just as I had transferred the display flowers from the window to the walk-in, the front door opened. A woman stood alone, looking confused in the empty space.

"Can I help you?" I asked, feeling impatient and ready to leave.

"Are you Victoria?"

I nodded.

"Earl sent me. He asked me to tell you he needs more of the same, exactly the same." She handed me thirty dollars. "He said to keep the change."

I placed the money on the counter and went into the walk-in, not sure if we had enough spider mums. I laughed aloud when I saw the giant bunch I had purchased that morning. What remained of the periwinkle sat forgotten on the floor, where I had left it the week before. Renata hadn't watered the plant, and it was dry but not dead.

"Why didn't Earl come?" I asked as I began the arrangement.

The woman's eyes flitted between my work and the window. She had the energy of a trapped bird.

"He wanted me to meet you."

I didn't say anything, and didn't look up. In my peripheral vision I could see her pull at the roots of her burgundy-brown hair, the color covering what was probably speckled gray.

"He thought you might be able to make me a bouquet — something special."

"For what reason?" I asked.

She paused, looking out the window again. "I'm single but don't want to be."

I looked around. My success with Earl had made me confident. She needed red roses and lilac, I decided, neither of which I had purchased. I tended to avoid them. "Next Saturday," I said. "Can you come back?"

She nodded. "Lord knows I can wait," she said, rolling her eyes. She watched my fingers fly in circles around the mums in silence. When she walked out the door ten minutes later, she seemed lighter, jogging up the block toward Earl's like a much younger woman.

I rode the bus to Main Library the next morning and waited on the steps until it opened. It didn't take me long to find what I was looking for. Books on the language of flowers were on the top floor, wedged between the Victorian poets and an extensive gardening collection. There were more than I had expected. They ranged from ancient, crumbling hardcovers like the one I carried to illustrated paperbacks that seemed to have come from antique coffee tables. All the volumes had one thing in common — they looked as though they hadn't been touched in years. Elizabeth had told me the language of flowers was once common knowledge, and it always amazed me that it had retreated into the virtual unknown. I stacked as many books as I could carry onto trembling arms.

At the nearest table I opened a leather-bound volume, its once-gilded title faded to a scattering of gold dust. The card in the inside pocket had last been stamped before I was born. The book contained a complete history of the language of flowers. It began with the original flower dictionary published in nineteenth-century France and included a long list of the royalty who had courted with the language, giving detailed descriptions of the bouquets they traded. I skimmed to the end of the book, which listed a brief dictionary of flowers. White poplar was not included.

I scanned a half-dozen more books, my anxiety growing with each volume. I was afraid to know the stranger's response but even more afraid that I wouldn't find the definition and would never know what he was trying to say. After twenty minutes of searching, I finally found what I was looking for, a single line between plum and poppy. Poplar, white. *Time.* I exhaled, relieved but also confused.

Closing the book, I pressed my head against its cool cover. Time, as a response to presumption, was more abstract than I had hoped. *Time will tell? Give me time?* His response was unspecific; he had clearly not learned from Elizabeth. I opened another book and then another, hoping for an extended definition of the white poplar, but a search of the entire collection did not yield a second reference. I was not surprised. It didn't seem that poplar, a tree, would be a plant of choice for romantic communication. There was nothing wistful about the passing of sticks or long strips of bark.

I was about to re-shelve the books when a pocket-sized volume caught my eye. The cover was illustrated with drawings of flowers in a grid of small squares, the definition in tiny print below each image. In the bottom row were delicately rendered drawings of roses in every hue. Under the faded yellow rose was the word *jealousy*.

Had it been any other flower, I might not have noticed the discrepancy. But I had never forgotten the sorrow that passed over Elizabeth's face when she gestured to her yellow rosebushes or the thoroughness with which she snipped every young bud in the spring, leaving them to shrivel in a pile by the garden fence. Replacing infidelity with jealousy — this changed the meaning entirely. One was an action, the other only an emotion. Opening the small book, I scanned the pages, then set it down and opened another.

Hours passed as I took in hundreds of pages of new information. I sat frozen, only the pages of the books turning. Looking up flowers one at a time, I cross-referenced ev-

erything I had memorized with the dictionaries stacked on the table.

It wasn't long before I knew. Elizabeth had
been as wrong about the language of flowers
as she had been about me.

13.

On the front steps, Elizabeth sat, soaking her foot in a pan of water. From where I stood at the bus stop, she looked small, her exposed ankles pale.

She looked up as I approached her, and I felt a rush of nerves — she wasn't done with me, this I knew. That morning, Elizabeth's shriek, followed by the loud thump of a wooden heel hitting the linoleum floor, had announced her discovery of the cactus spines. I'd risen, dressed, and raced downstairs, but by the time I entered the kitchen, she was already seated at the table, calmly eating her oatmeal. She didn't look up when I walked into the room, didn't say anything when I sat down at the table.

Her lack of reaction made me furious. *What are you going to do with me?* I'd screamed, and Elizabeth's response had floored me. Cactus, she told me, her eyes taunting, meant ardent love, and though her shoes might never recover, she did appreciate the sentiment. I shook my head wildly, but Elizabeth reminded me of what she had explained in her garden, that each flower has only one meaning, to avoid confusion. I'd picked up my backpack and started to the door, but Elizabeth was behind me, a bouquet pressed to the back of my neck. *Don't you want to see my response?* she asked. I spun around to face the tiny purple petals. *Heliotrope,* she said. *Devoted affection.*

I hadn't paused for breath, and what came out next was a fiery whisper.

Cactus means I hate you, I'd said, slamming the door in her face.

Now a full day of school had passed, and my anger had faded into something close to regret. But Elizabeth smiled when she saw me, her expression welcoming, as if she had completely forgotten my declaration of hatred only hours earlier.

"How was your first day of school?" she asked.

"Awful," I said. I took the stairs two at a time, my legs stretching their full length as I attempted to pass Elizabeth, but her bony fingers flew out and closed around my ankle.

"Sit," she said. Her tight grasp thwarted my attempt at escape. I turned and sat on

130

the step below her to avoid her eyes, but she pulled me up by the collar until I faced her.

"Better," she said, then handed me a plate of sliced pear and a muffin. "Now eat. I have a job for you that may take all afternoon, so you'll start as soon as you've finished this."

I hated that Elizabeth was such a good cook. She kept me so well fed that I had yet to go back for the American cheese in my desk drawer. The pears on the plate were peeled and cored; the muffin was full of warm chunks of banana and melted peanut-butter chips. I ate every bite. When I finished, I traded the plate for a glass of milk.

"There," she said. "Now you should be able to work for as long as it takes to remove every spine from the insides of my shoes." She handed me two leather gloves that were much too big for my hands, a pair of tweezers, and a flashlight. "When you're done, you'll put them on your feet and walk up and down the steps three times, so that I can see you've been successful."

I hurled the gloves down the stairs, and they landed like forgotten hands in the dirt. Thrusting my bare hands into the darkness of her shoe, my fingers searched the soft leather for spines. I found one and pinched it between my fingernails, drawing it out and flicking it onto the ground.

131

Elizabeth watched me work in quiet concentration: first the leather inside, then the sides, and ending with the point of the toe. The shoe that Elizabeth had stepped into was the hardest, her weight having hammered the spines all the way through the leather. I dug each one out with the tweezers like a sloppy surgeon.

"So, if not ardent love, what?" Elizabeth asked as I neared the end of my task. "If not your eternal devotion and passionate commitment to me, what?"

"I told you before school," I said. "Cactus means I hate you."

"It doesn't," Elizabeth said firmly. "I can teach you the flower for hate, if you like, but the word *hate* is unspecific. Hate can be passionate or disengaged; it can come from dislike but also from fear. If you'll tell me exactly how you're feeling, I'll be able to help you find the right flower to convey your message."

"I don't like you," I said. "I don't like you locking me out of the house or throwing me into the kitchen sink. I don't like you touching my back or grabbing my face or forcing me to play with Perla. I don't like your flowers or your messages or your bony fingers. I don't like anything about you, and I don't like anything about the world, either."

"Much better!" Elizabeth seemed genuinely impressed by my hate-filled monologue. "The flower you're looking for is clearly the common thistle, which symbolizes misanthropy. *Misanthropy* means hatred or mistrust of humankind."

"Does humankind mean everybody?"

"Yes."

I thought about this. *Misanthropy.* No one had ever described my feelings in a single word. I repeated it to myself until I was sure I wouldn't forget.

"Do you have any?"

"I do," she said. "Finish your task, and we'll look together. I have a phone call to make, and I'm not leaving the kitchen until I've made it. When we're both done, we'll go looking for thistle together."

Elizabeth hobbled inside, and when the screen door banged closed, I scurried up the steps, crouching below the window. I rubbed my hand against the soft leather of the shoes, feeling for straggling spines. If Elizabeth was finally going to make the phone call she had been attempting for days, I wanted to listen. It was intriguing, the thought that Elizabeth, who never seemed to trip over a single word, had something she found hard to say. Peering in the window, I saw her sitting on the kitchen counter. She dialed seven numbers quickly, listened to perhaps the first ring, and then hung up. Slowly, she dialed again. This time she held the phone to her ear. From where I sat outside the window, I could see she was holding her breath. She listened for a long time.

Finally, she spoke. "Catherine." She pressed her hand over the receiver and made a sound between a gasp and a sob. I watched her wipe at the corners of her eyes. She put the phone back to her mouth. "This is Elizabeth." She paused again, and I listened intently, trying to hear the voice coming through the line, but couldn't. Elizabeth continued, her voice fragile. "I know it's been fifteen years, and I know you probably thought you'd never hear from me again. To tell you the truth, *I* thought you'd never hear from me again. But I have a daughter now, and I can't stop thinking about you."

I realized then that Elizabeth was talking to an answering machine, not a person. Picking up speed, her words tumbled forth. "You know," she said, "all the women I've known who've had babies, the first thing they do is call their mothers; they want their mothers with them — even the women who hate their mothers." Elizabeth laughed then, and relaxed her shoulders, which had been lifted almost all the way to her ears.

She played with the spiraling cord with her finger. "So I understand that now, you know? In a completely different way. With our parents gone, all I have is you, and I think about you constantly — I almost can't think of anything else." Elizabeth paused, perhaps thinking about what she should say next, or how to say it. "I don't have a baby — I was going to, adopt one, that is — but I ended up with a nine-year-old girl. I'll tell you the whole story sometime, when I see you. I hope I'll see you. Anyway, when you meet Victoria, you'll understand — she has these wild animal eyes, like I had as a little girl, after I'd learned that the only way to get our mother out of her room was to start a grease fire on the stove or smash the entire season's canned peaches." Elizabeth laughed again, and wiped her eyes. I could see that she was crying, although she didn't look sad. "Remember? So — I'm just calling to say that I forgive you for what happened. It was so long ago, a lifetime ago, really. I should have called years before now, and I'm sorry I didn't. I hope you'll call, or come to see me. I miss you. And I want to meet Grant. Please." Elizabeth waited, listening, and then set the phone down gently, so that I could barely hear the click of the receiver.

Scrambling back down the stairs, I stared

at Elizabeth's shoes intently, hoping she wouldn't know I'd been listening. Finally, she emerged from the kitchen and limped down the steps. Her eyes were wiped dry but still glistened, and she looked lighter — happier, even — than I'd ever seen her. "Well, let me see if you've been successful," she said. "Try them on."

I put on her shoes, took them off, extracted a spine I'd missed underneath my big toe, and put them on again. I walked up and down the stairs three times.

"Thank you," she said, slipping a shoe on her uninjured foot and sighing with pleasure. "Much, much better." She stood up slowly. "Now run into the kitchen and grab an empty jam jar from the cupboard with the glasses, a dish towel, and the pair of scissors on the kitchen table."

I did as she asked, and when I returned she was standing on the bottom step, testing her weight on her hurt foot. She looked from the road to her garden and back again as if trying to decide where to go.

"Common thistle is everywhere," she said. "Which is perhaps why human beings are so relentlessly unkind to one another." She took her first step toward the road and grimaced. "You'll have to help me or we'll never make it," she said, reaching for my shoulder.

"Don't you have a cane or something?" I asked, shrinking away from her touch.

Elizabeth laughed. "No, do you? I'm not an old lady, despite what you may think." She reached toward me, and this time I didn't retract. She was so tall she had to bend at the waist to lean on my shoulder. We took slow steps toward the road. She stopped once to readjust her shoe, and we kept walking. My shoulder burned beneath her hand.

"Here," Elizabeth said, when we reached the road. She sat down on the gravel and leaned against the wooden post of the mailbox. "See? Everywhere." She gestured to the ditch separating the highway from the rows of vines. It was about as deep as I was tall, full of stiff, dry plants, without a flower anywhere.

"I don't see anything." I was disappointed.

"Climb down in there," she said. I turned around and slid down the steep dirt wall. She handed me the jam jar and scissors. "Look for dime-sized flowers that were once purple, although this time of year they've likely faded to brown like everything else in Northern California. They're sharp, though, so pick them carefully when you find them."

I took the jar and scissors, and crouched

137

down into the weeds. The brush was thick, golden, and smelled like the end of summer. I cut a dry plant at the root. It stood tall in its place, supported by weeds on all sides. Detangling it, I threw it onto Elizabeth's lap.

"Is that it?"

"Yes, but this one doesn't have flowers. Keep looking."

I scrambled up the side of the ditch a few inches to get a better view but still didn't see anything purple. I picked up a rock and threw it as hard as I could in frustration. It hit the opposite wall and flew back in my direction so that I had to jump out of the way. Elizabeth laughed.

Leaping back into the weeds, I parted the brush with my hands and examined every dry stalk. "Here!" I said finally, snatching a clover-sized bud and throwing it into the jar. The flower looked like a small golden puffer fish with a faded tuft of purple hair. I climbed back to Elizabeth to show her the flower, which was bouncing around inside the jar like a living thing. I clapped my hand over the top to keep it from escaping.

"Thistle!" I said, handing her the jar. "For you," I added. I reached out awkwardly and patted her once on the shoulder. It was perhaps the first time in my entire life I had initiated contact with another human being — at least the first time in my memory. Meredith had told me I was a clingy baby, reaching out and clutching hair, ears, or fingers if I could find them — the straps of my infant car seat if I could not — with pulsing purple fists. But I didn't remember any of this, and so my action — the quick connection of the palm of my hand to Elizabeth's shoulder blade — surprised me. I stepped back, glaring at her as if she had made me do it.

But Elizabeth just smiled. "If I didn't know the meaning, I would be thrilled," she said. "I think this is the kindest you've been to me, and all to express your hatred and mistrust of humankind." For the second time that afternoon her eyes filled, and, like before, she did not look sad.

She reached out to hug me, but before she could draw me in, I slipped out of her arms and back into the ditch.

14.

The solid form of the chair on which I sat began to liquefy. Without knowing how I got there, I lay on my stomach on the library floor, books spread in a semicircle around me. The more I read, the more I felt my understanding of the universe slip away from me. Columbine symbolized both *desertion* and *folly;* poppy, *imagination* and *extravagance.* The almond blossom, listed as *indiscretion* in Elizabeth's dictionary, appeared in others as *hope* and occasionally *thoughtlessness.* The definitions were not only different, they were often contradictory. Even common thistle — the staple of my communication — appeared as *misanthropy* only when it wasn't defined as *austerity.*

The temperature in the library rose with the sun. By mid-afternoon I was sweating, swiping at my forehead with a wet hand as if trying to wipe memories from a saturated mind. I had given Meredith peony, *anger* but also *shame*. Admitting shame was closer to an apology than I ever hoped to get with Meredith. If anything, she should be coming to me with bunches and bunches of peony, quilting peony-covered bedspreads, baking peony-covered cakes. If peony could be misinterpreted, how many times, to how many people, had I misspoken? The thought made my stomach turn.

My choices for the flower vendor hung as a threatening unknown. Rhododendron clung solidly to the definition of *beware* throughout every dictionary before me, but there were likely hundreds, if not thousands, more dictionaries in circulation. It was impossible to know how he had interpreted my messages or what he was thinking as he sat in the donut shop. It was past five o'clock. He would be waiting, his eyes on the door.

I had to go. Leaving books scattered on the library floor, I skipped down four flights of stairs and walked out into the darkening San Francisco sky.

It was almost six by the time I got to the donut shop. I opened the double glass doors and found him sitting alone in a booth, a half-dozen donuts in a pink box before him.

I walked over to the table but did not sit down.

"Rhododendron," I demanded, as Elizabeth once had.

"Beware."

"Mistletoe."

"I surmount all obstacles."

I nodded and continued. "Snapdragon?"

"Presumption."

"White poplar?"

"Time." I nodded again, scattering before him the few thistles I had collected on my walk across the city. "Common thistle," he said. *"Misanthropy."*

I sat down. It had been a test, and he had passed. My relief was disproportional to his five correct answers. Suddenly starving, I dug a maple bar out of the box. I hadn't eaten anything all day.

"Why thistle?" he asked, helping himself to a chocolate old-fashioned.

"Because," I said between huge bites, "it's all you need to know about me."

He finished his donut and started on another. He shook his head. "Not possible."

I took a glazed and a sprinkled donut out of the box and set them on a napkin. He was eating so fast I was afraid the box would be empty before I finished my first.

"So, what else is there?" I asked, my mouth full.

He paused, and then looked into my eyes.

"Where've you been for the past eight years?"

His question stunned me.

I stopped chewing and tried to swallow, but I'd put too much in my mouth. I spit a brown ball onto a white napkin and looked up.

All at once, I saw it. The realization was as shocking for its obviousness as for the fact that we had met again; I couldn't believe I hadn't recognized him instantly. The boy he had been lurked inside the man he had become, his eyes still deep and afraid, his body, filled out now, still curved in at the shoulders, protective. I flashed on the first time I'd ever seen him, a lanky teenager leaning against the back of a pickup truck, tossing roses.

"Grant."

He nodded.

My instinct was to run. I'd spent so many years trying not to think about what I'd done, trying not to remember all that I'd lost. But as much as I wanted to flee, my desire to know what had become of Elizabeth, of the grapes, was stronger.

I covered my face with my hands. They smelled of sugar. In the space between my fingers I whispered my question, not at all sure he would answer: "Elizabeth?"

He was silent. I peered at him through lines of flesh. He didn't look angry, as I'd expected, but tormented. He pulled at a patch of hair above his ear, the skin stretching away from his scalp. "I don't know," he said. "I haven't seen her since —"

He stopped, looking out the window and then at me. I dropped my hands from my face, searching for his anger. Still, he looked only distressed. The silence was thick between us.

"I don't know why you asked me here," I said finally. "I don't know why you'd want to see me, after everything that happened."

Grant exhaled, the tension in his eyebrows releasing. "I was afraid *you* wouldn't want to see *me*."

He licked a finger. The fluorescent light illuminated his eyes and reflected off the stubble on his chin. I was unaccustomed to men in general, having spent my adolescence in all-female group homes with only an occasional male therapist or teacher, and I couldn't remember having ever been in such proximity to a man who was both young and handsome. Grant was so different from everything I was used to — from the size of his hands, heavy on the table, to the low, quiet voice that echoed into the silence between us.

"Your mother taught you?" I asked, gesturing to the scattered thistle.

He nodded. "But she died seven years ago. Your rhododendron was the first message-laden flower I've received since. I was surprised I hadn't forgotten the definition."

"I'm sorry," I said. "About your mother." My words didn't sound heartfelt, but Grant didn't appear to notice. He shrugged.

"Elizabeth taught you?" he asked.

I nodded. "She taught me what she knew," I said, "but she didn't know everything."

"What do you mean?"

" *'The language of flowers is nonnegotiable, Victoria,'* " I said, my voice a stern imitation of Elizabeth's. "And today, in the library, I learned there are three contradictory definitions of the almond blossom."

"Indiscretion."

"Yes. And no." I told Grant that white poplar wasn't listed in my dictionary, and about my trip to the library and the sighting of the yellow rose.

"Jealousy," Grant said, when I described the small illustration on the cover of the book.

"Exactly what it said," I told him. "But not what I learned." I finished the last donut, licked my fingers, and retrieved my worn dictionary from my backpack. I opened to the *R*'s and scanned the page for *rose, yellow.* I pointed.

"*Infidelity.*" His eyes widened. "Whoa."

"Changes everything, right?"

"Yes," he said. "Changes everything."

He reached into his backpack and pulled out a book with a red cloth cover and stem-green endpapers. He turned to the page with yellow rose and set the dictionaries side by side. *Jealousy, infidelity.* This simple discrepancy, and the ways in which the yellow rose had altered both our lives, hung between us. Grant might have known the details, but I didn't, and I didn't ask. Being with him was enough; I had no desire to further uncover the past.

It didn't seem like Grant wanted to dwell on the past, either. He closed the empty donut box. "You hungry?"

I was always hungry. But even more, I wasn't ready to say goodbye. Grant wasn't angry; being with him felt like being forgiven. I wanted to soak it up, take it with me, face the next day a little less haunted, a little less hateful.

I took a breath. "Starving."

"Me, too." He closed both dictionaries and slid mine across the table toward my backpack. "Let's get dinner and compare. It's the only way."

Grant and I decided to eat dinner at Mary's Diner, because it stayed open all night. We had hundreds of pages of flowers to compare, and for every discrepancy, we debated the better definition. We agreed that the loser would cross the old definition out of their dictionary and write in the new one.

We got stuck on the very first flower. Grant's dictionary defined acacia as *friendship*, mine as *secret love.*

"Secret love," I said. "Next."

"Next? Just like that? You didn't make much of a case."

"It's thorny and pod-bearing. Just the sway of the tree makes you think of shifty-eyed men in convenience stores, untrustworthy."

"And how is *untrustworthy* related to *secret love?*" he asked.

"How is it not?" I shot back.

Grant appeared unsure how to respond, so he chose another approach. "Acacia. Subfamily: Mimosoideae. Family: Fabaceae. Legumes. They provide sustenance, energy, and satisfaction to the human body. A good friend provides the same."

"Blah," I said. "Five petals. So small they're almost hidden by a large stamen. Hidden," I repeated. "Secret. Stamen: love." My face flushed as I said this, but I didn't turn away. Grant didn't, either.

"Yours," he said finally, reaching for the black permanent marker on the table between us.

We continued this way hour after hour, eating and debating. Grant was the only person I had ever met who could match me bite for bite, and, like me, he seemed to never grow full. By sunrise we had ordered and eaten three meals apiece and were only halfway through the *C*'s.

Grant surrendered a *columbine* defeat and snapped his dictionary shut. I hadn't let him win, not once. "I guess I'm not going to the market today," he said, looking at me with a guilty expression.

I looked at my watch. Six a.m. Renata would already be there, throwing a surprised glance at Grant's empty stall. I shrugged. "November's slow, Tuesday's slow. Take a day off."

"And do what?" Grant asked.

"How should I know?" I was suddenly tired, ready to be alone.

I stood, stretched, and put my dictionary in my backpack. Sliding the check across the table toward Grant, I walked out of the restaurant without saying goodbye.

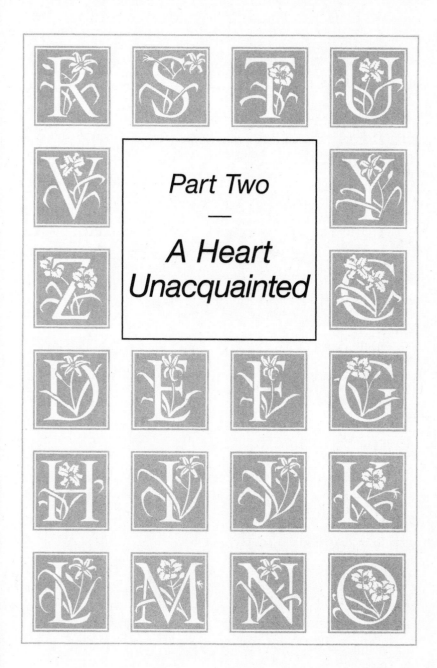

Part Two

—

A Heart Unacquainted

1.

Like Elizabeth, Grant was hard to forget. It was more than the intersection of our pasts, more than the drawing of the white poplar, which, in its obscurity, had led me to the truth about the language of flowers. It was something about Grant specifically, the seriousness with which he regarded the flowers, or the tone of his voice when he argued, simultaneously pleading and forceful. He'd shrugged his shoulders when I expressed sympathy at the death of his mother, and this, too, I found intriguing. His past — with the exception of the moments I'd glimpsed as a child — was a mystery to me. Group-home girls divulge their pasts relentlessly, and on the rare occasion I'd met someone unwilling to expose the details of her childhood, it was a relief. With Grant, I felt different. After only one night, I wanted to know more.

For a week I rose early and spent the library's open hours comparing definitions. I filled my pockets with smooth stones from a display in front of the Japanese teahouse in Golden Gate Park and used them as paperweights. Lining up dictionaries on two tables, I opened each to the same letter and placed rocks on the corners of the pages. Moving from one book to the next, I compared the entries flower by flower. Whenever I found conflicting definitions, I had long, drawn-out debates in my mind with Grant. Occasionally, I let him win.

On Saturday I arrived at the flower market before Renata. I handed Grant the scroll I had created, a list of definitions through the letter *J,* including revisions I'd made to the list we compiled together. When Renata and I returned to Grant's stall an hour later, he was still reading the scroll. He looked up to watch Renata finger his roses.

"Wedding today?" he asked.

Renata nodded. "Two. Small, though. One is my oldest niece. She's eloping but told me because she wanted me to give her flowers." Renata rolled her eyes. "Using me, the doll."

"An early day, then?" Grant asked, looking at me.

"Probably, the way Victoria works," she said. "I'd like to close the shop by three."

Grant wrapped Renata's roses and gave

her more change than she deserved. She had stopped bargaining with him; there was no need. We turned to leave.

"See you then," he called after us. I turned, my eyes quizzical. He held up three fingers.

The space below my rib cage expanded. The room felt unnaturally bright and filled with too much oxygen. I concentrated on exhaling, following Renata's orders without thinking. We had loaded everything into her truck before I remembered my promise of the week before.

"Wait," I said, slamming the truck door and leaving Renata inside the cab.

I raced through the market, looking for red roses and lilac. Grant had bucketsful, but I passed him without looking up. On the way back to the car, I passed him again. Shielding my face with a stalk of white lilac, I peeked in his direction. He held up three fingers again and cracked a shy smile. My face was hot, embarrassed. I hoped he didn't think the flowers in my arms were for him.

I worked all day in a nervous haze. The door opened and closed, and customers came in and out, but I never looked up.

At half past one, Renata lifted the hair off my forehead, and when I raised my head, her eyes were inches from mine.

"Hello? I've called you three times," she said. "There's a lady waiting for you."

I grabbed the roses and lilac from the walk-in and went into the showroom. The woman faced the door as if she might leave, her shoulders low.

"I didn't forget," I said when I saw her. She turned.

"Earl said you wouldn't." She watched me work, arranging the white lilac around the roses until the red was no longer visible. I wound sprigs of rosemary — which I had learned at the library could mean commitment as well as remembrance — around the stems like a ribbon. The rosemary was young and supple, and did not break when I tied it in a knot. I added a white ribbon for support and wrapped the whole thing in brown paper.

"First emotions of love, true love, and *commitment,"* I said, handing her the flowers. She handed me forty dollars. At the register I made change, but when I looked up, she was gone.

I returned to the worktable, and Renata examined me with a half-smile. "What were you doing out there?"

"Just giving the people what they want," I said, rolling my eyes the way Renata had the first day we'd met, when she stood on

154

the sidewalk with dozens of out-of-season tulips.

"Whatever they want," Renata agreed, clipping a row of sharp thorns off a yellow rose. A yellow rose for her niece's wedding: her fugitive, eloping, using niece. *Jealousy, infidelity.* The specifics of the definition didn't matter much in this case, I thought. The outcome did not look good. I finished my last table arrangement and looked at the clock. Two-fifteen.

"I'll just load these up," I said to Renata, grabbing as many vases as I could carry. They were too full, and water soaked into my shirt where it spilled over the tops.

"Don't worry about it," Renata said. "Grant's been waiting on the stoop for two hours. I told him if he was going to sit there, he better not scare away my customers, and he would do my heavy lifting as payment."

"He agreed?"

She nodded, and I set the vases down. Pulling on my backpack, I waved goodbye to Renata, avoiding her eyes. Grant sat on the sidewalk, leaning against the sun-warmed brick wall. He startled as I walked out the door, jumping to his feet.

"What're you doing here?" I was surprised by the accusation in my voice.

"I want to bring you to my farm. I have

disagreements with your definitions, and you'll understand better with my flowers in your hands. You know I'm no good at debating."

I looked up and down the hill. I wanted to go with Grant, but being with him made me nervous. It felt illicit. I didn't know if the feeling was left over from my time with Elizabeth or if it was just too close to romance or friendship, two things I'd spent a lifetime navigating around. I sat down on the curb, thinking.

"Good," he said, as if my sitting down was an act of assent. He held out his car keys and nodded across the street. "You can wait in the truck, if you want, while I carry Renata's flowers. I brought lunch."

With the mention of lunch, I overcame my reluctance. I grabbed his keys. In the truck, a white paper bag sat on the passenger seat. I picked it up and climbed inside. The truck was filled with the remains of flowers: Stem clippings littered the floor, and wilted petals worked themselves into the upholstery. I sunk into the seat and opened the bag. A sandwich on a thick French roll: turkey, bacon, tomato, and avocado, with mayonnaise. I took a bite.

Across the street, Grant carried vases two at a time up the hill. He paused only once at the top, looking downhill to where I sat in the parked car. He smiled and mouthed the words *Is it good?*

I hid my face behind the sandwich.

2.

The driver leaned away from me as I climbed onto the school bus. I recognized the look on his face — pity, dislike, and more than a little bit of fear — and I slammed my backpack against the empty seat as I sat down. The only reason he should feel sorry for me, I thought angrily, was because I had to look at his ugly, bald head all the way to school.

Perla sat down across the aisle from me and handed over her ham sandwich before I could demand that she do so. Two months into school, and she understood the drill. I ripped off large chunks and forced them into my mouth, thinking about the way Elizabeth had hurried out of the house that morning, leaving me alone to put my lunch in my backpack and find my shoes. I hadn't wanted to go to school — had begged to stay home for the first day of harvest. But she had ignored my appeals, even when they turned violent. *If you loved me, you'd want me here,* I said, hurling my math book at the back of her head as she hurried out the door. I wasn't fast enough. She disappeared through the doorway and jogged down the front steps, not even turning around at the sound of the book hitting the door frame. I could tell by the way she walked that she wasn't thinking of me. She hadn't been all morning. The stress of the harvest was all-consuming, and she wanted me gone, out of her hair. It was the first time I felt that I understood Elizabeth, and in my anger I yelled after her that she wasn't any different from all my other foster mothers. Stomping all the way to the bus stop, I ignored the stares of the workers arriving by the truckload.

The bus driver glared at me in the rearview mirror, following each bite of sandwich into my mouth with the same two eyes that should have been watching the road. I opened my mouth while I chewed, and the bus driver's face pinched in repulsion.

"So, don't watch!" I yelled, springing to my feet. "If it's so disgusting, just don't watch." I picked up my backpack, thinking vaguely that I would jump off the moving bus and walk the rest of the way to school, but instead I swung my bag high into the air and brought it down on the driver's shiny scalp. There was a satisfying smack as my full metal thermos collided with his skull. The bus swerved, the driver swore, and the children screeched at an almost deafening pitch. Somewhere within the layers of noise I heard Perla's small voice begging me to stop, and then she started to cry. When the bus skidded to a halt on the side of the road and the driver cut off the engine, Perla's sobs were the last remaining sound.

"Off," the driver said. A large knot was already forming on his head, and he pressed the palm of one hand against it while he reached for a radio with the other. I put on my backpack and climbed off the bus. Dust from the road swirled around me as I looked up through the open doors.

"Your mother's name," the driver demanded, pointing down at me.

"I don't have one," I said.

"Your guardian, then."

"The State of California."

"Then who do you fucking live with?" The radio crackled with harsh words, and the driver turned it off. The silence on the bus was complete. Even Perla had stopped crying and sat motionless.

"Elizabeth Anderson," I said. "I don't know her phone number or her address." My entire childhood I had refused to memorize phone numbers, so that I wouldn't be able to answer questions like these.

The bus driver threw the radio on the floor in anger. He glared at me, and I held his gaze in defiance. I hoped he would drive off and leave me alone on the side of the road. I would prefer to be left than continue on to school, and I relished the thought that my abandonment would likely cost the bus driver his job. He tapped his thumbs on the horn, and my anticipation stretched down the empty road.

Just then Perla stood up and stepped out in front of the driver. "You can call my father," she said. "He'll come for her."

I squinted my eyes at Perla. She looked away.

Carlos did come for me. He put me in the truck, listened to the bus driver's version of events, and then drove me back to the vineyard in silence. I looked out the window as we drove, paying attention to every detail as if taking in the landscape for the last time. Elizabeth would not keep me, not after this. My stomach lurched.

But when Carlos told Elizabeth what I'd done, his rough hand clamped around the back of my neck, forcing me to face her, she laughed. The sound was so unexpected and fleeting that the second she stopped laughing, I thought I'd imagined it.

161

"Thank you, Carlos," Elizabeth said, her face turning serious. She reached out to shake his hand and quickly released it, and the gesture was grateful and dismissive at once. Carlos turned quickly to leave. "Do the crews need anything?" Elizabeth asked as he walked away. Carlos shook his head. "I'll be back in an hour, then, maybe more. Watch over the harvest, please, while I'm gone."

"I will," he said, disappearing behind the sheds.

Elizabeth walked directly to her truck. When she turned and saw that I wasn't following, she walked back to where I stood. "You're coming with me," she said. "Now." She took a step toward me, and I remembered the way she'd carried me into the house, just two months before. I had grown since then, and gained back the weight I'd lost, but I didn't doubt she could still throw me inside the truck if it was her will to do so. Following her into the cab, I imagined what was to come: the drive to social services, the white-walled waiting room, Elizabeth leaving even before the social worker on call could check me in to the system. It had all happened before. Clenching tight fists, I stared out the window.

But as we started down the driveway, Elizabeth's words surprised me. "We're going to see my sister," she said. "This feud has gone on long enough, don't you think?"

My body turned rigid. Elizabeth looked to me as if for a response, and I nodded stiffly, the reality of what she had said sinking in.

She was going to keep me.

My eyes filled with tears. The anger I'd felt toward Elizabeth that morning dissolved, replaced immediately by shock. I had not, for even one moment, believed Elizabeth when she said there was nothing I could do to make her give me back. But here I was, only moments after having been sent home from school — a suspension would follow, if not an expulsion — listening to Elizabeth talk about her sister. Confusion and something unexpected — relief, maybe, or even joy — swirled within me. I sucked in my lips, trying not to smile.

"Catherine won't believe you hit the bus driver over the head while he was driving," Elizabeth said. "I mean, she won't believe it because I did it, too — the exact same thing! Maybe I was in second grade, though? I can't remember. At any rate, one minute he was driving, and the next minute he was glaring at me in the rearview mirror, and before I could stop myself, I was out of my seat, yelling, *'Keep your eyes on the road, you fat*

163

bastard!' And he *was* fat, let me tell you."

I started to laugh, and once I started, I couldn't stop. Folded over, my forehead pressed against the dashboard, my laughter escaped in a series of choking gulps that sounded like sobs. I covered my face with my hands. "My bus driver isn't fat," I said when I had calmed enough to speak, "but he's ugly."

I started to laugh again, but Elizabeth's silence quieted me.

"I don't want you to think I'm encouraging you," she said. "What you did was clearly wrong. But I feel bad that I ignored your anger, and that I sent you to school in the state you were in. I should have explained myself better, should have included you."

Elizabeth understood.

I pulled my forehead away from the dashboard and shifted my head onto her lap, suddenly feeling less alone than I ever had in my entire life. The steering wheel was only an inch from my nose, and I nuzzled the crown of my head into her stomach. If Elizabeth was surprised by my sudden affection, she didn't show it. She moved her hand from the gearshift to my hairline, stroking my temple and down the bridge of my nose.

"I hope she's home," she said, and I knew her thoughts had returned to Catherine. She switched on her blinker, waiting for a line of cars to pass before turning from the driveway onto the road.

Elizabeth had not stopped thinking about her sister in the weeks leading up to the harvest. I knew this because of the phone calls, dozens of them, all messages left on Catherine's answering machine. The first few were similar to the one I had overheard on the porch: moments of scattered reminiscing followed by a statement of forgiveness. But lately her messages had been different — chatty, and long — sometimes so long that the answering machine cut her off and she had to call back. She rambled on and on about the minutia of our daily lives, describing the endless tasting of the grapes and the cleaning of the picking bins. Often she described what she was cooking as she cooked it, tangling herself up in the long, spiraling cord as she moved from the stove to the spice rack and back again.

The more time Elizabeth spent talking to Catherine, or, more specifically, Catherine's answering machine, the more it struck me how little Elizabeth spoke to anyone else. She left the property only to go to the farmers' market, the grocer, the hardware store, and, occasionally, the post office. These visits were only to pick up plants she had mail-ordered from a gardening catalog, never to mail or receive letters. It was obvious that in the small community, she knew everyone — she asked the butcher to give her regards to his wife, and when she approached the vendors behind the stands at the farmers' market, she greeted each one by name. But she did not have conversations with these people. In fact, I thought, she had not had a single conversation that I had witnessed throughout the time I'd been with her. She spoke to Carlos as necessary but only about specific aspects of growing and harvesting grapes, and not once did their words meander off topic.

As we drove to Catherine's, my head in Elizabeth's lap, I compared my quiet existence at Elizabeth's to all the things I had previously understood to compose a life: large families, loud homes, welfare offices, busy cities, violent outbursts. I didn't want to go back. I liked Elizabeth. I liked her flowers, her grapes, and her concentrated attention. Finally, I realized, I had found a place I wanted to stay.

Pulling off the road, Elizabeth parked the truck and took a deep, nervous breath.

"What did she do to you?" I asked, suddenly interested in a way I had never been before.

Elizabeth looked unsurprised by my question but didn't answer right away. She stroked my forehead, my cheek, and my shoulder. When she finally spoke, her words were a whisper. "She planted the yellow roses."

Then she pulled the parking brake and reached for the door handle.

"Come on," she said. "It's time to meet Catherine."

3.

Grant drove through the city, his oversized truck slowing for tight turns in crowded intersections.

"Grant?" I asked.

"Yeah?"

I searched the crumpled white paper bag for crumbs but didn't find any. "I don't want to see Elizabeth."

"So?"

Like the white poplar, his response was unspecific. "So, what?"

"So, if you don't want to see her, don't see her."

"She won't come to the farm?"

"She hasn't visited since the day you came with her, and that was — what? — almost ten years ago?" Grant looked out at the water, and I couldn't see his face, but when he spoke next, his voice bordered on anger. "She didn't come for my mother's funeral, but you think she'll just show up today because you're here?"

He rolled down the window, and the wind became a wall between us.

Grant and Elizabeth had no contact. He had said this over donuts, but I hadn't believed it to be possible. Grant must know the truth, and if he did, what would have kept him from telling Elizabeth? I tried to think of an explanation for the remainder of the drive, but when he stopped in front of the locked metal gate, I still hadn't come up with anything. He parked and got out to open the gate, then returned to the car and drove through the opening.

The sight of the flowers eclipsed my contemplation. I jumped out of the car and dropped to my knees at the side of the road. There must have been a fenced property line somewhere, but it wasn't visible, and the stretch of the flowers felt infinite. A gardening stake scrawled with a scientific name I didn't recognize announced the genus and species of the nearest plant. I held fistfuls of the small yellow flowers to my face as if discovering water after many days in the desert. Pollen clung to my cheeks, and petals rained down on my chest and stomach and thighs. Grant laughed.

"I'll give you a minute," he said, climbing back into the truck. "When you're done here, walk behind the house." His truck kicked up dust as it bumped over the road.

I lay down in the dirt between the rows, disappearing from sight.

I found Grant behind the farmhouse, sitting at a weathered picnic table. On the table sat a box of chocolates, two glasses of milk, and the scroll I'd given him that morning. I sat down across from him and gestured to the sheet of paper with my head.

"So, what's the problem?"

Reaching for the chocolates, I scanned the selection. Dark chocolate, mostly, with nuts and caramel. Exactly what I would have chosen.

Grant ran his finger along the paper, pausing on a line and tapping a word I couldn't read upside down.

"Hazel," he said. *"Reconciliation.* Why shouldn't it be *peace?"*

"Because of the history of the Betulaceae family, divided for centuries into two families, Betulaceae and Corylaceae. Only recently brought together as subgroups within the same family," I explained. "Bringing together — reconciliation."

Grant looked down at the table, and I could tell by his expression that he already knew the history of the family. "I'm never

170

going to win with you, am I?"

"You know you aren't," I said. "Did you really bring me here to try?"

He looked at the house and then out into the fields.

"No," he admitted. "I didn't." He grabbed a handful of chocolates and stood up. "Eat chocolate. I'll be right back, and then we'll go for a walk."

I drank my milk. When Grant returned, he had an old camera around his neck, black and heavy on an embroidered strap. It looked as if it belonged in the Victorian era with the language of flowers.

He took off the camera and handed it to me. "For your dictionary," he said, and I immediately understood. I would create my own dictionary, and his flowers would illustrate the pages. "Make me a copy," he said, "so that we'll never have a misunderstanding."

This is all a misunderstanding, I thought to myself, taking the camera. *I don't ride in trucks with young men and sit at picnic tables and eat chocolate. I don't drink milk while discussing families, flower or otherwise.*

Grant walked away, and I followed. He led me to a dirt road heading west, the sun setting over the hills in front of us. The sky was undecided, alternating orange and blue behind approaching thunderclouds, full of the nervous anticipation of rain. I wrapped my arms tightly around myself and lagged a step behind. Grant pointed to the left at a long row of wooden sheds, all padlocked. There had been a dried-flower business, he explained, but he'd shut it down when his mother became ill. He didn't much care for the corpses of what had once been alive. On the right were acres of illuminated green-houses, long hoses running out of cracked open doors. Grant approached one and held the door open for me. I slipped inside.

"Orchids," he said, gesturing to shelves of staked pots. "Not ready for market." There wasn't a bloom in sight.

We stepped out and continued along the path, which climbed a hill and dipped down the other side. Somewhere beyond the fields of flowers the vineyard began, but the property line was too far away to see. Eventually, the path curved around the acres of green-houses and back through open fields until we stood again in front of the farmhouse.

Grant led me down a gradual slope into a rose garden. It was small, carefully tended, and looked like it belonged to the house and not the farm. Grant's hand brushed mine as we walked, and I took a step away.

"Have you ever given anyone a red rose?"

Grant asked. I looked at him as if he was trying to force-feed me foxglove. "Moss rose? Myrtle? Pink?" he pressed.

"Confession of love? Love? Pure love?" I asked, to make sure we shared the same definitions. He nodded. "No, no, and no."

I picked a pale blush-colored bud and shredded the petals one at a time.

"I'm more of a thistle-peony-basil kind of girl," I said.

"Misanthropy-anger-hate," said Grant. "Hmm."

I turned away. "You asked," I said.

"It's kind of ironic, don't you think?" he asked, looking around us at the roses. They were all in bloom, and not one was yellow. "Here you are, obsessed with a romantic language — a language invented for expression between lovers — and you use it to spread animosity."

"Why is every bush in bloom?" I asked, ignoring his observation. It was late in the season for roses.

"My mother taught me to prune thoroughly the second week of October, so we would always have roses for Thanksgiving."

"You cook Thanksgiving dinner?" I asked, glancing toward the farmhouse. The window of the peaked gable was still broken, all these years later. Someone had put plywood behind it.

"No," he admitted. "My mother did when I was young, before she began to spend most of her days in bed. I always pruned her roses just as she taught me, though, hoping the view from her window might beckon her into the kitchen. Only once did it work, the Thanksgiving before she died. Now that she's gone, I just do it out of habit."

I tried to remember whether Thanksgiving had already passed or if it was in the coming week. I paid little attention to holidays, although in the flower business they were hard to ignore. It must still be approaching, I thought. When I looked up, Grant was looking at me as if he was awaiting a response. "What?" I asked.

"Do you know your biological mother?"

I shook my head. He started to ask something else, but I cut him off. "Really. Don't waste your time asking — I don't know any more about her than you do." I walked away and knelt on the ground, holding the camera's viewfinder up to my eye. I snapped a blurry photo of knobby old wood and the tops of deep roots.

"It's manual. Do you know how to use it?" I shook my head. He pointed to the buttons and dials, defining photography terms I had never heard. I was paying attention only to the distance of his fingers from the camera hanging around my neck. Whenever he got too close to my chest, I took a step back.

"Try it," Grant said when he was done explaining. I held the camera up again and turned a dial to the left. An open pink blossom went from blurry to unrecognizable. "Other way," Grant said. I turned the dial to the left again, ruffled by his voice too close to my ear.

His hand closed around mine, and together we turned the dial to the right. His hands were soft and did not burn where they touched. "Yeah," he said. "That's right." He lifted my other hand to the top of the camera and pressed my index finger onto a round metal button. My heart stopped and started again. The lens clicked open and shut.

Grant withdrew his hands, but I did not lower the camera. I didn't trust my face. I didn't know if he would see joy or hatred in my eyes, fear or pleasure written on my bright-red cheeks. I didn't know what I felt except breathless.

"Wind the film to take another picture," he said. I didn't move. "Want me to show you?"

I stepped back. "No," I said. "That's enough."

"Too much information for one day?"

Grant asked.

"Yes," I said. I took off the camera and handed it to him. "Way too much."

We walked back toward the house. Grant did not invite me inside. He walked straight to his truck and opened the passenger door, holding out his hand to me. I paused and then took it. He helped me inside and closed the door.

We drove back to the city in silence. It began to rain, slowly at first, and then with a blinding, unexpected ferocity. Cars pulled over to wait out the storm, but it only strengthened. It was the first strong rain of the fall, and the earth opened to its long-awaited watering, releasing a metallic scent. Grant drove slowly, guided by his memory of the turns rather than the sight of the road. The Golden Gate Bridge was deserted. Water rose from the bay and fell from the sky with equal force. I imagined the water coming into the car, the level rising over our feet, knees, stomachs, and throats as we drove.

Nervous to reveal the location of Natalya's apartment, I asked Grant to drop me off in front of Bloom. It was still raining when he stopped in front of the store. I don't know if he waved; I couldn't see him through the water on the windshield.

Natalya and her band were setting up their instruments when I opened the door, and they nodded at me as I slipped up the stairs. Pulling my keys out of my backpack, I opened my small door, crawled inside, and curled up on the floor. The water from my wet clothes soaked into the fur carpet, and the whole world was wet and blue and cold. I shivered with my eyes wide open. I wouldn't sleep that night.

4.

"Ready?" Elizabeth asked.

I was surprised to see the short distance we'd traveled. Elizabeth had parked behind a locked metal gate, in a driveway. To the right was the parking lot where the farmers' market was held, and just beyond that, the vineyard. Somewhere beyond the vast expanse of asphalt, I realized, the two properties likely connected.

Stepping out of the truck, Elizabeth withdrew a skeleton key from her pocket. She slipped the key into the lock, and the gate swung open. I waited for her to come back to the truck, but she beckoned for me to get out.

"Let's walk," she said when I joined her. "It's been a long time since I've set foot on this land."

She walked slowly up the driveway toward the house, pausing to pinch wilted flowers and stick her thumb an inch into the soil.

Surrounded by flowers, I was struck by what I now understood as the magnitude of the sisters' quarrel. Nothing I could think of would make Elizabeth angry enough to give up not only her sister but also these endless acres of flowers for as long as she had. It must have been the worst kind of betrayal.

Elizabeth picked up her pace as she neared the house, smaller than ours, and yellow, but with a similar peaked-roof shape. As we walked up the front steps, I noticed the wood was soft, as if it hadn't quite dried out from the past spring's rain. The yellow paint was beginning to peel in large sections near the front door, and the gutter, knocked loose, hung low over the top step. Elizabeth ducked underneath it.

At the top of the steps, she approached the front door. A narrow rectangular window was set into the painted blue wood, and she leaned forward. Standing on my tiptoes, I pressed my head into the space below Elizabeth's chin. We peered inside. The glass was warped and dirty, and gave the effect of looking at a scene through water. The edges of the furniture blurred; framed photographs appeared to hover above a mantel. A thin floral carpet disappeared under the steam of our breath on the glass. I took in the room's emptiness: There were no people, dishes, newspapers, or any other sign of human activity.

But Elizabeth knocked anyway: softly, and then louder. She waited, and when no one approached, she began to knock continuously. Her taps grew punctuated with frustration. Still, no one came to the door.

Elizabeth turned and marched down the steps. Imagining the stairs caving under my feet, I tiptoed softly behind her. Ten paces away, she turned and pointed to a gable, the window shut but not curtained.

"See that window?" Elizabeth asked. "Inside used to be the attic, where we played as girls. When I was sent to boarding school — I was ten, so Catherine must have been seventeen — she converted it into a studio. She was talented, so talented. She could have gone to art school anywhere in the country, but she didn't want to leave our mother." Elizabeth paused, and we both looked up at the window. Water spots and dust reflected sunlight off the glass. I couldn't see inside the room. "She's in there right now," Elizabeth said. "I know she is. Do you think maybe she just didn't hear our knock?"

If she was inside, she had heard the knock. Though two stories, the house was not big. But Elizabeth's eyes were hopeful; I couldn't tell her the truth. "I don't know," I said.

"Maybe."

"Catherine?" Elizabeth called up. The window did not open, and I saw no motion behind it. "Maybe she's asleep."

"Let's just go," I said, pulling on her sleeve.

"Not until we know she's seen us. If she sees us and still won't come down, then she'll have made her feelings clear."

Elizabeth turned, kicking the dirt in front of the nearest row of flowers. She folded over and picked up a stone, rough and round, the size of a walnut. Aiming for the window, she threw the rock gently. It bounced off the shingled roof of the gable and returned to the ground, just paces from where we stood. Picking it up, she tried again, and again, her aim unimproved with practice.

Growing impatient, I grabbed a stone and hurled it at the upstairs window. It hit its target and went sailing through, a sound like a bullet traveling through glass, the break a perfect circle in the center. Elizabeth covered her ears with her hands, clenching her teeth and closing her eyes. "Oh, Victoria," she said, her voice pained. "Too hard. Much, much too hard."

She opened her eyes and lifted her face to the window. I followed her gaze. Inside, a thin, pale hand reached up, fingers closing around a gathering of cords. A shade dropped behind the shattered glass. Beside me, Elizabeth sighed, her eyes still fixed on the place where the hand had been.

"Come on," I said, grabbing her by the elbow. Her feet moved slowly, as if through sand, and I pulled her gently to the road. Helping her into the truck, I turned back and swung the metal gate closed.

5.

I was sleep-deprived and useless for an entire week. My fur floor didn't dry for days, and every time I went to lie down, the moisture soaked through my shirt like Grant's hands, a constant reminder of his touch. When I did sleep, I dreamt the camera was turned to my bare skin, capturing my wrists, the underside of my jawbone, and, once, my nipples. As I walked down deserted streets I would hear the click of the camera's shutter and spin around, expecting Grant just steps behind me. But there was never anyone there.

My inability to form coherent sentences and work the cash register did not escape Renata. It was Thanksgiving week, and the storefront was packed, but she relegated me to the back room with overflowing buckets of orange and yellow flowers and long stems of dried leaves in bright fall colors. She gave me a book with photographs of holiday arrangements, but I didn't open it. I wasn't completely awake, but flower arranging was something I could now do in my sleep. She brought me hastily scrawled orders and came back when they were done.

On Friday, the rush of the holiday past, Renata sent me to the workroom to sweep the floor and sand the table, which was beginning to bow and splinter under years of water and work. When Renata came to check my progress an hour later, I was asleep on my stomach on top of the table, my cheek against the rough wood.

She shook me awake. The sandpaper was still in my hand, the pads of my fingers textured where they clutched. "If you weren't in such demand, I would fire you," Renata said, but her voice was filled with amusement, not anger. I wondered if she believed me to be love-struck; the truth, I thought, was much more complicated.

"Get up," Renata said. "That same lady wants you." I sighed. There weren't any more red roses.

The woman leaned on folded elbows at the counter. She wore an apple-green raincoat, and a second woman, younger and prettier, stood next to her in a red coat of the same belted shape. Their black boots were wet. I looked outside. The rain had returned, just as my clothes and room had dried from the week before. I shivered.

"This is the famous Victoria," the woman said, nodding in my direction. "Victoria, this is my sister, Annemarie. And I'm Bethany." She reached her hand out to me, and I shook it. My bones melted within her strong shake.

"How are you?" I asked.

"I've never been better," Bethany said. "I spent Thanksgiving at Ray's. Neither of us had ever cooked Thanksgiving dinner, so we ended up throwing away a half-baked turkey and heating up cans of tomato soup. It was delicious," she said. It was obvious by the way she said it that she was referring to more than the soup. Her sister groaned.

"Who's Ray?" I asked. Renata appeared at the doorway with the broom, and I avoided her questioning stare.

"Someone I know from work. We've never shared more than complaints over ergonomics, but then Wednesday, there he was at my desk, asking me over."

Bethany had plans again the next night with Ray, and she wanted something for her apartment, something seductive, she said, blushing, but not obviously so. "No orchids," she said, as if this was a sexual flower and not a symbol of refined beauty.

"And for your sister?" I asked. Annemarie looked uncomfortable but didn't protest as her sister began to describe the details of her love life.

"She's *married*," Bethany said, emphasizing the word as if the roots of Annemarie's problems could be found in the very definition of the word. "She's worried her husband isn't attracted to her anymore, which — look at her — is ridiculous. But they don't — you know. And they haven't for a long time." Annemarie looked out the window and did not defend her husband or her marriage.

"Okay," I said, taking it all in. "Tomorrow?"

"By noon," Bethany replied. "I'll need all afternoon to clean my apartment."

"Annemarie?" I asked. "Is noon okay?"

Annemarie didn't answer right away. She smelled the roses and dahlias, the leftover oranges and yellows. When she looked up, her eyes were empty in a way that I understood. She nodded. "Yes," she said. "Please."

"I'll see you tomorrow," I said as they turned to go.

When the door closed, I looked up to see Renata, still in the doorway with the broom. "The famous Victoria," she chided me. "Giving the people what they want."

I shrugged and walked past her. Grabbing

186

my coat off the hook, I turned to leave.

"Tomorrow?" I asked. Renata had never given me a schedule. I worked when she told me to.

"Four a.m.," she said. "Early-afternoon wedding, two hundred."

I spent the evening sitting in the blue room, mulling over Annemarie's request. I was well acquainted with the opposite of intimacy: hydrangea, *dispassion,* had long been a favorite of mine. It bloomed in manicured gardens in San Francisco six months out of the year, and was useful for keeping housemates and group-home staff at a distance. But intimacy, closeness, and sexual pleasure — these were things for which I had never had a reason to look. For hours I sat underneath the naked bulb, the light yellowing the water-stained pages of my dictionary, scanning for useful flowers.

There was the linden tree, which signified *conjugal love,* but this didn't seem quite right. The definition felt more like a description of the past than a suggestion for the future. There was also the difficulty of identifying a linden tree, removing a small branch, and explaining to Annemarie why she should display the limb on her dining room table instead of a bouquet of flowers. No, I decided, the linden tree would not work.

Below me, Natalya's band started up, and I reached for a pair of earplugs. The pages of the book vibrated on my lap. I found flowers for *affection, sensuality,* and *pleasure,* but none, on their own, felt like enough to combat Annemarie's empty eyes. Growing frustrated, I reached the last flower in the book and turned back to the beginning. Grant would know, I thought, but I couldn't ask him. The asking alone would be too intimate.

As I searched, it occurred to me that if I couldn't find the right flowers, I could give Annemarie a bouquet of something bold and bright and lie about its meaning. It wasn't as if the flowers themselves held within them the ability to bring an abstract definition into physical reality. Instead, it seemed that Earl, and then Bethany, walked home with a bouquet of flowers expecting change, and the very belief in the possibility instigated a transformation. Better to wrap Gerber daisies in brown paper and declare sexual fulfillment, I decided, than to ask Grant his opinion on the subject.

I closed the book, closed my eyes, and tried to sleep.

Two hours later I got up and dressed for the

market. It was cold, and even as I changed my clothes and put on my jacket, I knew I could not give Annemarie Gerber daisies. I had been loyal to nothing except the language of flowers. If I started lying about it, there would be nothing left in my life that was beautiful or true. I hurried out the door and jogged down twelve cold blocks, hoping to beat Renata.

Grant was still in the parking lot, unloading his truck. I waited for him to hand me buckets and then carried them inside. There was only one stool in his booth; I sat down on it, and Grant leaned against the plywood wall.

"You're early," he said.

I looked at my watch. It was just past three in the morning. "You, too."

"I couldn't sleep," he said. I couldn't, either, but I didn't say anything.

"I met this woman," I said. I turned my stool away from Grant as if I would help a customer through the window, but the market was nearly empty.

"Yeah?" he said. "Who?"

"Just some woman," I said. "She came into Bloom yesterday. I helped her sister last weekend. She says her husband doesn't want her anymore. You know, in a —" I stopped, unable to finish.

"Hmm," Grant said. I felt his eyes all over my back, but I didn't turn to face him. "That's tough. It was the Victorian era, you know? Not a lot of talk about sex."

I hadn't thought of that. We watched the market begin to fill in silence. Renata would come through the door any minute, and I would think of nothing but someone else's wedding flowers for hours.

"Desire," Grant said finally. "I would go with *desire.* I think that's as close as you'll get."

I didn't know desire. "How?"

"Jonquil," Grant said. "It's a form of narcissus. They grow wild in the southern states. I have some, but the bulbs won't bloom till spring."

Spring wasn't for months. Annemarie didn't appear as though she could wait that long. "There's no other way?"

"We could force the bulbs in my greenhouse. I don't, usually; the flowers are so associated with spring, there isn't much of a market for them until late February. But we can try, if you want."

"How long will it take?"

"Not long," he said. "I bet you could see flowers by mid-January."

"I'll ask her," I said. "Thanks." I started to walk away, but Grant stopped me with his hand on my shoulder. I turned around.

"This afternoon?" he asked.

I thought about the flowers, his camera, and my dictionary. "I should be done by two," I said.

"I'll pick you up."

"I'll be hungry," I said as I walked away.

Grant laughed. "I know."

Annemarie looked more relieved than disappointed when I told her the news. January would be fine, she said, better than fine. The holidays were busy; the month would be a blur. She wrote down her phone number, wrapped her body tightly with the red belt of her coat, and walked out the door after Bethany, who was already halfway up the block. I had given her ranunculus: *You are radiant with charms.*

Grant was early, as he had been the week before. Renata invited him in. He sat at the table, watching us work and eating chicken curry out of a steaming foam container. A second container, unopened, sat beside him. When I finished the table arrangements, Renata said I could go.

"The boutonnieres?" I asked, looking into the box where she was lining up the bridesmaids' bouquets.

"I can finish them," she said. "I have

191

plenty of time. You just go on." She waved me out the door.

"You want to eat here?" Grant asked, handing me a plastic fork and a napkin.

"In the car. I don't want to waste light." Renata looked at us with curiosity but didn't ask. She was the least meddlesome person I had ever met, and I felt a twinge of affection for her as I followed Grant out the door.

The curry and our breath fogged the windows on the long drive to Grant's house. We drove in silence, the only noise the constant hum of the defroster. It was wet out, but the afternoon was clearing. By the time Grant opened the gate and drove past the house, the sky was blue. He went inside for the camera, and I was surprised to see him enter the square three-story building and not the house.

"What's that?" I asked when he returned, gesturing to the building from which he had just come.

"The water tower," he said. "I converted it into an apartment. You want to see inside?"

"Light," I said, looking to where the sun was already starting to descend.

"Right."

"Maybe after."

"Okay. You want another lesson?" Grant asked. He stepped toward me and dropped the camera strap around my head. His hands brushed against the back of my neck.

I shook my head no. "Shutter speed, aperture, focus," I said, turning dials and repeating the vocabulary he had thrown at me the week before. "I'll teach myself."

"Okay," he said. "I'll be inside." He turned and walked back into the water tower. I waited until I saw a light flip on in the third-story window before I turned toward the rose garden.

I would start with the white rose; it felt like a good place to begin. Sitting in front of a flowering bush, I dug a blank notebook out of my backpack. I would teach myself photography by documenting my successes and my failures. If, next week, I developed the film and saw that only one photo was clear, I needed to know exactly what I had done to produce the image. I numbered a sheet of paper from one to thirty-six.

In the waning light I photographed the same half-opened white rosebud, writing down in descriptive, nontechnical terms the reading of the light meter and the exact positions of the various dials and knobs. I recorded the focus, the position of the sun, and the angles of the shadows. I measured the distance of the camera to the rose in multiples of the length of my palm. When I ran out of light and film, I stopped.

Grant was sitting at his kitchen table when I returned. The door was open, and inside was as cold as outside. The sun had disappeared, and with it all warmth. I rubbed my hands together.

"Tea?" he asked, holding out a steaming mug.

I stepped in and closed the door behind me. "Please."

We sat across from each other at a weathered wood picnic table identical to the one outside. It was pushed up against a small window that framed a view of the property: sloping rows of flowers, the sheds and greenhouses, and the abandoned house. Grant stood up to adjust the lid on a rice cooker that was spewing liquid out of a small hole. He opened a cupboard and retrieved a bottle of soy sauce, which he set on the uneven table.

"Dinner's almost ready," he said. I looked at the stove. Nothing was cooking except the rice. "You want a tour?"

I shrugged but stood up.

"This is the kitchen." The cupboards were painted a pale green, the countertops gray Formica with silver trim. He didn't appear to own a cutting board, and the counters were dented and scraped from slicing. There was an antique white-and-chrome gas stove with a folding shelf, and on the shelf sat a row of empty green glass vases and a single wooden spoon. The spoon had a white sticker with a faded price on its tip, leading me to think it had either never been used or never been washed. Either way, I was not particularly anxious to sample his cooking.

In the corner of the room was a black metal staircase, spiraling through a small square hole. Grant began to climb, and I followed him up. The second floor contained a living room big enough for only an orange velour love seat and a floor-to-ceiling bookshelf. An open door led to a white tile bathroom with a claw-foot tub. There was no television and no stereo. I didn't even see a telephone.

Grant stepped back onto the staircase and led me to the third floor, which was covered wall to wall with a thick foam mattress. Crumbling foam was visible where the sheets had peeled away from the edges. Clothes sat in piles in two corners, one folded, the other not. Where there should have been pillows, there were stacks of books.

"My bedroom," Grant said.

"Where do you sleep?" I asked.

"In the middle. Closer to the books than the clothes, usually." He climbed across the foam mattress and switched off the reading lamp. I held on to the banister and climbed back down into the kitchen.

"Nice," I said. "Quiet."

"I like it that way. I can forget where I am, you know?" I did know. In Grant's water tower, settled in the absence of all things automatic and digital, it was easy to forget not just the location but also the decade.

"My roommate's punk band practices all night in the downstairs of our apartment," I said.

"That sounds awful."

"It is."

He walked over to the counter and spooned hot, soggy rice into large ceramic soup bowls. He handed me a bowl and a spoon. We began to eat. The rice warmed my mouth, throat, and stomach. It was much better than I had expected.

"No phone?" I asked, looking around. I'd thought I was the only young person in the modern world not attached to a communication device. Grant shook his head no. I continued: "No other family?"

Grant shook his head again. "My father left before I was born, went back to London. I've never met him. When my mother died, she left me the land and the flowers, nothing else." He took another bite of rice.

"Do you miss her?" I asked.

Grant poured on more soy sauce. "Some-times. I miss her as she was when I was a child, when she cooked dinner every night and packed my lunches with sandwiches and edible flowers. But toward the end of her life, she began to confuse me with my father. She'd go into a rage and throw me out of the house. Then, when she realized what she'd done, she would apologize with flowers."

"Is that why you live here?"

Grant nodded. "And I've always liked being alone. No one can understand that."

I understood.

He finished his rice and helped himself to another bowl, then reached for mine and filled it up as well. We ate the rest of the meal in silence.

Grant got up to wash his dish and set it up-side down on a metal drying rack. I washed my own and did the same. "Ready to go?" he asked.

"The film?" I grabbed the camera from where he had hung it on a hook and handed it to him. "I don't know how to release it."

He rewound the camera and unloaded the film. I pocketed it.

"Thanks."

We climbed into Grant's truck and started down the road. We were halfway back to the city when I remembered Annemarie's request. I sucked in my breath.

"What?" he asked.

"The jonquil. I forgot."

"I planted it while you were in the rose garden. It's in a paper box in the greenhouse — the bulbs require darkness until the foliage starts to grow. You can check on them next Saturday."

Next Saturday. As if we had a standing date. I watched Grant drive, his profile hard and unsmiling. I would check on them next Saturday. It was a simple statement but one that changed everything as completely as the discovery of the yellow rose.

Jealousy, infidelity. Solitude, friendship.

6.

It was dark out by the time I came in for dinner. The house was bright, and inside the frame of the open door, Elizabeth sat alone at the kitchen table. She had made chicken soup — the smell had reached me in the vines, the scent a physical draw — and she sat hunched over her bowl, as if studying her reflection in the broth.

"Why don't you have any friends?" I asked.

The words escaped without premeditation. For a week I'd watched Elizabeth manage the harvest with a heavy, dejected quality, and the image of her sitting at the kitchen table, alone and so obviously lonely, pushed the words right out of me.

Elizabeth looked over to where I stood. Quietly, she stood up, dumping the contents of her bowl back into the soup pot. With a match, she lit the blue ring of fire beneath it.

She turned to me. "Well, why don't you?"

"I don't want any," I said. Besides Perla, the only children I knew were from my class at school. They called me *orphan girl,* and it had gotten so that I doubted even my teacher remembered my real name.

"Why not?" Elizabeth pressed.

"I don't know," I said, my voice growing defensive. But I did know.

I had been suspended for five days for my attack on the school bus driver, and for the first time in my life, I was not miserable. Home with Elizabeth, I didn't need anyone else. Every day I followed behind as she managed the harvest, steering workers toward ripe vines and away from grapes that needed another day in the sun, another two. She popped grapes into her own mouth and then into mine, spewing numbers that correlated to the ripeness: 74/6, 73/7, and 75/6. *This,* she would say, when we located a ripe bunch, *is what you need to remember. This exact flavor — the sugars at seventy-five, the tannins at seven. This is a perfectly ripe wine grape, which neither machine nor amateur can identify.* By the end of the week, I had chewed and spit grapes from nearly every plant, and the numbers began to come to me almost before the grapes entered my mouth, as if my tongue was simply reading them like the number on a postage stamp.

The soup began to simmer, and Elizabeth stirred it with a wooden spoon. "Take off your shoes," she said. "And wash up. The soup's hot."

At the table, Elizabeth set out two bowls and loaves of bread as big as cantaloupes. I tore the bread in half, scooping out the soft, white middle and dipping it in the steaming broth.

"I had a friend, once," Elizabeth said. "My sister was my friend. I had my sister and my work and my first love, and there was nothing else in the world I wanted. Then, in an instant, all I had was my work. What I lost felt irreplaceable. So I focused every waking moment on running a successful business, on growing the most sought-after wine grapes in the region. The goal I set was so ambitious, and took so much time, that I didn't have even a minute to think about everything I'd lost."

Taking me in, I understood, had changed that. I was a constant reminder of family, of love, and I wondered if she regretted her decision.

"Victoria," Elizabeth asked abruptly. "Are you happy here?"

I nodded, my heartbeat suddenly racing. No one had ever asked me a question like that without immediately following with something like, *because if you were happy, if you had the sense to know that you were lucky to be here, you wouldn't act like such an ungrateful little brat.* But Elizabeth's smile, when it finally came, was only relieved. "Good," she said. "Because I'm happy you're here. In fact, I'm not looking forward to you going back to school tomorrow. It's been nice having you home; you've opened up a little. For the first time, you've seemed interested in something, and while I admit I'm a bit jealous of the grapes, it does bring me joy to see you engaging in the world."

"I hate school," I said. Just uttering the word made my soup bubble up at the back of my throat, a sick, nauseous feeling.

"Do you really hate school? Because I know you don't hate to learn."

"I really hate it." I swallowed once, and then told her what they called me, told her it was just like every school I'd ever been to, that I was singled out, labeled, watched, and never taught.

Elizabeth took her last bite of bread, and then carried her bowl to the sink.

"We'll withdraw you tomorrow, then. I can teach you more here than you'll ever learn in that school. And if you ask me, you've suffered enough for one lifetime." She came back to the table, retrieved my bowl, and refilled it to the brim.

My relief was so expansive I finished the second bowl, and then a third. Still, an internal lightness threatened to lift me off the chair and throw me, spinning, up the stairs and into bed.

7.

My photographs were awful. They were so bad I blamed the one-hour photo lab where I had them printed and took the negatives to a specialty store. The sign in front boasted that they printed only the work of professionals. It took them three days to make the prints, and when I picked them up, they were just as bad. Worse, even. My mistakes were more pronounced, the blurry green-and-white blobs more defined within the muddy background. I threw the photos into the gutter and sat down on the curb outside the photography store, defeated.

"Experimenting with abstraction?" I turned. A young woman stood behind me, looking at the photographs littering the street. She wore an apron and smoked a cigarette. The ash floated down around the photos. I wished they would catch fire and burn.

"No," I said. "Experimenting with failure."

"New camera?" she asked.

"No, new to photography."

"What do you need to know?"

I picked one of the prints up out of the street and handed it to her. "Everything," I said.

She stepped on her cigarette and considered the print. "I think it's a film-speed issue," she said, motioning for me to follow her inside. She led me to the film display, pointing out numbers on the corners of the boxes I hadn't even noticed. The shutter speed was too slow, she explained, and the film speed a poor match for the low light of late afternoon. I wrote everything she said down on the back of the prints and shoved the stack into my back pocket.

I was anxious to get off work the following Saturday. The store was empty; we didn't have a wedding. Renata was doing paperwork and didn't look up from her desk all morning. When I tired of waiting for her to release me, I stood close to her desk and tapped my foot on the concrete floor.

"All right, go," she said, waving me away. I turned and was halfway out the door when I heard her add, "And don't come back tomorrow, or next week, or the week after."

I stopped. "What?"

"You've worked twice as many hours as I've paid you for, you must know that." I hadn't been keeping track. It wasn't as if I could have gotten another job even if I'd wanted to. I had no high school diploma, no college degree, and no skills. I assumed Renata understood this and worked me as she wished. I didn't feel resentful.

"So?"

"Take a few weeks off. Stop in the Sunday after next and I'll pay you as if you'd worked — I owe you the money. I'll need you again around Christmas, and I have two weddings on New Year's Day." She handed me an envelope of cash, the one she should have given me the following day. I put it in my backpack.

"Okay," I said. "Thanks. I'll see you in two weeks."

Grant was in the parking lot of the market when I arrived, loading up a bucket of unsold flowers. I approached and held up the blurry photos, spread out like a fan. "Now you want a lesson?" he asked, amused.

"No." I climbed inside his truck.

He shook his head. "Chinese or Thai?"

I was reading the notes I had scratched on the back of the embarrassing prints and didn't answer. When he stopped for Thai, I waited in the car.

"Something spicy," I called through the open window. "With shrimp."

I had purchased ten rolls of color film, all different speeds. I would start with 100 in the bright afternoon light and work my way to 800 just after sunset. Grant sat on the picnic table with a book, glancing in my direction every few pages. I barely moved from a low crouch between two white rosebushes. All the flowers were open; in another week, the roses would be gone. As I had the week before, I numbered all my photographs and noted every angle and setting. I was determined to get it right.

When the darkness was nearly complete, I put away my camera. Grant no longer sat at the picnic table. Light shone from the windows of the water tower through a thick layer of steam. Grant was cooking, and I was starving. I gathered all ten rolls of film into my backpack and walked into the kitchen.

"Hungry?" He watched me zip up my backpack and inhale deeply.

"Are you really asking me that?"

Grant smiled. I walked to the refrigerator and opened the door. It was empty except for yogurt and a gallon of orange juice. I picked up the orange juice and drank it out of the container.

"Make yourself at home."

"Thanks." I took another swig and sat down at the table. "What're you making?"

He pointed to six empty cans of beef ravioli. I made a face.

"You want to cook?" he asked.

"I don't cook. Group homes have cooks, and since then, I've eaten out."

"You've always lived in group homes?"

"Since Elizabeth's. Before that I lived with lots of different people. Some were good cooks," I said, "others weren't."

He studied me as if he wanted to know more, but I didn't elaborate. We sat down with bowls of ravioli. Outside, it had started to rain again, a pounding rain that threatened to turn the dirt roads into rivers.

When we finished eating, Grant washed his dish and went upstairs. I sat at the kitchen table, waiting for him to come back down and drive me home, but he didn't. I drank more orange juice and looked out the window. When I grew hungry again, I searched the cupboard until I found an unopened package of cookies and ate every one. Grant still did not return. I put on a pot of tea and stood over it, warming my hands on the open blue flame. The kettle began to whistle.

Filling two mugs, I pulled tea bags from a box on the counter and climbed the stairs.

Grant was sitting on the orange love seat on the second floor, a book open on his lap. I handed him a mug and sat down on the floor in front of the bookshelf. The room was so small that even though I sat as far away from him as possible, he could have touched my knee with his toes by stretching his legs. I turned to the bookshelf. On the bottom was a stack of oversized books: gardening manuals, mostly, interspersed with biology and botany textbooks.

"Biology?" I asked, picking one up and opening it to a scientific drawing of a heart.

"I took a class at a community college. After my mother died, I thought briefly of selling the farm and going to college. But I dropped out of the class halfway through. I didn't like the lecture halls. Too many people, and not enough flowers."

A thick blue vein curved out of the heart. I traced it with my finger and looked up at Grant. "What're you reading?"

"Gertrude Stein."

I shook my head. I'd never heard of her.

"The poet?" he asked. "You know, 'A rose is a rose is a rose'?"

I shook my head again.

"During the last year of her life, my

mother became obsessed with her," Grant said. "She'd spent most of her life reading the Victorian poets, and when she found Gertrude Stein, she told me she was a comfort."

"What does she mean, 'A rose is a rose is a rose'?" I asked. Snapping the biology book shut, I was confronted with the skeleton of a human body. I tapped the empty eye socket.

"That things just are what they are," he said.

" 'A rose is a rose.' "

" 'Is a rose,' " he finished, smiling faintly.

I thought about all the roses in the garden below, their varying shades of color and youth. "Except when it's yellow," I said. "Or red, or pink, or unopened, or dying."

"That's what I've always thought," said Grant. "But I'm giving Ms. Stein the opportunity to convince me." He turned back to his book.

I pulled another book off the shelf, higher up. It was a thin volume of poetry. Elizabeth Barrett Browning. I had read most of her work in my early teens, when I'd discovered the Romantic poets often referenced the language of flowers, and read everything I could get my hands on. The pages of the book were earmarked with notes scribbled in the margins. The poem I opened to was eleven verses, all beginning with the words *Love me.* I was surprised. I had read the poem, I was sure, but didn't remember the dozens of references to love, only the references to flowers. I replaced the book and withdrew another, and then another. All the while, Grant sat, silently turning pages. I looked at my watch. Ten past ten.

Grant looked up. He checked his own watch and then looked out the window. It was still raining. "You want to go home?"

The roads were wet; the drive would be slow. I would get soaked in the two blocks between Bloom and the blue room, and Natalya's band would be practicing. Renata did not expect me at work the following day. No, I realized, I did not particularly want to go home.

"Do I have another choice?" I asked. "I'm not sleeping here with you."

"I won't stay here. You can have my bed. Or sleep on the couch. Or wherever."

"How do I know you won't come back in the middle of the night?"

Grant pulled his keys out of his pocket and detached the key to the water tower. He handed it to me and walked down the stairs. I followed him out.

In the kitchen he grabbed a flashlight out

of a drawer and a flannel jacket off a hook. I opened the door, and he walked out, lingering under the cover of the stoop. Rain ran in sheets around the protected step. "Good night," he said.

"Spare key?" I asked.

Grant sighed and shook his head, but he was smiling. He leaned over and picked up a rusted watering can, half full of rainwater. He poured the water through the spout as if he was watering the sodden gravel. In the bottom was a key. "It's probably rusted beyond use. But here you go, just in case." He handed me the key, and our hands clasped around the wet metal.

"Thanks," I said. "Good night." He stood still as I inched the door closed and turned the lock.

I breathed in the emptiness of the water tower and climbed the stairs. On the third floor, I pulled the blanket off Grant's bed and returned to the kitchen, curling up underneath the picnic table. If the door opened, I would hear it.

But all I heard, all night, was the rain.

Grant knocked on the door at half past ten the next morning. I was still asleep under the table. It had been twelve hours, and my body was stiff and slow to rise. At the door I paused, leaning against the solid wood and rubbing my eyes, my cheekbones, and the back of my neck. I opened the door.

Grant stood in the clothes he'd worn the night before and looked only slightly more awake than I felt. Stumbling into the kitchen, he sat down at the table.

The storm had passed. Outside the window, under the cloudless sky, flowers glistened. It was a perfect day for photography.

"Farmers' market?" he asked. "On Sundays I sell down the road instead of in the city. You want to come?"

December was a bad time of year for fruit and vegetables, I remembered. Oranges, apples, broccoli, kale. But even if it had been midsummer, I wouldn't have wanted to go to the farmers' market. I didn't want to risk seeing Elizabeth. "Not really. I need film, though."

"Come with me, then. You can wait in the truck while I sell what I have left over from yesterday. Then I'll take you to the drugstore."

Grant changed his clothes upstairs, and I brushed my teeth with toothpaste and my finger. Splashing water on my face and hair, I went to wait in the truck. When Grant joined me a few minutes later, he had shaved and put on a clean gray sweatshirt and only slightly dirty jeans. He still looked tired, and he pulled up his hood as he locked the door of the water tower.

The road had flooded in places, and Grant drove slowly, his truck swaying like a boat in deep water. I closed my eyes.

Less than five minutes later, he stopped the truck, and when I opened my eyes, we were in a crowded parking lot. I slunk down in my seat while Grant jumped out. Pulling his hood low over his forehead, Grant slid the buckets out of his truck. I closed my eyes and pressed my ear against the locked door, trying not to hear the noises of the busy market or remember the many times I'd been there as a child. Finally, he returned.

"Ready?" he asked.

Grant drove to the nearest store, a country drugstore with fishing gear and pharmaceuticals. Being out in the world, in such close proximity to Elizabeth, made me nervous.

I paused, my hand on the door of the truck. "Elizabeth?"

"She won't be here. I don't know where she shops, but I've been coming here for over twenty years, and I've never seen her."

Relieved, I walked inside and went straight to the photo counter, dropping my canisters in an envelope and pushing them through a slot.

"One hour?" I asked a bored-looking clerk in a blue apron.

"Less," she said. "I haven't had any film to print in days."

I ducked into the nearest aisle. The store was having a sale on T-shirts — three for five dollars. I picked the top three off a tall pile and put them in my basket with rolls of film, a toothbrush, and deodorant. Grant stood at the checkout counter, eating a candy bar, watching me walk up and down the rows. I poked my head out of the aisle. When I saw that the store was empty, I joined him at the counter.

"Breakfast?" I asked, and he nodded. I picked up a PayDay and ate out the peanuts until it was nothing but a gooey caramel strip.

"Best part," Grant said, nodding to the caramel. I handed it to him, and he ate it quickly, as if I would change my mind and take it back. "You must like me more than you let on," he said, grinning.

The door opened, and an elderly couple walked toward us, holding hands. The woman's back bent forward, and the man had a stiff left leg, so it looked as if she was dragging him through the door. The old man looked me up and down, and his smile was youthful and out of place on his age-spotted skin.

"Grant," he said, winking and nodding in my direction. "Good work, son, good work."

"Thank you, sir," said Grant, looking at the ground. The man wobbled past, and after a few steps, he stopped and slapped his wife on the backside. He turned and winked at Grant.

Grant looked from me to the old man and shook his head. "He was a friend of my mother's," he said when the couple was out of earshot. "He thinks that will be us in sixty years."

I rolled my eyes, picked up a second Pay-Day, and walked to the photography counter to wait. There was nothing in the world less likely than Grant and me holding hands in sixty years. The clerk handed me the first roll, which had already been printed, the negatives cut and pressed into a clear envelope. I lined up the photographs on the bright yellow counter.

The first ten were blurry. Not indistinguishable white blobs, like my first attempt, but blurry. Beginning with the eleventh, they became passably clear, but nothing of which I could be proud. The clerk continued to pass me one roll at a time, and I continued to line them up, being careful to maintain the order.

Grant stood nearby, fanning himself with five empty candy wrappers. I walked over and held up the print. It was the sixteenth shot on the eighth roll — a perfect white rose, bright and clear, the contrast with the dark background a natural frame. Grant leaned over as if to smell it, and nodded. "Nice."

"Let's go," I said. I paid for the things in my basket and Grant's candy wrappers, and began to walk out the door.

"Your photos?" Grant asked, pausing and looking at the sea of prints I had left on the photo counter.

"This is all I need," I said, holding up the single image.

8.

I listened to the click of Elizabeth's rag mop, my spine pressed against the trunk of a thick vine. I was supposed to be out for my morning walk, but I didn't feel like walking. Elizabeth had opened every window in the house to let in the first warm spring air, and from my position in the row nearest the house, I could hear her every movement.

For six months I'd been home with Elizabeth, and I'd grown accustomed to her concept of home-school. I did not have a desk. Elizabeth did not purchase a chalkboard, or a textbook, or flash cards. Instead, she had posted a schedule on the refrigerator door — a wispy sheet of rice paper with delicate script, the corners curling around silver circular magnets — and I was responsible for the activities and chores on the thin sheet of paper.

Elizabeth's list was detailed, exhausting, and exact but never grew and never changed.

Every day, after breakfast and my morning walk, I wrote in the black leather-bound journal she had purchased for me. I was a good writer and an excellent speller, but I made purposeful mistakes to keep Elizabeth by my side, sounding out words and proofing pages. When I finished, I helped her prepare lunch, and we measured, and poured, and doubled recipes, and halved them. Silverware in neat stacks became fractions and cups of dry beans complicated word problems. Using the calendar by which she tracked the weather, she taught me to calculate averages, percentages, and probabilities.

At the end of each day, Elizabeth read to me. She had shelves and shelves of children's classics, dusty hardcovers with stamped gold titles: *The Secret Garden, Pollyanna,* and *A Tree Grows in Brooklyn.* But I preferred her viticulture textbooks, the illustrations of plants and chemical equations clues to the world that surrounded me. I memorized vocabulary — nitrate leaching, carbon sequestration, integrated pest management — and used them in casual conversation with a seriousness that made Elizabeth laugh.

Before bed, we marked off each day on a calendar in my room. Throughout January, I simply scratched a small red *X* in the box underneath the date, but by the end of March, I wrote the high and low temperatures, as Elizabeth did on her own calendar, what we had eaten for dinner, and a list of the day's activities. Elizabeth cut a stack of Post-its the size of the calendar's squares, and many evenings I filled five or six sheets before crawling into bed.

More than a nightly ritual, the calendar was a countdown. August second — the day after my supposed birthday — was highlighted, the entire box colored pink. In black felt-tip, Elizabeth had written eleven a.m., third floor, room 305. The law mandated I live with Elizabeth for a full year before my adoption could be finalized; Meredith had scheduled our court date for a year to the day from my arrival.

I checked the watch Elizabeth had given me. Another ten minutes before she would let me back inside. I leaned my head against the vine's bare branches. The first bright green leaves had sprouted from tight buds, and I studied them, perfect, fingernail-sized versions of what they would become. Smelling one, I nibbled a corner, thinking I would write in my journal about the taste of a grapevine, before the grapes. I checked my watch again. Five minutes.

Out of the quiet, I heard Elizabeth's voice.

It was clear, confident, and for a moment I thought she was calling me. Scampering back to the house, I stopped midstride when I realized she was on the phone. Though she had not mentioned her sister once since our visit to the flower farm, I knew in an instant she had called Catherine. I sat down in the dirt beneath the kitchen window, shocked.

"Another crop," she said. "Safe. I'm not a drinker, but I have more sympathy for Dad these days. The appeal of waking up to a shot of whiskey — 'to numb the fear of frost,' as he used to say — I can understand it." Her pause was brief, and I realized that, again, she was speaking only to Catherine's answering machine. "Anyway, I know you saw me that day in October. Did you see Victoria? Isn't she beautiful? You obviously didn't want to see me, and I wanted to respect that, to give you more time. So I haven't called. But I can't wait any longer. I've decided to start calling again, every day. More than once a day, probably, until you agree to talk to me. I need you, Catherine. Don't you understand? You're all the family I have."

I shut my eyes at Elizabeth's words. *You're all the family I have.* For eight months we had been together, eating three meals a day at the kitchen table, working side by side. My adoption was less than four months away. Still, Elizabeth did not consider me family. Instead of sorrow, I felt rage, and when I heard the phone click, followed by the gushing sound of dirty water being poured down a drain, I pounded up the front steps. I struck the door with clenched fists, trying to knock it in. *What am I, then?* I wanted to scream. *Why are we pretending?*

But when Elizabeth opened the door and I looked into her surprised face, I started to cry. I could not remember ever having cried, and the tears felt like a betrayal of my anger. I slapped at my face where tears ran down in streams. The sting of each slap made me cry harder.

Elizabeth didn't ask why I was crying, just pulled me into the kitchen. She sat on a wooden chair and drew me awkwardly into her lap. In a few months I would be ten. I was too old to sit on her lap, too old to be held and comforted. I was also too old to be given back. Suddenly I was both terrified of being placed in a group home and surprised that Meredith's scare tactic had worked. Burying my face in Elizabeth's neck, I sobbed and sobbed. She squeezed me. I waited for her to tell me to calm down, but she didn't.

Minutes passed. A timer on the kitchen stove buzzed, but Elizabeth did not stand up. When I finally lifted my head, the kitchen was filled with the scent of chocolate. Elizabeth had made a soufflé to celebrate the turn in the weather, and the scent was rich and sweet. I wiped my eyes on the shoulder of her blouse and sat up, pushing myself back to look at her. When our eyes met, I saw that she had been crying, too. Tears clung and then dropped from the edge of her jawbone.

"I love you," Elizabeth said, and I started to cry all over again.

In the oven, the chocolate soufflé began to burn.

9.

Grant left for the flower market early Monday morning, but I did not go with him. When I awakened hours later, I was surprised to find I was not alone on the property. Men shouted to one another between rows, and women knelt on the wet soil, pulling weeds. I watched it all happen from the windows: the pruning, tending, feeding, and harvesting.

It had never crossed my mind that anyone but Grant tended the acres and acres of plants, but once I saw the workers in action, it seemed ridiculous that I ever imagined it any other way. The job was enormous; the tasks were many. And while I didn't like having to share the property with anyone, especially on the first day Grant had left me alone, I was grateful for the workers who coaxed the hundreds of varieties of flowers into bloom.

I changed into a clean white T-shirt and

brushed my teeth. Grabbing a loaf of bread and my camera, I walked outside. The workers greeted me with a deep nod and a smile but didn't attempt to make conversation.

I entered the first greenhouse. It was the one Grant had opened for me on our first walk, and it contained mainly orchids, with a single wall of hibiscus varieties and amaryllis. It was warmer, and I was comfortable in my thin T-shirt. I began on the top shelf of the left wall. Numbering my notebook, I took two photographs of every flower and recorded the scientific name of each one instead of the camera settings. Afterward, I used one of Grant's gardening books to determine the common name for each flower, scrawling it in the margins and opening my flower dictionary to put an *X* by the flowers I photographed. I shot four rolls of film and put sixteen *X*'s in my dictionary. It would take me all week to shoot what was in bloom, and all spring to wait for what was not. Even then, I would likely be missing flowers.

Only steps from the back wall, my eye buried in the viewfinder, I tripped on a large object in the middle of the aisle. When I looked down I saw a closed cardboard box. The word *Jonquil* was scratched onto the top in thick black marker.

I peered inside the box. Six ceramic pots

were packed side by side, their sandy soil wet, as if they had been watered that morning. I stuck my finger an inch into the dirt, hoping to feel a shoot on the verge of emerging, but there was nothing. Closing the box, I continued on my path, the camera clicking and the film advancing every time I found a new plant with an open bloom.

The days continued this way. Grant left before I awoke in the mornings. I spent long afternoons alone in the greenhouses, passing courteous laborers on my walks between my work and the water tower. Most nights Grant would bring home takeout, but other nights we would eat canned soup and whole loaves of bread or frozen pizzas.

After dinner we read together on the second floor, sometimes even sharing the love seat. On these nights, I would wait for the dizzying need for solitude to overcome me, but just as the air in the room would start to thin, Grant would stand up, bid me good night, and disappear down the spiral staircase. Sometimes he would come back an hour later, sometimes not until the next evening. I didn't know where he went or where he slept at night, and I didn't ask.

I had been at Grant's nearly two weeks when he came home one late afternoon with a chicken. Raw.

"What're we going to do with this?" I asked, holding up the cold, plastic-wrapped bird.

"Cook it," he said.

"What do you mean, 'cook it'?" I asked. "We don't even know how to clean it."

Grant held up a long receipt. On the back he'd written instructions, and he read them aloud to me. They started with preheating the oven and ended with something about rosemary and new potatoes.

I turned on the oven. "That's my contribution," I said. "You're on your own from here on out." I sat down at the table.

He got out a baking sheet and washed the potatoes, then cut them into cubes and sprinkled on rosemary. Putting them on the tray with the chicken, he rubbed the whole thing with olive oil, salt, and spices from a small jar. Washing his hands, he put the tray in the oven.

"I asked the butcher for the easiest recipe possible, and that's what he came up with. Not bad, right?"

I shrugged.

"The only problem," he added, "is that it takes over an hour to cook."

"Over an hour!" The thought of waiting made my head hurt. I hadn't eaten since breakfast, and my stomach was empty to the point of nausea.

Grant lit a candle and produced a deck of cards. "To distract us," he said. He set a kitchen timer and sat down across from me.

We played war by candlelight, the only game either of us knew. It kept us just entertained enough to avoid passing out on the table. When the timer buzzed, I set plates on the table and Grant cut the breast of the chicken into thin slices. I pulled a leg off the golden-brown bird and started to eat.

The meal was delicious, the flavor inversely proportional to the amount of effort that had gone into the preparation. The meat was hot and tender. I chewed and swallowed huge mouthfuls, then pulled off the other drumstick before Grant could reach for it, eating the seasoned skin first.

Across from me, Grant ate a slice of breast with his knife and fork, cutting bites one at a time and eating slowly. His face showed both the pleasure of the food and the pride of the accomplishment. He put down his knife and fork, and when he looked across the table, I could see he was enjoying the sight of my ravenous hunger. His watchfulness made me uncomfortable.

I put down my second drumstick, all bones. "You know it won't, right?" I asked.

"Be us?"

Grant looked at me with confusion.

"At the drugstore, the old couple, the slapping and winking; it won't be us. You won't know me in sixty years," I said. "You probably won't know me in sixty days."

His smile faded. "Why are you sure?"

I thought about his question. I *was* sure, and I knew he could tell. But it was hard to explain why I was so sure. "The longest I've ever known anyone — unless you count my social worker, which I don't — is fifteen months."

"What happened after fifteen months?"

I looked at him, my eyes pleading. When he realized the answer, he looked away, embarrassed.

"But why not now?" It was the exact right question, and when he asked it, I knew the answer.

"I don't trust myself," I said. "Whatever you imagine our life would be like together, it won't happen. I'd ruin it."

I could see Grant thinking about this, trying to grasp the chasm between the finality in my voice and his vision of our future, and bridging the divide with a combination of hope and lies. I felt something, a combination of pity and embarrassment, for his desperate imaginings.

"Please don't waste your time," I said. "Trying. I tried, once, and failed. It's not possible for me."

When Grant looked back to me, the expression on his face had changed. His jaw was clenched, his nostrils slightly flared.

"You're lying," he said.

"What?" I asked. It was not the response I had expected.

Grant pinched the skin along his hairline with the fingers of one hand, and when he spoke, his words were slow and careful. "Don't lie. Tell me you'll never forgive me for what my mother did, or tell me every time you look at me you feel sick. But don't sit here and lie to me, talking about how it's your fault we can never be together."

I picked up the chicken bones, peeling fat away from the tendons. I couldn't look at him, needed time to process what he was saying. *What my mother did.* There was only one explanation. When I'd first met Grant, I had searched his face for anger, and when I didn't find it, I claimed forgiveness. But the reality was something else entirely. Grant was not angry with me because even he didn't know the truth. I didn't know how it was possible that he'd lived with his mother at the time and still didn't know, but I didn't ask.

"I'm not lying." It was all I could think of to say.

Grant dropped his fork, the metal clattering against the ceramic plate. He stood up. "You're not the only one whose life she ruined," he said, then walked out of the kitchen and into the night.

I locked the door behind him.

10.

July was crowded at the farmers' market. Strollers heaped with produce and nectarine-smeared toddlers blocked aisles, and elderly men with pushcarts waved impatient arms at distracted mothers. Under my feet, discarded pistachio shells crunched. I skipped to keep up with Elizabeth. She was making her way toward the blackberries.

After lunch, Elizabeth told me, we would make blackberry cobbler and homemade ice cream. It was a bribe to keep me inside the house, away from the record-breaking heat and her quickly ripening grapes, and I had reluctantly agreed. All spring, Elizabeth and I had worked side by side at the vineyard, and I didn't want to leave the plants alone now that there was little to do but wait. I missed the long mornings suckering the vines, trimming shoots that sprouted from the base of the trunk to keep the strength of the vine focused. I missed carrying a kitchen knife and following behind the small tractor Elizabeth used to disk the rows, pulling the remaining weeds by hand as she had taught me to do: first loosening the roots with the sharp point of the knife, then extracting the plants from the soil. I had been wielding the knife for more than three months before I told Elizabeth that allowing children in foster care to use knives was against the child-welfare code. But she didn't take it away. *You're not a foster child,* she had said simply. And though I no longer felt like a foster child (felt, in fact, so different from the girl who had arrived almost a year before that most mornings I studied my face in the bathroom mirror long after Elizabeth called me to breakfast, looking for physical signs of the change I knew to have occurred), this was not entirely the truth. I *was* still a foster child, and would be until after my court appearance in August.

Pushing my way through a thick crowd, I reached Elizabeth's side. "Blackberries?" she asked, passing me a green paper tray. On a red-cloth-covered table the vendor had displayed tall stacks of blackberries, ollalieberries, raspberries, and boysenberries. I plucked one from the tray and put it in my mouth. It was fat and sweet, and stained my fingertips purple where I touched it.

Elizabeth dumped six paper trays in a plastic bag and paid for her purchase, then moved on to the next stand. I followed her around the hot market, carrying the bags that wouldn't fit in her overflowing canvas sack. At a dairy truck, she handed me a milk jug, the glass of the bottle sweating. "Done?" I asked.

"Almost. Come," she said, beckoning me toward the far end of the market. Before she had even passed the Blenheim apricots, the last vendor in the line we knew, I understood where we were going. Tucking the slick bottle under my arm, I skipped to Elizabeth, holding her sleeve and pulling her back. But she only walked faster. She didn't stop until she reached the flower stand.

Bunches of roses lined the table. Up close, the perfection of the flowers was startling: each petal stiff and smooth, pressed one on top of the other, the tips a neat coil. Elizabeth stood still, studying the flowers as I did. I gestured to a mixed bouquet, hoping she might choose a bundle, pay, and turn to leave without speaking. But before she could make a purchase, the teenager swept the remaining flowers from the table, tossing them into the back of his truck. My eyes widened. He would not sell to Elizabeth. I watched her face for a reaction, but she was unreadable.

"Grant?" she said. He did not respond, did not glance in her direction. She tried again. "I'm your aunt. Elizabeth. You must know this." Leaning over the bed of his truck, he arranged a tarp over the layer of flowers. His eyes focused on the roses, but his ears peeled back slightly, his chin raised. Up close, he looked older. Light fuzz covered his upper lip, and his limbs, which I'd believed to be spindly, were defined. He wore only a plain white undershirt, and the curve of his shoulder blades caused a rise and fall in the thin material that I found mesmerizing.

"Are you going to ignore me?" Elizabeth asked. When he didn't respond, her voice changed, the way I remembered it from my first few weeks in her home: strict, patient, and then unexpectedly angry. "Look at me, at least, won't you? Look at me when I speak to you."

He didn't.

"This doesn't have anything to do with you. It never has. For years I've watched you grow up from a distance, and I've wanted more than anything to run over here and scoop you into my arms."

Grant secured the tarp with a rope, the muscles in his arms taut. It was hard to imagine anyone scooping him up, hard to imagine he wasn't always this strong. Tightening a final knot, he turned.

"You should have, then, if that's what you wanted to do." His voice was cold, unemotional. "No one was stopping you."

"No," Elizabeth said, shaking her head. "You don't know what you're talking about." Her words were low, underlined by a deep vibration I recognized from previous foster placements as the predecessor to an attack. But she did not leap at him, as I half expected her to do. Instead, she said something so surprising that Grant spun to face me, his eyes meeting mine for the first time.

"Victoria's making blackberry cobbler," she whispered. "You should come over."

11.

The image of Grant's face, disappointed and desperate, kept me awake. I gave up trying to sleep before dawn and sat at the kitchen table, waiting for the sound of the truck's engine. Instead, I was startled by a quiet knock. When I opened the door, Grant walked sleepily past me and up the stairs. The water started in the shower. I realized it was Sunday.

I wanted to return to the blue room, to Renata, to payday and the approaching frenzy of holiday arranging. I had stayed at Grant's too long. But he wouldn't be driving to the city. I sat down on the bottom step and thought about how to convince him of the three-hour round trip on his day off.

I was still thinking when Grant's foot pushed on the triangle between my shoulder blades. The unexpected pressure caused me to slip off the bottom step and onto the kitchen floor. I scrambled to my feet.

"Get up," he said. "I'm taking you back."

His words were familiar. I flashed on the variations of the phrase I'd heard throughout the years: *Pack your things. Alexis doesn't want to share her room anymore. We're too old to go through this again.* More often than not, it was simply *Meredith's coming,* with an occasional *I'm sorry.*

To Grant, I said what I always said: "I'm ready."

I grabbed my backpack, heavy with his camera and dozens of rolls of film, and climbed into the truck. Grant drove quickly down the still-dark country roads, swerving into oncoming traffic to pass pickups loaded with produce. He took the first exit south of the bridge, and then pulled onto the shoulder of the busy off-ramp. There wasn't a bus stop in sight. Unmoving, I looked up and down the street.

"I have to get back to the farmers' market," he said. He wouldn't look at me.

Grant cut the engine and walked around the front of the truck. He opened the passenger door and reached inside to grab my backpack from where it rested on my feet. His chest brushed my knees, and when he pulled back, the heat between our bodies dispersed in a cold rush of December air. I jumped out and grabbed my backpack.

So this is how it ends, I thought, with a camera full of images of a flower farm to which I would never return. I missed the flowers already but would not permit myself to miss Grant.

It took four buses to get back to Potrero Hill, but only because I took the 38 in the wrong direction and ended up at Point Lobos. It was mid-morning when I arrived at Bloom, and Renata was just opening the shop. She smiled when she saw me.

"No work and no help for two weeks," she said. "I've been bored out of my mind."

"Why don't people marry in December?" I asked.

"What's romantic about bare trees and gray skies? Couples wait for spring and summer, blue skies, flowers, vacation, all that."

Blue and gray were equally unromantic in my opinion, I thought, and harsh light was unflattering in photographs. But brides were irrational; I had learned this from Renata, if nothing else.

"When do you need me to work?" I asked.

"I have a big Christmas Day wedding. Then I'll need you every day through the first weekend in January."

I agreed, and asked Renata what time I

should arrive.

"On Christmas? Oh, sleep in. The wedding's late, and I'll buy the flowers the day before. Just make sure you're here by nine."

I nodded. Renata withdrew an envelope of cash from the register. "Merry Christmas," she said.

Later, in the blue room, I opened the envelope and saw that she'd paid me twice as much as she'd promised. *Just in time to buy holiday gifts,* I thought wryly, tucking the money into my backpack.

I spent most of my bonus on a case of film at a wholesale photography supplier and the remainder at an art store on Market. My dictionary would not be a book; instead, I bought two cloth-covered photo boxes, one orange, the other blue, archival black cardstock cut in five-by-seven-inch rectangles, a spray can of photo mount, and a silver metallic marker.

There were ten days until Christmas. With the exception of shooting my neglected garden in McKinley Square — the heath and helenium surviving despite the bad weather and desertion — I took a break from photography. I had taken twenty-five rolls of film at Grant's, and it took me the full ten days to have the film developed, sort the prints, mount them on cardstock, and label them.

Under each flower photograph, I wrote the common name, followed by the scientific, and on the back I printed the meaning. I made two sets of each flower and placed one in each photo box.

On Christmas Eve, every photo had been mounted and dried. Natalya and her band had gone wherever people go for the holidays, and the apartment was deliciously quiet. Carrying the photo boxes downstairs, I spread the cards out in the empty practice room in neat rows, with aisles wide enough for me to walk down. The cards for the orange box I placed flower side up, the cards for the blue box flower side down. I paced the aisles for hours, alphabetizing first the flowers, then the meanings. When I was done, I replaced all the cards in the boxes and opened Elizabeth's flower dictionary to admire my progress. It was the middle of winter, and my illustrated dictionary was already half finished.

The pizzeria at the top of the hill was deserted. I took my pizza to go and ate it on Natalya's bed, looking down over the empty street below. Afterward, I lay down in the blue room. Even though it was quiet, warm, and dark, my eyes kept popping open. A sliver of pale white light shone from the streetlight into Natalya's room and pushed its way through the crack in the closet door. The light was pencil-thin and drew a line down the wall opposite and through the middle of my photo boxes. The blue box was exactly the same color as the wall, and the orange box, sitting on top of it, looked like it was floating in air. It didn't belong there.

It belonged on Grant's bookshelf, across from his orange couch. I had chosen the color specifically for that purpose, even though I hadn't admitted it to myself. Grant was gone. The need to avoid flower-language miscommunications no longer existed, yet I had purchased an extra box, an orange box, and made a second set of cards. I unlocked the half-door leading to the living room and put the orange box out.

12.

Grant did not come over for blackberry cobbler. *He should have,* I thought, licking the bottom of the dish the next morning. It was delicious.

As I set the dish in the sink, Elizabeth swept through the back door, breathless. Her hair was loose around her shoulders, and I realized that I had never, in nearly a year, seen her without a tight bun at the back of her neck. She smiled, her eyes filled with an unrestrained happiness I'd never seen.

"I've figured it out!" she said. "It's absurd I didn't think of it sooner."

"What?" I asked. Her joy made me inexplicably nervous. Licking congealed blackberry juice off a spoon, I watched her.

"When I was at boarding school, Catherine and I wrote letters — until my mother started intercepting them."

"Intercepting?"

"Taking. She read them all — she didn't

trust me, thought somehow my letters would corrupt Catherine, even though I was a child and Catherine was already nearly an adult. For years we didn't write at all. But just after my sister's twentieth birthday, she discovered a Victorian flower dictionary on my grandfather's bookshelf. She started sending me drawings of flowers, the scientific name printed neatly in the bottom right-hand corner. She sent dozens before following with a simple note that read, 'Do you know what I'm telling you?' "

"Did you know?" I asked.

"No," Elizabeth said, shaking her head as if remembering her adolescent frustration. "I asked every librarian and teacher I could find. But it was months before my roommate's great-grandmother, visiting one day, saw the drawings on my wall and told me about the language of flowers. I found my own dictionary in the library and sent my sister a note immediately, with pressed flowers, not drawings, because I was a hopeless artist."

Elizabeth walked into the living room and returned with a stack of books. She set them on the kitchen table. "For years it was the way we communicated. I sent poems and stories by connecting dried flowers on strings, intertwined with typed words on little slips of paper: *and, the, if, it.* My sister continued to send drawings, sometimes whole landscapes, with dozens of floral varieties, all labeled and numbered, so I would know which flower to read first to decode the sequence of events and emotions in her life. I lived for those letters, checked the mailbox dozens of times a day."

"So, how will this help you win her forgiveness?" I asked.

Elizabeth had started toward the garden but stopped suddenly and whirled to face me. "*I'm* forgiving *her,*" she said. "Don't you forget that." After a deep breath, she continued. "But I'll tell you how it will help. Catherine will remember how close we were; she'll remember how I understood her better than anyone else in the world. And even if she's too remorseful to answer the phone, she'll answer with flowers. I know she will."

Elizabeth went outside. When she returned, she held a bouquet of three flowers, all different. Retrieving a cutting board from the counter, she set it on the kitchen table, the flowers and a sharp knife arranged on top.

"I'll teach you," Elizabeth said. "And you'll help me."

I sat down at the kitchen table. Elizabeth had continued to teach me flowers and their meanings but not in a formal or structured way. The day before we'd passed a hand-made purse at the farmer's market, the fabric printed with small white flowers. *Poverty for a purse,* Elizabeth had said, shaking her head. She pointed to the flowers and explained the defining features of clematis.

Sitting next to her now, I was thrilled at the prospect of receiving a formal lesson. I pushed my chair as close to Elizabeth as possible. She picked up a walnut-sized dark purple flower with a yellow sun center.

"Primrose," she said, twirling the pin-wheel-shaped flower between her thumb and index finger before placing it, face up, on her smooth white palm. *"Childhood."*

I leaned over her hand, my nose only inches from the petals. The primrose had a sharp scent, sugared alcohol and someone's mother's perfume. Pulling my nose away, I pushed the air out of my nostrils with force.

Elizabeth laughed. "I don't like the smell, either. Too sweet, as if it was trying to mask its true, undesirable smell."

I nodded in agreement.

"So, if we didn't know this was a primrose, how would we find out?" Elizabeth put down the flower and picked up a pocket-sized book. "This is a field guide of North American wildflowers, divided by color. Primrose should be with the violet-blues." She handed me the book. I turned to the violet-blues, flipping through the pages until I found the drawing that matched the flower.

"Cusick's primrose," I read. "Primrose family, Primulaceae."

"Good." She picked up the second of the three flowers, large and yellow, with six pointed petals. "Now this. Lily, *majesty.*"

Searching the yellows, I found the drawing that matched. I pointed with a damp fingertip and watched the water mark spread. Elizabeth nodded.

"Now, let's pretend you couldn't find the drawing, or you weren't sure you had found the right one. This is when you need to know about flower parts. Using a field guide is like reading a Choose Your Own Adventure book. It begins with simple questions: Does your flower have petals? How many? And each answer leads you to a different set of more complicated questions."

Elizabeth picked up a kitchen knife and sliced the lily in half, its petals falling open on the cutting board. She pointed to the ovary, pressed my fingertip against the sticky top of the outstretched stigma.

We counted petals, described their shape. Elizabeth taught me the definition of symmetry, the difference between inferior and

247

superior ovaries, and the variations of flower arrangements on a stem. She quizzed me using the third flower she had picked, a violet, small and wilting.

"Good," she said again, when I had answered an uninterrupted stream of questions. "Very good. You learn quickly." She pulled back my chair, and I slid down. "Now go sit in the garden while I cook dinner. Spend time in front of every plant you know, and ask yourself the same questions I asked you. How many petals, what color, what shape. If you know it's a rose, what makes it a rose and not a sunflower?"

Elizabeth was still rattling off questions as I skipped toward the kitchen door.

"Pick out something for Catherine!" she called.

I disappeared down the steps.

248

13.

Renata looked surprised to see me sitting on the curb at seven a.m. when she parked her truck on the empty street. I had been up all night, and looked it. She raised her eyebrows and smiled.

"Stay up waiting for Santa?" she asked. "Didn't anyone ever tell you the truth?"

"No," I said. "No one ever did."

I followed Renata into the walk-in and helped her pull out the buckets of red roses, white carnations, and baby's breath. They were my least favorite flowers. "Please tell me this was at the request of a dangerous bride."

"She threatened me with my life," she said. We shared a disdain for red roses.

Renata left, and when she came back with two cups of coffee, I had already finished three centerpieces.

"Thanks," I said, reaching for the paper cup.

"You're welcome. And slow down. The faster we finish, the more time I'll have to spend at my mother's Christmas party."

I picked up a rose and cut off the thorns in slow motion, lining up the sharp spikes on the table.

"Better," she said, "but not quite slow enough."

We worked with exaggerated sluggishness for the rest of the morning, but we were still finished by noon. Renata picked up the order and checked and double-checked our arrangements. She set down the list.

"That's it?"

"Yes," she said, "unfortunately. Just the delivery and then the Christmas party — you're coming with me."

"No thanks," I said, taking a final sip of cold coffee and putting on my backpack.

"Did that sound optional to you? It's not."

I could have fought her on it, but I was feeling indebted for the bonus, and I was in the mood for holiday food if not holiday cheer. I didn't know anything about Russian food, but it had to be better than the processed ham I had planned on eating right out of the package.

"Whatever," I said. "But I have somewhere to be by five."

Renata laughed. She must have known it was inconceivable that I had anywhere to be on Christmas.

Renata's mother lived in the Richmond District, and we took the longest route possible across the city.

"My mother's too much," Renata said.

"In what way?" I asked.

"In every way," she said.

We pulled up in front of a bright pink house. A Christmas flag flew on a wooden pole, and the small porch was crowded with glowing plastic creatures: angels, reindeer, chipmunks in Santa hats, and dancing penguins with knit scarves.

Renata pushed the door open, and we walked into a wall of heat. Men and women sat on the cushions, arms, and back of a single couch; school-age boys and girls lay on their stomachs on the shag carpet, toddlers crawling over their skinny legs. I stepped in and took off my jacket and sweater, but the path to the coat closet, where Renata greeted someone about my age, was completely blocked by small body parts.

As I stood by the door, an older, softer version of Renata pushed her way through the crowd. She carried a large wooden tray with sliced oranges, nuts, figs, and dates.

"Victoria!" she exclaimed when she saw me. She handed the tray to Natalya, who was lounged on the couch, and climbed over the children blocking her way to where I stood. When she hugged me, my face pressed into her armpit and the flared sleeves of her gray wool sweater wrapped around my back like living things. She was a tall woman, and strong — and when I finally wriggled away, she grasped my shoulders and tilted my face up to look at her. "Sweet Victoria," she said, her long, wavy white hair spilling forward and tickling my cheeks. "My daughters have told me so much about you — I loved you even before I met you."

She smelled of primrose and apple cider. I peeled myself away. "Thank you for inviting me to your party, Mrs. —" I stopped, realizing Renata had never told me her name.

"Marta Rubina," she said. "But I only answer to Mother Ruby." She reached forward as if to shake hands, then laughed and hugged me again. We were wedged into the corner, and only the thick plaster walls behind my back kept me standing. She pulled me forward, her arm around my shoulders, and led me around the room. The children scattered out of the way, and Renata, perched on a folding chair in the corner, watched with an amused smile.

Mother Ruby guided me into the kitchen, where she sat me at a table with two heaping plates of food. The first held a large baked fish, whole, with spices and some kind of root vegetables. The second held beans, peas, and potatoes with parsley. She handed me a fork and a spoon, and a bowl of mushroom soup. "We ate hours ago," she said, "but I saved you food. Renata told me you'd be hungry — which pleased me greatly. I love nothing more than feeding family."

Mother Ruby sat down across from me. She boned my fish, poked her finger in my peas, and reheated them after exclaiming over the temperature. She introduced me to everyone who walked by: daughters, sons-in-law, grandchildren, boyfriends and girlfriends of various family members.

I looked up and nodded but did not put down my fork.

I fell asleep at Mother Ruby's. I hadn't meant to. After dinner, I escaped into an empty guest room, and between the heavy food and the previous night's insomnia, I was unconscious almost before I lay down.

The smell of coffee pulled me out of bed the next morning. Stretching, I wandered down the hall until I found the bathroom. The door was open. Inside, Mother Ruby was in the shower behind a clear plastic curtain. When I saw her, I spun around and ran back down the hall.

"Come in!" she called after me. "There's only one bathroom. Don't pay any attention to me!"

I found Renata in the kitchen, pouring coffee. She handed me a mug.

"Your mother's in the shower," I said.

"With the door open, I'm sure," she said, yawning.

I nodded.

"Sorry about that."

I poured a cup of coffee and leaned against the kitchen sink.

"My mother was a midwife in Russia," Renata said. "So she's used to seeing women naked just moments after meeting them. America in the seventies worked for her just fine, and I don't think she's noticed that times have changed."

Mother Ruby came into the kitchen then, tied up in a bright coral terry-cloth robe. "What's changed?" she asked.

Renata shook her head. "Nudity."

"I don't think nudity's changed since the birth of the first human," Mother Ruby said. "Only society has changed."

Renata rolled her eyes and turned to me. "My mother and I have been having this

254

argument since I was old enough to talk. When I was ten, I told her I wouldn't have kids because I never wanted to be naked in front of her again. And look at me — fifty and childless."

Mother Ruby broke an egg into a pan, and it crackled. "I delivered all twelve of my grandchildren," she told me with pride.

"You're still a midwife?"

"Not legally," she said. "But I still get two a.m. calls from all over this city. And I go every time." She handed me a plate of eggs over easy.

"Thank you," I said. I ate them and then walked down the hall to the bathroom, locking the door behind me.

"A little more warning next time," I told Renata as we drove to Bloom later that morning. We had a full week of weddings ahead of us, and we were both rested and well fed.

"If I had warned you," Renata said, "you wouldn't have come. And you needed a little rest and nutrition. Don't try to tell me you didn't."

I didn't argue.

"My mother's a bit of a legend in the midwifery circle. She's seen everything, and her outcomes are far better than the outcomes of modern medicine, even when they shouldn't be. She'll likely grow on you; she does on most people."

"Most people," I guessed, "but not you?"

"I respect my mother," Renata said, pausing. "We're just different. Everyone assumes there's some kind of biological consistency between mothers and their children, but that's not always the case. You don't know my other sisters, but look at Natalya, my mother, and me." She was right; the three couldn't have been more different.

All day, as I organized orders and made lists of flowers and quantities for upcoming weddings, I thought about Grant's mother. I remembered the pale hand reaching out of the darkness the afternoon Elizabeth and I visited. What had it been like to be Grant as a child? Alone except for the flowers, his mother slipping from the past to the present as she walked from room to room. I would ask Grant, I decided, if he would talk to me again.

But he wasn't at the flower market that week, or the week after. His stall stood empty, the white plywood peeling and abandoned-looking. I wondered if he would come back, or if the thought of seeing me again was enough to keep him away permanently.

Consumed by thoughts of Grant's absence, the quality of my work suffered. Renata began sitting beside me at the worktable, and instead of our usual silence, she told me long, humorous stories about her mother, her sisters, her nieces and nephews. I only half listened, but the constant narration was enough to keep me focused on the flowers.

The new year came and went, a flurry of white weddings and silver-bell-trimmed bouquets. Grant still had not returned to the flower market. Renata gave me the week off, and I holed up inside the blue room, coming out only to eat and to use the bathroom. Every time I emerged through my half-door, I came face-to-face with the orange photo box, and I was flooded with a vague sense of loss.

Renata had not requested my help until the following Sunday, but on Saturday afternoon there was a knock on my door. I poked my head out and saw Natalya, still in her pajamas, clearly annoyed.

"Renata called," she said. "She needs you. She said to take a shower and come as fast as you can."

Take a shower? It seemed like an odd request from Renata. She probably needed me to accompany her to a delivery, and rightly assumed I'd been asleep and unbathed for most of the week.

I took my time in the shower, soaping and

shampooing and brushing my teeth with mouthfuls of water as hot as I could stand it. When I dried myself with a towel, my skin was red and splotchy. I put on my nicest outfit: black suit pants and a soft white blouse, the material sewn in tucks like an old-fashioned tuxedo shirt. Before leaving the bathroom, I trimmed my hair with precision and blow-dried the snips of hair off my shirt.

As I neared Bloom I saw a familiar figure sitting on the deserted curb, an open cardboard box in his lap. Grant. So that was why Renata had called. I stopped walking and took in his profile, serious and watchful. He turned in my direction and stood up.

We walked toward each other, our short steps matched, until we met in the middle of the steep hill, Grant looming above me. We were far enough apart that I couldn't see the contents of the box, which he held below his chin.

"You look nice," he said.

"Thank you." I would have returned the compliment, except he didn't. He had been working all morning; I could tell by the dirt on his knees and the fresh mud on his boots. He smelled, too, not like flowers but like a dirty man: equal parts sweat, smoke, and soil.

"I didn't change," he said, seeming suddenly aware of his appearance. "I should have."

"It doesn't matter," I said. I meant the words to be gracious, but they sounded dismissive. Grant's face fell, and I felt a flash of anger (not at Grant but at myself, for never having mastered the subtleties of tone). I moved a step closer to him, an awkward gesture of apology.

"I know it doesn't," he said. "I just stopped by because I thought you'd want these — for your friend." He lowered the box. Inside I saw the six ceramic pots of jonquil, the yellow flowers tall and open in bouncing clusters. An intoxicating sweetness wafted from the blossoms.

I reached inside and grabbed the pots, attempting to extract all six simultaneously. I wanted to surround myself in the color. Grant lowered the box, and through a gentle tug-of-war I succeeded in lifting all six. I buried my face in the petals. For only a moment they balanced in my arms, and then the middle two slipped out of my grasp. The pots shattered on the sidewalk, the bulbs coming unburied and the stalks bending at angles. Grant dropped to his knees and began to gather the flowers.

I hugged the remaining four to my body,

lowering them so that I could watch him over the petals. His strong hands cupped the bulbs and straightened the stems, and he wound long, pointed leaves around the stalks where they had been weakened by the fall.

"Where do you want these?" he asked, looking up.

I dropped down, kneeling beside him.

"Here," I said, and motioned with my chin for him to lay the flowers on top of the ones I held. He parted the clusters and set the exposed bulbs on top of the soil, the broken flowers nestled among the rest. His hands idled among the stems, and in his slow, regular breaths, I could feel him preparing to leave.

I loosened my arms, and the flowerpots slid out of my lap as if in slow motion, settling by my thighs on the steep sidewalk. Grant's hands fell onto my knees. I picked them up and brought them to my face, pressing them to my lips, my cheeks, and my eyelids. I wrapped his hands around the back of my neck and pulled him closer. Our foreheads touched. I closed my eyes, and our lips touched. His lips were full and soft, even as his upper lip scratched my own. He held his breath, and I kissed him again, harder this time, hungry. On my knees, I shuffled up the hill, knocking over the pots in a desire to be closer to Grant, to kiss him harder, longer, to show him how much I'd missed him.

When we pulled apart, finally, out of breath, a single pot had rolled to the bottom of the hill, its blossoms straight and tall and almost blindingly yellow in the winter sun.

Maybe I was wrong, I thought, watching the clusters sway in the breeze. Maybe the essence of each flower's meaning really was contained somewhere within its sturdy stem, its soft gathering of petals.

Annemarie, I knew, would be satisfied with the jonquil.

14.

Sitting on the front porch, I sifted through the pile of tiny white chamomile blossoms at my feet. A five-foot string connected Elizabeth and me, a needle on each end. We worked quickly, spearing spongy yellow centers and pushing flowers into the middle. Every few minutes I stopped, distracted by an insect or a splinter of wood, but Elizabeth did not pause in her movements. After an hour the task was complete, a delicate, petaled ribbon connecting us.

"Definition?" I asked. Elizabeth was folded over, stringing a square of paper onto the end of the ribbon. I glimpsed August and the number 2, along with a repetition of the word *please,* and a line that struck me as a lie: *I can't do this without you.*

Elizabeth coiled the flowered rope. *"Energy in adversity."*

Nothing could have more succinctly captured her mind-set. Since deciding to communicate with her sister through flowers, Elizabeth had been constantly in motion, planting seeds, watering, checking the progress of half-open buds, and waiting — a waiting that was like an action itself, dynamic and pacing — for a response.

"Come with me," Elizabeth said, climbing into her truck and setting the coiled chamomile between us.

We drove to Catherine's. Elizabeth left the engine running as she hopped out, wound the flowered string around the wooden post of Catherine's mailbox, and tucked the note inside. Climbing back into the truck, she continued driving down the road, away from the vineyard.

"Where are we going?" I asked.

"Shopping," Elizabeth said. Her hair flapped around her face in the wind, and she pulled it back into a rubber band quickly, steering with her knees. She shot a mischievous smile in my direction.

"Where?" I asked. There was a general store less than a mile away, where Elizabeth had purchased my rain parka and gardening shoes, but it was in the opposite direction.

"Chestnut Street," she said. "San Francisco. They have a whole row of children's boutiques, the kind with two-hundred-dollar velour sweat suits for newborns, toddler dresses made out of silk organza — that sort of thing. One dress for your adoption will cost me more than what I can get for two tons of grapes — but if not now, when? You're ten, you know? Next week you'll be *my* little girl, but you won't be a little girl much longer. I have to dress you up while I can." She smiled at me again, her smile an invitation.

I inched closer to her, pressing my head into her shoulder as we drove. She'd taught me to sit up straight and away from her in the truck, so that we wouldn't get pulled over for a seat belt violation, but today, her smile said, was an exception. She drove with one arm on the steering wheel, the other around my shoulders, squeezing me to her. I'd never been taken shopping for new clothes, not once, and it seemed to me the perfect way to start my life as someone's daughter. I hummed along with the oldies on the radio as we drove over the bridge and into the city, struggling with the conflicting emotions of wanting the day to last forever and wanting the day to be over and the next two as well. My court date was only three days away.

On Chestnut Street, Elizabeth parked the car, and I followed her into an open doorway. The shop was empty except for a saleswoman standing at a glass counter, arranging diamond-studded clips to a felt cutout of a tree. "May I help you?" she asked, her smile taking me in with what appeared to be genuine interest. "Looking for something special?"

"Yes," Elizabeth said. "Something for Victoria."

"And how old are you, sweetheart? Seven? Eight?"

"Ten," I said.

The saleswoman looked embarrassed, but her words didn't offend me. "I was warned never to guess," she said. "Let me show you what I have in your size." I followed her to the back of the store, where a single row of dresses hung opposite a mirror with a wooden ballet bar. Elizabeth grasped the bar and did an exaggerated squat, her knees bending deeply at angles, her toes pointed out. She was thin and pointy like a classical ballerina, but not even close to graceful. We both laughed.

I thumbed through the dresses once, then a second time. "If there isn't anything you like," Elizabeth said from behind me, "there're other shops."

But that wasn't the problem. I liked all the dresses, every single one. My hand settled on the velvet ribbons of a halter. Pulling the dress off the bar, I held it up against my body. It was only a size eight but reached well below my knees. The light blue top was separated from the patterned skirt by a brown velvet ribbon that tied behind the back. It was the pattern of the full skirt I was drawn to: raised brown-velvet flowers over a background of blue. The concentric petals reminded me of hundred-petaled roses or chrysanthemum. I looked at Elizabeth.

"Try it on," she said.

In the small dressing room, I took off my clothes. Standing in front of the mirror in my white cotton underpants, Elizabeth seated behind me, I took in my pale image, skin light and unmarked, my waist straight over narrow hips. Elizabeth studied my body with such pride I imagined it to be the way a mother looked at a biological daughter, whose every limb had been formed within her body.

"Arms up," she said. Slipping the dress over my head, she tied the ribbons of the halter-top under my hair and the second set of ribbons above my waistline.

The dress fit me perfectly. I gazed at my reflection, my arms held out stiffly on either side of the full skirt.

When my eyes met Elizabeth's, her face was so full of emotion I couldn't tell if she would laugh or cry. She pulled me to her, her forearms under my armpits, hands clasped over my chest. The back of my head pressed into her ribs.

"Look at you," she said. "My baby." And somehow, in that moment, her words spoke the truth. I had the vague sense of being a very young child — a newborn, even — tightly held and cradled in her arms. It was as if the childhood I had lived belonged to someone else, a girl who no longer existed, a girl who had been replaced by the one in the mirror.

"Catherine will love you, too," Elizabeth whispered. "You'll see."

15.

Before the start of wedding season, Renata hired me full-time. She offered me benefits or a bonus — not both. I was perfectly healthy and tired of relying on Grant to drive me to and from the flower farm, so I took the cash.

The drummer in Natalya's band sold me his old hatchback. His new drum kit — which seemed significantly louder than his old one — did not fit inside, so he took my bonus and gave me the pink slip. It seemed like a fair exchange, but I knew nothing about the value of cars. I didn't have a license and didn't know how to drive. Grant towed the hatchback from Bloom to the farm on the back of his flower truck and didn't let me out of the front gate for weeks. When he did, it was just to drive to the drugstore and back. Still, I was terrified. It took another month before I was ready to drive into the city alone.

That spring I spent mornings working for Renata and afternoons searching for the remaining flowers for my dictionary. After capturing everything on Grant's farm, I moved on to Golden Gate Park and the waterfront. All of Northern California was a botanical garden, with wildflowers springing up between busy freeways and chamomile thriving in sidewalk cracks. Sometimes Grant accompanied me; he was good at plant identification but tired quickly of small, square-block city parks and skinny sunbathers.

On weekends, if Renata and I finished in time, Grant and I went hiking in the redwoods north of San Francisco. We always sat in the parking lot long enough to see which hiking trails were the most crowded before choosing our direction. Alone in the forest, Grant was content to watch me photograph for hours, and he would talk in detail about every plant species and its relation to the others in the ecosystem. When he finished telling me what he knew, he would lean back against the soft moss covering the trunk of a redwood tree and look up through the branches to the pale sky. Silence stretched between us, and I always expected him to bring up Elizabeth, or Catherine, or the night he accused me of lying. I spent hours thinking of what I would say, how

I would explain the truth without turning him against me forever. But Grant did not bring up the past, not in the forest or anywhere else. It seemed he was content to keep our life together confined to the flowers and the present moment.

Many nights I slept in the water tower. Grant had taken up cooking in a serious way, and his kitchen counter was stacked with illustrated cookbooks. As I sat at the kitchen table and read, or looked out the window, or told an obnoxious bride story, Grant chopped and seasoned and stirred. After dinner he would kiss me, only once, and wait to see my reaction. Sometimes I kissed him back, and he would pull me to him, and we would stand intertwined in the doorway for half an hour; other times my lips remained cold and unmoving. Even I didn't know how I would react on any given day. About our deepening relationship, I felt fear and desire in equal, unpredictable parts. At the end of each night he walked outside to wherever it was he slept, and I locked the door behind him.

On a weeknight in late May, after months of this ritual, Grant leaned forward as if to kiss me but stopped just inches from my lips. He put his hands on the small of my back and pulled me to him so that the length of our bodies touched but not our faces. "I think it's time," he said.

"For what?" I asked.

"For me to have my bed back."

I clicked my tongue against the roof of my mouth and looked out the window.

"What're you afraid of?" he asked, when I had been quiet for a long time.

I thought about his question. He was right, I knew, that it was fear that kept us apart; but of what, specifically, was I afraid?

"I don't like to be touched," I said, repeating Meredith's long-ago words. But even as I spoke them, I knew they sounded ridiculous. Our entire bodies were pressed together, and I didn't pull away.

"Then I won't touch you," he said. "Not unless you ask me to."

"Not even when I'm asleep?"

"Especially not then." I knew he wouldn't.

I nodded. "You can sleep in your bed," I said. "But I'm sleeping on the couch. And I better not wake up with you beside me or I'm driving straight home."

"You won't," Grant said. "I promise."

That night I lay awake on the love seat, trying not to fall asleep until Grant did, but he wasn't sleeping, either. I heard him rolling around above me, rearranging the covers, knocking over a stack of books. Finally, after a long period of silence, when I was sure he had fallen asleep, I heard a soft tapping on the ceiling above me.

"Victoria?" A whisper came spiraling down the stairs.

"Yeah?"

"Good night," he said.

"Good night." I pressed a smile into the orange velour.

After a full season of jonquil, Annemarie was a different person. She came in every Friday morning for a fresh bouquet, and her skin was pinker and her body, finally free from the belted jacket, curved underneath thin cotton sweaters. Bethany, she told me, had gone to Europe for a month with Ray and would come back engaged. She said it with certainty, as if it had already happened.

Annemarie brought her friends, many with frilly-dressed little girls and all with disappointing marriages. They leaned on the counter while their children pulled flowers out of buckets taller than they were and spun around the room. The women discussed the details of their relationships, trying to reduce their problems to a single word. I had explained the importance of specificity, and the ladies clung to my words.

The conversations were sad, and amusing, and strangely hopeful all at the same time. The relentlessness with which these women tried to repair their relationships was foreign to me; I didn't understand why they didn't simply give up.

I knew that if it were me I would have let go: of the man, of the child, and of the women with whom I discussed them. But for the first time in my life, this thought did not bring me relief. I began to notice the ways in which I kept myself isolated. There were obvious things, such as living in a closet with six locks, and subtler ones, such as working on the opposite side of the table from Renata or standing behind the cash register when I talked to customers. Whenever possible, I separated my body from those around me with plaster walls, solid wood tables, or heavy metal objects.

But somehow, over six careful months, Grant had broken through this. I not only permitted his touch, I craved it, and I started to wonder if, perhaps, change was possible for me. I began to hope my pattern of letting go was something that could be outgrown, like a childhood dislike of onions or spicy food.

By the end of May I had nearly completed my dictionary. I captured images of many of the remaining, elusive plants at the Conservatory of Flowers in Golden Gate Park. After printing, mounting, and labeling each photo, I put X's in my dictionary and scanned the pages to see how many flowers were left. Only one: the cherry blossom. I was upset with myself for the omission. There were plenty of cherry trees in the Bay Area, dozens of varietals in the Japanese Tea Garden alone. But their bloom period was short — weeks or even days, depending on the year — and I had been too distracted by spring to capture their brief moment of beauty.

Grant would know where to find a cherry blossom, even now, long past its season. I wrote the single missing flower on a scrap of paper and taped it to the outside of the orange box. It was time to bring it to him.

I put the box in the backseat of my car and strapped it in with a seat belt. It was Sunday, and I got to the water tower before Grant got home from the farmers' market. Letting myself in with the spare key, I opened the cupboard and helped myself to a loaf of raisin bread. The box, bright orange on the weathered wood table, took up more space than it should have. It felt loud and new in the small kitchen of quiet antique appliances. I was about to take it upstairs when I heard Grant's truck settle into the gravel.

He opened the door and went immediately to the box.

"Is this it?" he asked.

I nodded, handing him the scrap of paper with the missing flower. "But not quite complete."

Grant let the scrap of paper fall to the floor and opened the lid. He flipped through the cards, admiring my photographs one at a time. I turned one over to show him the printed flower meanings, then replaced it and shut the lid on his fingers.

"You can look later," I said, retrieving the note from the floor and flapping it in the air in front of him. "Right now I need help finding this."

Grant held up the paper and read the missing flower. He shook his head. "A cherry blossom? You'll have to wait until next April."

My camera tapped against the table. "Almost a full year? I can't wait that long."

Grant laughed. "What do you want me to do? Transplant a cherry tree into my greenhouse? Even then, it wouldn't bloom."

"So, what can I do?"

He thought for a moment, knowing I wouldn't give up easily. "Look in my botany textbooks," he suggested.

I wrinkled my nose and leaned forward

until I was close enough to kiss him, but I didn't. Instead, I rubbed my nose against his stubbly cheek and bit his ear. "Please?"

"Please what?" he asked.

"Please suggest something more beautiful than a textbook illustration."

Grant looked out the window. He seemed to be debating something internally. It was almost as if he had possession of a late-blooming cherry blossom in his pocket and was trying to decide if I was important and trustworthy enough to receive it. Finally, he nodded.

"Okay," he said. "Follow me."

Grant walked out the door. I put my camera around my neck and walked in his footsteps. We crossed the gravel and climbed the steps of the main house. He withdrew a key from his pocket and unlocked the back door, which opened into a laundry room. A pale pink woman's blouse fluttered on the drying rack. Grant led me into the kitchen, where the curtains were drawn, and the counters were dusty and dark. All the appliances were unplugged, and the absolute quiet of the refrigerator was unsettling.

From the kitchen we walked through a swinging door to the dining room. The table had been pushed to the side and a sleeping bag was spread out on the wood floor. I recognized Grant's sweatshirt and balled socks beside it.

"When you had evicted me from my own home," he said, smiling and pointing to the pile.

"Don't you have a bedroom here?"

Grant nodded. "I haven't slept there for a decade, though," he said. "To tell you the truth, I've only been upstairs once since my mother died."

The stairs loomed on my left, a wide wooden banister curving up the side of the room. Grant took a step toward them.

"Come on," he said. "There's something I want to show you." At the top of the stairs we came to a long hall, with doors shut on both sides of the corridor. The hallway ended in front of five steps. We walked up and ducked through a low door.

The small room was hotter than the rest of the house, and filled with the smell of dust and dried paint. I knew before locating the gabled, boarded-up window that we were in Catherine's studio. When my eyes adjusted to the light, I took in the paneled walls, the long drafting table, and the shelves of art supplies. Half-empty glass jars of purple paint lined the top shelf, paintbrushes frozen in hard pools of lavender and periwinkle. A string circling the room displayed drawings — large, intricately rendered flowers in graphite and charcoal — hung with wooden clothespins.

"My mother was an artist," Grant said, gesturing to the work. "She spent hours of every day up here. For most of my life, she drew only flowers: rare ones, tropical ones, or short-blooming, delicate ones. She had a fear of not having the right flower to express what she wanted to say at any given moment."

He led me to an oak file cabinet in the corner of the room and opened the middle drawer. It was labeled *L–Q*. Every file was marked with a plant name, and each held a file folder with a single drawing: parsley, passionflower, peppermint, periwinkle, pineapple, and pink. He thumbed through the *P*'s until he got to poplar, white. He withdrew the file folder and opened it; it was empty. The drawing was in the blue room, still wrapped in a silk ribbon with the inked day and time of our first date.

Grant closed the drawer and opened another, looking through the files until he found a drawing of a cherry blossom. He placed it on the empty drafting table and disappeared through the door.

I sat down, admiring the work. The lines were quick, confident, the shadows deep and complex. The blossom filled the entire paper, and its beauty was nearly overwhelming. I bit my lip.

Grant returned, watching my expression as I studied the paper. "Definition?" he asked.

"Good education," I said.

He shook his head. *"Impermanence.* The beauty and transience of life."

This time, he was right. I nodded.

Grant held up a hammer he had retrieved and pried the board off the window. Light flooded through the broken glass and onto the tabletop like a spotlight. He placed the drawing in the rectangles of light and sat on the edge of the table. "Shoot," he said, caressing first the camera and then my body beneath it.

He watched as I extracted the camera from its case and turned to the image. I shot from every angle: standing on the floor, on a chair, and then in front of the window, blocking the harsh light. I adjusted the shutter speed and the focus. Grant's eyes were on my fingers, my face, and my feet crouched on the tabletop. I went through an entire roll. His eyes did not waver as I loaded a second roll and then a third. My skin lifted under his gaze as if the surface of my body were reaching toward him without the permission of my mind.

When I was done, I returned the drawing to the file folder. The next day I would have the film developed, and my dictionary would be complete. I turned the camera to where Grant sat, unmoving, on the table, and studied his face through the viewfinder.

Sunlight illuminated his profile. Circling, I captured his face in light and shadow. The camera clicked as I walked around him, starting at the top of his head and following his hairline down to the collar of his shirt. I rolled up his sleeves and photographed his forearms, the tight, protruding muscle in his wrist, his thick fingers and dirt-filled fingernails. I took off his shoes and shot the bottoms of his feet. When I ran out of film, I took off the camera.

I unbuttoned my blouse and took it off, too.

The bumps disappeared from the skin of my arms and appeared on Grant's. I climbed onto the table.

He folded his feet under him and moved to face me, then pressed his hands flat onto my stomach and held them there. His fingers lifted and fell as I breathed deep into my belly. My own fingers, clutching the edge of the table, were white.

He moved his hands around my back to my bra, unhooking it gently, one clasp at a time. Peeling my fingers from the tabletop, he slipped the bra off one arm, then the other. I reached for the table's edge again, squeezing as if trying to maintain balance on a rocking boat.

"Are you sure?" he asked.

I nodded.

He lay me down on the table, supporting my head as it eased onto the hard surface. He removed the rest of my clothes, and then his own.

Lying down next to me, Grant began to kiss my face. I turned my head toward the window, afraid I would be repulsed by his nudity. The only adult I had ever seen naked was Mother Ruby, and the image of her wet, hanging flesh had plagued me for months afterward.

Grant's fingers traveled my body with skill. He took as much care with me as he would have with a delicate sapling, and I tried to focus on his touch, the warmth he pulled to the surface of my skin, the weaving of our bodies together. He wanted me, and I knew he had wanted me for a long time. But directly below the window was the rose garden, and even as my body responded to his touch, my mind seemed to hover among the plants, thirty feet below. Grant moved on top of me. The rose garden was at the height of its bloom, the flowers open and heavy. I counted and categorized the individual bushes, starting with the reds, navigating up and down the rows: sixteen, from light red to deep scarlet. Grant's mouth traveled to my ear, open and wet. There were twenty-two pink rosebushes, if I didn't count the corals separately. Grant began to move quickly, his own pleasure eclipsing his attentiveness, and I closed my eyes at the pain. Behind my eyelids were the white roses, uncounted. I held my breath until Grant rolled off me.

My body turned to face the window, and Grant pressed himself against my back. His heart beat against my spine. I counted the white roses bursting under the setting sun, thirty-seven in all, more than any other color.

I inhaled deeply, my lungs filling with disappointment.

16.

For three frantic days we left messages for Catherine: Aloe, *grief,* taped in a row of spikes like a picket fence to her kitchen window; blood-red pansies, *think of me,* clustered in a tiny glass jar on her front porch; boughs of cypress, *mourning,* woven between the metal bars of the wrought-iron gate.

But Catherine made no sign of having received them, and gave Elizabeth nothing in return.

17.

My clothes migrated to Grant's in the trunk of my car. My shoes followed, then my brown blanket, and finally my blue box. It was everything I owned. I still paid rent to Natalya on the first of every month, and occasionally took naps on my white fur floor after work, but as the summer progressed, I spent less and less time in the blue room.

My flower dictionary was complete. The photograph I had taken of Catherine's drawing finished my set, and Elizabeth's flower dictionary and field guide retired to a dusty existence on the top of Grant's bookshelf. The blue and orange photo boxes sat side by side on the middle shelf, Grant's alphabetized by flower and mine by meaning. Two or three times a week Grant or I would set the dinner table with flowers or leave a stem of stock on the other's pillow, but we rarely consulted the boxes. We had both memorized every card, and we didn't argue over the definitions as we had when we first met.

We didn't argue over anything, really. My life with Grant was peaceful and quiet, and I might have enjoyed it if not for the overwhelming certainty that it was all about to end. The rhythm of our life together reminded me of the months before my adoption proceeding, when Elizabeth and I disked the rows, marked my calendar, and enjoyed being together. That summer with Elizabeth had been too hot; this one with Grant, the same. The water tower, lacking air-conditioning, filled up with heat as if with liquid, and Grant and I spread out on different floors in the evenings and tried to breathe. The humidity felt like the weight of what went unspoken between us, and more than once I went to him with the intention of confessing my past.

But I couldn't do it. Grant loved me. His love was quiet but consistent, and with each declaration I felt myself swoon with both pleasure and guilt. I did not deserve his love. If he knew the truth, he would hate me. I was surer of this than I had ever been of anything in my life. My affection for him only made it worse. We had grown increasingly close, kissing in greeting and parting, even sleeping beside each other. He stroked my hair and cheeks and breasts, at the dinner table and on all three floors of the water tower. We made love frequently, and I even learned to enjoy it. But in the moments afterward, when we lay naked beside each other, he wore an expression of open fulfillment that I knew, without looking, my face did not mirror. I felt my true, unworthy self to be far away from his clutching grasp, hidden from his admiring gaze. My feelings for Grant, too, felt hidden, and I began to imagine a sphere surrounding my heart, as hard and polished as the surface of a hazelnut, impenetrable.

Grant did not appear to notice my detachment in the midst of our connection. If he did, on occasion, feel my heart to be an unreachable object, he never mentioned it to me. We came together and parted ways in a predictable rhythm. Weekdays, our paths crossed for an hour in the evenings. Saturdays, we spent much of the day together, carpooling to work in the early morning and stopping afterward to eat or hike or watch the kites in the Marina. Sundays, we kept our distance. I did not accompany Grant to the farmers' market and was always gone when he returned, eating lunch in a restaurant by the bay or walking across the bridge alone.

I always returned to the water tower in time for dinner on Sundays, to take advantage of Grant's most creative and complicated meals. He spent the entire afternoon cooking. When I walked through the door, there would be appetizers on the kitchen table. The finger food, he learned, would keep me from pestering him until the entrée was complete, often not until well past nine o'clock.

That summer Grant moved beyond the cookbooks — which he carried upstairs and tucked under the love seat — and he began inventing every meal from scratch. He felt less pressure, he told me, if he wasn't comparing his results to the photograph beside the recipe. And he must have known his meals were better than anything he could have created from a cookbook, better than anything I had eaten since leaving Elizabeth's.

On the second Sunday in July I drove home from a long walk down Ocean Beach hungrier than usual, my stomach turning from emptiness and nerves. I had walked past The Gathering House, and the young women in the window, none of whom I knew, made my stomach ache. Their lives would not turn out as they dreamed. I understood this, even as mine had turned out far better than

I would have hoped, had I permitted myself to hope for anything at all. I was the exception, I knew, and even my own good fortune I believed to be a fleeting moment in what would be a long, hard, solitary life.

Grant had set out slices of a baguette stuffed with something — cream cheese, maybe, or something fancier — with bits of chopped herbs, olives, and capers. The appetizers were arranged in rows on a square ceramic plate. I started at one end and went up and down the rows, popping each circle into my mouth whole. I looked up before I ate the last one, and Grant was watching with a smile.

"You want it?" I asked, pointing to the last slice.

"No. You'll need the sustenance to wait for the next course; the rib roast still has forty-five minutes."

I ate the last one and groaned. "I don't think I can wait that long."

Grant sighed. "You say that every week, and then every week, after you've eaten, you tell me it was worth the wait."

"I do not," I said, but he was right. My stomach digested the cheese with a loud churning. I folded over onto the table and closed my eyes.

"You okay?"

I nodded. Grant prepared the rest of the meal in silence while I dozed at the table. When I opened my eyes, the steaming steak was beside me. I rolled onto one elbow.

"Will you cut it for me?" I asked.

"Sure." Grant rubbed my head, neck, and shoulders, and kissed my forehead before picking up the knife and slicing my meat. It was red in the middle, the way I liked it, and crusted with something peppery. The sauce was a combination of exotic mushrooms, red potatoes, and turnips. It was the best thing I had ever tasted.

My stomach, however, did not agree with my mouth's assessment of the quality. I had taken only a few bites when I knew, without a doubt, that my dinner would not stay within the confines of my stomach. Flying up the stairs, I locked myself in the bathroom and expelled the contents of my stomach into the toilet bowl. I flushed and turned on the water in the sink and in the shower, hoping the noise would drown out the series of retches that followed.

Grant knocked on the door, but I didn't open it. He went away and came back a half-hour later, but I still didn't answer his soft tapping. There wasn't enough room to lie flat on the bathroom floor, so I lay folded over on my side, my legs pressed against the door and my back curved against the ceramic tub. My fingers traced the white hexagonal tile and drew patterns of six-petaled flowers. It was after eleven when I emerged, the shapes of the tile etched deeply into the flesh of my cheek and exposed shoulder.

I hoped Grant would be asleep, but he was sitting upright on the love seat, all the lights turned out.

"Was it the food?" he asked.

I shook my head. I didn't know what it was, but it definitely wasn't the food. "The roast was incredible."

I sat down beside him, our thighs touching through matching dark denim. "Then what?" he asked.

"I'm sick," I said, but I avoided his eyes. I didn't believe that to be the truth, and I knew he didn't, either. As a child I had vomited from closeness: from touch or the threat of touch. Foster parents towering over me, shoving my uncooperative arms into a jacket, teachers ripping hats from my head, their fingers lingering too long on my tangled hair, had forced my stomach into uncontrollable convulsions. Once, shortly after moving in with Elizabeth, we had eaten a picnic dinner in the garden. I had overeaten, as I did at every meal that fall, and, unable to move, I had allowed Elizabeth to pick me up and carry me back to the house. She had barely set me down on the porch before I threw up over the side of the railing.

I looked at Grant. He had been touching me, intimately, for months. Without being aware of it, I had been waiting for this to happen.

"I'll sleep on the couch," I said. "I don't want you to catch it."

"I won't," Grant said, taking my hand and pulling me up. "Come upstairs."

I did as he asked.

18.

The morning of my adoption hearing, I awoke at sunrise.

Sitting up, I turned and leaned against the cool wall, the comforter pulled up to my chin. Light traveled lazily through the window, the soft beam illuminating my dresser and open closet door. In many ways, the room looked the same as it had when I'd entered a year before; it contained the same furniture, the same white comforter, and the same stacks of clothes, many of which I had yet to grow into. But all around me were signs of the girl I had become: library books stacked on the desk with titles such as *Botany on Your Plate* and *The Ultimate Book of Mix-It-Yourself Concoctions for Your Garden,* a photograph of Elizabeth and me that Carlos had taken, our bright pink winter cheeks pressed close together, and a wastepaper basket full of flower drawings for Elizabeth, none of which I'd deemed good enough to give her.

It was my last morning in the room as a foster child, and I gazed around, as I always did — surveying objects as if they belonged to someone else. *Tomorrow*, I thought. *Tomorrow I will feel different. I will wake up, look around, and see a room — a life — that is mine and will never be taken away from me.*

Moving quietly down the hall, I listened for Elizabeth. Though it was early, I was surprised to hear the house quiet, to see her bedroom door shut. I had imagined her to be as sleepless as I was. The day before had been my birthday, and though Elizabeth had made cupcakes and we'd frosted them with thick purple roses, the anticipation of my adoption had mostly eclipsed the celebration of the day. After dinner, we'd distractedly licked off the frosting, our gazes shifting out the window, waiting for the sky to darken so the new day would begin. Lying awake in bed, my body wrapped in the long floral nightgown Elizabeth had given me as a present, I'd been more excited than on every Christmas Eve of my life put together. Perhaps Elizabeth had been unable to sleep, too, I thought, and was sleeping in because she'd been up half the night.

In the bathroom was the dress we'd purchased together, hanging in plastic on a hook behind the door. I washed my face and brushed my hair before pulling it off the hanger.

It was hard to put on without Elizabeth, but I was determined. I wanted to see the look on her face when she awoke to find me dressed and sitting at the kitchen table, waiting. I wanted her to understand that I was ready. Sitting on the edge of the bathtub, I pulled the dress on backward, zipped it up, and then twisted it around until the zipper ran the length of my spine. The ribbons were thick and hard to tie. After multiple failed attempts, I settled for a loose square knot at the back of my neck. Around my waist I did the same.

When I went downstairs, the clock on the stove read eight o'clock. Opening the refrigerator, I scanned the full shelves and chose a small container of vanilla yogurt. I peeled back the seal, poking at a layer of thick cream with a spoon, but I wasn't hungry. I was nervous. Elizabeth had never slept in, not once in the year I'd been with her. For a full hour I sat at the kitchen table, my eyes on the clock.

At nine o'clock, I climbed the stairs and knocked on her bedroom door. The knot around my neck had loosened, and the front of the dress hung too low, exposing my protruding chest bone. I didn't look as glamorous, I knew, as I had in the store. When Elizabeth did not answer or call out, I tried the doorknob. It was unlocked. Pushing the door quietly, I stepped inside.

Elizabeth's eyes were open. She stared at the ceiling, and she did not shift her gaze when I crossed the room to stand by the side of the bed.

"It's nine o'clock," I said.

Elizabeth did not respond.

"We have to see the judge at eleven. Shouldn't we go, to get checked in and everything?"

Still, she did not acknowledge my presence. I stepped closer and leaned in, thinking she might be asleep, even though her eyes were wide open. I'd had a roommate who slept that way once, and every night I waited for her to fall asleep first, so that I could shut her eyelids. I didn't like the feeling of being watched.

I started to shake Elizabeth, gently. She did not blink. "Elizabeth?" I said, my voice a whisper. "It's Victoria." I pressed my fingers into the space between her collarbones. Her pulse beat calmly, seeming to tick away the seconds until my adoption. *Stand up,* I pleaded silently. The thought of missing our court date, of having it postponed for a month, a week, even just another day, was incomprehensible. I began to shake her, my hands clutching her shoulders. Her head wobbled loosely on her neck.

"Stop," she said finally, the word barely audible.

"Aren't you getting up?" I asked, my voice breaking. "Aren't we going to court?"

Tears leaked out of Elizabeth's eyes, and she did not lift her hand to wipe them. I followed their path with my eyes and saw the pillow was already wet where they landed. "I can't," she said.

"What do you mean? I can help you."

"No," she said. "I can't." She was quiet a long time. I leaned so close that when she finally spoke again, her lips grazed my ear. "This isn't a family," she said softly. "Just me and you alone in this house. It isn't a family. I can't do this to you."

I sat down on the foot of the bed. Elizabeth didn't move, didn't speak again, but I sat where I was for the rest of the morning, waiting.

19.

The nausea didn't go away, but I learned to hide it. I vomited in the shower every morning until the drain started to clog. After that, I didn't shower, racing to my car before Grant got up, blaming Renata and an impossible summer wedding schedule. The feeling followed me throughout the day. The scent of the flowers at work made it worse, but the coolness of the walk-in brought relief. I took afternoon naps among the chilled buckets.

I don't know how long things would have continued this way if Renata hadn't confronted me in the walk-in. The heavy metal door closed behind her with a loud click, and she toed me awake in the darkness.

"You think I don't know you're pregnant?" she asked.

My heart beat against its nut-hard shell. *Pregnant.* The word floated in the room between us, unwanted. I wished it would slip under the door, onto the street, and into the body of someone who wanted it. There were plenty of women dreaming of motherhood, but neither Renata nor I was one of them.

"I'm not," I said, but without as much force as I'd intended.

"You can stay in denial as long as you want, but I'm getting you health insurance before that baby is full term and you're standing there birthing it in front of my store."

I didn't move. Renata went to kick me again, but it turned into a gentle nudge on what I now noticed was my fattening middle.

"Get up," she said, "and sit at the table. The stack of papers you have to sign will take most of the afternoon."

I stood up and walked out of the walk-in, past the papers stacked high on the worktable, and out onto the sidewalk. Dry-heaving into the gutter, I started to run. Renata called my name, repeatedly and with increasing volume, but I didn't look back.

When I reached the grocery store on the corner of 17th and Potrero, I was exhausted and out of breath. I collapsed onto a curb and heaved. An old woman with a bagful of groceries stopped and put her hand on my shoulder, asking me if I was okay. I slapped her hand away, and she dropped her groceries. In the commotion of the gathering crowd, I slipped into the store. I bought a three-pack of pregnancy tests and walked back to the blue room, the light paper box a stone in my backpack.

Natalya was still asleep, her bedroom door open. She had stopped closing it months ago, when I'd all but stopped living there, and slammed it shut whenever I surprised her with an appearance. Closing her door silently, I shut myself in the bathroom.

I peed on all three sticks and lined them up on the edge of the sink. It was supposed to take three minutes, but it didn't.

Sliding open the bathroom window, I threw them out one at a time. They bounced and settled on the flat gravel roof just a foot below the window, the results still readable. I sat down on the lid of the toilet and put my head in my hands. The last thing I wanted was for Natalya to know; Renata was bad enough. If Mother Ruby found out, she'd be living in the blue room with me, feeding me fried eggs day and night, and placing her hands on my stomach every five minutes.

I walked into the kitchen and climbed onto the counter. Natalya and her band often climbed onto the roof this way, but I'd never tried it. The window over the kitchen sink was small but not impossible to get through, even with my body in its widening state.

The roof was littered with cigarette butts and an empty vodka bottle. Crawling over them, I gathered the pregnancy tests and put all three in my pocket. I stood up slowly, dizzy from the exertion and the height, and looked around.

The view was astounding, as much because I had never noticed it as for the actual sight. The roof was long — the distance of an entire city block — and surrounded by a low concrete wall. Beyond the wall was the city, from downtown to the Bay Bridge to Berkeley, a perfect illustration of itself, the motion of taillights on freeways the blur of red pigment. I walked to the edge of the roof and sat down, breathing in the beauty, forgetting, momentarily, that everything in my life was about to change, again.

The pads of my fingers traveled from my neck to my navel. My body was mine no longer. It had been inhabited, taken over. It wasn't what I wanted, but I didn't have any options; the baby would grow within me. I couldn't have an abortion. I couldn't go to a clinic, and undress, and stand naked in front of a stranger. The thought of anesthesia, of losing consciousness while a doctor did whatever he would with my body, was an offense beyond consideration. I would have the baby, and then I would decide what to do with it.

A baby. I repeated the words to myself again and again, waiting for warmth or emotion, but I felt nothing. Within my paralysis, I held only a single conviction: Grant could never, ever know. The excitement in his eyes, the instant vision he would hold of the family we would be together, was more than I could bear. I could picture exactly the way it would unfold: me, sitting at the picnic table, waiting for Grant to sit down so that I could choke out the life-changing words. I would begin to cry before I finished speaking, but still, he would know. And he would want it. The light in his eyes would be proof of his devotion to our unborn child, and my tears would be proof of my unfitness to be a mother. The knowledge that I would let him down (and the unknown of how it would happen, and when) would keep me far from his excitement, sealed from his professions of love.

I had to leave, quickly, silently, before he discovered the reason for my departure. It would hurt him, but not as much as it would hurt him to watch, helpless, as I packed my bags and took his child away from him forever. The life he desired with me was not possible.

It was better for him never to know how close we had come.

20.

It was four o'clock in the afternoon, and Elizabeth was still in bed. I sat at the kitchen table, eating peanut butter out of a jar with my thumb. I'd thought about making her dinner, chicken soup or chili, something with a magnetic scent. But so far I'd only learned how to make desserts: blackberry cobbler, peach pie, and chocolate mousse. It didn't feel right to eat dessert without dinner, especially today, when we had nothing at all to celebrate.

Putting the peanut butter away, I began to rummage through the pantry when I was surprised by a knock. I didn't need to look out the window to see who it was. I had heard the knock enough times in my life to know. Meredith. She pounded harder. In another moment she would try the door, and it would be unlocked. I ducked into the pantry. The sound of the front door slamming traveled into the darkness. The beans and rice lining the shelves rattled in their canisters.

"Elizabeth?" Meredith called. "Victoria?" She walked through the living room and into the kitchen. Her footsteps traveled around the table and paused in front of the window over the sink. I held my breath, imagining her eyes traveling over the leafy vines, looking for signs of movement. She wouldn't find any. Carlos had taken Perla camping again, for their annual trip. Finally, I heard her turn and walk up the stairs. "Elizabeth?" she called again. And then, quietly: "Elizabeth? Are you all right?"

Creeping up the stairs, I stopped on the top step and leaned into the wall, out of sight.

"I'm resting," Elizabeth said quietly. "I just needed a little rest."

" 'Resting'?" Meredith asked. Something in Elizabeth's voice had angered Meredith, and her tone had turned from concerned to accusing. "It's four o'clock in the afternoon! And you missed your court date. You left the judge and me sitting there staring at each other, wondering where you and Victoria —" She stopped midsentence. "Where's Victoria?"

"She was just here a minute ago," Elizabeth said, her voice weak. *Hours,* I wanted to yell. I was there hours ago; I'd left her bedside at noon, when I knew for certain we were not going to court. "Did you check the kitchen?"

When Meredith spoke next, she sounded closer to me. "I checked," she said. "But I'll check again." I stood up and began to tiptoe down the stairs, too late. "Victoria," Meredith said. "Come back here."

Turning, I followed Meredith into my bedroom. I had changed out of the dress and into shorts and a T-shirt earlier in the day, and the dress lay across the top of my desk. Meredith sat down and began to run her fingers over the top of the velvet flowers. I snatched the dress from her, crumpled it into a ball, and threw it under the bed.

"What's going on?" Meredith demanded, her voice as accusing as it had been with Elizabeth. I shrugged.

"Don't think you're going to stand there and say nothing. Everything's going great, Elizabeth loves you, you're happy — and then a no-show for your adoption proceeding? What did you do?"

"I didn't do anything!" I shouted. For the first time in my life, it was true, but there was no reason for Meredith to believe me. "Elizabeth's tired, you heard her. Just leave us alone." I crawled into bed, pulled up the covers, and turned to face the wall.

Exhaling a loud, impatient sigh, Meredith stood up. "Something's going on," she said. "Either you did something horrific, or Elizabeth isn't mentally fit to be a mother. Either way, I'm not sure this is a good placement for you anymore."

"It isn't your place to decide what is or is not good for Victoria," Elizabeth said quietly. I sat up and turned to look at her. She leaned heavily against the door frame, as if she would fall over without its support. A pale pink bathrobe crisscrossed her body. Her hair fell in tangled bunches over her shoulders.

"It's exactly my place to decide," Meredith said, stepping toward Elizabeth. She was neither taller nor stronger, but she towered over Elizabeth's wilted figure. I wondered if Elizabeth was afraid. "It wouldn't have been my place anymore if you'd appeared in court at eleven a.m. this morning, and believe me, I was ready to give up control of this child. But it seems that isn't to be. What did she do?"

"She didn't do anything," Elizabeth said.

I couldn't see Meredith's face, couldn't see if she believed her. "If Victoria didn't do anything, I'll have to write you up. Give you a written warning for missing a court date, for suspicion of neglect. Has she eaten anything today?" I lifted my shirt away from my skin, where streaks of peanut butter remained from my snack, but neither Meredith nor Elizabeth looked at me.

"I don't know," Elizabeth said.

Meredith nodded. "That's what I thought." She moved toward the bedroom door, stepping past Elizabeth. "We'll finish in the living room. Victoria doesn't need to be a part of the conversation we're about to have."

I didn't follow them down the stairs, didn't want to hear. I wanted everything to be as it was the day before, when I believed Elizabeth would adopt me. Rolling to the edge of the bed, I reached underneath until I found my wrinkled ball of a dress. I pulled it into bed with me, squeezing it into my chest and pressing my face into the velvet. The dress still smelled like the store, new wood and glass cleaner, and I remembered the feeling of Elizabeth's arms underneath my armpits and tight across my chest, the look on her face as our eyes met in the mirror.

From downstairs I heard snippets of an argument: Meredith mostly, her voice raised. *She has you or she has nothing,* she said at one point. *It's bullshit for you to say you want more for her. An excuse.* Didn't Elizabeth know that she was all I wanted? That she was all I would ever want? Huddled under the com-

306

forter, I found the summer heat thick and suffocating. I struggled for breath.

I'd been given a chance, a final chance, and somehow, without meaning to, I'd ruined it. I waited for Meredith to march up the stairs and deliver the words I never thought I'd hear: *Elizabeth's given notice. Pack up.*

21.

On Sunday morning, I ate soda crackers and waited for the nausea to subside. It didn't. I got into my car anyway and drove across the city, vomiting into storm drains on three different occasions. The worldwide population expansion was not a phenomenon I could comprehend as I rolled to a stop at one grate after another.

Grant wasn't home, as I knew he wouldn't be. He would be standing behind his truck, handing cut flowers to lines of locals. I had been away only three nights, not an unusually long time for me or for our relationship, and I imagined him hurrying through his work, thinking about the extravagant dinner he planned to create. It would never cross his mind that I would miss a Sunday-night meal. At least I'd warned him, I thought, as I let myself in with the rusty spare key. It wasn't my fault if he'd forgotten.

Listening for the sound of his truck, I

packed quickly. I took everything that belonged to me and many things that didn't, including Grant's duffel bag, a large, army-green canvas tube that would camouflage well beneath the heath. I stuffed in clothes, books, a flashlight, three blankets, and all the food he had in the cupboard. Before zipping the bag, I shoved in a knife, a can opener, and the cash he kept in the freezer.

I crammed my belongings into the backseat of my car and went back for my blue photo box, Elizabeth's dictionary, and the field guide. In the car, I secured them into the front seat with the seat belt and then went back up the spiral staircase to the second floor. I pulled Grant's orange box off the bookshelf. Opening it, I thumbed through the photos, considering whether or not I should take it. I had made it; everything inside belonged to me. But the idea of having an extra in a safe location comforted me, especially as the next few months of my life would likely be anything but safe. If something happened to my blue box, I could always come back for the orange one.

I left the box in the middle of the floor and withdrew a small square of paper from my backpack. It was folded in half so that it stood up on top of the box like a place marker at a formal dinner. In the center, I had glued a quarter-sized photo of a white rose from a pile of scraps in the blue room, having trimmed it with precision so that only the flower remained. Below the image, in the place where a name would go, I had written a single sentence in permanent ink.

A rose is a rose is a rose.

Grant would understand, if not accept, that this was the end.

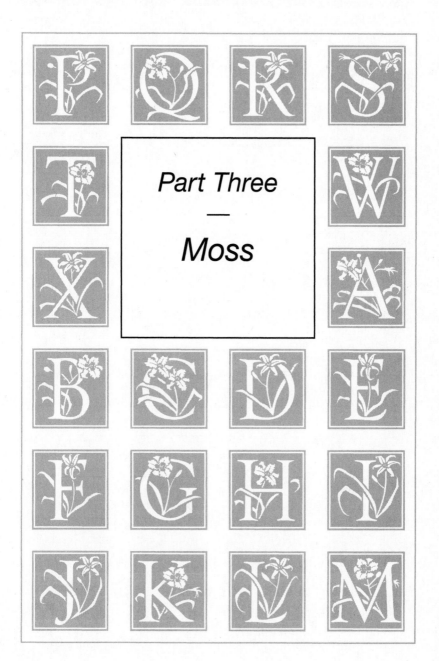

Part Three

—

Moss

1.

I would go back to the blue room; I would have the baby within its watery walls. I knew this in the same way I knew that Grant was looking for me, without evidence and without doubt. Grant didn't know the location of the blue room, but he knew enough to find it, I was sure. Until he had given up, I had to stay away. It could take months or most of the year. I was prepared to wait.

No longer squeamish in the presence of intoxicated teenagers, I moved back in to my garden in McKinley Square. I had a knife and a sexual past. They couldn't attempt anything that hadn't already been done, and, looking at my reflection in a gas station mirror, I doubted anyone would try. Feeling numb toward both my changing body and my homelessness, I didn't change my clothes, didn't seek out showers or wealthy neighborhoods. The weeks began to show on my skin.

I missed Renata, and missed my job, but I couldn't go back to Bloom. It was the first place Grant would look for me. Instead, I hid under the heath bushes, which had grown and multiplied in my absence. The seeds of heath could exist in the soil for months or years — decades, even — before bursting forth new life, and the familiar plant comforted me as I curled up with Grant's duffel bag beneath its branches. The rest of my things I left in my car, which I moved to a different street every day. If Grant saw the hatchback, he would recognize it — even with the license plate removed and the blue box well hidden under my belongings — so I kept it far from Potrero Hill, in Bernal Heights or Glen Park, sometimes as far as Hunters Point. I had been sleeping in the park for weeks before it dawned on me that I could sleep in my car at night. But I didn't want to. The smell of the soil, saturated from overwatering, entered my dreams and calmed my nightmares.

In mid-August, perched at the top of the play structure in McKinley Square, I spotted Grant. He was coming straight up Vermont Street, climbing the hill with his eyes scanning the modern lofts and old Victorians. He stopped and exchanged words with a painter on slanted scaffolding. Turquoise paint dripped from a brush and landed on a drop cloth near Grant's shoe. He reached down and touched the wet paint, then called something up to the painter, and the man shrugged. Grant was three blocks down the hill, and I couldn't hear his words, but I could see he wasn't out of breath even after the steep climb.

I scrambled through the bushes, zipped my bag, and pulled it across the street and into the corner store. When I'd first moved back to McKinley Square, I'd told the store's owner I was running from an abusive family. I asked him to hide me if my brother ever came looking. The owner had refused, but as time passed and I purchased every meal from his always-empty neighborhood store, I knew I would not be turned away.

The owner looked up when I ran in with my heavy bag and quickly opened the door behind him. I raced around the counter, through the door, and up a flight of stairs. Dropping to my knees, I crawled to the front window of the small, sparsely furnished apartment. The hardwood floor smelled like lemon oil and felt slick against my shins. The walls were painted bright yellow. Grant would not look up twice.

Crouching low under the bay window, my eyes peered over the sill. Grant had already climbed the stairs to the park and passed the swings, the empty seats swaying in the breeze. He spun in a circle, and I ducked down. When I lifted my head again, he stood at the edge of the grass, where thick green sod met the wild forest undergrowth. He pressed a boot into the trunk of a redwood tree before walking across the soft layer of duff and kneeling in front of the white verbena. I held my breath as Grant looked around the sloping hillside, afraid he would notice the carved-out heath bush and the outline of my body, belly round, beneath it.

But he didn't pause at the heath. He turned back to the verbena and bowed his head. I was too far away to see the delicate clustered petals in which he dipped his nose, too far away to hear his hushed words, but I knew he was praying.

My forehead pressed against the glass, and I felt my body being pulled toward him by the strength of my own desire. I missed his sweet, earthy smell, his cooking, and his touch. The way he placed his square palms over each side of my face as he looked into my eyes, and the way his hands smelled of soil, even after they had just been washed. But I could not go to him. He would make promises, and I would repeat his words because I wanted to believe in his vision of our life together. But over time we would both find my words meaningless. I would fail; it was the only possible outcome.

Closing my eyes, I forced my body away from the window. My shoulders fell forward, belly pressed against parted thighs. The sun warmed my back. If I had known how, I would have joined Grant in prayer. I would have prayed for him, for his goodness, his loyalty, and his improbable love. I would have prayed for him to give up, to let go, and to start over. I might have even prayed for forgiveness.

But I didn't know how to pray.

Instead, I stayed as I was, folded over on the floor of a stranger's living room, waiting for Grant to give up, forget about me, and go home.

2.

"Six months," Elizabeth said.

I watched Meredith drive away. After visiting weekly for two months, she had finally decided to set a new court date. Six months away.

Elizabeth slipped an extra strip of bacon into a sandwich and set it in front of me. I picked it up, took a bite, and nodded. She hadn't given notice, as I'd expected, but she was different than she'd been before the failed adoption, nervous and apologetic.

"The time will go quickly," she said, "with the harvest and the holidays and everything."

I nodded again and swallowed hard, wiping my eyes, refusing to cry. In the time since our missed court appearance, I had replayed scenes from the year before in my head endlessly, looking for clues to what I had done wrong. The list was long: cutting down the arm of the cactus, hitting the bus driver over the head, and more than one declaration of hatred. But Elizabeth seemed to have forgiven me for my violent outbursts. These, she seemed to understand. I'd come to the conclusion that her sudden ambivalence was because of my growing clinginess, or else my tears. Feeling my eyes well again, I shut them and folded over, my forehead pressed against the table.

"I'm really sorry," Elizabeth said quietly. She had said it hundreds of times in the previous weeks, and I believed her. She seemed sorry. What I didn't believe, though, was that she still wanted to be my mother. Pity, I knew, was different from love. From what I'd heard of their conversation in the living room, Meredith had made my options clear to Elizabeth. I had her or I had no one. It was out of a sense of obligation, I decided, that Elizabeth hadn't given notice. Finishing my sandwich, I rubbed my hands clean on my jeans.

"If you're done," Elizabeth said, "wait for me on the tractor. I'll clean up and meet you out there."

Outside, I leaned against the tall tire, surveying the vines. It was turning out to be a good year. Elizabeth and I had thinned and fertilized in just the right amounts; the grapes that remained were fat and starting to sweeten. I'd spent all fall working beside Elizabeth on the vineyard, writing three-paragraph essays on seasons, soil, and grape growing; memorizing field guides and plant families. In the evenings, just as I had the autumn before, I accompanied Elizabeth on her tasting tours.

I checked my watch. We had a long night of tasting ahead of us, and I was anxious to start. But Elizabeth didn't come, not after five minutes, and not after ten. I decided to go back inside. I would drink some milk and watch Elizabeth finish cleaning the kitchen.

When I reached the front porch, I heard her voice, half angry, half pleading. She was on the phone. All at once I realized why Elizabeth had kept me waiting by the tractor, and just as suddenly I realized that the failed adoption was not my fault. It was Catherine's. If she'd shown up, if she'd responded with words or flowers, if she hadn't left Elizabeth so alone, everything would have been different. Elizabeth would have gotten out of bed and tightened the ribbons on my dress and driven us to court, Grant and Catherine in tow. Filling with rage, I stormed into the kitchen.

"I fucking hate that woman!" I shouted.

Elizabeth looked up. She moved her hand to cover the mouthpiece. Springing forward,

I ripped the phone out of her hand. "You fucking ruined my life!" I shouted, and then slammed it against the base. The call disconnected, but the phone bounced off the hook, hitting the hardwood floor and then dangling an inch above the ground. Elizabeth folded her head into her hands and leaned against the counter. She appeared neither surprised nor offended by my unexpected outburst. I waited for her to speak, but she was quiet for a long time.

"Victoria, I know you're angry," she said finally. "You have every right to be. But don't be mad at Catherine. I'm the one who messed up. Blame me. I'm your mother — don't you know that's what mothers are for?" The corners of her mouth turned up slightly, a wry, tired smile, and she met my gaze.

Squeezing my hands into fists, I rocked backward on my heels, begging myself not to attack her. Even in the height of my anger, I understood that above all else, I wanted to stay with Elizabeth.

"No," I said, when I'd calmed enough to speak. "You're not my mother. You would have been, if Catherine hadn't ruined my life."

Storming over to the stairs, I was startled by a flash of motion out the front window. A truck sped up the driveway. In profile, I saw Grant hunched over the steering wheel. Brakes squealed and gravel flew as he parked in front of the house.

I sprinted upstairs at the same time Grant pounded up the front porch. At the top, I leaned against the wall, out of sight. Grant didn't knock and didn't wait for Elizabeth to come to the door.

"You have to stop," he said, out of breath.

Elizabeth crossed the room. I imagined her standing in front of him, only the screen separating their bodies.

"I won't stop," she said. "Eventually, she'll accept my forgiveness. She has to."

"She won't. You don't know her anymore."

"What? What do you mean?"

"Just that. You don't know her."

"I don't understand," Elizabeth whispered, her voice barely audible over a persistent tapping. It sounded like Grant's foot on the porch, or his knuckles on the frame of the screen. The noise was nervous, impatient.

"I only came over to tell you to stop calling — please." There was silence between them.

"You can't tell me to forget her. She's my sister."

"Maybe," Grant said.

" *'Maybe'?*" Elizabeth's voice rose suddenly.

I could picture her face flushed, hot. Had Elizabeth been stalking the wrong woman? Was Grant even her nephew?

"All I mean is, she isn't the sister you knew. Please believe me."

"People change," Elizabeth said. "Love doesn't. Family doesn't."

There was silence again, and I wished I could see their faces, to see if they were angry, or indifferent, or on the verge of tears.

"Yes," Grant said finally. "Love does." I heard footsteps, and I knew he was leaving. When his voice reached me again, it was from far away. "She keeps filling jam jars with lighter fluid. Lining them up on the kitchen windowsill. Says she's going to burn down your vineyard."

"No." Elizabeth did not sound shocked or afraid, only disbelieving. "She wouldn't do it. I don't care how much she's changed in fifteen years. She wouldn't do that. She loves these vines as much as I do. She always has."

His truck door slammed. "I just thought you should know," he said. The engine started, a quiet hum, and it idled there, in the driveway. I imagined Grant's and Elizabeth's gazes meeting, each searching the other for the truth.

Finally, Elizabeth called out to him. "Grant?" she said. "You don't have to leave. There's leftovers from dinner, and you're welcome here."

Wheels turned in the gravel. "No," he said. "I shouldn't have come, and I won't come again. She can never know."

3.

I waited a second month, and then a third, just to be certain, slipping rent under Natalya's door when it was due. By the end of October, the nausea had lessened. It returned only when I didn't eat enough, which was rare. I had plenty of money for meals. Grant's cash and my own savings would have kept me well fed throughout my pregnancy, but I knew I wouldn't have to wait that long.

As the leaves fell, I became sure that Grant had given up. I imagined looking through the windows of his water tower and watching him box up the romantic poets and cover the orange box with an opaque cloth, the calculated actions of a man with a past to forget. And soon, I told myself, he would forget. There would be many women at the flower market, women who were more beautiful, exotic, and sexual than I would ever be. If he hadn't already found one, he would. But even as I tried to convince myself, Grant's image passed through my mind, his hooded sweatshirt pulled low over his forehead. Not once had I seen him look up at a woman passing his stall.

The day I felt the baby kick for the first time, I returned to the blue room. I lugged the duffel bag across the city to my car and drove to the apartment. Letting myself in the front door, I carried everything up the stairs in three trips. Natalya's door was open, and I stood over her bed, watching her sleep. She had recently dyed her hair again, and the pink had rubbed off in streaks on the white pillowcase. She smelled like sweet wine and cloves, and she didn't stir. I shook her awake.

"Has he come?" I asked.

Natalya covered her eyes with her elbow and sighed. "Yeah, a few weeks ago."

"What did you tell him?"

"Just that you were gone."

"I was."

"Yeah. Where'd you go?"

I ignored her question. "Did you tell him I was still paying rent?"

She sat up and shook her head. "I wasn't entirely sure the money was from you." She reached out and placed her hand on my stomach. In just the past few weeks, I had gone from looking fat to looking undeniably pregnant. "Renata told me," she said.

The baby kicked again, its fingers and feet pressing into my internal organs, scraping the walls of my liver, my heart, my spleen. I gagged and ran into kitchen, throwing up into the sink. Dropping down to the floor, I felt the nausea ebb and flow with the motion of the baby. I thought I was past the sickness of early pregnancy; I also thought I had overcome the urge to vomit every time I was touched. One of my two assumptions was inaccurate.

Renata had told Natalya. If she had told Natalya, there was no reason to think she hadn't told Grant. I climbed my way up the kitchen cabinets and threw up into the sink a second time.

There was a new sign in the window of Bloom. Shorter hours, closed on Sundays. When I arrived in the early afternoon, the storefront was dark and locked, even though the sign said it should be open. I knocked, and when Renata didn't come, I knocked again. The key was in my pocket, but I didn't use it. I sat down on the curb and waited.

Fifteen minutes later, Renata returned, the silver tube of a wrapped burrito in her hand. I watched the light reflect off the aluminum and onto the walls of the buildings she passed. I stood up but did not look at her, even when she was standing directly in front of me. My eyes studied my feet, still visible beneath the curve of my stomach.

"Did you tell him?" I asked.

"He doesn't know?" The shock and accusation in her voice pushed me backward. I stumbled off the curb and into the street. Renata steadied me with her hand on my shoulder. When I looked up, her eyes were kinder than her words had been.

She nodded to my stomach. "When are you due?"

I shrugged. I didn't know, and it didn't matter. The baby would come when it did. I would not see a doctor, and I would not give birth in a hospital. Renata seemed to understand all this without me having to tell her.

"My mother will help you. And she won't charge you anything. She considers it the work for which she was put on this earth." I could hear Renata's words coming out of Mother Ruby's mouth, her accent thicker and her hands on my body. I shook my head.

"Then what do you want from me?" Renata demanded, her frustration escaping in short, punctuated words.

"I want to work," I said. "And I want you

not to tell Grant — that I'm back or that I'm having a baby."

She sighed. "He deserves to know."

I nodded. "I know he does." Grant deserved a lot of things, all of them better than me. "You won't tell him?"

Renata shook her head. "No. But I won't lie for you. You can't work for me, not with Grant asking me every Saturday if you've returned to your job. I've never been a good liar, and I don't want to learn now."

I crumpled onto the curb, and Renata sat beside me. When I checked my pulse underneath the wristband of my watch, the beat was imperceptible. I couldn't get another job. Even before getting pregnant, the likelihood was slim, and it would be impossible in my current, increasingly visible, condition. The money I had saved would eventually run out. I wouldn't be able to feed myself or buy whatever it was that made children so infamously expensive.

"Then what will I do?" My despair became anger as it left my body, but Renata didn't flinch.

"Ask Grant," she said.

I stood up to leave.

"Wait a minute," she said. She unlocked the door to Bloom and opened the cash register. Lifting the cash drawer, she extracted a sealed red envelope, my name printed neatly across the front, and a stack of twenty-dollar bills. Walking back outside, she held out the cash.

"Your final paycheck," she said. I didn't count the money she handed me, but I could tell it was much more than I had earned. When I had put it in my backpack, she handed me the envelope and her unopened burrito. "Protein," she said. "That's what my mother always says. It builds the baby's brain. Or maybe it's the bones — I can't remember."

I thanked her, turning to walk down the hill.

"If you ever need anything," she called after me, "you know where to find me."

The rest of the day I spent in the blue room, fighting off waves of nausea as the baby fluttered inside me. The red envelope lay on the white fur floor like a bloodstain, and I sat cross-legged beside it. I couldn't decide whether to open it or to slip it under the rug and forget about it.

Finally, I decided I had to know. It would be hard to read Grant's words but even harder to go through the pregnancy without knowing if he had guessed the reason for my abrupt parting.

But when I opened the envelope, it was not

what I had expected. It was a wedding invitation: Bethany and Ray, the first weekend in November, Ocean Beach. The wedding was less than two weeks away. I was invited, Bethany wrote on the back, as a guest, but would I also do the flowers? What she wanted most, she wrote, was permanence, and after that, passion. *The opposite of the cherry blossom,* I thought, cringing at the memory of the afternoon in Catherine's studio and everything that moment had become. I would suggest honeysuckle, I decided, *devotion.* The very strength of the vine suggested a permanence I had never experienced but hoped Bethany would.

Bethany had included her phone number and asked me to call by the end of August. The date had long passed, and she had likely found another florist, but I had to try. It was the only foreseeable source of income in what would be a long, idle winter.

Picking up on the second ring, Bethany gasped at the sound of my voice.

"Victoria!" she said. "I'd given up! I found another florist, but that woman is about to lose a job, deposit or no."

She and Ray could meet the following day, she said. I gave her directions to my house.

"I hope you'll stay for the wedding," she said before she hung up. "You know, I credit your bouquet as the beginning of every-thing."

"I will," I said. And I would bring some-thing resembling business cards.

I asked Natalya if I could meet with Bethany and Ray downstairs, and she agreed. Early the following morning, I bought a card table and three folding chairs at a flea market in South San Francisco. They fit inside the back of my car, the hatchback tied down with a rope. In addition to the furniture, I bought a rose-colored cut crystal vase with a discreet chip for a dollar and a white lace tablecloth with a pink plastic liner for three. I wrapped the vase in the tablecloth and took the side streets home.

Before Bethany and Ray arrived, I set up the card table in the empty office space. Cov-ering it with the lace cloth, I set the crystal vase in the center, full of flowers from my garden in McKinley Square. Next to the vase sat my blue photo box. I checked and rechecked my alphabetization while I waited for the door to open.

Finally, it did, and Bethany stood in the empty doorway more beautiful than I re-membered, Ray more handsome than I imagined. They would make a breathtaking couple, I thought, draping honeysuckle in long lines through the white sand.

Bethany opened her arms to hug me, and I allowed it, my belly a ball between us. Looking down, she gasped and placed her hands on my stomach. I wondered how many times I would have to endure this in the coming months, from acquaintances and strangers on the street. Pregnancy seemed to remove the unspoken societal laws of personal space. I disliked it almost as much as the feeling of another human being growing within my body.

"Congratulations!" Bethany said, hugging me again. "When are you due?"

It was the second time I'd been asked in two days, and I knew the frequency would increase along with my size. I counted the months in my head.

"February," I said. "Or March. The doctors aren't sure."

Bethany introduced me to Ray, and we shook hands. Motioning to the table and chairs, I asked them to sit down. I sat across from them, apologizing for taking so long to call.

"We're just so glad you did," Bethany said, squeezing Ray's thick arm. "I've told Ray all about you."

I pushed the blue box toward the couple. It glowed under the fluorescent office lights.

"I can do anything you want for your wedding. Nearly everything is available at the flower market, even out of season." Bethany opened the lid, and I cringed as if she was again touching my body.

Ray picked up the first card. In the years that followed, I watched many men squirm in front of my flower dictionary, the fluorescent lights casting a sickly shadow on their nervous faces. But Ray wasn't one of them. His bulk was deceiving; he discussed emotions like Annemarie's lady friends, with loquacious enthusiasm and indecision. They got stuck on the first card, acacia, as Grant and I had, but for completely different reasons.

"Secret love," he said. "I like that."

" 'Secret'?" Bethany asked. "Why secret?" She said it with mock offense, as if he was suggesting they hide their love from the world.

"Because what we have *is* secret. My friends, when they talk about their girlfriends or wives, complaining or bragging, I just keep quiet. What we have — it's different. I want to keep it that way. Untouched. Secret."

"Mmm," Bethany said. "Yes." She turned over the card and viewed the photo of the acacia blossom, a feathery golden sphere-shaped flower hanging on a delicate stem. There was more than one acacia tree in McKinley Square. I hoped they were in bloom. "What can you do with this?" she asked.

"It depends on what else you want. Acacia isn't a centerpiece flower. I would probably drape it around the edge of a nosegay, half concealing your hands."

"I like that," said Bethany. She turned back to Ray. "What else?"

In the end, they decided on fuchsia moss roses with pale pink lilac, cream-colored dahlia, honeysuckle, and the golden acacia. They would have to return the bridesmaid's dresses; the burgundy silk would clash. Bethany was relieved they were from a department store and that she hadn't special-ordered. The flowers were the most important, she said with confidence, and Ray agreed.

As they stood up to go, I told them I would deliver the flowers at noon and return for the two-o'clock wedding. "I can adjust your bouquet at the last minute," I told her, "if it needs anything."

Bethany hugged me again. "That would be wonderful," she said. "My greatest fear is that the roses will suddenly snap when the wedding music starts to play, and both my wedding and my good fortune will be shattered."

"Don't worry," I said. "Flowers don't spontaneously combust." I looked from Bethany to Ray as I said it. She smiled. I was talking about Ray, not the flowers, and she understood.

"I know," she said.

"Do you mind if I bring business cards?" I asked. "I'm just starting out here." I nodded to the white walls.

"Of course!" she said. "Bring cards! And bring a guest; we forgot to tell you that." Bethany nodded to my stomach and winked. The baby kicked; my nausea returned.

"I will," I said, "bring cards — not a guest. Thank you."

Bethany looked embarrassed, and Ray, flushing, pulled her to the door. "Thank you," she said. "Really. I can't thank you enough."

Standing at the glass door, I watched them walk up the hill to their car. Ray wrapped his arm around Bethany's waist. I knew he was comforting her, assuring her that the strange, solitary young woman with the magical way with flowers was happy to be having a fatherless child.

I was not.

4.

I bought a black dress in Union Square and four dozen purple irises from a bucket on Market Street. The black dress concealed my bulge and would lessen the brazen hands; the irises would become my business cards. I cut lavender paper into rectangles and punched a hole in each. On one side I wrote *Message* in a scripty, Elizabeth-inspired hand. On the other I wrote *Victoria Jones, Florist,* in my own plain print. I included Natalya's phone number.

There was only one stumbling block, and it turned out to be more complicated than I had thought. I still had Renata's wholesale card, but I couldn't buy my flowers at the flower market. Grant was there every day except Sunday. It wouldn't be possible to buy flowers on Sunday for a wedding the following Saturday. I had planned to drive to San Jose or Santa Rosa for the nearest wholesale market, but when I began to look,

I learned there weren't any others in all of Northern California. Florists drove for hundreds of miles in the middle of the night to buy flowers in San Francisco.

I considered buying the flowers at a retail shop, but after calculating the cost, I realized I wouldn't make a profit this way; it might even end up costing me money. So, on the Friday before the wedding, I drove to The Gathering House, walked up the cement stairs, and knocked on the heavy door.

A thin girl with white-blond hair let me in.

"Anyone here need a job?" I asked. The blond girl walked down the hall and didn't come back. A cluster of girls on the couch looked at me with suspicion.

"I used to live here," I said. "I'm a florist now. I have a wedding tomorrow, and need help buying flowers." A few of the girls stood up and crossed the room to join me at the dining room table.

By way of an interview, I asked the girls three questions, listening to their responses one at a time. The first question — Do you have an alarm clock? — elicited a solemn series of nods. The second — Do you know how to get to 6th and Brannan by bus? — eliminated a short, overweight redhead at the end of the table. She did not, under any circumstance, she told me, ride the bus. I flicked her away with my thumb and forefinger.

I asked the remaining two girls why they needed the money. The first to respond, a Latina girl named Lilia, rattled off a long list of desires, some essential, but many self-indulgent. Her highlights were growing out, she said, she was almost out of lotion, and she didn't have any shoes that matched the outfit her boyfriend had given her. She mentioned rent as an afterthought. I liked her name but not her answers.

I couldn't see the last girl's eyes under her long bangs. When she occasionally wiped them off her face, she would leave her hand in their place over her forehead. But her answer to my question was simple and exactly what I was waiting for. If she didn't make rent, she said, she would be evicted. Her voice choked as she said it, and she slid her face down into her turtleneck sweater until only her nose peeked above the knit. I was looking for someone desperate enough to hear an alarm clock at three-thirty a.m. and actually get out of bed; this girl would not disappoint me. I told her to meet me at the bus stop on Brannan, a block from the flower market, at five a.m. the following day.

The girl was late. Not late enough to hinder my ability to complete the arrangements on time but enough to make me worry. I didn't have a backup plan, and I would rather leave Bethany at the altar without a bouquet than risk seeing Grant. Every time I thought of him, my body ached and the baby squirmed. But the girl arrived, sprinting and out of breath, fifteen minutes after we had agreed. She had fallen asleep on the bus and missed her stop, she said, but would work fast and make up the time. I handed her my wholesale card, a stack of cash, and a list of flowers.

While the girl was inside, I patrolled the outside of the building, fearful that she would try to make a run for it with the money. The many emergency exits worried me; I hoped they were alarmed. But half an hour later, the girl emerged, her arms full of flowers. She handed them to me with the change, and then went back inside for the second half. When she returned, we loaded the flowers into my car, driving back to Potrero Hill in silence.

I had covered the downstairs floor with thick painter's plastic. Natalya said I could do whatever I wanted with the downstairs during the day, as long as it didn't interfere with her band's ability to practice at night. The vases I had purchased on sale at a dollar store were lined up in the center of the room, already filled with water, and a roll of ribbon and pins sat beside them.

We set to work on the ground. As the girl watched, I demonstrated how to de-thorn roses, trim leaves, and cut stems at an angle. She prepared the flowers while I began the arrangements. We worked until my legs began to cramp, the weight of my body heavy on the floor. I went upstairs to stretch, and retrieved the acacia and honeysuckle I had gathered. It sat on the middle shelf of the refrigerator, next to a package of cinnamon rolls and a gallon of milk. I gathered everything and carried it downstairs, holding the pastry box out to the girl.

"Thanks," she said, taking two. "My name's Marlena, in case you forgot."

I had forgotten. There was little memorable about Marlena. Everything about her was plain, and even her plainness was hidden by long hair and baggy clothes. She shook her head and blew forcefully over her upper lip so that her bangs parted and settled on either side of her brown eyes. Her face, which I could finally see, was round, with smooth, unblemished skin. She wore an enormous fleece sweatshirt that hung almost to her knees and made her look like a lost child. When she finished eating, her bangs fell onto her face again; she didn't move them.

"I'm Victoria," I said. I handed her a tall iris from a vase by the table. She read the card.

"You're lucky," she said. "A businesswoman with a baby on the way. I don't think many of us are going to make it like you have."

I didn't tell her about my months in McKinley Square, or the dread I felt every time I remembered that the churning mass growing inside me would become a child: a screaming, hungry, living thing.

"Some will, some won't," I said. "Same as everywhere." I finished my cinnamon roll and started back to work. Hours passed, and occasionally Marlena would ask a question or compliment my arrangements, but I worked beside her in silence. My mind was full of memories of Renata, my first morning with her at the flower market, learning to buy flowers, and later that same day, sitting at her long table, the nod of her approval punctuating each bouquet I assembled.

When we were done, Marlena helped me put the flowers in my car, and I got out my cash. "How much do you need?" I asked.

Marlena was prepared for the question. "Sixty dollars," she said. "To pay rent on the first. Then I can stay another month."

I counted out three twenties, paused, and

gave her a fourth. "Here's eighty," I said. "Call me at the number on the card every Monday. I'll tell you when I have more work."

"Thank you," she said. I could have taken her home — the wedding was only a few blocks from The Gathering House — but I had tired of company. I waited for her to walk around the corner before climbing into the car and driving to the beach.

The wedding was perfect. The roses did not snap; the honeysuckle draped but did not tangle. Afterward, I stood at the entrance to the parking lot and handed an iris to every guest. No one touched my stomach. I did not attend the reception.

I hadn't told Natalya about my business, so I rarely left the house and always answered the phone. "Message," I would say into the receiver, my intonation a mixture of question and statement. Natalya's friends would leave her a message, and I would tape notes to her bedroom door. Customers would introduce themselves and explain their events, and I would pinpoint their desires through a chain of questions or invite them downstairs for a consultation. Bethany's friends were wealthy, and no one, even once, asked the price of a flower. I charged more when

I needed the money, less as my business began to grow.

As I waited for the phone to ring and my appointment book to fill, I made two additional sets of boxes. I didn't like the idea of strangers sitting at the table, fingering my blue box, and I needed a box organized by flower, as Grant's had been. From the negatives I'd kept, I printed new photographs, mounted them on plain white cardstock, and filed them in shoeboxes I scavenged. One set I placed on the downstairs table, the second set I gave to Marlena, telling her to memorize every card. My blue box I returned to my room, safe behind the row of deadbolts.

I was called for a baby shower in Los Altos Hills, a toddler's birthday party in a wood-floored flat on California Avenue, and a wedding shower in the Marina, across the street from my favorite deli. I had three holiday parties and a New Year's party at Bethany and Ray's. Everywhere I went, I brought a silver bucket of irises, all tagged. By January, Marlena had made enough to pay first and last months' rent for her own apartment, and I had sixteen summer weddings scheduled.

I didn't take requests for anything for the entire month of March, and my February engagements made me nervous. Four plastic one-gallon containers of dittany sat in the corners of the blue room. Without light, the plant would never bloom. I kept the light off and tried to delay the inevitable.

But the baby within me, despite my dread, continued to grow. My stomach was so big by late January that I had to tilt the seat of my small car as far back as it would go. Even then, there was only an inch between my belly and the steering wheel. When the baby jabbed an elbow or a foot forward, it felt as though it was reaching out to take control of the car. I wore men's clothes, T-shirts and sweatshirts that were too big and too long, and elastic-waist pants pulled low over my stomach. Occasionally, I passed as overweight, but most of the time I still fell prey to curious hands.

I met with clients as little as possible in the final month of my pregnancy, and delivered flowers well before guests arrived, leaving the bucket of iris behind. My ever-sloppier appearance was out of place among the well-dressed women, and I could see, though they pretended otherwise, that it made them uncomfortable.

Mother Ruby began to appear with frequency, only halfheartedly making excuses for her visits. Natalya was looking thin, she told me the first time, and she had baked a tofu casserole. Neither Natalya, who was not looking thin, nor I ate it. Tofu was one of the few foods I couldn't stomach. When Natalya left to go on her first monthlong tour — the spread of her fan base had widened — I threw the casserole away in its heavy glass dish. Alone in the apartment, I began looking out the window before leaving, and if Mother Ruby sat on the sidewalk below, I would return to the blue room and lock all six locks.

Renata had told her mother of my pregnancy, I knew. Natalya wouldn't have invited the frequent visits, and Renata, despite firing me, cared about my well-being, and had, inexplicably, from the moment we met. In the early mornings, as I arranged flowers on the downstairs floor, I would see her drive by, her truck heavy on the way to her shop. Our eyes would catch, and she would wave, and sometimes I would wave back, but she never stopped, and I never stood up.

In preparation for the baby, I gathered minimal newborn supplies: blankets, a bottle, formula, pajamas, and a hat. I couldn't think of anything else. Wrapped in a numb paralysis, I purchased it all without anticipation or anxiety. I was not afraid of childbirth. Women had given birth since the beginning of time. Mothers died, babies died; mothers lived, and babies lived. Mothers raised babies and abandoned them, boys and girls, healthy and defected. I thought of all the possible outcomes, and not one seemed more tolerable than any of the others.

On the twenty-fifth of February I awoke swimming in water, and the pain started immediately after.

Natalya was still touring, and I was grateful for that. I had imagined biting pillows to muffle the sounds of childbirth, but there was no need. It was a Saturday, the adjacent office buildings were closed, and our apartment was empty. I opened my mouth at the first wavelike contraction, and a low growl came from somewhere within me. I did not recognize my voice or the burning pain in my body. When it passed, I closed my eyes and imagined myself floating on a deep blue sea.

I floated for a minute, maybe two, before the pain returned, sharper than before. Rolling onto my side, I felt the walls of my stomach like steel, closing in around the baby, pushing it down. The fur floor came out in wet clumps under the grasp of my fingers, and when the pain passed, I drummed angry fists against the bare patches.

The smell of dittany and damp soil seemed to be beckoning the baby, and all I wanted was to leave. It would be different on the cold cement sidewalk, I thought, amid traffic and noise. The baby would understand that there was no space in the world for a gentle entrance, nothing soft or welcoming. I would walk to the Mission and buy a donut, and the baby would get high on chocolate glaze and decide to remain unborn. Sitting in a hard plastic booth, the pain would stop; it had to.

Crawling out of the blue room, I tried to stand up. But I couldn't. The contractions were a sweeping undertow, pulling me down. On all fours, I crept to the stool pushed against the kitchen counter, my neck dangling on the low metal bar. Perhaps my neck would snap, I thought with some optimism. Perhaps my head would roll off, severed, and this would be over. I opened my mouth and bit down on the metal as the next contraction overwhelmed me.

When the pain released, I craved water. Sliding across the wall to the bathroom, I bent over the sink, turned on the faucet, and cupped handfuls into my open mouth. It wasn't enough. I turned on the water in the shower and pulled myself into the bathtub, the steady stream running into my mouth and down my throat. Turning around, I let the water soak through my clothes and down the length of my body. I stayed that way, the top of my head against the wall and the pressure drumming my lower back, until I ran out of hot water and stood, shivering, in dripping clothes.

Outside the shower, I leaned over the sink and began to swear, my voice deep and angry. I would hate my child for this. Mothers must all secretly despise their children for the inexcusable pain of childbirth. I understood my own mother in that moment as clearly as if we had just been introduced. I imagined her sneaking out of the hospital alone, her body split in two, abandoning her perfect swaddled baby, the baby she had exchanged for her own once-perfect body, her own once-pain-free existence. The pain and sacrifice were not forgivable. I did not deserve to be forgiven. Looking in the mirror, I tried to imagine my mother's face.

The searing of the next contraction caused me to double over, my forehead pressed against the curved metal faucet. When I lifted my head and looked back into the mirror, it was not my imagined mother's face I saw but Elizabeth's. Her eyes were glazed, the way they got during the harvest, wild and full of anticipation.

I wanted, more than anything, to be with her.

5.

"Elizabeth!" I called.

My voice was frenzied, desperate. An early moon rose above Perla's trailer, and the low rectangular structure cast a dark shadow up the hill to where I stood. Elizabeth responded to my voice immediately, turning to race along the edge of the shadow. She slipped in and out of the darkness until she stood before me. Moonlight illuminated the few silver hairs curling around her temples. Her face, in shadows, was a compilation of angles and lines accented by two soft, round eyes.

"Here," I said. My heart beat audibly. I held out a single wine grape, polished it against my damp T-shirt, and held it out to her again.

Elizabeth took the grape and looked at me. Her mouth opened and closed. She chewed once, expelled seeds, chewed, swallowed, and chewed again. Her face changed. The strain lifted, and the sugar from the grape seemed to sweeten her skin; she flushed a youthful pink, smiled, and, without a moment's hesitation, enclosed me in her strong arms. My great accomplishment expanded into the air around us until we were enveloped, protected in a bubble of our mutual joy. I leaned into her, proud, glowing, wrapping my arms around her waist, my feet still and my heart racing.

Holding me at arm's length, she looked into my eyes. "Yes," she said. "Finally."

We had been searching for the first ripe grape for nearly a week. A sudden rise in temperatures had caused a spike in sweetness so sudden it was impossible to accurately evaluate the thousands of plants. Elizabeth, frantic, began to order me around as if I was an extension of her own tongue. Acres went untouched while Elizabeth and I split up and went row by row, sucking out centers, chewing skin, and spitting seeds. Elizabeth gave me a pointed stick, and in front of every vine I tasted I was to draw an O or an X, her symbols for sun and shade, followed by my sugar-tannin count. I started by the road: O 71:5, moved to behind the trailers: X 68:3, and then climbed the hill above the wine cellar: O 72:6. Elizabeth paced acres far from where I tasted but eventually came back to retrace my steps, tasting every second or third row and comparing it to my notes.

She hadn't needed to question my ability, and she knew that now. She kissed my forehead, and I rocked toward her on my toes. For the first time in months, I felt wanted, cherished. Elizabeth sat down on the hillside and pulled me to her. We sat together in silence, watching the moon rise.

Our required focus on the approaching harvest had dulled Grant's warning. There had been no time to think about Catherine or her threat. Now, surrounded by ripe grapes, our veins pounding with love for each other and for the vineyard, his words returned. I felt a rush of nerves.

"Are you worried?" I asked.

Elizabeth was quiet, her expression thoughtful. Before she spoke, she turned and brushed my bangs away from my eyes, stroking the side of my face. She nodded. "About Catherine, yes," she said. "Not the vineyard."

"Why?"

"My sister isn't well," she said. "Grant didn't say much, but he didn't have to. He was terrified. You'd understand if you'd seen his face, and also if you knew my mother."

"What do you mean?" I didn't understand how Elizabeth's dead mother had anything to do with Catherine's present condition, or the fear in Grant's face.

"My mother was mentally ill," Elizabeth said. "I didn't even see her for the last few years of her life. I was too afraid. She didn't remember me, or she'd remember some awful thing I'd done and blame me for her illness. It was horrific, but I shouldn't have just left her alone, left Catherine with the burden."

"What could you have done?" I asked.

"I could have cared for her. It's too late now, obviously. She passed away almost a decade ago. But I can still care for my sister — even if she doesn't want me to. I've already talked to Grant about it, and he agrees that it's a good idea."

"What?" I was shocked. Elizabeth and I had tasted grapes twelve hours a day for a week. I couldn't imagine when she'd had time to talk to Grant.

"He needs us, Victoria, and Catherine does, too. Their house is almost as big as ours — there'll be plenty of room for all of us." I shook my head back and forth slowly, and then picked up speed as what she was suggesting sank in. My hair flapped around my ears and hit my nose. She wanted us to move in with Catherine. She wanted me to live with, help care for, the woman who had ruined my life.

"No," I said, jumping up and away from Elizabeth. "You can go, but I won't."

When I looked at her, she turned away, and my words hung in the air between us.

6.

I wanted Elizabeth.

I wanted her to hold me as she had among the vines, clean my sweat-drenched face and shoulders with the same thorough, gentle touch she had used to clean my thorn-punc-tured palms. I wanted her to wrap me in gauze and carry me to breakfast and tell me not to climb trees.

But she was unreachable.

And even if I did somehow reach her, she wouldn't come.

Without warning, I threw up into the sink and gasped for air. There wasn't any time to breathe. The contractions hit me like a wall of water, and I was sure that I would drown. Picking up the phone, I dialed the number for Bloom. Renata answered. Through my desperate gasping, I heard her voice regis-ter understanding. She slammed down the phone.

Minutes later she was in the living room.

I had crawled back into the blue room on all fours, my feet sticking out the half-door. "I'm glad you called," Renata said. I drew my feet into the room until I was curled into a ball on my side. When Renata tried to peek in, I closed the door in her face.

"Call your mother," I said. "She has to come get this baby out of me."

"I already did," Renata said, "and she was nearby. Probably on purpose. She has premonitions about these things. She'll be here any minute."

I screamed and rolled over onto my hands and knees.

Without hearing her enter, Mother Ruby was there, undressing me. Her hands were all over my body, inside and out, but I didn't care. She would get the baby out. Whatever she had to do, I was ready. If she'd produced a knife to slice me open on the spot, I wouldn't have looked away.

Reaching for me, she held a paper cup and straw to my lips. I sipped something cold and sweet. Afterward, she wiped the corners of my mouth with a cloth.

"Please," I said, "please. Whatever you have to do. Just get it out."

"You're doing it," she said. "You're the only one that can get this baby out."

The blue room was on fire. Water is not

supposed to be flammable, but there I was, drowning and burning simultaneously. I could not breathe; I could not see. There was no air; there was no exit.

"Please," I said, my voice breaking.

Mother Ruby crouched down, her eyes level with mine, our foreheads touching. She placed my arms around her shoulders, and I moved from knees to feet as if she might pull me out of the blazing water, but she didn't move. We were low to the ground, and she was listening.

"The baby's coming," she said. "You're bringing her here. Only you can do it."

It was right then that I understood what she was telling me. I started to cry, my moaning wails remorseful. This time, there was no escape. I could not turn away, could not leave without accepting what I had done. There was only one way to the other side, and that was through the pain.

Finally, my body surrendered. I stopped fighting, and the baby began to move — slowly, excruciatingly — down the birth canal and into Mother Ruby's waiting arms.

7.

It was a girl. She was born at noon, just six hours after my water broke. It felt like six days, and if Mother Ruby had told me it had been six years, I would have believed her. I emerged from the birth with a sense of peaceful exultation, and the smile that greeted me in the bathroom mirror hours later did not belong to the angry, hateful child who transported buckets of thistle from roadside ditches. I was a woman, a mother.

Mother Ruby said it was a perfect birth and a perfect baby, and she told me I would be a perfect mother. She bathed her while Renata went to the store for diapers, and then placed the warm bundle in my arms for the first time. I expected her to be asleep, but she wasn't. Her eyes were open, taking in my tired face, short hair, and pale skin. Her face twitched into what looked like a squinty smile, and in her wordless expression I saw gratitude, and relief, and trust. I wanted, desperately, not to disappoint her.

Mother Ruby lifted my shirt, cupped my breast, and pressed the baby's face against my uplifted skin. The baby opened her mouth and began to suck.

"Perfect," Mother Ruby said again.

She *was* perfect. I knew this the moment she emerged from my body, white and wet and wailing. Beyond the requisite ten fingers and ten toes, the beating heart, the lungs inhaling and exhaling oxygen, my daughter knew how to scream. She knew how to make herself heard. She knew how to reach out and latch on. She knew what she needed to do to survive. I didn't know how it was possible that such perfection could have developed within a body as flawed as my own, but when I looked into her face, I saw that it clearly was.

"Does she have a name?" Renata asked when she returned.

"I don't know," I said, stroking the baby's fuzzy ear as she continued to suck. I hadn't ever thought about it. "I don't know her yet."

But I would. I would keep her, and raise her, and love her, even if she had to teach me how to do it. Holding my own daughter in my arms, only hours old, I felt that everything in the world that had been so far out of my reach was now possible.

The feeling stayed with me for exactly a week.

Mother Ruby stayed until almost midnight and returned early the next morning. In the eight hours I spent alone with the baby, I listened to her breathing, counted her heartbeats, and watched her fingers stretch open and close into fists. I smelled her skin, her saliva, and the oily white cream that had resisted Mother Ruby's washcloth and nestled in the creases of her arms and legs. Rubbing every inch of her body, my own fingers became slick with the thick residue.

Mother Ruby had told me the baby would sleep for six or more hours the first night, exhausted from the birth. *It's the first gift that a child gives its mother,* she had told me before she left. *Not the last. Take it, and sleep.* I tried to sleep, but my mind was full of wonder at the existence of a child, a child who had not existed in the world only the day before, a child whose life had come from within my own body. Watching my baby sleep, I understood that she was safe, and that she knew it. I felt a rush of adrenaline at this simple accomplishment. The next morning, when I heard Mother Ruby fit a key into the downstairs lock, I hadn't slept for even a moment.

Mother Ruby pulled her great birthing bag up the steps and unzipped it at the door of the blue room. The baby was awake and nursing. When she pulled away from my breast, Mother Ruby listened to her heart and slipped her into a cloth sling with a metal spring that was somehow also a scale. She exclaimed at the ounces the baby had gained — unusual, she said, in the first twenty-four hours. The baby whimpered and began to suck air. Mother Ruby pressed her against my other breast, checking the baby's latch with her index finger.

"Keep eating, big girl," she said.

We both watched the baby nurse, her eyes closed, temples beating. It was the last thing in the world I had ever expected to do, breast-feed a baby. But Mother Ruby insisted it was what was best for us both; that the baby would thrive and we would bond and my body would regain its shape. Mother Ruby was proud, and told me so two or three times an hour. Not all mothers have the patience, she said, or the selflessness, but she knew I would. I had not disappointed her.

I was proud, too. Proud that my body was producing everything my baby needed, and proud that I could tolerate the relentless clamping of the baby's jaw, the sensation of liquid transferring from deep within my body to deep within my daughter's. The baby nursed for more than an hour, but I didn't mind. The feeding gave me time to study her face, memorize her short, straight eyelashes; her naked brow; the pinprick white dots scattering her nose and cheeks. When her eyes flitted open, I studied the dark gray, looking for signs of the brown or blue they would become. I wondered if she would resemble me or Grant, or if she would look like a maternal or paternal relative, none of whom I had met. I did not yet recognize anything about her.

Mother Ruby scrambled eggs while reading aloud from a book on newborn care. She fed me small bites while quizzing me on the text. I listened to every word and repeated every answer verbatim. Mother Ruby stopped reading when the baby fell asleep and refused to continue, even when I pleaded with her to keep going.

"Sleep, Victoria," Mother Ruby said, closing the book. "It's the most important thing. Postpartum hormones can warp reality if they aren't tempered with generous stretches of sleep." She reached her arms out for me to hand her the baby. Although sleep was already pulling me under, I was reluctant to hand her my daughter. Separation, I feared, could be irreversible. The pleasure I found in the baby's touch was new and unreliable; I was afraid if I gave her up I wouldn't be able to bear her touch when she was returned.

But Mother Ruby did not understand my hesitation. She reached in and withdrew the baby, and before I could protest, I was asleep.

Mother Ruby was not the only one to visit that first week. The day after the birth, Renata shopped for a featherbed for the blue room and a Moses basket for the baby, carrying them upstairs in two trips. She came back every afternoon with lunch for both of us. I lay on my new featherbed with the half-door open, the baby asleep with her cheek pressed against my bare breast, as I ate noodles or sandwiches with my hands. Renata perched on a bar stool. We rarely talked; neither she nor I could communicate in the presence of my nakedness, but our silence grew more comfortable as the days passed. The baby ate and slept and ate again. As long as she stretched across my body, skin to skin, she was content.

On Tuesday, while Renata and I ate in our accustomed silence, Marlena came to the door. I'd stopped answering the phone, and we had an anniversary dinner the following day. Renata let her in, and she delighted over the baby. She held and rocked and shushed her with a naturalness that caused Renata to raise her eyebrows and shake her head. I asked Renata to retrieve cash from my backpack and give it to Marlena; she would have to do the flowers for the dinner herself.

"No," Renata said. "You keep her here. I'll do the flowers." She got out the cash and also my event calendar, where I had written the purchasing list and the address of the restaurant. Renata scanned the book. I had nothing else for thirty days.

"I'll be back with lunch tomorrow," she said. "And I'll show you the centerpieces. You can approve them."

She turned to Marlena and shook her hand awkwardly under the sleeping ball of baby. "I'm Renata," she said. "Stay here as long as you can today, and come back tomorrow as well. I'll pay you whatever hourly rate you usually make."

"Just to hold the baby?" Marlena asked.

Renata nodded.

"I will," Marlena promised. "Thank you." She spun in slow motion, and the baby sighed, sound asleep.

"Thank you," I said to Renata. "I could use a nap." I hadn't slept deeply in days, always aware, even in sleep, of the baby's location and needs. It seemed I had inherited a maternal gene after all, I thought, remembering Renata's words on the drive to our first dinner together.

Renata walked over to where I lay on the featherbed, my hand reaching out the half-door and stretching into the living room. She stood over me as if trying to figure out how to hug me but gave up and nudged my hand gently with her big toe. I squeezed her foot, and she smiled. "See you tomorrow," she said.

"Okay."

Renata's boots padded down the stairs. The metal frame of the door rattled as she walked out.

"What's her name?" Marlena asked, kissing the baby's sleeping forehead. She settled onto one of the bar stools, but the baby stirred. Standing up again, she walked the length of the room and back with a slow sway.

"I don't know," I said. "I'm thinking about it."

I hadn't actually thought about it, but I knew I needed to start. Even though I wasn't doing anything but feeding and diapering and swaddling, there didn't seem to be space, mental or otherwise, for anything else. Marlena moved into the kitchen, the baby nuzzling the length of her chest and pressing her pink cheek against Marlena's shoulder. She began to cook with one hand. Easily. I couldn't cook, and I definitely couldn't cook one-handed with a baby on my shoulder.

"Where'd you learn?" I asked.

"To cook?"

I nodded. "And babies."

"My last foster home had a daycare. The woman kept me because I home-schooled and helped with the infants. I didn't mind. It was better than high school."

"You home-schooled?" I asked. My mind flashed back to the task list on Elizabeth's refrigerator door; I checked my watch reflexively.

"Yeah," she said, "the last few years. I was so far behind, the county thought it might help me get caught up, but I just got further behind. When I turned eighteen, I gave up on school and moved in to The Gathering House."

"I was home-schooled, too," I said. One o'clock. Elizabeth would have been just drying and putting away the last dish, drilling me on my eights, maybe my nines.

Something simmered on the stove, and Marlena added salt. I was surprised she had found anything to cook in the empty cabinets. The baby startled awake, and Marlena transferred her to the other shoulder. She angled the baby so she could see what she was cooking and mumbled something soft, a prayer or a poem, that I couldn't make out. The baby closed her eyes.

"You're better with kids than flowers," I said.

"I'm learning," Marlena said, not appearing offended.

"Yeah," I said, watching her work. "Me, too."

As Marlena chopped, the baby's head jiggled gently. "You should sleep," she said. "While the baby is happy. You know she'll be hungry again soon."

I nodded. "Okay," I said. "Wake me up if she needs anything."

"I will." Marlena turned back to the stove.

I closed the half-door, waiting for sleep. Marlena's soft lullaby floated through the crack, the tune familiar. As I drifted around the edge of consciousness, I wondered if someone had sung to me when I was a baby, someone who didn't love me, someone who would give me back.

On Saturday morning, a week after the birth, Mother Ruby arrived and began her daily routine. She asked me a hundred questions about my bleeding, after-pains, and appetite. She checked for evidence I had eaten dinner the night before, and listened to the baby's heart before wrapping her in the cloth scale.

"Eight ounces," Mother Ruby announced. "You're doing great." She unwrapped the baby and changed her diaper. In the process, the baby's umbilical cord, which I never touched and tried not to look at, snapped off.

"Congratulations, angel," Mother Ruby whispered into my daughter's sleeping face. The baby arched her back and reached out, her eyes still closed.

She cleaned the baby's belly button with something in an unlabeled bottle. Re-swaddling her, she handed her back to me. "No infections, eating, sleeping, and gaining weight," she said. "And you're getting help?"

"Renata brought food," I said. "And Marlena was here for a few days."

"Good." Roaming the room, she packed up her books, blankets, towels, bottles, and tubes.

"Leaving?" I asked with surprise. I was used to her spending most of the morning with me.

"You don't need me anymore, Victoria,"

she said, sitting next to me on the couch and putting her arm around my shoulders. She pulled me to her until my face was pressed against her breast. "Look at you. You're a mother. Believe me when I tell you there are many women out there who need me more than you do."

I nodded into her chest and did not protest.

She stood up and took a final loop around the small apartment. Her eyes settled on the cans of formula I had purchased before the baby was born. "I'll donate these," she said, stuffing them into her already-full bag. "You won't need them. I'll be back next Saturday, and then two Saturdays after that, just to check the baby's weight gain. Call me if you need anything."

I nodded again and watched her walk lightly down the stairs. She had not left her phone number.

You're a mother, I repeated to myself. I was hoping the words would reassure me, but instead I felt something familiar trembling inside of me. It started deep in my stomach and picked up momentum as it tumbled into the cavernous space that had once held the baby.

Panic.

I tried to breathe, willing it away.

8.

I regretted my ultimatum.

Choose me or choose your sister, my words had demanded. Elizabeth, by not running after me, had made her choice clear.

All night and well into the morning, I plotted. My desire was simple: to stay with Elizabeth, and Elizabeth alone. But I could think of no way to convince her. I could not whine or beg. *Do you even know me?* she would ask, her eyes amused, as I begged to eat her muffin batter. I could not hide; Elizabeth would find me, as she always did. I could not tie myself to the bedposts and refuse to move; she would cut the ropes and carry me.

There was only one possibility, and that was to turn Elizabeth against her sister. She had to see Catherine for what she was: a selfish, hateful woman unworthy of her care.

And then, all at once, I saw the solution. My heartbeat grew deafening as I lay still, turning the idea around in my head, looking for problems. There were none. As surely as Catherine had ambushed my adoption, she had provided me with the ammunition I needed to stay with Elizabeth, and Elizabeth alone. I would win the battle she had unconsciously waged, even before she knew she had waged it.

Slowly, I stood up. I slipped off my nightgown and pulled on a pair of jeans and a T-shirt. In the bathroom, I scrubbed my face with cold water and hand soap harder than usual, my fingernails scratching lines in the white soap residue. Looking at myself in the mirror, I searched for signs of fear, or anxiety, or apprehension of what was to come. But my eyes were flat, my chin set with determination. There was only one way to get what I wanted. It could not be ignored.

In the kitchen, Elizabeth washed dishes. A bowl of cold oatmeal sat on the table.

"The crews are already here," Elizabeth said, motioning with her head in the direction of the hill on which we'd stood the night before. "Eat your breakfast and put on your shoes before I leave you behind." She turned back to the sink.

"I'm not coming," I said, and in the drop of Elizabeth's shoulder blades, I could see disappointment but not surprise.

I opened the pantry and plucked an empty

canvas bag off a hook.

It was warm on the front porch, even though it was still early. I walked slowly down the long driveway, toward the road. Again, Elizabeth did not come after me. I wished it was cooler, wished I'd packed a bagful of food. I would be hot and hungry as I sat in the ditch in front of the flower farm. But I would wait. As long as it took for Grant to leave, even if I had to spend the night by the side of the road, I would wait. Eventually, his truck would rumble through the open gate, leaving the farmhouse exposed.

When it did, I'd sneak inside for what I needed.

9.

Renata did not come on Sunday. Neither did Marlena. I stayed in the blue room for what I thought was most of the day, nursing the baby and sleeping, but when I emerged with a full bladder and an empty stomach, it was only ten o'clock in the morning.

Leaning against the bar stool, I debated between showering and preparing a meal. The baby was asleep in the blue room, and I was hungry, but the scent of my own body, sour breast milk mixed with apricot baby oil, was causing me to lose my appetite. I decided on a shower.

I closed and locked the bathroom door out of habit, stripping and stepping under the hot water. My eyes closed, and I guiltily enjoyed the brief moment of solitude. Picking up a bar of soap, I heard a high-pitched wail. It was muffled by the locked door but piercing all the same. Inhaling, I continued to soap my body. *Just one minute,* I thought.

Just a quick shower and I'll be back. Hold on.

But the baby couldn't hold on. Her cry picked up both pitch and volume, and came around moments of quiet, desperate gasping. I began to shampoo my hair with frantic speed and let the water run into my ears, attempting to block out the sound. It didn't work. I had a strange sensation that I could have walked down the stairs, out the door, and across the city, and I still would have been able to hear her, that her cry was connected to my body through more than the physical waves of sound. She needed me, craved me like hunger, and the hunger spread from her body into my own.

Giving in to the sound, I jumped out of the shower, suds clinging to my hair and running in white rivers down my legs. I ran across the living room and reached into the blue room, picking up the rigid, screaming baby. I pressed her to my soapy breast. She opened her mouth and gasped and choked and sucked and repeated it all two or three times before she calmed down enough to nurse. In the shower, the water flowed into the empty ceramic tub and down the drain.

I slid down the wall and sat in the puddle at my feet. If I had owned a clean towel, I might have retrieved it. But there weren't any, and there wouldn't be any for a long time. I was no Marlena. I couldn't carry the baby and a bag of laundry up the hill, pressing quarters into vibrating machines with a hungry mouth on my exposed breast. I wished I had thought about the laundry before the baby was born.

I wished I had thought of a lot of things, now that it was too late. I should have bought diapers, and groceries, and baby clothes. I should have gathered the take-out menus of every restaurant on the hill and memorized the number of a delivery service. I should have found a daycare, or a nanny, or both. I should have bought a stack of parenting books and read every one. I should have decided on a name.

I couldn't do any of that now.

The baby and I would use dirty towels, sleep on dirty sheets, and wear dirty clothes. The idea of doing anything other than nursing and trying to nourish my own body was too overwhelming to consider.

We survived Monday, Tuesday, and Wednesday, alone except for a brief food drop from Renata. It was spring; business was picking up, and Renata had never replaced me. Marlena called to tell me she was taking the month to visit relatives in Southern California. She would be back, she said, in time for our April engagements. The phone did not ring again.

On Thursday the baby ate all day. She awoke for her first feeding just after six in the morning and nursed continuously, falling asleep mid-suck every half-hour. If I attempted to remove her from my breast, she startled awake with a deafening shriek. She would sleep only with her face pressed against my naked skin, and when I tried to set her down, no matter how deep in sleep she appeared, she would cry out for more milk.

I resigned myself to my own hunger, spending the morning listening to the sounds of spring enter the apartment through the open kitchen window. Birds, brakes, an airplane, a school bell. I stroked the baby's soft shoulder as she slept, and told myself that physical hunger was a reasonable sacrifice to make for a baby as beautiful as she. But as the day progressed, the hunger traveled from my stomach to my brain. I began to hallucinate, not sights but smells: phantom meatballs, a sauce simmering, and something dark chocolate baking.

By mid-afternoon I had convinced myself of the existence of a multicourse meal in my kitchen. I climbed out of the blue room with the baby still attached to my breast. When I saw the stove turned off, the burners bare, and the oven empty, I almost cried. I placed the baby on the kitchen counter and patted her distractedly while searching for something to eat. At the back of the cupboard I found a can of soup. The baby whimpered and started to cry. The sound weakened the muscles in my hands until it was impossible for me to turn the dial of the can opener. Giving up halfway around the can, I pried the lid back with a spoon and drank the soup cold, without pausing for breath. When it was empty, I threw the aluminum can into the sink. The baby startled at the loud sound and stopped crying long enough for me to press her face back to my breast. I carried her back to the blue room, my hunger unappeased.

Friday began as Thursday had, except that I was twenty-four hours more exhausted and as hungry as the never-satisfied baby. I ate peanuts in bed while the baby nursed. Mother Ruby had warned me that the baby would go through growth spurts, and I comforted myself with this thought. The end must be growing near. I didn't have much more to give her, I thought, slipping my finger under the flap of skin that had once been a round, full breast.

At noon I pulled the sleeping baby away

from my chest and saw that her lips were red. My nipples were dry and had cracked under the constant suction. The baby was drinking my blood as well as my milk; no wonder I was exhausted. Soon there would be nothing left of me. I eased her gently onto the bed, praying that just this once, she would stay asleep. There was one tray of Marlena's cooking left in the freezer.

But the baby awoke as I set her down, lifting her chin toward my sore nipple. I sighed. She couldn't possibly still be hungry, but I picked her back up and let her attempt to extract more milk from my deflated chest.

The baby sucked only two or three times before falling back asleep, her mouth falling open, but awoke again when I tried to set her down. She made a gurgling, sucking sound and puckered her lips.

I put her back to my breast more forcefully than I had intended. "If you're hungry, eat," I said, growing frustrated. "Don't fall asleep." The baby grimaced and latched on.

I sighed, regretting my impatient touch.

"That's good, big girl," I said, trying out Mother Ruby's words. They sounded forced and insincere on my tongue. I stroked the baby's hair, a wispy black tuft growing over her ear.

When she'd fallen back to sleep, I stood up

slowly and walked her to the Moses basket. Perhaps she would find comfort in the small, padded enclosure, I thought, lowering her a centimeter at a time. I had succeeded in putting her down but had not even withdrawn my arms when she started crying again.

Standing above her, I listened to her cry. I needed to eat. My grasp on reality was slipping with each additional empty-stomached hour, but I couldn't stand the sound of her wail. Good mothers did not let their babies cry. Good mothers put the needs of their babies first, and I wanted, more than anything, to be a good mother. It would make up for all the harm I had caused, if I could do something right, just this once, for another person.

Picking her up, I walked the length of the room and back again. My nipples needed a rest. I hummed and jiggled and paced as I had seen Marlena do, but the baby wouldn't be calmed. She twisted her face from side to side and began to suck in the cool oxygen, searching. I sat on the couch and pressed a soft, round pillow against her cheek. She was not fooled. She began to cry harder, sucking air and choking and stretching her short arms over her head. She could not possibly be hungry, I told myself again; she didn't need to eat.

The baby's face turned as red as the blood still leaking from my nipple. Walking over to the Moses basket, I set her inside.

In the kitchen, I banged my fists on the tile counter. I was hungry; the baby was not. I needed to take care of myself. I needed her to wait just an hour, while I filled my stomach and rested my nipples. From across the room, I could see her face, now near purple with desperation. She wanted me; she didn't understand that my body was not her own.

I walked out of the room, away from the noise, and stood at Natalya's window. I couldn't bring her to my breast. Not after nursing for nearly thirty-six hours straight. She had consumed all my milk, I was sure, and had moved on to something deeper, more precious, something connected to my heart or nervous system. She wouldn't be satisfied until she had devoured all of me, until she had sucked every fluid, thought, and emotion from me. I would be an empty shell, incoherent, and she would still be hungry.

No, I decided, she couldn't have any more. Mother Ruby would not be back until the next day, and there was no sign of Renata. I would go to the store for formula and feed her with a bottle until my nipples healed. I would leave her in her basket and run the whole way to the market and back. Bringing her to the grocery store would be too risky. Someone would hear her hungry, broken-hearted wail and understand my incompetence. Someone would take her away from me.

Grabbing my wallet, I sprinted down the stairs before I could change my mind. I ran up a hill and down the other side, not stopping for cars or pedestrians. I passed everyone. My body, still healing from the birth, felt as if it was splitting in half. A fire burned from between my legs and spread up my spinal cord to the back of my neck, but still I ran. I would be back before the baby even knew I was gone, I told myself. I would feed her a bottle in my arms, and she would finally, after days of nursing, be full.

The light was red at the busy intersection of 17th and Potrero. I stopped running and waited. Catching my breath, I watched the cars and pedestrians hurry in all directions. I heard a driver honk and swear, a teenager on an orange Schwinn singing something loud and cheerful, and a dog on a short leash growling at a brazen pigeon. But I did not hear my daughter. Even though I was blocks from the apartment, I was surprised. Our separation was simple and shockingly complete.

My heart regained its normal rhythm. I watched the light turn green, then red, then green again. The world continued its patterns, busy and oblivious to the crying baby six blocks away, the baby I had birthed but whose cries I could no longer hear. The neighborhood existed as it had a week ago and two weeks before that, as if nothing at all had changed. The fact that my life had turned upside down did not matter to anyone, and out on the sidewalk, removed from the source of the upheaval, my panic seemed unwarranted. The baby was fine. She was well fed and could wait.

I crossed at the next green light and walked slowly to the market. I bought six cans of formula, trail mix, a half-gallon of orange juice, and a turkey sandwich from the deli. Walking the long way home, I devoured fistfuls of almonds and raisins. My breasts filled and began to leak. I would let her nurse one last time, I thought, tenderness seeping into the space I had created between us.

I walked inside and up the stairs. The apartment was silent and looked empty, and for one moment it was easy to imagine I was coming home after delivering flowers for a shower and a nap, alone. My steps were silent on the carpet, but the baby awoke anyway, as if she could sense my presence. She began to cry.

I lifted her out of the basket, and we settled onto the couch, the baby attempting to nurse through the thin soaked cotton of my T-shirt. I pulled my shirt up, and she began to suck. Her wrinkled hands squeezed my outstretched finger as she latched on, the fact of my nipple in her mouth not enough to prove my return. As she nursed, I ate the turkey sandwich. A thin sliver of turkey escaped from my mouth and landed on her temple, rising and falling with her frantic suck. I leaned over, eating the turkey right off her face and kissing her at the same time. She opened her eyes and looked into mine. Where I expected anger or fear, I saw only relief.

I would not leave her again.

10.

It was dark when I returned to Elizabeth's.

From the dull glow of the upstairs windows, I imagined her sitting at my desk, heavy textbooks open before her, waiting. I had never missed dinner; she would be worried. Hiding the heavy canvas bag under the back porch steps, I walked inside. The screen door squeaked when I opened it.

"Victoria?" Elizabeth called down the stairs.

"Yeah," I said. "I'm home."

11.

Mother Ruby returned on Saturday, as she had promised she would. She sat down on the floor outside the blue room. I turned my face away. The weight of what I had done tormented me, and I was sure Mother Ruby would know. A woman who traveled to a neighborhood for a birth before being called would know when a baby was in danger. I waited for the accusation.

"Give me that baby, Victoria," she said, confirming my fears. "Come on, hand her over."

I slipped my pinkie finger between my nipple and the baby's gums as Mother Ruby had taught me to do. The suction released. I rubbed the baby's mouth with my thumb in an attempt to remove the dried blood from her upper lip but was unsuccessful. I passed the bundle over my shoulder without turning around.

Mother Ruby breathed her in. "Oh, big

girl," she said. "I've been missing you."

I waited for Mother Ruby to stand up and walk out the door, taking my daughter with her, but I heard only the sound of the springy scale. "Twelve ounces!" came Mother Ruby's elated voice. "Have you been eating your mama alive?"

"Pretty much," I murmured. My words soaked into the walls, unheard.

"You come out of there, Victoria," Mother Ruby said. "Let me rub your feet or cook you a grilled cheese sandwich. You must be exhausted caring for this baby like you have." I didn't move. I didn't deserve her praise.

Mother Ruby reached in and began to stroke my forehead. "Don't make me come in there," she said, "because you know I will."

Yes, I knew she would. The formula I had purchased was at my feet, still in the bag, evidence of my crime. I kicked it farther into the corner, rolled over, and crawled out feetfirst. Sitting on the couch, I waited for Mother Ruby to see the truth. But she didn't look at my face. She lifted my shirt and rubbed something from a lavender tube onto my cracked nipples. It was cooling and numbed the stinging pain.

"Keep this," Mother Ruby said, closing my palm around the tube. She turned my chin and looked into my eyes, my guilty, drowning eyes. "Are you sleeping?" she asked.

I considered the previous night. After finishing the sandwich, the baby and I had gone straight to the blue room, where she reattached herself to my body and closed her eyes. She sucked and swallowed and slept in an excruciating rhythm, and I let her, accepting the pain as punishment. I did not sleep.

"Yeah," I lied, "pretty well."

"Good," she said. "Your daughter is thriving. I'm so proud of you."

I looked out the window and did not respond.

"Are you hungry?" Mother Ruby asked. "Are you getting enough help? Do you want me to make you something before I leave?" I was starving, but I couldn't take another compliment. I shook my head.

Mother Ruby handed the baby back to me and put away her scale. "Okay, then," she said. Her eyes were on my face, studying me as if for clues, and I strained my neck away. I didn't want her to see me.

She stood to go, and I jumped up to follow. Suddenly, I was not afraid she would look into my face and see my trespass; it was more terrifying to think of her leaving in oblivion, without knowing what I had done, without doing something to stop me from doing it again. But Mother Ruby only smiled and leaned in to kiss my cheek before walking away.

I wanted to tell her, to come clean and beg forgiveness, but I didn't know what to say. "It's hard," was all I could manage, my whisper directed at her back as she descended the stairs. It wasn't enough.

"I know, love," Mother Ruby said. "But you're doing it. It's in you to be a mother, a good one." She walked down the stairs.

No, it isn't in me, I thought bitterly. I wanted to tell her that I had never loved anyone, and ask her to explain how a woman incapable of giving love could ever be expected to be a mother, a good one. But even as I thought the words, I knew they were not the truth. I had loved, more than once. I just hadn't recognized the emotion for what it was until I had done everything within my power to destroy it.

Mother Ruby stopped when she reached the bottom of the stairs and turned around. She looked small and ignorant, and my reliance on her felt misplaced. She was an intrusive old woman, I thought, nothing else. A switch flipped inside me, and I felt the return of the angry child I had once been. I wanted only for Mother Ruby to leave.

"Name?" she called up to where I stood. "Does that big girl have a name yet?"

I shook my head. "No."

"It'll come to you," she said.

"No," I said harshly, "it won't."

But Mother Ruby had already walked out the door.

After Mother Ruby left, I set the baby in her Moses basket, and through a small miracle she slept peacefully for most of the afternoon. I took a long, hot shower. My body was filled with a palpable despair — a numb, tingling sensation — and I scrubbed my limbs as if the irritation was external and could be washed down the drain. When I got out of the shower, my skin was pink and scraped red in patches. The despair had moved to a deeper, quieter place. I pretended I was clean and renewed, ignoring its low, persistent buzz. Dressing in loose pants and a sweatshirt, I rubbed the cream from the lavender tube on the patches of raw skin on my arms and legs.

I poured myself a glass of orange juice and sat on the floor, looking into the baby's basket. When she awoke, I would nurse her, and when she was done eating, we would go for a walk. I would carry the basket down the stairs and out the door, and the fresh air would be good for us both. Maybe I would carry her up to McKinley Square and give her a lesson in the language of flowers. She wouldn't respond, but she would understand. She had the kind of eyes, when they were open, that made me believe she understood everything I said and much of what went unspoken. They were deep, mysterious eyes, as if she was still connected to the place from which she had come.

The longer the baby slept, the more the despair subsided until I could almost make myself believe I had overcome its gravity. Perhaps my brief escape to the grocery store had not caused permanent damage, and I was, as Mother Ruby insisted, capable of the task before me. It was unrealistic to think I could make a clean break from the way I had lived for nineteen years. There would be setbacks. I had spent my life being hateful and solitary, and I could not, overnight, become loving and attached.

Lying down on the floor next to the baby, I breathed in the damp-straw smell of the basket. I would sleep. But before I had closed my eyes, her rhythmic breathing was replaced by the familiar sound of her open, searching mouth.

I peered into the basket, and she looked at me, her eyes wide open, her mouth moving.

391

She had given me an opportunity to sleep, and I had wasted it. There would not be another for hours, if not days. I picked her up. My eyes welled, and when her jaw clamped down, the tears leaked onto my cheeks. I brushed them away with the back of my hand. The relentless suction on my breast pulled the despair up from wherever it was that it had receded, whistling forth like the quiet roar of a conch shell, a reflection of something greater.

The baby nursed for an eternity. Transferring her from one side to the other, I checked my watch. It had been a full hour, and she was only half done. My sigh became a low moan as she latched on again.

When she finally fell asleep, I tried to replace my nipple, still tight between her lips, with my pinkie finger, but she cracked her tired eyes open and began to grunt in complaint.

"Well, I'm done," I said. "I need a break." I set her on the couch and stretched. Her grunts became a series of soft cries. I sighed. I knew what she wanted, and I knew how to give it to her. It seemed like it should be so simple. Maybe it was simple for other mothers, but it wasn't for me. I had handled her touch for hours, for days, for weeks, and I needed just a few moments to myself. As

I walked to the kitchen, she began to cry harder. The sound pulled me back.

I sat down and picked her up.

"Five more minutes," I said, "and then we're leaving. You don't need any more."

But when I placed her in the basket five minutes later, she cried as if I was sending her downriver, as if she would never see me again.

"What do you want?" I asked, the despair in my voice bordering on anger. I tried to jiggle the basket like Marlena had done, but when I shook it, she bounced and cried harder.

"You can't be hungry," I pleaded, leaning close to her small ear so that she could hear me over the sound of her own cry. She turned her face to mine and tried to attach herself to my nose. A hysterical sound escaped my body; a snorting that would have been mistaken for a laugh by an observer unaware of my approaching implosion.

"Fine," I said. "Here." I lifted my shirt and forced her onto my breast. She struggled to open her mouth against the pressure of my hand. When she finally got it open, she stopped crying and began to suck.

"This is it," I told her. "You better enjoy it." My words were threatening, and I listened to them as if they were coming from someone else.

Still nursing, I held on to the baby with one hand and crawled into the blue room, reaching in for the bag of formula and dumping it out. Six cans scattered on the floor. I reached to pick one up, and the baby lost her hold on my nipple. She began her heartbroken wail.

"I'm right here," I said as I crossed the room and set her on the kitchen counter, but my words didn't comfort either of us. The baby writhed on the countertop as I poured the can of formula into a bottle and screwed on the lid. Resting the plastic nipple against the baby's lips, I waited for her to open her mouth. When she didn't, I opened her lips with my fingers and forced the nipple inside. She gagged.

I took a breath and tried to calm myself. Carrying the baby and the bottle to the couch, I sat down and adjusted her position until her head was tucked into my elbow. I kissed her between the eyebrows. She tried to latch on to my nose again, and I slipped the bottle into her open mouth. She sucked once and then turned away, the formula dribbling out of the side of her mouth. She began to scream.

"Then you aren't hungry," I told her, setting the bottle down too hard next to me.

A thin stream of liquid shot out the top. "If you won't eat this, you aren't hungry."

I set her back in the basket gently. I would let her cry for two or three minutes, just to prove I was serious. When I picked her up again, she would take the bottle. She had to.

But she didn't. I let her cry another five minutes, and then another ten. I tried holding her. I tried feeding her in the basket. I tried laying her on my featherbed and reaching inside with the bottle, but still she refused to suck. Finally I gave up and closed the half-door. The baby cried out in the darkness of the blue room, alone.

Lying down on the living room floor, my eyes closed involuntarily. The sound of the cry became something distant and unpleasant but no longer overwhelming. For stretches I forgot the source of the sound or why I had tried to stop it. It passed over my body, leaving me untouched. The fog of my exhaustion was impenetrable.

It wasn't until the crying stopped that I jolted awake. I felt a rush of fear that I had killed the baby. It was dark outside. I had no idea how much time had passed. Perhaps hours without food and a room without light was enough to kill a newborn. I knew so little about newborns, about children, about human beings. It felt like a horrible joke to leave me alone with a baby, responsible for another life. I threw open the door to the blue room, but before I could even reach out to feel for her pulse, she began to cry.

My body was flooded with emotion, relief but also undeniable disappointment, followed immediately by shame. I held the baby to my body, kissing her head in an attempt to mask the desperation I could no longer bury. I stuck the bottle in the baby's mouth. She would learn to drink formula. Breast-feeding was too much for me. I would never be able to maintain it, and if I wanted to keep the baby, I needed to find a way to be a mother that I could handle. This time the baby tried to suck, but her lips were weak with hunger and the plastic was stiff and unresponsive.

The nipple must be defective. It was the clear explanation for my baby's stubborn refusal. Of the hundreds on the shelf, I had purchased the cheapest. I hurled the bottle into the kitchen, and it bounced off the wall and onto the floor. The baby began to cry.

I set her in the basket and walked away. My breasts were full and dripping onto the stained office carpet, but I would not give her milk from my body. It was too much. I would get her a new bottle, and she would take it. My panic would subside.

I took the steps two at a time, her cry growing louder as the distance between us increased. Running out onto the sidewalk, I sprinted the block faster than I ever had in my life. I crossed streets recklessly, running in the same direction I had to buy the formula just the day before. But when I got to Vermont Street, I turned left instead of right. I didn't think about where I was going, and I did not stop running until I reached the steps of McKinley Square. Digging heavy feet into the mowed lawn, I fell into the white verbena, rolling into my cavern beneath the heath and closing my eyes. I would give myself five minutes. Just five minutes in the park, and when I returned to the baby, I would be able to handle it. I covered my head with my arm, searching in the darkness for the brown wool blanket that wasn't there. Sleep pulled me under again, and I was protected, rocked, comforted. There was nothing but the darkness, the solitude, and the white petals of the verbena praying for me and for the child I wouldn't let myself remember.

12.

"I missed you today," Elizabeth said when I walked into the room.

She didn't ask where I'd been, and I didn't offer an explanation. I crawled into bed, pulling the covers up over my head and rolling onto my side, my back to the desk where she sat.

"I love you, Victoria," she said quietly. "I hope you know that." The first time she'd declared her love, I'd believed her. Now her words ran over my heart like water over a stone. The desk chair scraped against the wood floor as she stood, and I felt the mattress dip as she moved to the edge of the bed. She placed one hand on my shoulder.

"What did she do?" I asked.

The question was sudden and unplanned, and I felt Elizabeth's body flinch. She was quiet for a long time. Finally, she lay down on her back next to me.

"I loved a man, once," she said simply.

"It was a long time ago. He was English, here for an internship with one of the bigger wineries, just a few miles up the road. I was happier than I'd ever been. And then Catherine — my sister, my best friend — took him away from me."

Elizabeth rolled onto her side and draped her arm over my body. I stiffened but did not protest, waiting for her to continue. "A year later, Grant was born. For years I couldn't look at him without remembering his father, without replaying in my mind everything I'd lost. But his father was gone; I don't know if he ever knew Catherine was pregnant. She raised Grant completely alone."

Elizabeth inched closer until her bent legs tucked into the space behind my kneecaps. When she spoke next, her face was pressed into the blanket covering the top of my head so that I had to strain to hear her words.

"I had a chance to forgive her," she whispered. "Once, when Grant was still a baby, Catherine approached me at the farmers' market. She apologized, crying, and told me how much she missed me. It was my chance to have her back in my life, but instead I turned her away. I shouldn't have done it. I said awful things, things that keep me up at night."

She deserved it, I thought. Catherine de-

399

served everything Elizabeth had said and more. The idea that Elizabeth was about to move in to the home of the woman who had betrayed her made my chest fill with rage. I took a deep breath, willing myself to be patient.

For what seemed like hours, I waited for Elizabeth to speak, tense in her gentle grasp. But she was quiet, her story complete. Just as I began to worry that she had fallen asleep, she stood up and tiptoed out of the room. The faucet in the bathroom sink turned on and off, the toilet flushed, her bedroom door closed, and then all was quiet. I slipped out of bed.

Downstairs, I sneaked through the kitchen and out the back door. The canvas bag was underneath the steps where I had stashed it, full and heavy. I picked it up and hugged it to my chest. Inside, the glass jars clattered and resettled.

I had decided earlier, crouched in the ditch, exactly where I would go, and I walked quickly in the direction of the road. There was no moon, but the stars illuminated the property as I walked to the northeast corner. Here, wedged between the concrete of the farmers' market and the highway, the grapes were dusty and constantly dry. In the fall, they remained sour long after the other acres had ripened.

I unscrewed the lid of the first jam jar. Lighter fluid seeped over the edges and spiraled through the ridges at the lip of the glass. Slowly, I emptied it onto the trunk of the vine, holding the jar away from my body, so the fluid wouldn't run back to my bare toes. When the first jar was empty, I opened the second, moving down the row. The bag felt bottomless, and I began to move quickly, sloppily, the lighter fluid a wild spray from my hands to the vines. When I reached the end of the row, I retraced my steps, picking up the empty jars that littered the ground.

On the top porch step — in the same place Elizabeth and I had once sat, stringing chamomile — I lined up the jam jars, one after the other, and then went into the kitchen for matches.

I started back toward the road, looking for the wet trail. It ended by the driveway. I stepped back. Holding a fistful of matches together, I struck them on the wide, sandpapery strip of the box. One lit, and the others followed in a rush, until I held a flickering, glowing orb. The flame descended toward the tips of my fingers, and I waited until the heat grew uncomfortable, and then painful, before flicking it onto the ground.

There was a pause, and then a rushing

noise — like a river, tumbling — followed by a quick series of loud pops. Then the heat. Turning, I ran toward the house, as I had planned, for a pot of water. But the fire was faster than I was. Looking over my shoulder, I saw the flames fleeing away from me, following an invisible trail through the brush and vines. I had expected the fire to be contained to the trunks of the vines I'd soaked, to flicker there until I ran inside for buckets of water, but the fire didn't wait.

I leapt up the steps three at a time, racing into the kitchen. Replacing the matches, I screamed for Elizabeth. She rose immediately. I heard her thumping into my bedroom, calling my name.

"Downstairs!" I yelled. I was at the sink, filling a soup pot with water. The pipes of the old house clanked, and water emerged slowly, in breathy waves.

Clutching the full pot, I crossed the kitchen at the same moment Elizabeth descended the stairs, and we turned, shoulder to shoulder, our gaze drawn to the light.

The sky was purple. The stars were gone. As we watched, the fire dipped into the roadside ditch, a quarter-mile of dry thistle igniting in a single moment. The wall of flames that rose seemed to climb halfway to the sky. Beyond it, the surrounding properties disappeared, leaving Elizabeth and I completely alone.

Like electricity on wires, the fire spread in lines across the vineyard.

13.

I awoke when the sun rose. My body was sore, my cheek textured with the imprint of the forest. I'd slept six hours, maybe seven. Pushing up into a sitting position, I adjusted myself away from the two circular puddles under the heath.

The city was waking up. Engines sputtered to life, brakes screeched, birds sang. On the street below me, a school-age girl stepped off a bus. She was alone and walked quickly down the street, a bouquet of flowers in her hands. I couldn't see what she carried.

I exhaled. I wanted more than anything to be that girl, to be a child again and carry crocus or hawthorn or larkspur instead of buckets of thistle. I wanted to search the North Bay until I found Elizabeth, and apologize, and beg forgiveness. I wanted to start my life over, on a course that would not lead to this moment, this waking up alone in a city park, my own daughter alone in an empty apartment building. Every decision I'd ever made had led me here, and I wanted to take it all back, the hatred and the blame and the violence. I wanted to have lunch with my angry ten-year-old self, to warn her of this morning and give her the flowers to point her in a different direction.

But I couldn't go back. There was only now: this forest within a city and my own daughter, waiting. The thought filled me with dread. I did not know what I would find when I returned to the apartment. I did not know if she still screamed, or if time, solitude, and hunger had collapsed my daughter's lungs as completely as a rising tide.

I had failed my daughter. Less than three weeks after giving birth and making promises to us both, I had failed, and failed again. The cycle would continue. Promises and failures, mothers and daughters, indefinitely.

14.

My arms began to shake violently, water from the soup pot sloshing onto Elizabeth. The cold spray snapped her into action. She ran to the phone in the kitchen as I sprinted out the front door, tripping over the jam jars as I flew down the steps.

The water in the pot was not enough to save even one vine. Looking at the fire, I knew this. Yet I had to try. Acres burned, the heat dizzying. Everything Elizabeth had spent her life cultivating would be gone if I did not act. She would be left on scorched earth, homeless and alone. I had to put it out. If I didn't, I would never be able to look at her again.

Halfway to the road, I launched the water on a row of burning vines. If there was a sizzle, if even one flame surrendered, I didn't hear or see it. Up close, the roar of the fire was deafening, the smell of the smoke sugary. The scent reminded me of Elizabeth caramelizing apples, and I realized the sweet smell came from the grapes, the perfectly ripe grapes, charring.

From the porch, Elizabeth called me. I turned. In her glassy, helpless eyes the fire reflected. She clutched one hand over her mouth and the other over her heart. I turned away, the enormity of my error as thick as the smoke in my lungs. That I hadn't meant to cause so much damage didn't matter. That I had done it only to stay with her, because I loved her, would never matter. I had to put out the fire. If I didn't, I would lose everything.

Without making a conscious decision to do so, I ripped off my nightgown and began swatting at the flames, trying to suffocate them. The thin cotton, splattered with lighter fluid, exploded in my hands. Elizabeth ran toward me, frantic. She yelled at me to back away from the fire, but I continued flapping my flaming nightgown around my head wildly. Sparks flew from the scorched material, so that Elizabeth had to duck under them as she ran to me.

"Are you out of your mind?" Elizabeth screamed. "Get back to the house!"

I stepped closer to the fire, the heat intense and threatening. A stray spark singed my hair, traveling up a cluster of strands and melting into my scalp. Elizabeth slapped at my smoldering hairline, and the sting of the slap felt good, deserved.

"I'm putting it out!" I screamed. "Leave me alone!"

"With what?" Elizabeth demanded. "Your bare hands? The fire trucks are coming. You'll get killed standing here like an idiot, waving your hands in the air."

Still, I didn't back away. The flames leapt closer to where I stood.

"Victoria," Elizabeth said. She had stopped screaming, and her wide eyes filled. I strained to hear the words she uttered over the roar of the fire. "I'm not losing my vineyard and my daughter on the same night. I won't." When I didn't move, she lunged at me, grabbing me by the shoulders, shaking me. "Do you hear me?" she shouted. "I won't!" I wriggled free from her hands, and she caught me by one arm, pulling me toward the house. As I fought, she pulled harder, and I felt my shoulder pop out of the socket. She yelped and let go. Collapsing onto the ground, I pulled my knees in to my bare chest. The fire circled me like a blanket, and through the heat I heard the faraway sound of the trailer door slamming. Elizabeth screamed for me to get up, pulled at my feet, and kicked me in the ribs. When she tried to carry me, I screamed and bit at her like a wild animal.

Finally, she let me be.

15.

The baby was awake in the Moses basket when I returned. Her wide eyes blinked up at the ceiling, and she did not cry out when she saw me. I retrieved her bottle from the kitchen, emptied the day-old formula into the sink, and refilled it with a fresh can. Standing over the baby, I rested it on her lips. She opened her mouth but did not suck. I squeezed the nipple and watched the liquid run in a thin stream down her waiting tongue. She swallowed twice before falling asleep in the basket.

I showered and ate a bowl of cereal on the rooftop. Every time I walked by the baby's basket, I would pause and study her face, and if she opened her eyes, I would put the bottle to her lips. She learned to suck, slowly, placidly, without the urgent ferocity with which she had once devoured my breast. It took her all day to finish a single can of formula. She did not cry. She did not even whimper.

Before going to bed, I changed her sodden diaper but did not take her out of the basket. She seemed comfortable there, and I was afraid to break the fragile peace we had reached, afraid my panic would return at the sound of her first scream. Instead, I moved her basket to the couch, where we settled into a square of moonlight. I offered her a fresh bottle, and her lips formed a perfect circle around the amber-colored plastic. Tiny bubbles ran the length of the bottle as she persuaded water, iron, calcium, and protein through microscopic holes. Her eyes were wider than I had ever seen them, concentric circles and small triangles of white scanning my face. When she was done eating, the rubber nipple slipped from her mouth, and she reached her tiny fingers toward my face. I lowered my head until my nose was only inches from her hands, my eyes looking into hers. She opened and closed her fingers in the empty space between us, squeezing tight.

Before I realized I was crying, a tear dropped from the tip of my chin onto the baby's cheek. It ran in a thin line to the edge of her mouth, and her red lips puckered in surprise. I laughed, and the tears ran faster. The open forgiveness in her eyes, the uncensored love, terrified me. Like Grant, my daughter deserved so much more than I could give her. I wanted her to carry hawthorn, laugh easily, and love without fear. But I could not give her this, could not teach her what I didn't know. It would be only a matter of time before my toxicity would taint her perfection. It would leak out of my body, and she would swallow it with the willingness of a ravenous infant. I had hurt every person I had ever known; I wanted, desperately, to save her from the dangers of being my daughter.

I would bring her to Grant in the morning.

He would preserve her goodness and teach her everything she needed to know. Renata was right; Grant deserved to know his daughter. He deserved her sweetness, her beauty, and her unwavering loyalty.

When I pulled my face away, the baby's eyes were closed. I left the basket on the couch and shut myself in the blue room.

That night I smelled moss, dried leaves, and damp soil in my apartment of plaster and concrete, blocks and blocks from anything green or growing.

In the morning I hurried out of the apartment. Feeding the baby what was left of the formula in the bottle from the night before,

I carried her in her basket to my car. She was awake as we drove across the city. She had slept through the night, or, if she hadn't, she had not cried out. I had slept deeply and without dreams but awoke with the agitated alertness of the overtired. My body ached, my full breasts on fire, and I was hot in the cool morning. I rolled down the windows, and the baby grimaced in the strong wind.

Driving north on the freeway, I crossed the bridge and took the first wooded exit. I didn't have time to drive to one of the lush state parks, but it wouldn't matter. It had been a wet spring. I would find what I needed in any dense, shaded forest. I pulled in to a parking lot at a vista point overlooking the bay and the Golden Gate Bridge, which was rust-colored and glowing in the early-morning sun. Already the parking lot was half full with hikers pulling on boots and filling brightly colored plastic bottles with water.

Grabbing the basket by its woven handles, I started down a trailhead. The trail split and split again. I chose the path with the least sun and shuddered as I walked into the cool undergrowth. Hikers passed and cooed over the baby until I turned off the main trail and onto one marked *Reforestation. Do Not Trespass.* I lifted the basket over the thin chain and dropped out of sight into a circle of redwoods.

The baby didn't make a sound as I lay her down on the forest floor, the bald patch on the back of her head pressing against the soft duff. She looked up through the redwoods, her blurred, blue-eyed vision scanning the tall trees, patches of light, gray sky, and perhaps even what lay beyond it. I didn't doubt her.

I pulled out the large, flat putty knife I had stuck in the back pocket of my jeans and began to strip the spongy green moss from the trunks of the redwood trees. The moss fell to the ground in long, hairy patches, and I arranged them carefully around the bottom and sides of the basket, making sure the softest and most fragrant pieces would surround her tiny head.

When the basket was completely covered, I put the knife back in my pocket, picked up the baby, who had fallen asleep, and lay her down gently on the blanket of moss.

Maternal love.

It was all I could give her. Someday, I hoped, she would understand.

The spare key to Grant's door was where it had always been, inside the rusted tin watering can on the front stoop. I unlocked the door and carried the moss-lined basket into the kitchen, setting it down beside the spiral staircase in the corner of the room. From where the baby lay, she could look up three stories, and it seemed to amuse her well enough. She continued her quiet squinting while I moved about the kitchen, lighting the stove with a match and filling a kettle with water for tea. It had been nearly a year since I'd made tea in this kitchen, but everything was exactly as it had been before.

I sat down at the table while I waited for the water to boil. The baby was so quiet it was easy to forget her, easy to imagine I had returned only to surprise Grant with a cup of tea at the splintering table. I missed him. Sitting in his water tower, looking out over his flower farm, the feeling was impossible to ignore. And soon I would miss the baby. I pushed the thought from my mind and kept my focus on the flowers stretching across the fields below.

The baby made a sound between a sigh and a squawk just as the water started to boil. Steam clouded the kitchen window. I wondered if she could drink peppermint tea. It seemed like it might be good for her stomach, soothing, and I had brought the near-empty bottle but forgotten a can of formula. Dumping the congealing liquid down the drain, I rinsed the bottle and filled half with boiling water, half with tap water. I dropped in a tea bag and screwed on the top. The baby's nose wrinkled in surprise as she tasted the tea, but her lips worked the nipple hungrily and without complaint. Steam from the still-boiling water settled down on us. The moss glowed greener from the moisture in the air.

I balanced the bottle against the side of the basket so the baby could suck while I filled a soup pot with water and lit another burner. I wanted the moss to live for as long as possible. As the baby sucked, the water tower filled with hot, billowing steam. I carried the basket up the two flights of stairs to Grant's bed. The baby was asleep by the time I got to the top — a deep, motionless sleep that made me nervous about my choice of nourishment. Setting the basket down in the middle of the foam mattress, I lay down next to her, lowering my face until I could feel her quick exhales on my upper lip.

I stayed there — our noses nearly touching, our exhales joined — until the sun was dangerously high in the sky and Grant's arrival was imminent. Closing my eyes, I withdrew my face. The baby made the air-sucking whimper I remembered from the release of my nipple from her mouth, and my breasts ached with the memory. I pulled a small square of moss off the edge of the basket and rubbed it against her cheek, her chin, and tucked it into the crease where her neck would be, someday, when she was strong enough to lift her head. The moss pulsed with the beating of her heart.

Pulling myself away, I walked down the stairs. The pot on the stove was almost empty. I filled it to the brim, returned it to the stove, and slipped silently out the door.

My hatchback skidded down the long dirt driveway, and I continued toward the highway without looking back. What had started as a dull, dislocated ache had become centralized in my left breast. When I touched the nipple, a pain shot through my flesh and down my spine. I started to sweat. The windows were down, and I turned on the air-conditioning as well, but still I was hot. Glancing in the rearview mirror, I saw the empty seat where the baby had been. There was nothing but a thin spray of dirt and a single hair-fine coil of bright green moss.

I turned on the radio and spun the dial until I found something loud and vibrating, too many cymbals and a voice without words. It reminded me of Natalya's band. I drove faster, flying over the bridge and through intersections, neither red nor yellow lights slowing me down. I needed the blue room. I needed to lie down and close my eyes and sleep. I wouldn't emerge for a week, if I emerged at all.

Screeching to a stop in front of the apartment, I came bumper to bumper with Natalya's car. The trunk was open. Boxes and suitcases were stacked on the sidewalk. It was hard to tell if she was coming or going. I got out of the car quietly, hoping I could slip inside the blue room and lock all the locks without her noticing.

I tiptoed across the empty office space and nearly collided with Natalya at the bottom of the stairs. She did not step aside. I looked up and could tell by her expression that my face looked as hot as it felt.

"You all right?" Natalya asked. I nodded and tried to get by, but still she did not move. "Your face is pinker than my hair."

She reached out, touching my forehead, and recoiled as if she'd been burned. I pushed past her but tripped and fell on the bottom step. I didn't even try to stand but crawled on my hands and knees up the stairs. Natalya followed. Collapsing into the blue room, I pulled the door closed behind me.

Natalya tapped on the half-door. "I have to leave," she said, her voice a whisper, full of fear. "Our tour has been extended — I'll be gone for six months at least. I just came to get some things and tell you to use my bedroom if you want."

I didn't say anything.

"I really have to go," she said again.

"So go already," I managed to say.

Something loud hit the door, likely Natalya's foot. "I don't want to return in six months to the smell of your rotting corpse," she said, kicking the door again. The next thing I heard was the sound of her shoes stomping down the stairs and a car door slamming. The engine of her car sputtered and started. Then she was gone.

Would she call her mother? I wondered. Would she realize the baby was gone, and report me to the authorities? If she was going to call someone, I hoped she decided on the police; I'd rather do time than face Mother Ruby and her disappointment.

I lay on my left side on the featherbed, the hard rubber ball of my breast supported by the mattress. My body, which did not feel like my own, shook uncontrollably. I was freezing. I put on every sweatshirt I owned and pulled up the brown blanket. When that didn't warm me, I crawled underneath the featherbed. I stayed there, barely able to breathe, my body and mind an ice storm under a heavy cloud. My chill became something black and swirling, and I had the fleeting, comforting thought that the sleep I was entering was eternal, a state from which I might never return.

From far away, sirens whirled, growing louder, nearer, until they sounded as if they were coming from Natalya's bedroom. Flashing lights soaked under my door. And then, just as suddenly, they stopped.

For just a moment the room was black and silent as death; then the door was pushed in and I heard the trampling of feet on the stairs.

16.

I lay in an ambulance, strapped to a white cloth board. I couldn't remember how I got there. I was still in only my underwear, and someone had draped a hospital gown across my chest.

Beside me, Elizabeth sobbed.

"Are you her mother?" a voice asked. I opened one eye. A young man in a navy uniform sat near my head. Whirling lights shone through the window and flashed across his sweaty face.

"Yes," Elizabeth said, still crying. "I mean no. Not yet."

"She's a ward of the court?" he asked.

Elizabeth nodded.

"You'll need to report it, then, immediately. Or I will." The man looked apologetic, and Elizabeth wept harder. He handed her a heavy black phone, connected to the side of the ambulance by a cord that spiraled like the one in Elizabeth's kitchen. I closed my

421

eyes again. We drove through the night for what felt like hours, and Elizabeth didn't stop crying.

When the ambulance stopped, hands tucked the hospital gown under my arms. The doors opened. Cool air rushed in, and when I opened my eyes, I saw Meredith, waiting. She was still in her pajamas, a trench coat thrown on over them.

As we passed, she leaned forward, her hand reaching out to pull Elizabeth away from me. "I can take over from here," she said.

"Don't touch me," Elizabeth said. "Don't you dare touch me."

"Wait in the lobby."

"I'm not leaving her," Elizabeth said.

"You'll wait in the lobby or I'll have you escorted out by security," Meredith said.

I watched over my receding toes as Meredith left Elizabeth standing in the hall, shocked. She followed me into a room.

A nurse examined my body, recording my injuries. I had burns on my scalp and in a ring where the elastic of my cotton underwear had melted into my stomach. A dislocated arm fell limp at my side, and my chest and back were bruised where Elizabeth had kicked. Meredith recorded the nurse's findings in a notebook.

Elizabeth had hurt me. Not in the way that Meredith believed, but still, she had hurt me. The marks were indisputable evidence. They would be photographed and recorded in my file. No one would ever believe Elizabeth's story: that she had been trying to save me from running headlong into a raging blaze. Even though it was the truth.

And suddenly I saw, in the markings on my body, an undeniable escape route, a path away from Elizabeth's pain-filled eyes; a path away from the guilt, the regret, and the scorched vineyard. I could not face the pain I had caused Elizabeth. I would never be able to face it. It wasn't just the fire; it was a year's worth of transgressions, many small, some unforgivable. Mothering me had changed her. A year after I'd moved in to her home, she was a different woman, softened in a way that allowed suffering. With me in her life, she would only continue to suffer. She didn't deserve it. She didn't deserve any of it.

The nurse walked into the hall. Meredith pulled the door of the small room closed behind her, and we were alone.

"Did she beat you?" she asked.

I bit my bottom lip so hard it split. When I swallowed, it was blood and saliva, both. Meredith stared at me. I took a deep breath.

My eyes scanned the holes in the acoustic tile before dropping to answer her question in the only way I could, in the way Meredith expected.

"Yes," I said.

She left the room.

One word, and it was over. Elizabeth might try to visit, but I would refuse to see her. Meredith and the nurses, believing her to be dangerous, would protect me.

That night, for the first time, I dreamed of fire. Elizabeth hovered above me, wailing. The sound was almost inhuman. I tried to move toward her, but my toes were sealed to the ground, as if my flesh had melted into the earth. She began to shout then, her words blurred with agony. My body was charred black before I understood her to be proclaiming her love for me, over and over again. It was worse than the wailing.

I woke up burning, my body wet with sweat.

17.

I spent three days in the hospital, recovering from mastitis. The paramedics found me with a temperature of 105 degrees. My fever did not break until after a full forty-eight hours of intravenous antibiotics, which, the doctors discussed as I fell in and out of sleep, they had never seen. Mastitis was a common infection for breast-feeding mothers, painful but localized and easily treated. For me, mastitis had become an inflammation of nearly my entire body. Skin boiled on my breasts, but also on my arms, my neck, and the insides of my thighs. The doctors said there were no cases like mine on record.

When the fever subsided, the aching for my daughter replaced the burning. My face, my chest, and my limbs blazed with longing. Worried the doctors would ask questions about a new mother alone in the hospital, with no baby in sight and no visitors, I fled before being released, pulling out my IV and sneaking down a back staircase.

I took a taxi back to the empty apartment and called a locksmith to change the locks. If Natalya returned, I would make her a key. Until then, I didn't want Mother Ruby or Renata, both of whom had taken to walking in without knocking, stopping by to see the baby. I didn't have the strength to tell them what I had done.

That very afternoon Mother Ruby came. She knocked until I was sure the glass doors would break. I peeked out the window in Natalya's room, then returned to the kitchen to take the phone off the hook before crawling into the blue room and closing the door. In the evening it was Renata, who pounded even harder and threw a small stone against the upstairs window. I gave no sign that I had returned. The next morning a different, softer knock woke me from a deep sleep and I knew that Marlena was back. It was time to go back to work. I would tell her the truth.

Stumbling down the stairs, I squinted in the bright light. Marlena burst through the doors. "She must be enormous!" she exclaimed. "What's her name?" She flew up the stairs, and I followed slowly behind. When I got to the top, Marlena was spinning in a circle in the living room, the emptiness of the apartment settling over her. She looked at me, her eyes holding a single question.

"I don't know," I said, answering her spoken question but not her unspoken one. "Her name. I didn't name her." Marlena's eyes did not move from my body, the question they held the same: *Where is she?*

I started to cry. Marlena came to me, placing a soft hand on my shoulder. I wanted to tell her. I wanted her to know that the baby was safe, and would be loved, and might even be happy.

Minutes passed before I could speak, and when I did, I told the story simply, without embellishment. I left her with her father, who would raise her. I wasn't able to be the mother I wanted to be. The loss was incapacitating, but I had made the best decision for my daughter.

"Please," I said when I had finished. "Let's not talk about her again." I walked across the room for a box of tissues and my appointment book. I scrawled a short list on a lined sheet of paper and folded it into Marlena's fingers with enough cash for the purchase. "I'll see you tomorrow," I said. I did not wait for her to leave but crawled into the blue room and locked the door.

The spoken truth rocked me to sleep.

It was not Marlena's quiet tap that woke me

the following morning but Renata's punctuated pounding. I covered my head with a
pillow, but her voice reached me though the
feathers.

"I'm not going anywhere, Victoria," she
called up. "I just saw Marlena at the flower
market, and I know you're inside. If you
don't open up, I'll just sit here until Marlena
arrives, and she'll let me in."

There was no way to avoid it any longer. I
had to face her. Walking downstairs, I unlocked the double glass doors and inched
one open.

"What?" I demanded.

"I saw her," Renata said. "This morning,
at the market. I thought you had left with
the baby, left without telling any of us where
you were going, and then there she was in
his arms."

My eyes filled, and I lifted my shoulders by
way of asking what she wanted from me.

"You told him?" Renata asked. "You gave
him the baby?"

"I didn't tell him anything," I said. "And I
don't want you to tell me anything. Ever." I
swallowed hard.

Renata softened then. "She looked happy,"
she said, "and Grant looked tired. But —"

"Please," I said to Renata as I inched the
door closed. "I don't want to know. I can't

take it."

I closed and locked the door. Renata and I stood on opposite sides of the glass in silence. The doors were not thick enough to block conversation, but neither of us spoke. Renata looked into my eyes, and I let her. I hoped she could see the longing, the loneliness, and the despair. It was hard enough to let my baby go. It would be harder with constant updates from Renata. She had to understand that the only way I could survive my decision was to try to forget.

Marlena drove up in my car, the hatchback open and flowers spilling out. Midway through unloading, she stopped, examining Renata and me.

"Everything okay?" she asked. Renata looked at me, and I turned my face away.

Renata didn't answer. She turned up the hill to Bloom, her arms defeated at her sides.

I closed and locked the door. Kerria and I stood on opposite sides of the glass in the lounge. The doors were not thick enough to block conversation, but neither of us spoke. Kerria looked into my eyes, and I let her. I hoped she could see the love and the loneliness, and the despair. It was hard enough to let my baby go. It would be harder with constant updates from Kerria. She had to understand that the only way I could survive was if my decision was to let go forever.

Marcia drove up in my car, the hatchback open and flowers spilling out. Halfway through the drive, she stopped, returning Kerria and me.

"Everything okay?" she asked. Kerria looked at me, and I turned my face away.

Kerria didn't answer. She turned up the hill to Elburn, her arms dejected at her side.

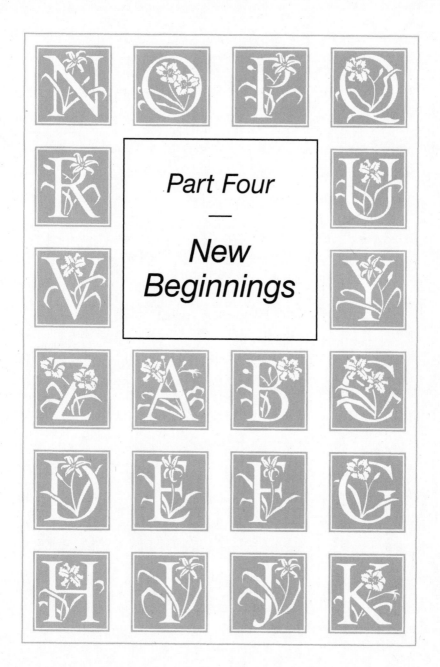

Part Four

—

New Beginnings

1.

Message grew exponentially in the months that followed. I accepted only cash, up front, and the underground quality attracted a cultlike following. I did not advertise. After the first few buckets of tagged iris, my phone number spread faster than it would have if I'd purchased a blinking billboard on the entrance to the Bay Bridge. Natalya did not return from her tour, and I took over the apartment, sending an envelope full of hundred-dollar bills to the landlord on the first of June. Marlena continued to work as my assistant, organizing the calendar, answering calls, filling purchase orders, and making deliveries. I supervised the flower arranging and met with clients on the folding flea-market chairs in the empty office space, the shoeboxes open under the harsh fluorescent lights.

My pre-wedding consultations were as in demand as my arrangements. Couples treated their appointments like visits to a fortune-teller or a priest; they told me, often for hours, the many hopes they held for their relationships, and also the challenges they faced. I recorded only a couple's own words, taking notes on a sheet of transparent rice paper, and when they finished speaking, I handed them the paper, rolled into a scroll with a ribbon. Yet as the couples referenced the scroll to choose their flowers and craft their wedding vows, they credited me with forecasting their life together. Bethany and Ray were happily married. Countless other couples sent me cards from their honeymoons, describing their relationships with words like *peace, passion, fulfillment,* and an infinite number of flower-inspired qualities.

The rapid growth of Message — combined with an outpouring of florists offering consultations in the language of flowers to the streams of brides Marlena and I turned away — caused a subtle but concrete shift in the Bay Area flower industry. Marlena reported that peony, marigold, and lavender lingered in their plastic buckets at the flower market while tulips, lilac, and passionflower sold out before the sun rose. For the first time anyone could remember, jonquil became available long after its natural bloom season had ended. By the end of July, bold brides carried ceramic bowls of strawberries or fragrant clusters of fennel, and no one questioned their aesthetics but rather marveled at the simplicity of their desire.

If the trajectory continued, I realized, Message would alter the quantities of anger, grief, and mistrust growing in the earth on a massive scale. Farmers would uproot fields of foxglove to plant yarrow, the soft clusters of pink, yellow, and cream the cure to a broken heart. The prices of sage, ranunculus, and stock would steadily increase. Plum trees would be planted for the sole purpose of harvesting their delicate, clustered blossoms, and sunflowers would fall permanently out of fashion, disappearing from flower stands, craft stores, and country kitchens. Thistle would be cleared compulsively from empty lots and overgrown gardens.

Summer afternoons, as I worked in the rooftop greenhouse I'd constructed with PVC pipes and plastic sheeting, tending hundreds of small ceramic pots on wire racks, I tried to take solace in this small, intangible contribution to the world. I told myself that someone, somewhere, would be less angry, less grief-stricken, because of the rampant success of Message. Friendships would be stronger; marriages would last. But I didn't believe it. I couldn't take credit for an abstract contribution to the world when in every tangible human interaction I'd ever had I'd caused only pain: with Elizabeth, through arson and a false accusation; with Grant, through abandonment and an unnamed, unsupported child.

And then there was my daughter. That I had abandoned her did not leave my mind, not even for a moment. I could have moved in to Natalya's old bedroom, but instead I still slept in the blue room, curled up alone in the space we'd once occupied together. Every morning upon waking, I counted her age to the month and day. Sitting across from chatty brides, I tried to remember her nearly hairless eyebrows, curved up at me in question, her lips opening and closing in rhythm. Her absence in the empty apartment began to feel as real as she'd once been, rattling the plastic sheeting of the greenhouse, seeping like light under the crack of the blue room's door. In the tap of the rain on the flat roof, I heard her ravenous suck. Every twenty-nine days the moonlight traveled in a slow square across the futon where we sat on our last night together, and each month I half expected it to bring her back to me. Instead, the moonlight illuminated my solitude, and I sat upright in its pale glow, remembering her as she had been, imagining her as she had become. Miles and miles away, I felt my daughter changing, each day growing and developing, without me. I longed to be with her, to witness her transformation.

But as much as I wanted to be reunited, I would not go to her. My desire for my daughter felt selfish. Leaving her with Grant had been the most loving act I had ever accomplished, and I did not regret it. Without me, my daughter would be safe. Grant would love her like he had loved me, with unearned devotion and tender care. It was everything I wanted for her.

I had only one regret, and it had nothing to do with my daughter. In a life of trespasses, many violent and most undeserved, I regretted only the fire. A collection of jam jars, a fistful of matches, and an absence of judgment had created an inferno that blazed well past the extinguishing of the final flame. It burst forth into the lie that had taken me away from Elizabeth, ignited fights throughout eight years of institutional placements, and smoldered in my mistrust of Grant. I had refused to believe that he loved me, or that he would continue to love me if he knew the truth.

Grant believed his mother had lit the fire that ruined both our lives; though he didn't talk about it, I knew he had not forgiven her.

But she wasn't the one to blame. It was my fault the vines went up in flames, my fault Elizabeth did not go to Catherine, my fault Grant spent the following year alone, caring for his sick mother. I didn't know the details of Catherine's unraveling, but they were clear in the way Grant loved me, delicately and in isolation. He had needed Elizabeth as much as I had.

Now it was too late. The vineyard had ignited. Grant spent his entire life (with the exception of the six months with me) alone. I'd lost the only woman who had ever tried to mother me, and it was too late to go back, too late to salvage my own childhood. But even though it was too late, it was this thought that plagued me: I wanted to go back to Elizabeth. I wanted, more than anything, to be Elizabeth's daughter.

Mid-August, exhausted from an unrelenting summer wedding schedule and equally unrelenting thoughts of my daughter, Elizabeth, and Grant, I retreated to the blue room. For the first time since starting Message, I locked all six locks and slept through every appointment on our calendar. Marlena covered for me. The whistle of the kettle drifted into my dreams as she prepared tea for our clients, but I didn't emerge. The locks kept me from climbing into my car and driving straight to the water tower, racing to the third floor, and taking my baby back. In my fantasies, she still lay helpless in her basket, staring up at the ceiling. In reality, she would be six months old, sitting up, reaching out, and maybe even crawling across the floor.

I stayed in the blue room for nearly a week. Marlena did not disturb me, but each morning she slid a photocopied sheet of paper through the crack under my door. It was our September calendar, the squares growing increasingly crowded as the days passed. I had expected business to taper off as the weather cooled, but if anything, we seemed to be getting busier, and my anxiety over the mounting work finally surpassed my depression. I grabbed a banana from a fruit bowl Marlena had filled and walked downstairs.

Marlena sat at the table, chewing the end of a pen. She smiled when she saw me.

"I was about to go to The Gathering House," she said, "and hire another assistant."

I shook my head. "I'm here. What's first?"

She scanned the calendar. "Nothing major until Friday. But then we have to work sixteen days straight."

I groaned, but in reality I felt relieved. Flowers were my escape. With flowers in my hands, perhaps I could survive the fall. And maybe, as the months passed, things would get easier. It was what I had expected, but so far it hadn't proven to be true. In fact, the opposite seemed to be occurring; with each passing day, I felt more desolate, the consequences of my decisions less bearable. I turned to walk back upstairs.

"Going back to your cave?" Marlena asked. She sounded disappointed.

"What else would I do?"

Marlena exhaled. "I don't know." She paused, and I turned back around. It seemed she did know but was having trouble finding the words. "There's a new sandwich shop next to Bloom," she said finally. "I thought maybe we could grab some lunch and then go for a drive."

"A drive?"

"You know." She looked out the front windows to the street. "To see her."

Marlena meant my daughter. But for a split second before I realized this, I thought she meant Elizabeth, and it seemed to me to be exactly the thing I needed to do. I knew where she lived, and I knew how to get there. It might be too late to be a child in her home, but it wasn't too late to apologize for what I had done.

When I didn't respond right away, Marlena looked to me, her expression hopeful.

I shook my head. I'd asked her never to speak of my daughter, and until now, she'd done as I'd asked. "Please don't," I said.

Her chin dropped to her chest, and she looked for a moment as neckless as a newborn.

"I'll see you on Friday," I said, turning to walk up the stairs.

All night I imagined driving to see Elizabeth. I pictured the long, dusty driveway, the late-summer grapes heavy on the vines. The afternoon sun would cast a rectangular shadow from the peeling white farmhouse, and the porch steps would squeak as I climbed them. At the kitchen table, Elizabeth would sit with her arms folded, her eyes on the door, as if she'd been waiting for me.

The vision shattered with the realization that all this could be gone. Not only the acres of vines but also the kitchen table, the screen door, the entire house. In all the time I'd spent with Grant, I'd never once asked him how much damage the fire had caused, and I'd never driven down the road past the entrance to the flower farm. I hadn't wanted to know.

I couldn't go. I couldn't bear to see it, not even to apologize to Elizabeth.

But once sparked, I couldn't let go of the idea. If I could apologize, then maybe, finally, I could forget. Maybe my dreams would cease and I could settle into a quiet, if lonely, life, knowing Elizabeth understood my remorse. Huddled in the blue room, I thought about how to accomplish the task. It would be simple enough to write a letter. Once I'd learned the address, I'd never forgotten it. But I couldn't write my return address on the envelope without fear of Elizabeth showing up at my door, and without a return address, Elizabeth couldn't answer my letter. Though I didn't think I could live looking constantly out the window, half expecting her old gray truck to pull up to the curb, I wanted desperately to know her response. Written, I could handle her anger, her disappointment. It might even bring some relief from the years of guilt.

When the sun rose I knew what I had to do: I would write Elizabeth a letter and use Bloom as the return address. Renata would bring me a letter if one arrived. Inching open the door of the blue room, I listened for sounds of Marlena. The apartment was quiet. Walking downstairs, I sat at the table as I would during a flower consultation, reaching for a sheet of rice paper and a blue felt-tip pen. My hand shook as the pen hovered above the paper.

I wrote the date first in the upper-right-hand corner, as Elizabeth had taught me to do. Still trembling, I scrawled her name. I couldn't remember if a colon or a comma should follow; after a pause, I put both. I looked down at what I had written. My script was sloppy from nerves, a far cry from the perfection Elizabeth had always demanded. I crumpled the paper and threw it to the floor, starting again.

An hour later I reached for my last piece of paper. Balled attempts littered the room all around me. This one, no matter what, would have to do. The pressure of the final sheet made my hand shake even more, and my handwriting looked like that of a young child, unsure of the shape of each letter. Elizabeth would be disappointed. Still, I continued, slowly, purposefully. Finally, I succeeded in inking out a single line:

I lit the fire. I'm sorry. I've never stopped being sorry.

I signed my name. The letter was short, and I worried Elizabeth would think it rude or insincere, but there was nothing else to say. I folded the paper into an envelope, and sealed, addressed, and stamped it. The stamps I had purchased the previous spring held a drawing of a daffodil — *new beginnings* — yellow and white on a red background, gold letters celebrating the Chinese New Year. Elizabeth would notice.

Walking quickly to the end of the block, I pulled the heavy metal handle of the mailbox, dropping the letter through the slot before I had time to change my mind.

2.

On an afternoon in September I sat in the cavernous office space, checking the alphabetization of my cards out of habit and waiting for a couple to arrive. The couple would not marry until the following April but had insisted on meeting with me now. The bride wanted to coordinate everything — from the color of the place settings to the words in the song of their first dance — to her flower choices. Over the summer I had worked with countless brides, but coordinating music and flowers was new even to me. I was not looking forward to the meeting.

I checked my watch. Four forty-five. Fifteen minutes until my clients were set to arrive. It was time to make tea. I drank only a strong chrysanthemum tea I bought in Chinatown, the blossoms uncurling and suspending in the dark liquid. It was a nice touch for my sessions, and something my clients had come to expect.

In the kitchen, I brewed a pot and drank a cup before descending the stairs. The bride had arrived, sitting on the stoop in front of the glass doors. She sat alone, looking up and down the street. In the straight line of her back I could see her impatience. Her fiancé was late or absent. It was a bad sign for a marriage, and brides knew it. The long-term success of my business, I had decided months before, was dependent on the fact of arranging flowers only for couples whose marriages would last; I'd refused more than one couple for tardiness or spiteful conversations over the cards.

I set down the tray and walked to the door. Pressing my palms against the glass, I stopped suddenly. Outside, brakes squealed. Then, in front of my door, an old gray pickup truck lurched past, Elizabeth behind the wheel. At the stop sign on the steep corner, the truck rolled back before peeling into the intersection and disappearing up the hill. Turning, I raced up the stairs and into Natalya's old bedroom, where I crouched down below the window to wait for the truck to return.

In less than five minutes, it did. Elizabeth drove more easily down the hill than she had up, and in a moment she'd turned the corner and was out of sight. I took the stairs two at a time and walked outside. The bride on the

446

curb stood up when she saw me.

"I'm sorry," she said quickly. "He'll be here any minute."

He wouldn't, though. There was something rehearsed about her apology, as if she'd used the same words to excuse her fiancé for months or years.

"No," I said, "he won't." Maybe it was the chrysanthemum tea, but I suddenly wanted this woman to know the truth. She opened her mouth as if to protest, but the expression on my face stopped her.

"You won't do our flowers, will you?" She turned away from me, knowing the answer to her question. She would try Renata next; they always did. Renata had the only other flower dictionary identical to mine. I'd asked Marlena to make her a copy a few months before, when we began to have more business than we could handle. Daily, we directed clients to Bloom.

I started up the hill, and from the top I saw Renata descending. We met in the middle, as Grant and I had once done, the afternoon he brought the jonquil. In her hand was a pale pink envelope. My fingers trembled as I took it. I sat down on the curb and placed the envelope in my lap. Renata sat down next to me.

"Who is she?" Renata asked.

447

The envelope felt hot, and I moved it onto the sidewalk between us. I studied the lines of my empty palms as if looking for the answer to her question.

"Elizabeth," I said quietly.

We were silent. Renata did not ask more, but when I glanced up, her face was still pinched in question, as if I had not responded at all. I looked back down at my hands. "She wanted to be my mother once, when I was ten years old."

Renata made a clicking sound with her tongue. With a short fingernail, she picked at a glint of metal trapped in the concrete, but it did not come loose. "So?" she asked. "What did you do?"

It was a question Meredith would have asked, but coming from Renata, it sounded less accusatory than interested.

"I lit a fire."

It was the first time I had said the words aloud, and a lump rose in my throat at the image they produced. I squeezed my eyes shut.

"My little fire starter," Renata said. She placed a gentle arm around my shoulders, pulling me to her. "Why doesn't that surprise me?"

I turned to study her. She did not smile, but her eyes were warm. "So?" I asked.

"Why doesn't it?"

Renata pushed a clump of hair away from my eyes, her fingertips brushing my forehead. Her skin was soft. I leaned into her, my ear pressed against her shoulder so that her words, when she spoke, were muffled. "Do you remember the morning we met?" she asked. "When you stood on my stoop, looking for work, and then came back hours later with proof of what you could do? You handed me those flowers like an apology, even though you hadn't done anything wrong, even though your bouquet was as close to perfection as I'd ever seen. I knew right then that you felt unworthy, that you believed yourself to be unforgivably flawed."

I remembered the morning well. Remembered worrying that she'd know the truth about my homelessness, the truth about my history. "Then why did you hire me?" I asked.

Renata ran her hand along the line of my cheekbone. When she reached my chin, she tilted my face up. I looked into her eyes.

"Do you really think you're the only human being alive who is unforgivably flawed? Who's been hurt almost to the point of breaking?"

She looked at me deeply. When she looked away, I knew she understood that yes, I did

449

believe I was the only one. "I could have hired someone else. Someone less flawed, perhaps, or at least better at hiding it. But none of them would have had the talent you have with flowers, Victoria. It's truly a gift. When you work with flowers, everything about you changes. The set of your jaw loosens. Your eyes glaze with focus. Your fingers manipulate the flowers with a gentle respect that makes it impossible to believe you are capable of violence. I'll never forget the first day I saw it. Watching you arranging sunflowers at the back table, I felt like I was looking at a completely different girl."

I knew the girl of whom she was speaking. It was the same one I'd glimpsed in the dressing room mirror with Elizabeth, after nearly a year in her home. Perhaps that girl had survived somewhere within me after all, preserved like a dried flower, fragile and sweet.

Renata picked up the envelope and flapped it in the air between us.

"Shall I?" she asked.

3.

At the sound of the gavel, I blew the white, cottony buds I'd arranged in a line off the table. They scattered to the floor of the courtroom. Elizabeth stood up.

The flowers had been at my seat when I'd arrived, the tangle of baby's breath — *everlasting love* — reflecting on the polished tabletop, soft, round orbs bobbing deep within the glossy wood. They were stiff and dry against my fingertips, as if Elizabeth had purchased them for our first court date, before the hearing had been continued, and continued again. Baby's breath did not wither or mold. With time it grew increasingly brittle, but otherwise it did not change. There had been no reason for Elizabeth to purchase a fresh bunch.

As she stood before the judge, systematically denying a long list of accusations, I snapped the brown, budless stems into inchlong pieces, arranging them like a bird's nest in the center of the table. There was a pause, and the courtroom fell silent. Elizabeth's request echoed in my ears: *I would ask that you return Victoria to my custody, effective immediately.* I didn't dare look up, afraid my eyes would betray my desire. But when the judge spoke again, it was only to ask Elizabeth to return to her seat. Her request, it seemed, did not deserve a response. She sat back down.

Meredith sat between Elizabeth and me at the long table, flanked by attorneys. My attorney was a short, heavy man. He looked uncomfortable in his suit, leaning forward as the judge spoke and pulling his shirt away from the back of his neck. His notepad was blank, and he did not appear to be carrying a pen. Under the table, he checked the time on his watch. He was ready to leave.

I was ready to leave, too. Only half listening as Meredith and the judge debated my level of need, I manipulated the collection of broken stems on the tabletop, arranging them into the shape of a three-finned fish, a pointed crown, and then a lopsided heart. The brittle pile distracted me from the proximity of Elizabeth, less than five arm lengths away. A level-ten group home, the judge ordered, pending availability. Meredith wrote the decision on my case plan, crossing the courtroom to the bench with a thick stack of papers in her hand. The judge paused, told Meredith to add my name to all the waiting lists for transitional housing, and then signed the top sheet. When I emancipated in eight years, I would still be alone. Without stating it in precise terms, the judge's words defined my future.

The judge cleared her throat. Meredith returned to her seat. In the silence that followed, I understood that the judge was waiting for me to look up, but I did not. With my finger, I poked a hole in the twiggy heart I'd created from the stems, pulling it open until I saw my own face reflected in the tabletop within. I was surprised by how old I looked, and also how angry. Still, I did not look up.

"Victoria," the judge said finally. "Do you have anything to say?"

I didn't respond. On the other side of my attorney, the county prosecutor tapped her long, polished fingernails against the table, red ovals pressed onto wrinkled hands. She wanted me to testify against Elizabeth in criminal court, but I'd refused.

I stood up slowly. From my pockets I pulled handfuls of red carnations, browning heads I'd plucked from a holiday bouquet in the hospital gift shop. Over two months after the night of the fire, I was still in the hospital, moved from the burn unit to the psychiatric ward until Meredith could find a placement for me.

I ducked under the table and crossed the courtroom.

"I want you to think about the consequences of refusing to testify," the judge said as I stood before her. "This is more than just about standing up for yourself, and standing up for justice. This is about protecting other children."

The adults in the room believed Elizabeth to be a threat. I almost laughed, the idea was so absurd. But I knew if I laughed I would start to cry, and if I started to cry, I might never stop.

Instead, I piled the red carnations on the bench. *My heart breaks.* It was the first time I'd ever given a flower to someone who didn't understand the meaning. The gift felt subversive and strangely powerful. As I turned to go, Elizabeth stood, taking in the meaning of the flowers. Our bodies faced each other, and in the brief, quiet moment, the energy between us was as hot as the fire that had torn us apart.

I started to run. The judge pounded the gavel; Meredith called me back. Throwing open the doors of the courtroom, I raced down six flights of stairs, pushing open an emergency exit and walking outside. I stopped in the bright afternoon light. It didn't matter which way I ran. Meredith would catch me. She would drive me back to the hospital, place me in a group home, or lock me in a detention center. For eight years, I would move from one placement to the next, whenever she came for me. Then, on my eighteenth birthday, I would emancipate, and I would be alone.

I shivered. It was a cold December day, the bright blue sky deceptive. I lay down on the ground where I stood, pressing my cheek against the warm cement.

I wanted to go home.

4.

Ten years had passed, and still, Elizabeth wanted me.

Her letter, folded into a small square and tucked inside my bra, pressed into my skin as I worked beside Marlena that evening. *I let you down,* she'd written. *I've never stopped being sorry, either.* And then, at the very bottom, just above her name: *Please, please, come home.* Two or three times an hour I removed and reread the short sentences, until I'd memorized not only the words on the page but the exact shape of every letter. Marlena didn't ask, just worked harder to make up for my distraction.

I would go to Elizabeth. I had decided this the moment I read her letter, sitting on the curb beside Renata. Standing up, I'd meant to walk straight to my car, drive immediately over the bridge and through the countryside to her vineyard. But instead I'd seen Marlena working through the window, stopped in to rearrange a bouquet, then paused and reached for another. Hours passed. We had an anniversary party the following day, followed by two weddings, back-to-back. The fall had officially become as busy as the summer months had been, full of demanding, superstitious brides who would rather marry on a Sunday in late autumn than use another florist. They were my least favorite. Not wealthy enough to have simply outbid other brides for the summer months and planned extravagant weddings with grace and gratitude but wealthy enough to run in the same circles and feel the grief of constant comparison. Fall brides were insecure, and the men they were marrying overindulgent. In the past month, Marlena and I had been called in for last-minute consultations for three different brides, in which everything we had planned was scrapped and we started over the day before a wedding.

But it was more than just the demands of our schedule that kept me idling beside Marlena. The thrill of knowing that Elizabeth still wanted me had dulled the pain of the past decade, dulled even my constant aching for my daughter. As long as I did not go to her, the promise of Elizabeth's letter remained intact. If I knocked on her door, I risked coming face-to-face with a woman different from the one I remembered — older, without a doubt, but perhaps also sadder or angrier — and this felt like too great of a risk to take.

That night I slept fitfully, waking every few hours with the urge to drive to Elizabeth's. But by morning, the pull of the vineyard had weakened. I would wait a week, I decided, two at the most, and then I would go to her, fully prepared for whatever I would find.

I had showered and dressed when the phone rang. Caroline. I'd been expecting her call. During our consultation, she hadn't known what she wanted from a florist or from a relationship, and got weepy every time I asked a question she couldn't answer, which was anytime I asked anything more complicated than her name or the date of her wedding. I should have turned her away, but I liked her fiancé, Mark, which I suppose was why I kept the job; he teased her in a way that somehow sounded encouraging instead of belittling.

I answered her call on the first ring. Just as I was trying to decide whether to tell her to come over or lie and say I was busy, I walked through the bedroom and saw her sitting on the curb across the street. She looked up at me, Mark at her side. Her fists were clenched, but she opened one hand slowly to wave. I slid open the window and hung up the phone.

"Okay, give me a minute," I said, just as Natalya had the first time I knocked on the door, and, like Natalya, I took my time. I went into the kitchen and made a cup of tea, poached eggs, and toast. If we were going to start over on the bouquets — and I knew we were — I would likely be working the next twenty-four hours straight. I took my time eating and drank two glasses of milk before descending the stairs.

Caroline hugged me when I opened the door. She was probably almost thirty but wore her hair in two long braids, and the hairstyle made her appear much younger. When she sat down at the table across from me, I saw that her blue eyes were watery.

"The wedding's tomorrow," she said, as if this fact had somehow escaped me. "And I think I got it all wrong." She gasped and pounded her heart with a flat palm.

Mark sat down next to her and patted her on the back with a fist. She laughed and hiccupped. "She's trying not to cry," he said. "If she cries this close to the wedding, it will definitely show in the photographs."

Caroline laughed again, and a tear escaped. She swatted at it with a manicured fingernail and kissed Mark. "He doesn't understand the significance," she said. "He's never met Alejandra and Luis, and doesn't know about what happened on their honeymoon."

I nodded as if I remembered this couple and the flowers I had chosen for them. "So, what can I do for you?" I asked as patiently as I could manage.

"You know that old question, if you could eat only five foods for the rest of your life, what would they be?" I nodded, even though no one had ever asked me that question. "Well, I keep thinking about that. Choosing flowers for a wedding is like picking the five qualities you want in a relationship *for the rest of your life.* How can you possibly choose?"

"She says *for the rest of your life* like marriage is a terminal disease," said Mark.

"You know what I mean," she said, examining her hands.

I was only half listening to their conversation, thinking about the five foods I would choose. Donuts, definitely. Did I have to specify a type, or could I just say assorted? Assorted, I decided, with an emphasis on maple.

Caroline and Mark were debating red roses and white tulips, *love* versus *the declaration of love.* "But if you love me and don't tell me, how will I know?" she asked.

460

"Oh, you'll know," Mark said, raising his eyebrows and running his fingers from her knee to the top of her thigh.

I looked out the window. Donuts, roasted chicken, cheesecake, and butternut squash soup, extra hot. One more. It should be a fruit or a vegetable if I was to survive more than a year on this imaginary diet, but I couldn't think of any I liked enough to eat every day. I drummed my fingers on the card table and looked out the window at the unseasonably blue sky.

And just then I knew exactly what it would be, and I knew I had to leave, right then, to see Elizabeth. The grapes were ripe. I'd been counting the warm fall days, twelve in a row, and just now, the sun shining in sharp, dust-filled angles through the dark room, I knew the grapes were ready for harvest. I also knew that Elizabeth had not yet discovered them. I don't know how I knew this, but I did, in the way that I had heard some mothers and daughters, once connected by an umbilical cord, know before being told when the other was sick or in danger. I stood up. Caroline and Mark had moved on to heliotrope versus wild geranium, but I had missed who had won the tulip-rose debate.

"Why are you limiting yourself?" I asked, more harshly than I had intended. "I never

461

told you to limit yourself to a certain number of flowers for your bouquet."

"But who ever saw a bride carrying a bouquet with fifty different types of flowers?" she asked.

"So, start a trend," I said. Caroline was the type who would like the possibility of starting a trend. I pulled out my spiral notebook and a pen. "Go through the boxes one card at a time and write down every single quality you want in your relationship. We'll get together everything we can at the last minute," I said. "But give up on matching your bridesmaids' dresses."

"The dresses are chartreuse," Caroline said sheepishly, as if she had purchased them in anticipation of this exact moment. "They'll match anything."

I was already halfway up the stairs. I needed to call Marlena. She was capable of filling the order without me, and would do it quickly and professionally. Her arrangements were not beautiful — she had improved little over time — but she knew the flowers and definitions by heart and would not confuse oak-leaf with pencil-leaf geranium. The reputation of Message depended on the content of the bouquet, not on the artistic merit of the arrangements, and in the area of content Marlena was flawless.

She answered after one ring, and I knew she'd been awaiting this call, too.

"Come over," I said. Marlena groaned. I hung up without telling her that I wouldn't be here when she arrived, or that Caroline and Mark were in the midst of compiling quite possibly the most complex bouquet in the history of San Francisco weddings. No reason to alarm her.

I grabbed my keys and took the stairs two at a time.

"Marlena is on her way," I said to Caroline and Mark as I walked past the table and out the door.

I drove the country roads as I had so many times before, with Grant, alone, and then with the baby, the last time I had come. Passing the flower farm, I pressed my palm into my left temple to block my peripheral vision. I didn't see the farmhouse, the water tower, or the flowers. I had mustered up the courage to see Elizabeth but could not bear the thought of glimpsing Grant or my daughter on the same day.

Across from Elizabeth's driveway, I pulled onto the shoulder of the road. A school bus passed, and then a crowded brown station wagon. When the road was empty, I stepped out into the quiet countryside and looked across the road.

On first glance, the vineyard was exactly how I remembered it. The long driveway, the farmhouse in the center, the vines running in stripes parallel to the road. I leaned back against my car, looking for signs of the damage I had caused. The vineyard had been replanted, the charred earth turned, and the ashes were long gone; even the thistle had returned to the ditch, as tall and dry as it had been the night I lit the fire. Only the thickness of the vines revealed the history of the blaze: On the southeastern quadrant of the property, the trunks of the grapevines were half as thick as those on the opposite side of the driveway. The leaves of the younger plants were a brighter shade of green, and noticeably more fruit hung on the vines. I wondered if the quality of the fruit on the new vines had yet reached Elizabeth's standards.

I walked across the road. The house looked unchanged, but the row of sheds had disappeared — burned, I imagined, to the ground. Carlos's trailer was gone, too, but I doubted the metal had melted; it was more likely he'd found another job or moved away, and Elizabeth had disposed of the trailer. Without the dilapidated outbuildings, the house looked more like a bed-and-breakfast than a working vineyard. The white paint was bright and spotless, and a pair of red wooden rocking chairs sat on the front porch. Inside the lace-covered window, the kitchen light was on.

Pausing on the bottom step, I heard a soft sound like a rush of wind, followed by a quiet splash. Elizabeth was in the garden. My back pressed against the white clapboard, I crept around the side of the house. Elizabeth squatted barefoot in the dirt just paces from where I stood, her back to me. Mud oozed into the wrinkles on the backs of her heels, and when she leaned forward, I saw that the arches of her feet were clean and pink.

"Again?" she asked, holding up a round wire ring with a worn wooden handle.

I moved away from the wall to get a better view of the garden. On a path in front of the roses sat a galvanized washbasin half-full of bubble solution, iridescent swirls reflecting in the thick liquid. With one hand squeezing the edge of the basin, a round-eyed baby reached for the metal ring. She sat on the ground in only a cloth diaper, and her naked body swayed, her full belly teetering on her unstable bottom. With her free hand, Elizabeth reached behind the baby's back to steady her, and in the moment of distraction, the baby succeeded in grabbing the ring and pulling it, still soapy, into her mouth. She gummed it fiercely.

"Excuse me, little one," Elizabeth said, tugging unsuccessfully on the wooden handle. "This is a bubble wand, not a teething ring."

The baby did not react to the admonition. After a pause, Elizabeth tickled her bare belly until she giggled, releasing her clamped jaw from the metal ring. Elizabeth wiped the soapy residue from the baby's mouth with her thumb.

"Now watch," Elizabeth said. She dipped the wand and blew through the ring. Bubbles rained down on the baby, leaving wet circles as they popped on her shoulders and forehead.

Her hair had grown; dark ringlets covered the top half of her ears and curled up at the back of her neck. From hours in the garden, I imagined, her skin had browned to a darker shade of cream, and she'd sprouted two bottom teeth where months before I'd run my finger along her slick gums. I may not have recognized her at all except for her eyes — her round, deep, gray-blue eyes — which turned and fixed on my face in question, as they had the morning I'd left her in the moss-lined basket.

Backing silently away, I spun around and ran to the road.

5.

Sitting among the decades-old plants, I surveyed the scarce blooms. Grant had pruned the roses. A quarter-inch below each sliced end, a fat red bud pushed out of the stem, the point from which a new flower would emerge. Grant would have roses, as he did every year, for Thanksgiving.

Twenty-five years alone, and Grant had reconnected with Elizabeth. Stunned, I'd driven immediately to the flower farm, ditching my car on the road and — having long before thrown away the key — climbing over Grant's locked gate. But instead of knocking on the water tower's door, I'd retreated into the rose garden. My daughter's shy smile played behind my eyelids; her joy, swirling like the soapy water in the basin, filled me. She was with Elizabeth, and she was happy. The ease of their interaction made me think her home was permanently on the vineyard, and the thought caused me to feel Grant's loneliness as acutely as I'd experienced my daughter's joy.

An hour passed. Still swooning from the unexpected glimpse of my baby girl, I heard Grant's boots approach from behind me. My heart echoed as it had in the flower market the first time we met, and I pulled my knees to my chest as if to muffle the sound. Grant lined his boots up with my own and sat down next to me, his shoulders touching mine. He tucked something behind my ear, and I withdrew it. A white rose. I held it up to the sun, and its shadow fell upon us. We sat in silence for a long time.

Finally, I slid away and turned to him. It had been more than a year since I'd seen Grant, and he seemed to have aged more than the time should have allowed. Thin lines etched across his serious brow, but his strong soil scent was as I remembered. I inched myself back until our shoulders touched again.

"What's she like?" I asked.

"Beautiful," he said. His voice was quiet, thoughtful. "Shy at first, usually. But when she's ready, when she reaches for you and holds both your ears with her fat little hands, there's nothing like it in the world." He paused for a moment, pulling a petal from the rose I held and holding it to his lips.

"She loves flowers, too, picks them, smells them, will eat them if you don't watch her closely enough."

"Really?" I asked. "Loves them like we do?"

Grant nodded. "You should see the way she smiles when I rattle off the names of the orchids in the greenhouse: *oncidium, dendrobium, bulbophyllum,* and *epidendrum,* tickling her face with each blossom. I wouldn't be surprised if 'Orchidaceae' was her first word."

I pictured her round face, cheeks flushed from the heat of the greenhouse, pressed into Grant's chest to avoid the tickling flowers.

"I'm trying to teach her the science behind the plants, too," Grant said. The smile that stretched his lips was full of memory. "But so far it's not going so well. She falls asleep when I start to ramble on about the history of the Betulaceae family or the way moss grows without roots."

Moss grows without roots. His words took my breath away. Throughout a lifetime studying the biology of plants, this simple fact had eluded me, and it seemed now to be the one fact I needed, desperately, to have known.

"What's her name?" I asked.

"Hazel." *Reconciliation.* Grant pulled at

a stubborn root of crabgrass, avoiding my eyes. "I thought, someday, she'd bring you back to me."

She had, in this moment, brought us back together. The root of the crabgrass popped loose. Grant followed the dry shoot to the point of its next engagement with the earth.

"Are you mad?" I asked.

Grant didn't answer for a long time. Another root broke free, and he pulled up the entire plant, twisting the long strand of grass around his thick index finger. "I should be."

He was quiet again, looking out over his property. "I've rehearsed my anger a hundred times since discovering Hazel. You deserve to hear me out."

"I know I do," I said. "Go ahead." I looked at him, but he didn't meet my gaze. He would not deliver the words he'd practiced. Though he had every right to be, he wasn't angry, and didn't want to make me suffer. It wasn't in him.

After a time, Grant shook his head, exhaling. "You did what you had to do," he said. "And I did what I had to do."

I understood his words to mean that I was right when I'd guessed my daughter lived on the vineyard; Grant had given her to Elizabeth.

471

"Dinner?" Grant asked suddenly, turning back to me.

"Are you cooking?" I asked.

He nodded, and I stood up.

I started toward the water tower, but Grant took my hand and led me to the front porch of the main house. I let him guide me, noticing for the first time that the house had been repainted and the windows replaced.

The dining room table was set, the long, polished wood exposed except for two placemats on one end, folded cloth napkins, polished silver, and thin white china plates with indistinguishable blue flowers ringing the edge. I sat down, and Grant poured water into a crystal glass from a pitcher before disappearing through the swinging door that led to the kitchen. He came back with a whole roasted chicken on a silver platter.

"You cook this much for yourself?" I asked.

"Sometimes," he said. "When I can't get you out of my head. But today I cooked it for you. When I saw you jump the fence, I turned on the oven."

He removed both drumsticks with a knife and placed them on my empty plate before slicing the breast. From the kitchen, he retrieved a boat of gravy and a long tray of roasted vegetables: beets, potatoes, and pep-

472

pers in vibrant colors. While he served me vegetables, I finished sucking the meat off the bones of the first drumstick. I set the clean bone down in a pool of gravy, and Grant took his seat in the chair opposite mine.

I had so many questions. I wanted him to describe every day that had passed since he discovered the baby in the moss-lined basket. I wanted to know how he felt when he looked into his daughter's eyes for the first time, if he felt love or terror, and how she came to live with Elizabeth.

I wanted to ask, but instead I ate the chicken, ferociously, as if I had not had a meal since the last time Grant cooked for me. I ate both drumsticks and both wings and started on the breast. The taste of the meat was entwined in my memory with the taste of Grant, his kisses after cooking, the way he touched me, only when I asked, in the studio and in all three stories of the water tower. I had left him, and his touch, and his cooking, and nothing, ever, had replaced it. When I looked up, he was watching me eat, as he had done so many times before, and I could tell by the look in his eyes that nothing had replaced me, either.

When I finished eating, the chicken on the silver platter was a statue of bones. I looked at Grant's plate. It was hard to tell if he'd eaten anything. I hoped so. I hoped I hadn't devoured the entire bird. But when he asked me if I wanted to see Hazel's room, and I tried to stand up, I felt the weight of the meat inside me. I let Grant half-carry me up the stairs. He opened the last door in the long hallway and helped me to the edge of a twin bed. I lay down. Grant picked up my head and placed a pillow beneath my neck. He crossed in front of a rocking chair and pulled a pink leather scrapbook off a bookshelf.

"Elizabeth made this for her," he said, opening the book. The first page held a picture of a hazel blossom that Catherine had drawn. It had been pulled from its file, laminated with clear plastic, and secured to the album with gold photo corners. Below the drawing was my daughter's name, Hazel Jones-Hastings, in Elizabeth's elegant script, and her birthday, March 1, which wasn't her birthday at all. He turned the page.

In a mounted photograph, Hazel lay in her moss-lined basket, exactly as I had left her. It made my stomach churn, my eyes well, to remember my love for her in that moment, overwhelming and incapacitating. On the next page, Hazel's head pressed against Grant's chest in a baby carrier, a floppy white hat tied under her chin. She was asleep. There were two or three photos from each month of her life, her first smile and first teeth and first food all captured with loving attention.

I closed the book and handed it back to Grant. It was everything I had wanted to know.

"This is her room?" I asked.

"When she visits," he said. "Saturday afternoons, usually, or after the farmers' market on Sundays." He ran his hand along the railing of an empty crib as he returned the photo album to its shelf. When he lay down next to me, his body was hot where it touched my arm.

I looked around the room. Catherine's floral drawings, one-foot graphite squares, hung in thick white mats with pink wooden frames. The frames matched the pink furniture: the crib, a rocking chair, a nightstand, and a bookshelf, all stenciled with white daisies.

"The house looks good," I said. "You've done so much in a year."

Grant shook his head. "A year and a half," he said. "I started the day after I showed you my mother's art studio. Afternoons you worked late, I'd rush home to peel wallpaper, refinish the floors. I wanted it to be a

475

surprise. I hoped someday we'd live here together."

I'd left without saying goodbye, without even telling Grant I was pregnant. And all the while, he'd been building me a home, never knowing if or when I would return.

"I'm sorry," I said. In the silence that followed, I remembered the early months of my pregnancy, sleeping for the second time in McKinley Square, nauseated, dirty, and disheveled. The image made me uncomfortable. I'd been in shock to the point of fearlessness, all sense of self-preservation gone.

"I'm sorry, too," Grant said.

I peeled away from him and looked into his eyes. He was talking about our daughter, her room, empty, surrounding us.

"You gave her away?" I asked. It wasn't an accusation, and for once the tone of my voice communicated what I wanted to say, that my curiosity was blameless and all-consuming.

Grant nodded. "I didn't want to. I loved her the moment I saw her. I loved her so much I forgot to eat and sleep and tend my flowers for the entire month of March." So it had been the same for Grant, I thought: too much.

He turned toward me, his thick body wedged between the wall and my side. "I wanted so much to make her happy," he said. "But I kept making mistakes. I'd feed her too much or forget her diapers or leave her too long in the sun while I worked. She never cried, but the guilt kept me up at night. I thought I was letting her down, and you, too. I couldn't be the father I wanted to be, not alone, not without you. And I was afraid, even as I named her, that you weren't ever coming back."

Grant lifted a heavy hand and ran it through my hair. He pressed his cheek into my scalp, and I felt his unshaven jawbone tickle my skin. "I took her to Elizabeth," he said. "It was the only thing I could think of to do. When I showed up on her front porch with the baby in the basket, she cried and took us into her kitchen. I didn't leave her home for two weeks, and when I did, I didn't take the baby with me. Hazel smiled for the first time in Elizabeth's arms; I couldn't bear the thought of separating them."

Grant wrapped his arms around me and leaned his face into my ear. "Maybe it was just my excuse for leaving her," he whispered. "But I couldn't do it."

I slipped my arm under his chest. When he squeezed me to him, I squeezed back.

"I know," I said. I couldn't do it, either, and he knew it without me having to say it. We held on to each other as if we were drowning, neither looking for shore, and we stayed that way a long time, not talking, barely breathing.

"You told Elizabeth about me?" I asked.

Grant nodded. "She wanted to know everything. She thought I should be able to recite every moment of every day you'd lived since the last time she saw you in court, and kept getting frustrated when I couldn't." Grant told me about sitting at Elizabeth's table, a pot roast in the oven, Hazel asleep in his arms. *Why didn't you ask?* she would say, when Grant didn't know what I'd done for my sixteenth birthday, if I'd gone to high school, or what I liked best for breakfast. "She laughed when I told her you don't like lilies, and she told me you don't much care for cactus, either." I pulled my face out of Grant's chest to look at him. The corner of his mouth turned up, and I knew he had heard the whole story.

"She told you everything?" I asked. Grant nodded. I dropped my head back down, speaking my next words into his chest. "Even about the fire?"

He nodded again, his chin pressing into my forehead. We were quiet for a long time. Finally, I asked the question I had long held. "How could you have not known the truth?"

Grant didn't answer right away. When he did, the words came out with a long sigh. "My mother's dead."

I believed his statement to signal an end to my questioning, and did not press. But after a pause, he continued.

"It's too late to ask her. But I think she thought she lit the fire. By that time, she didn't recognize me most days. She was forgetting to eat, refusing her medicine. The night of the fire, I found her in her studio, watching. Tears streamed down her face. She began to cough spastically, and then choke, as if she had smoke in her lungs. I went to her, put my arms around her shoulders. She felt so small. I'd probably grown a foot since the last time I'd been in her arms. Between sobs, she muttered the same sentence, over and over again: *I didn't mean to do it.*"

I imagined the purple sky, Catherine and Grant's silhouette in the window, felt the return of the despair I'd experienced in the heat of the fire. Catherine had felt it, too. In that moment, we were the same, each of us destroyed by our limited understanding of reality.

"And after?" I asked.

"She spent a year drawing hyacinth; in pencil, charcoal, ink, pastel. Finally, she began to paint, on everything from huge canvases to tiny postage stamps, tall purple stalks with hundreds of small blossoms. All for me, she said. Not one was good enough for Elizabeth. Every day, she tried again."

Hyacinth. *Please forgive me.* I remembered the jars of purple paint on the top shelf of Catherine's studio.

"It was a good year," Grant said. "One of the best we had. She took her medicine, tried to eat. Every time I crossed the grounds below her broken window, she called down that she loved me. I still look up sometimes when I cross the front of the house, expecting to see her."

Catherine had never, not even in illness, left Grant. Unsupported and alone, she had managed what neither Grant nor I had been able to do: keep and raise a child. The respect that hit me was deep and unexpected. I looked at Grant, to see if he felt it, too. His eyes, glassy and full, were fixed on his mother's drawings.

"She loved you," I said.

His tongue curled out of his mouth, pressed against his upper lip. "I know."

There was a hint of surprise in his voice, and I didn't know if he was surprised that his mother had loved him so much or surprised that he finally understood the depth of her feeling. Her mothering had been far from perfect. But Grant, grown now, was strong, loving, and a successful farmer. Sometimes he was even happy. No one could say she hadn't raised him well, or at least well enough. I felt a wave of gratitude for the woman I would never meet, the woman who had created the man I loved.

"How did she die?" I asked.

"One day she didn't get out of bed. When I went to her, she wasn't breathing. Alcohol and her prescriptions, the doctors said. She knew she wasn't supposed to drink, but she often snuck a bottle to bed. In the end, it was too much."

"I'm sorry."

I was. I was sorry for Grant, and sorry I wouldn't meet her. Sorry Hazel would never know her grandmother.

I squeezed Grant a final time. Inching my arm out from underneath him, I kissed his forehead.

"You've been good to Hazel," I said, my voice unsteady. "So good. Thank you." I crawled over his body and stood up.

"Don't go," he said. "Stay here with me. Please. I'll cook you dinner every night."

I scanned the drawings on the wall: crocus, primrose, and daisy, flowers for a young girl. I could not look at Grant, could not think about his cooking. If I looked into his eyes even one more time or smelled anything in the oven, it would be impossible for me to leave.

"I have to go," I said. "Please don't ask me to stay. I care too much about my daughter to interrupt her life now, when she's happy, cared for, and loved."

Grant stood up. He wrapped his arms around my waist and pulled me to him. "But she doesn't have her mother," he said. "Nothing makes up for that."

I sighed. His words were not guilt-ridden, forceful, or said to be persuasive.

They were true.

I walked down the stairs, and Grant followed close behind. He passed me in the dining room and swept open the front door. I walked through the passageway quickly.

"Come for Thanksgiving," he said. "There'll be roses."

I started walking toward the road, my steps slow and heavy. Though I'd refused Grant's invitation to stay, I didn't, in fact, want to leave. Having heard my daughter's giggle, having witnessed Elizabeth as a mother, again — her voice as firm and gentle as I remembered — I couldn't bring myself to walk away. I didn't want to drive back across the bridge and retreat into my blue room. More than anything, I realized with surprise, I didn't want to be alone.

I waited for the front door to click shut. When it did, I turned and ducked into the first greenhouse.

I needed flowers.

6.

The bouquet I had assembled at Grant's bobbed between my knees as I drove the short distance back to Elizabeth's.

I parked at the entrance to the property, jogging up the long driveway. From the kitchen window, soft orange light glowed. This late in October, I had expected to find Elizabeth already on her nightly tasting tour, Hazel in tow, but it looked as if they were still finishing dinner. I wondered how she had managed the vineyard with a baby, and whether the quality of the harvest would suffer as a result. I couldn't imagine her allowing it.

On the porch, I paused, peering in the front window. Hazel sat at the kitchen table, buckled into a high chair. She'd been bathed and dressed since I'd glimpsed her in the garden. Her wet hair, darker and curlier, was parted on the side and pulled back with a clip. A glossy green bib fastened behind her neck was splattered with something white and creamy, and she licked the remains of what she'd eaten from her fingertips. Elizabeth's back was to me, washing dishes at the sink. When I heard the water turn off, I stepped behind the closed front door.

Bowing my head, I dipped my nose into the bouquet I'd assembled. There was flax, and forget-me-not, and hazel. There were white roses and pink ones, helenium and periwinkle, primrose, and lots and lots of bellflower. Between the tightly wrapped stems I'd packed velvety moss, barely visible, and I had sprinkled the bouquet with the purple and white petals of Grant's Mexican sage. The bouquet was enormous, and not nearly enough. Taking a deep breath, I knocked on the door.

Elizabeth crossed in front of the window and swung the door open. Hazel straddled her hip, her cheek against Elizabeth's shoulder. I held out the flowers.

A smile spread across Elizabeth's face. Her expression held recognition and joy but not the surprise I had expected. As she looked me up and down, I felt like a daughter returning from summer camp to a mother who had worried unnecessarily. Except instead of summer camp it had been my entire adolescence, emancipation, homelessness, and single parenthood, and I couldn't rightly say that Elizabeth's worry had been unwarranted. But now, the years that had passed since I'd left her home felt short and far away.

Pushing open the screen, she reached past the bouquet and wrapped her arm around the back of my neck. I fell against the shoulder Hazel hadn't claimed, and we stood there, in an awkward embrace, until Hazel began to slip off Elizabeth's hip. She jostled her back up, and I pulled away to look at them both. Hazel's face was hidden; Elizabeth wiped tears away from the corners of her eyes.

"Victoria," she said. She closed her hand around my fingers, and we clutched the bouquet together. Finally, she took it from me. "I've missed you."

Elizabeth held the screen door open and motioned with her head for me to come inside. "Have you eaten? There's leftover lentil soup, and I made vanilla ice cream this afternoon."

"I just ate," I said. "But I'll have ice cream."

Hazel lifted her head from Elizabeth's shoulder and clapped her hands together.

"You had yours already, little one," Elizabeth said, kissing the top of Hazel's head and walking into the kitchen. She set her down on the floor, where the baby clung to the backs of Elizabeth's legs. Leaning from the freezer to the cupboard without taking a step, Elizabeth succeeded in retrieving a metal tub of ice cream, a dish, and a spoon.

"Up you go," she said when the bowl was full. Hazel reached up, and Elizabeth bent down to scoop her up with one arm. "Let's sit at the table with your mother."

My heart raced at Elizabeth's casual reference to my motherhood, but Hazel, of course, did not flinch.

I washed my hands at the sink and sat down. Elizabeth slid the high chair to face me, but when she bent to put the baby inside, Hazel shrieked and held on to the back of Elizabeth's neck.

"No thank you, Aunt Elizabeth," she said calmly, cutting Hazel's scream short. She pulled the high chair out of the way and slid a chair into its place, then sat down with Hazel pressed against her, chest to chest.

"She'll get used to you," Elizabeth said. "It takes her a minute to warm up."

"Grant told me."

"You saw Grant?"

I nodded. "Just now. I came here first, but when I saw you out in the garden, with Hazel, I was so surprised I turned and ran."

"I'm glad you came back," she said.

"Me, too."

Elizabeth pushed the bowl of ice cream across the table, and our eyes met. I had come back. Maybe it wasn't too late, after all.

I took a cold, creamy bite. When I looked up, Hazel had turned. She peered shyly at me, her thin lips parted. I refilled the spoon, lifted it in slow-motion to my lips, and just before taking a bite, turned the spoon to her waiting tongue. She swallowed, smiled, and hid her face in Elizabeth's chest. Then, looking up, she opened her mouth again. I scooped up a second bite of ice cream and slipped it between her lips.

Elizabeth's gaze flicked from the baby's face to mine. "How've you been?" she asked.

"Fine," I said, avoiding her stare.

She shook her head. "No way. I want to know *exactly* how you've been, since the moment I last saw you in court. I want to know everything, starting with where you went when you ran from the courthouse."

"I didn't get far. Meredith caught me and put me in a group home, as she'd promised."

"Was it awful?" Elizabeth asked. There was dread in her eyes, and I knew she was

488

waiting for me to confirm her worst nightmares of what my life had been like for the past decade.

"For the other girls in the home," I said wryly, remembering the adolescent I'd been and all the harm I'd caused. "For me, it was only awful because I wasn't here, with you."

Elizabeth's eyes welled. In her lap, Hazel banged impatient fists on the table. I fed her another bite, and she reached out, as if she wanted me to pick her up. I looked at Elizabeth.

She nodded, encouraging. "Go ahead."

With trembling hands, I grasped Hazel underneath her armpits, lifting her up and pulling her to me. She was heavier than I expected. When I set her down in my lap, she wiggled her diapered bottom back against my abdomen and tucked her head under my chin. I dipped my face into the back of her hair. She smelled like Elizabeth: cooking oil, cinnamon, and citrus soap. I inhaled, wrapping my arms around her waist.

Hazel reached into the bowl, submerging her fingers in the melted cream. Elizabeth and I watched her eat, the ice cream dripping onto her bibless linen dress. Her brow, in concentration, was as serious as her father's.

"Where do you live?" Elizabeth asked.

"I have an apartment. A business, too. I arrange flowers for weddings, anniversaries, that kind of thing."

"Grant says you're amazing. He told me women line up for blocks, wait months to buy flowers from you."

I shrugged. "Everything I know," I said, "I learned here."

I looked around, remembering the afternoon Elizabeth sliced open a lily on a cutting board at this same kitchen table. Everything was exactly as I remembered — the table and chairs, the clean countertop, and the deep white porcelain sink. The only addition was a painting, a matchbox-sized rendering of purple hyacinth, floating in a blue glass frame and placed in the windowsill next to the row of blue bottles.

"From Catherine?" I asked, nodding to the painting.

Elizabeth shook her head. "From Grant. Catherine died before painting a hyacinth she liked well enough to give me. But this was Grant's favorite, and he wanted me to have it."

"It's beautiful."

Elizabeth nodded. "I love it." She stood and brought it to the table, setting it between us. I studied the way the individual flowers clustered around the single stalk, their sharp points fitting together like pieces of a puzzle. Something about the configuration of the petals made me believe that forgiveness should come naturally, but in this family, it hadn't. I thought about the decades of misunderstandings, from the yellow rose to the fire, the thwarted attempts at forgiving and being forgiven.

"Everything's changed," Elizabeth said, as if responding to my thoughts. "Grant and I, after so many years, are a family again. I hope you've come back to be a part of it. We've all missed you enough, haven't we, Hazel?"

Hazel's attention was on the bowl, empty now. She turned it upside down, picking it up again and studying the creamy ring on the table. With her fingers, she spread the cream around in circles, a wild, sugary abstraction on the wood.

Elizabeth's hand inched toward mine on the table. She offered it to me, and in doing so it felt like she was offering me a path back into the family, the family in which I was loved, as a daughter, as a partner, as a mother. I reached for her hand. Hazel slipped hers, sticky and warm, between our palms.

But even with the clear forgiveness in Elizabeth's words, I had one more question.

"What happened to the vineyard?" I asked. The dread I felt was the same as the dread in Elizabeth's voice when she had asked me about my adolescence in group homes. We had both imagined the worst.

"We replanted. The loss was substantial, but it was overshadowed completely by losing you. For years the new vines were thin, the weeds thick. I left the house only in the fall, to do the tasting, and only because Carlos practically broke down my door every evening."

The trailer was gone now. Carlos, too.

"He moved back to Mexico a year ago, after Perla went to college," Elizabeth explained. "His parents were old, and ill. I'd finally learned to manage my grief, and my vineyard, too. I didn't need him anymore."

The loss of my own daughter would have gotten easier, then, if I had waited long enough. But a decade is a long time to wait. I pressed my nose down into Hazel's curly hair, inhaling again her sweet smell.

"The grapes must be close," I said.

"Probably. I haven't checked for three days. It's harder now" — she nodded toward Hazel — "but worth it."

"Do you want my help?" I asked, gesturing to the vineyard.

Elizabeth smiled. "Yes," she said. "Let's go." She picked up a damp dishcloth from the drying rack and wiped Hazel's hands and face as she squirmed.

Outside, we climbed onto the red tractor. Elizabeth first, then, after passing up Hazel, I followed. Hazel sat in Elizabeth's lap, her arms reaching out to touch the steering wheel, but when the engine started, she turned and buried her face in Elizabeth's chest, pressing one ear into her armpit to muffle the sound. We bumped up the road past the place the trailer had been, onto the hill where I'd found the ripe grape, the year I started the fire. Elizabeth cut the engine.

The vineyard was silent. Hazel pulled away from Elizabeth, looking out over the grapevines, to the house. Her sleepy eyes tracked the roofline to the upstairs windows. When she turned in my direction, she startled, as if she'd forgotten I was there, and then she smiled, a slow, shy, radiant smile. Reaching for me, she squealed in delight, and the high-pitched noise broke a fine line into my nut-covered heart as cleanly as it would have split a delicate crystal glass.

I pulled her to me. We slid down from the tractor and crouched in the vines. Hazel pressed her face into a cluster of grapes, and I joined her. Picking one, I pierced it open with my teeth and gave a tiny sliver to Hazel. She had already been taught. Together we chewed the skin, swished the soft middle from cheek to cheek.

I smiled. 75/7. The grapes were ripe.

7.

I placed my blue box on the bookshelf, in the empty space next to Grant's orange one. The cloth-covered boxes fit snuggly between a botany textbook and a poetry anthology, in the space they'd occupied when Grant and I had lived in the water tower together the year before.

It was Thanksgiving Day. All morning I'd helped Grant, chopping vegetables and whipping potatoes and cutting roses for the table. Any moment, Elizabeth would arrive. Hazel, too. Grant wanted everything to be perfect. When I'd left him in the kitchen, he'd been pacing in front of the gravy, checking the temperature of the oven often enough to let out most of the hot air. The turkey wouldn't be ready until late evening, but it didn't matter to me. I wasn't going anywhere.

I'd left the vineyard only twice since tasting the grapes with my daughter, once to help Marlena with a five-hundred-guest wedding

— our biggest yet — and the second time, just the day before, to pack up my things. After emptying the apartment, I'd driven to The Gathering House and knocked on the front door, offering free rent in exchange for work as a floral assistant. Two girls volunteered, and I hired them on the spot, driving them back to the apartment. Marlena had been waiting, nervous, and I watched as she showed the girls around and then went over the calendar. They listened quietly as she described the many tasks for which they would be responsible. Afterward, I turned to leave, confident I would not be needed in the near future, but Marlena pulled me aside, desperation in her eyes. "But they don't know the flowers," she'd whispered.

"Neither did you," I'd reminded her, but she didn't look entirely reassured. I promised her I'd be back, soon. I just needed a little more time.

Pulling Grant's heavy green duffel bag to the third floor, I thought about the promise I'd made to Marlena. I loved Message, loved the look on my brides' faces when I handed over their wedding scrolls, loved the thank-you cards that poured in every day with the mail. We were building something, Marlena and I. Bethany and Ray had already booked Message for their first, fifth, and tenth wedding anniversaries. Bethany credited me for the fulfillment she'd found in her relationship; I credited her with the growing success of my business. I would not let her down, and I would not let Marlena down, either.

It would be possible, someday, to have a business and a family, both. I would commute back to San Francisco in the mornings and return in time for dinner like any other working mother. I would pick Hazel up from Elizabeth's and buckle her into her car seat, drive her back to the flower farm, and sit with her at the long dining room table. Grant would have dinner made, and we would chop Hazel's food into tiny pieces and talk about our day, marveling over the growth of our businesses, our daughter, our love. On days off we would take Hazel to the beach, Grant carrying her on his shoulders until she was old enough to run safely among the waves, her footprints in the sand growing with each passing month.

One day, I would be able to do it all.

But not yet.

Right now, I knew it would require all my strength and attention to rejoin my family. Though she was worried, Marlena understood. The task ahead of me was great. I needed to accept Grant's love, and Elizabeth's, and earn the love of my daughter. I needed to never, under any circumstance, leave any of them again.

The idea filled me with equal parts joy and terror.

I'd lived with Grant before, and failed. I'd lived with Elizabeth; I'd lived with Hazel. Each time, I had failed.

This time, I told myself, looking around Grant's old bedroom, it would be different. This time, I would take smaller steps, and enter our unconventional family in a way that I knew I could handle. From breast-feeding I had learned the dangers of throwing myself fully into something and risking a complete collapse. It was why I had decided, for now, to live in the water tower alone. Hazel would remain with Elizabeth, visiting more and more often, and for longer periods of time. As my fear eventually turned to trust — in my family, but mostly in myself — I would move in to the main house with Grant, and we would bring Hazel to live with us. Less than a mile away, Elizabeth would be our support. And the water tower, Grant promised, would always be mine for a brief escape, a moment of solitude. It was everything I needed to stay.

I unzipped my bag and began to transfer my belongings, stacking jeans and T-shirts and shoes in the corners, hanging blouses and belts on a row of rusty nails on the wall. Outside, the front gate squeaked open. I went to the window and watched Elizabeth push a stroller through the opening, returning to latch the gate. Hazel's patent-leather shoes peeked out from beneath a wide canvas hat, pulled low to shield the sun from her face.

I found my only dress inside the duffel bag and shook it out. Undressing quickly, I slipped it over my head. The dress was a black cotton shirtwaist with a thin, cloth-covered belt of the same fabric. I pushed my feet into my dark red flats and fastened a crystal necklace Elizabeth had given me around my neck, one Hazel liked to grab.

Combing my fingers through my short hair, I returned to the window. Elizabeth had reached the bottom porch step, where she braked the stroller and pushed up the shade. Hazel squinted into the sunlight. Her eyes traveled up the water tower, and I waved from behind the third-story window. She smiled and reached up, as if wanting me to pull her out of the stroller.

Elizabeth saw her outstretched arms and leaned over to pick her up. With the baby on her hip, she reached under the stroller and pulled something out of a storage area beneath the seat, holding it up for me to see.

A ladybug-shaped backpack. Inside, I

knew, were Hazel's pajamas, diapers, and a change of clothes. Elizabeth's face was joyful and determinedly brave; mine, I knew, was the same. Looking at my daughter filled me with a love I once thought myself incapable of feeling, and I thought about what Grant had said the afternoon I reappeared in his rose garden. If it was true that moss did not have roots, and maternal love could grow spontaneously, as if from nothing, perhaps I had been wrong to believe myself unfit to raise my daughter. Perhaps the unattached, the unwanted, the unloved, could grow to give love as lushly as anyone else.

Tonight, my daughter would spend the night for the first time. We would read books and rock in her rocking chair. Afterward, we would try to sleep. Maybe she would be scared, and maybe I would feel overwhelmed, but we would try again the next week and the one after that. Over time, we would learn each other, and I would learn to love her like a mother loves a daughter, imperfectly and without roots.

VICTORIA'S DICTIONARY
OF FLOWERS

Abutilon (*Abutilon*) . . . *Meditation*
Acacia (*Acacia*) . . . *Secret love*
Acanthus (*Acanthus*) . . . *Artifice*
Agapanthus (*Agapanthus*) . . . *Love letter*
Allium (*Allium*) . . . *Prosperity*
Almond blossom (*Amygdalus communis*)
    . . . *Indiscretion*
Aloe (*Aloe vera*) . . . *Grief*
Alstroemeria (*Alstroemeria*) . . . *Devotion*
Alyssum (*Lobularia maritima*) . . . *Worth
    beyond beauty*
Amaranth (*Amaranthus*) . . . *Immortality*
Amaryllis (*Hippeastrum*) . . . *Pride*
Anemone (*Anemone*) . . . *Forsaken*
Angelica (*Angelica pachycarpa*) . . .
    Inspiration
Apple (*Malus domestica*) . . . *Temptation*
Apple blossom (*Malus domestica*) . . .
    Preference

Aster (*Aster*) . . . *Patience*

Azalea (*Rhododendron*) . . . *Fragile and ephemeral passion*

Baby's breath (*Gypsophila paniculata*) . . . *Everlasting love*

Bachelor's button (*Centaurea cyanus*) . . . *Single blessedness*

Basil (*Ocimum basilicum*) . . . *Hate*

Bay leaf (*Laurus nobilis*) . . . *I change but in death*

Begonia (*Begonia*) . . . *Caution*

Bellflower (*Campanula*) . . . *Gratitude*

Bells of Ireland (*Moluccella laevis*) . . . *Good luck*

Bird of paradise (*Strelitzia reginae*) . . . *Magnificence*

Blackberry (*Rubus*) . . . *Envy*

Black-eyed Susan (*Rudbeckia*) . . . *Justice*

Bluebell (*Hyacinthoides non-scripta*) . . . *Constancy*

Bougainvillea (*Bougainvillea spectabilis*) . . . *Passion*

Bouvardia (*Bouvardia*) . . . *Enthusiasm*

Broom (*Cytisus*) . . . *Humility*

Buttercup (*Ranunculus acris*) . . . *Ingratitude*

Cabbage (*Brassica oleracea*) . . . *Profit*

Cactus (*Opuntia*) . . . *Ardent love*

Calla lily (*Zantedeschia aethiopica*) . . . *Modesty*

Camellia (*Camellia*) . . . *My destiny is in your hands*

Candytuft (*Iberis*) . . . *Indifference*

Canterbury bells (*Campanula medium*) . . . *Constancy*

Carnation, pink (*Dianthus caryophyllus*) . . . *I will never forget you*

Carnation, red (*Dianthus caryophyllus*) . . . *My heart breaks*

Carnation, striped (*Dianthus caryophyllus*) . . . *I cannot be with you*

Carnation, white (*Dianthus caryophyllus*) . . . *Sweet and lovely*

Carnation, yellow (*Dianthus caryophyllus*) . . . *Disdain*

Celandine (*Chelidonium majus*) . . . *Joys to come*

Chamomile (*Matricaria recutita*) . . . *Energy in adversity*

Cherry blossom (*Prunus cerasus*) . . . *Impermanence*

Chervil (*Anthriscus*) . . . *Sincerity*

Chestnut (*Castanea sativa*) . . . *Do me justice*

Chicory (*Cichorium intybus*) . . . *Frugality*

Chrysanthemum (*Chrysanthemum*) . . . *Truth*

Cinquefoil (*Potentilla*) . . . *Beloved daughter*

Clematis (*Clematis*) . . . *Poverty*

Clove (*Syzygium aromaticum*) . . . *I have loved you and you have not known it*

Clover, white (*Trifolium*) . . . *Think of me*

Cockscomb (*Celosia*) . . . *Affectation*

Columbine (*Aquilegia*) . . . *Desertion*

Coreopsis (*Coreopsis*) . . . *Always cheerful*

Coriander (*Coriandrum sativum*) . . . *Hidden worth*

Corn (*Zea mays*) . . . *Riches*

Cosmos (*Cosmos bipinnatus*) . . . *Joy in love and life*

Cowslip (*Primula veris*) . . . *Pensiveness*

Crab-apple blossom (*Malus hupehensis*) . . . *Ill-tempered*

Cranberry (*Vaccinium*) . . . *Cure for heartache*

Crocus (*Crocus*) . . . *Youthful gladness*

Currant (*Ribes*) . . . *Thy frown will kill me*

Cyclamen (*Cyclamen*) . . . *Timid hope*

Cypress (*Cupressus*) . . . *Mourning*

Daffodil (*Narcissus*) . . . *New beginnings*

Dahlia (*Dahlia*) . . . *Dignity*

Daisy (*Bellis*) . . . *Innocence*

Daisy, Gerber (*Gerbera*) . . . *Cheerfulness*

Dandelion (*Taraxacum*) . . . *Rustic oracle*

Daphne (*Daphne*) . . . *I would not have you otherwise*

Daylily (*Hemerocallis*) . . . *Coquetry*

Delphinium (*Delphinium*) . . . *Levity*

Dianthus (*Dianthus*) . . . *Make haste*

Dittany (*Dictamnus albus*) . . . *Childbirth*

Dogwood (*Cornus*) . . . *Love undiminished by adversity*

Dragon plant (*Dracaena*) . . . *You are near a snare*

Edelweiss (*Leontopodium alpinum*) . . . *Noble courage*

Elder (*Sambucus*) . . . *Compassion*

Eucalyptus (*Eucalyptus*) . . . *Protection*

Euphorbia (*Euphorbia*) . . . *Persistence*

Evening primrose (*Oenothera biennis*) . . . *Inconstancy*

Everlasting pea (*Lathyrus latifolius*) . . . *Lasting pleasure*

Fennel (*Foeniculum vulgare*) . . . *Strength*

Fern (*Polypodiophyta*) . . . *Sincerity*

Fern, maidenhair (*Adiantum capillus-veneris*) . . . *Secrecy*

Feverfew (*Tanacetum parthenium*) . . . *Warmth*

Fig (*Ficus carica*) . . . *Argument*

Flax (*Linum usitatissimum*) . . . *I feel your kindness*

Forget-me-not (*Myosotis*) . . . *Forget me not*

Forsythia (*Forsythia*) . . . *Anticipation*

Foxglove (*Digitalis purpurea*) . . . *Insincerity*

Freesia (*Freesia*) . . . *Lasting friendship*

Fuchsia (*Fuchsia*) . . . *Humble love*

Gardenia (*Gardenia*) . . . *Refinement*

Gentian (*Gentiana*) . . . *Intrinsic worth*

Geranium, oak-leaf (*Pelargonium*) . . . *True friendship*

Geranium, pencil-leaf (*Pelargonium*) . . . *Ingenuity*

Geranium, scarlet (*Pelargonium*) . . . *Stupidity*

Geranium, wild (*Pelargonium*) . . . *Steadfast piety*

Ginger (*Zingiber*) . . . *Strength*

Gladiolus (*Gladiolus*) . . . *You pierce my heart*

Goldenrod (*Solidago*) . . . *Careful*

encouragement
Grapevine (*Vitis vinifera*) . . . *Abundance*
Grass (*Poaceae*) . . . *Submission*

Hawthorn (*Crataegus monogyna*) . . . *Hope*
Hazel (*Corylus*) . . . *Reconciliation*
Heath (*Erica*) . . . *Solitude*
Heather (*Calluna vulgaris*) . . . *Protection*
Helenium (*Helenium*) . . . *Tears*
Heliotrope (*Heliotropium*) . . . *Devoted affection*
Hibiscus (*Hibiscus*) . . . *Delicate beauty*
Holly (*Ilex*) . . . *Foresight*
Hollyhock (*Alcea*) . . . *Ambition*
Honesty (*Lunaria annua*) . . . *Honesty*
Honeysuckle (*Lonicera*) . . . *Devotion*
Hyacinth, blue (*Hyacinthus orientalis*) . . . *Constancy*
Hyacinth, purple (*Hyacinthus orientalis*) . . . *Please forgive me*
Hyacinth, white (*Hyacinthus orientalis*) . . . *Beauty*
Hydrangea (*Hydrangea*) . . . *Dispassion*

Ice plant (*Carpobrotus chilensis*) . . . *Your looks freeze me*

Impatiens (*Impatiens*) . . . *Impatience*
Iris (*Iris*) . . . *Message*
Ivy (*Hedera helix*) . . . *Fidelity*

Jacob's ladder (*Polemonium*) . . . *Come down*
Jasmine, Carolina (*Gelsemium sempervirens*) . . . *Separation*
Jasmine, Indian (*Jasminum multiflorum*) . . . *Attachment*
Jasmine, white (*Jasminum officinale*) . . . *Amiability*
Jonquil (*Narcissus jonquilla*) . . . *Desire*

Laburnum (*Laburnum anagyroides*) . . . *Pensive beauty*
Lady's slipper (*Cypripedium*) . . . *Capricious beauty*
Lantana (*Lantana*) . . . *Rigor*
Larch (*Larix decidua*) . . . *Audacity*
Larkspur (*Consolida*) . . . *Lightness*
Laurel (*Laurus nobilis*) . . . *Glory and success*
Lavender (*Lavandula*) . . . *Mistrust*
Lemon (*Citrus limon*) . . . *Zest*
Lemon blossom (*Citrus limon*) . . . *Discretion*

Lettuce (*Lactuca sativa*) . . .
   Coldheartedness
Liatris *(Liatris)* . . . *I will try again*
Lichen (*Parmelia*) . . . *Dejection*
Lilac (*Syringa*) . . . *First emotions of love*
Lily (*Lilum*) . . . *Majesty*
Lily of the valley (*Convallaria majalis*) . . .
   Return of happiness
Linden tree (*Tilia*) . . . *Conjugal love*
Lisianthus (*Eustoma*) . . . *Appreciation*
Lobelia (*Lobelia*) . . . *Malevolence*
Lotus (*Nelumbo nucifera*) . . . *Purity*
Love-in-a-mist (*Nigella damascena*) . . .
   Perplexity
Love-lies-bleeding (*Amaranthus caudatus*)
   . . . *Hopeless but not helpless*
Lungwort (*Pulmonaria*) . . . *You are my life*
Lupine (*Lupinus*) . . . *Imagination*

Magnolia (*Magnolia*) . . . *Dignity*
Marigold (*Calendula*) . . . *Grief*
Marjoram (*Origanum*) . . . *Blushes*
Marsh marigold (*Caltha palustris*) . . . *Desire
   for riches*
Meadow saffron (*Colchicum autumnale*)
   . . . *My best days are past*
Meadowsweet (*Filipendula ulmaria*) . . .
   Uselessness

Michealmas daisy (*Aster amellus*) . . . *Farewell*

Mignonette (*Reseda odorata*) . . . *Your qualities surpass your charms*

Mimosa (*Mimosa*) . . . *Sensitivity*

Mistletoe (*Viscum*) . . . *I surmount all obstacles*

Mock orange (*Pittosporum undulatum*) . . . *Counterfeit*

Monkshood (*Aconitum*) . . . *Chivalry*

Morning glory (*Ipomoea*) . . . *Coquetry*

Moss (*Bryopsida*) . . . *Maternal love*

Mullein (*Verbascum*) . . . *Take courage*

Mustard (*Brassica*) . . . *I am hurt*

Myrtle (*Myrtus*) . . . *Love*

Narcissus (*Narcissus*) . . . *Self-love*

Nasturtium (*Tropaeolum majus*) . . . *Impetuous love*

Nettle (*Urtica*) . . . *Cruelty*

Oats (*Avena sativa*) . . . *The witching soul of music*

Oleander (*Nerium oleander*) . . . *Beware*

Olive (*Olea europaea*) . . . *Peace*

Orange (*Citrus sinensis*) . . . *Generosity*

Orange blossom (*Citrus sinensis*) . . . *Your purity equals your loveliness*
Orchid (*Orchidaceae*) . . . *Refined beauty*
Oregano (*Origanum vulgare*) . . . *Joy*

Pansy (*Viola*) . . . *Think of me*
Parsley (*Petroselinum crispum*) . . . *Festivity*
Passionflower (*Passiflora*) . . . *Faith*
Peach (*Prunus persica*) . . . *Your charms are unequaled*
Peach blossom (*Prunus persica*) . . . *I am your captive*
Pear (*Pyrus*) . . . *Affection*
Pear blossom (*Pyrus*) . . . *Comfort*
Peony (*Paeonia*) . . . *Anger*
Peppermint (*Mentha*) . . . *Warmth of feeling*
Periwinkle (*Vinca minor*) . . . *Tender recollections*
Persimmon (*Diospyros kaki*) . . . *Bury me amid nature's beauty*
Petunia (*Petunia*) . . . *Your presence soothes me*
Phlox (*Phlox*) . . . *Our souls are united*
Pineapple (*Ananas comosus*) . . . *You are perfect*
Pink (*Dianthus*) . . . *Pure love*
Plum (*Prunus domestica*) . . . *Keep your promises*

Poinsettia (*Euphorbia pulcherrima*) . . . *Be of good cheer*

Polyanthus (*Primula*) . . . *Confidence*

Pomegranate (*Punica granatum*) . . . *Foolishness*

Pomegranate blossom (*Punica granatum*) . . . *Mature elegance*

Poplar, black (*Populus nigra*) . . . *Courage*

Poplar, white (*Populus alba*) . . . *Time*

Poppy (*Papaver*) . . . *Fantastic extravagance*

Potato (*Solanum tuberosum*) . . . *Benevolence*

Potato vine (*Solanum jasminoides*) . . . *You are delicious*

Primrose (*Primula*) . . . *Childhood*

Protea (*Protea*) . . . *Courage*

Purple coneflower (*Echinacea purpurea*) . . . *Strength and health*

Queen Anne's lace (*Ammi majus*) . . . *Fantasy*

Quince (*Cydonia oblonga*) . . . *Temptation*

Ranunculus (*Ranunculus asiaticus*) . . . *You are radiant with charms*

Raspberry (*Rubus*) . . . *Remorse*

Redbud (*Cercis*) . . . *Betrayal*

Rhododendron (*Rhododendron*) . . . *Beware*

Rhubarb (*Rheum*) . . . *Advice*

Rose, burgundy (*Rosa*) . . . *Unconscious beauty*

Rose, moss (*Rosa*) . . . *Confession of love*

Rose, orange (*Rosa*) . . . *Fascination*

Rose, pale peach (*Rosa*) . . . *Modesty*

Rose, pink (*Rosa*) . . . *Grace*

Rose, purple (*Rosa*) . . . *Enchantment*

Rose, red (*Rosa*) . . . *Love*

Rose, white (*Rosa*) . . . *A heart unacquainted with love*

Rose, yellow (*Rosa*) . . . *Infidelity*

Rosemary (*Rosmarinus officinalis*) . . . *Remembrance*

Saffron (*Crocus sativus*) . . . *Beware of excess*

Sage (*Salvia officinalis*) . . . *Good health and long life*

Saint-John's-wort (*Hypericum perforatum*) . . . *Superstition*

Saxifraga (*Saxifraga*) . . . *Affection*

Scabiosa (*Scabiosa*) . . . *Unfortunate love*

Scarlet Pimpernel (*Anagallis arvensis*) . . . *Change*

Snapdragon (*Antirrhinum majus*) . . .

Presumption

Snowdrop (*Galanthus*) . . . *Consolation and hope*

Sorrel (*Rumex acetosa*) . . . *Parental affection*

Speedwell (*Veronica*) . . . *Fidelity*

Spirea (*Spiraea*) . . . *Victory*

Star-of-Bethlehem (*Ornithogalum umbellatum*) . . . *Purity*

Starwort (*Stellaria*) . . . *Welcome*

Stephanotis (*Stephanotis floribunda*) . . . *Happiness in marriage*

Stock (*Malcolmia maritima*) . . . *You will always be beautiful to me*

Stonecrop (*Sedum*) . . . *Tranquility*

Strawberry (*Fragaria*) . . . *Perfection*

Sunflower (*Helianthus annuus*) . . . *False riches*

Sweet briar (*Rosa rubiginosa*) . . . *Simplicity*

Sweet pea (*Lathyrus odoratus*) . . . *Delicate pleasures*

Sweet William (*Dianthus barbatus*) . . . *Gallantry*

Tansy (*Tanacetum*) . . . *I declare war against you*

Thistle, common (*Cirsium*) . . . *Misanthropy*

Thrift (*Armeria*) . . . *Sympathy*

Thyme (*Thymus*) . . . *Activity*
Trachelium (*Trachelium*) . . . *Neglected beauty*
Trillium (*Trillium*) . . . *Modest beauty*
Trumpet vine (*Campsis radicans*) . . . *Fame*
Tuberose (*Polianthes tuberosa*) . . . *Dangerous pleasures*
Tulip (*Tulipa*) . . . *Declaration of love*
Turnip (*Brassica rapa*) . . . *Charity*

Verbena (*Verbena*) . . . *Pray for me*
Vetch (*Vicia*) . . . *I cling to thee*
Violet (*Viola*) . . . *Modest worth*

Wallflower (*Cheiranthus*) . . . *Fidelity in adversity*
Water lily (*Nymphaea*) . . . *Purity of heart*
Waxflower (*Hoya*) . . . *Susceptibility*
Wheat (*Triticum*) . . . *Prosperity*
White Monte Casino (*Aster*) . . . *Patience*
Willow herb (*Epilobium*) . . . *Pretension*
Winter cherry (*Physalis alkekengi*) . . . *Deception*
Wisteria (*Wisteria*) . . . *Welcome*
Witch hazel (*Hamamelis*) . . . *A spell*

Yarrow (*Achillea millefolium*) . . . *Cure for a broken heart*

Zinnia (*Zinnia*) . . . *I mourn your absence*

AUTHOR'S NOTE

When I began *The Language of Flowers,* I owned only one flower dictionary: *The Floral Offering: A Token of Affection and Esteem; Comprising the Language and Poetry of Flowers,* written in 1851 by Henrietta Dumont. It was an ancient, crumbling hardcover, with dry flowers pressed between the pages. Scraps of poetry, collected by previous owners and stored between the yellowed pages, slipped to the floor as I scanned the book for meanings.

Three chapters into Victoria's story, I myself made the discovery of the yellow rose. In the table of contents at the beginning of Ms. Dumont's beautiful book, the yellow rose appears as jealousy. Hundreds of pages later, in the very same book, the yellow rose appears again: this time as infidelity.

Reading through the book more carefully, I found no explanation for the discrepancy, so I went in search of additional dictionaries, hoping to determine the "correct" definition of the yellow rose. Instead, I found that the problem was not specific to the yellow rose; nearly every flower had multiple meanings, listed in hundreds of books, in dozens of languages, and on countless websites.

The dictionary included here was created in the manner in which Victoria compiled the contents of her boxes. Lining up dictionaries on my dining room table — *The Flower Vase* by Miss S. C. Edgarton, *Language of Flowers* by Kate Greenaway, *The Language and Sentiment of Flowers* by James D. McCabe, and *Flora's Lexicon* by Catharine H. Waterman — I scanned the meanings, selecting the definition that best fit the science of each flower, just as Victoria would have done. Other times, when I could find no scientific reason for a definition, I chose the meaning that occurred most often or, occasionally, simply the one I liked best.

My goal was to create a usable, relevant dictionary for modern readers. I deleted plants from the Victorian dictionaries that are no longer common, and added flowers that were rarely used in the 1800s but are more popular today. I kept most food-related plants, as Victoria would have, and deleted most nonflowering trees and shrubs because, as Victoria says, there is nothing wistful about the passing of sticks or long strips of bark.

I am grateful for the assistance of Stephen Zedros of Brattle Square Florist in Cambridge and Lachezar Nikolov at Harvard University. This dictionary would not exist without their vast knowledge and generous support.

ACKNOWLEDGMENTS

In a book filled with mother-daughter relationships, I would like to thank my own mother first: Harriet Elizabeth George, a strong, brave woman who learned to be a mother through purposeful study, fierce love, and a community of support. My relentless optimism and belief in the possibility of creating positive change, both internally and externally, would not exist without her.

I would also like to thank the community of women who mothered me: my stepmother, Melinda Vasquez; my mother-in-law, Sarada Diffenbaugh; my grandmothers, Virginia Helen Fleming, Victoria Vasquez, Irene Botill, Adelle Tomash, Carolyn Diffenbaugh, and Pearl Bolton; and the fathers in my life, for making each of us better mothers: my own father, Ken Fleming; my stepfather, Jim Botill; my father-in-law, Dayanand Diffenbaugh; my brother-in-law Noah Diffenbaugh; and my husband, PK Diffenbaugh.

I wouldn't have had the knowledge, confidence, or time to write this book without all of your love and support.

I am grateful to my early readers and dear friends: Maureen Wanket believed in this book and in my potential from the very first page, and her belief was contagious; Tasha Blaine read my first draft and told me the truth — I will love her for it, forever; Angela Booker sat next to me and encouraged me as I rewrote the end — again, and again, and again; Jennifer Jacoby and Lindsey Serrao talked me through the storms of my own motherhood and inspired me with their joyful mothering; Polly Diffenbaugh taught me to dissect a flower and use a field guide, and (more than once) lectured me on the intricacies of scientific classification; Jennifer Olden shared her expertise on attachment disorder; Priscillia de Muizon told me lovely, vivid stories of her childhood on a vineyard; Janay Swain answered my endless questions about foster care; Barbara Tomash sat beside me on the edge of Papa's lake and dreamed up section titles; Rachel McIntire painted the blue room and shared the inner workings of the floral-arranging world; Mark Botill inspired me with his intelligence and humor; Amanda Garcia, Carrie Marks, Isis Keigwin, Emily Olavarri, and Tricia Stirling

522

read my first draft and told me to keep writing; Wendi Everett, Wendi Imagire, Tami Trostel, Josie Bickinella, Sara Galvan, Sue Malan, and Kassandra Grossman loved my babies and gave me time to write; and Christie Spencer cried over my plot summary and reminded me of the power of a good story.

My agent, Sally Wofford-Girand, is the person responsible for seeing the potential in my early drafts and pushing me to be better. I will never be able to thank her enough for her vision, encouragement, and commitment to this book. Jenni Ferrari-Adler made me think about pacing, character, and plot just when I thought I was done (and I was, of course, far from done!), and Melissa Sarver kept us all focused and motivated. Jennifer Smith, my brilliant editor at Ballantine, has made this book immeasurably better through her careful reads and wise suggestions. She has been a delight to work with from the very beginning.

I would like to thank my writing teachers, in the order they appeared in my life: Charlotte Goldsmith, for teaching me to write letters in a tray of sand; Linda Holm, for giving me a journal and demanding I fill it; Chris Persson, for reading my first short story, telling me I was a writer, and then helping me to become one; and Keith Scribner and

Jennifer Richter, who, in addition to teaching me much of what I know about writing, helped me survive college by offering me a glimpse into their own lives as young writers, teachers, and parents.

Finally, I would like to thank my children, for teaching me to be a mother and loving me through my mistakes: Tre'von, Chela, Miles, Donavan, Sharon, Krystal, Wayneshia, Infinity, and Hope. And Megan, wherever you are.

ABOUT THE AUTHOR

Vanessa Diffenbaugh was born in San Francisco and raised in Chico, California. After studying creative writing and education at Stanford, she went on to teach art and writing to youth in low-income communities. She and her husband, PK, have three children: Tre'von, eighteen; Chela, four; and Miles, three. Tre'von, a former foster child, is attending New York University on a Gates Millennium Scholarship. Diffenbaugh and her family currently live in Cambridge, Massachusetts, where her husband is studying urban school reform at Harvard.

CAMELLIA
NETWORK

In the language of flowers, camellia means *my destiny is in your hands*. Author Vanessa Diffenbaugh is launching the Camellia Network in order to create a nationwide movement to support youth making the transition from foster care to independence.

www.camellianetwork.org

We hope you have enjoyed this Large Print book. Other Thorndike, Wheeler, Kennebec, and Chivers Large Print books are available at your library or directly from the publishers.

For information about current and upcoming titles, please call or write, without obligation, to:

Publisher
Thorndike Press
295 Kennedy Memorial Drive
Waterville, ME 04901
Tel. (800) 223-1244

or visit our Web site at:

http://gale.cengage.com/thorndike

OR

Chivers Large Print
published by AudioGO Ltd.
St James House, The Square
Lower Bristol Road
Bath, BA2 3SB
England
Tel. +44(0) 800 136919
email us at: info@audiogo.co.uk

All our Large Print titles are designed for easy reading, and all our books are made to last.